PENGUIN

MR. HOGARTH'S WILL

Catherine Helen Spence, born in Scotland in 1825, migrated with her family to the new colony of South Australia in 1839. She became a teacher, a journalist, an untiring philanthropist, wrote eight novels, travelled the world twice and worked as a propagandist for proportional representation. She was Australia's first woman candidate for political office (unsuccessful) and, when she died in 1910, was described as 'the grand old woman of Australia'. Spence's life demonstrated that a nineteenth-century Australian woman could achieve a lifestyle which, even in today's terms, could be described as satisfyingly liberated.

Helen Thomson is a senior lecturer in the English department at Monash University. Melbourne-born, she completed her first degree at Monash and has lived in England and Germany. Her current research interests are nineteenth-century feminism and contemporary theatre. She writes theatre criticism for the *Australian* newspaper. She is married to a fellow academic and they have two children.

Series Editor: Dale Spender

The Penguin Australian Women's Library will make available to readers a wealth of information through the work of women writers of our past. It will include the classic to the freshly re-discovered, individual reprints to new anthologies, as well as up-to-date critical re-appraisals of their work and lives as writers.

Other books in the Penguin Australian Women's Library

The Penguin Anthology of Australian Women's Writing
edited by Dale Spender

Kirkham's Find by Mary Gaunt
Introduced by Kylie Tennant. Afterword by Dale Spender

A Bright and Fiery Troop: Australian Women Writers of the Nineteenth Century edited by Debra Adelaide

Her Selection: Nineteenth-Century Australian Women's Writings
edited by Lynne Spender

The Peaceful Army edited by Flora Eldershaw
Introduced by Kylie Tennant and Dale Spender

CATHERINE HELEN SPENCE

MR. HOGARTH'S WILL

PENGUIN BOOKS

Penguin Books Australia Ltd,
487 Maroondah Highway, PO Box 257
Ringwood, Victoria, 3134, Australia
Penguin Books Ltd
Harmondsworth, Middlesex, England
Viking Penguin Inc.
40 West 23rd Street, New York, NY 10010, USA
Penguin Books Canada Limited
2801 John Street, Markham, Ontario, Canada, L3R 1B4
Penguin Books (N.Z.) Ltd
182-190 Wairau Road, Auckland 10, New Zealand

First published by Richard Bentley, London, 1865

Typeset in Garamond by Allset Graphics Pty Ltd
Made and Printed in Australia by
The Book Printer, Maryborough, Victoria

CIP

Spence, Catherine Helen, 1825-1910.
Mr. Hogarth's will.

ISBN 0 14 011233 2.

I. Title. (Series: Penguin Australian women's Library).
A823'.1

CONTENTS

Introduction i

Volume One

I The Will 1
II Disappointment and Hope; Prose and Poetry 17
III Closed Doors 32
IV An Evening at Mr. Rennie's 47
V A Humble Friend 61
VI A Bundle of Old Letters 66
VII Up and Down 77
VIII Peggy Walker's Adventures 87
IX Peggy Walker's Adventures 93
X Elsie's Literary Venture, and its Success 110
XI Some Grave Talk in Gay Company 117
XII Mr. Brandon in Edinburgh 126
XIII Peggy's Visitors, and Francis' Resolution 138
XIV Good News for Francis 144

Volume Two

I	How Francis Received the Good News	153
II	Jane's Situation	162
III	Elsie's Situation	179
IV	Elsie Refuses an Excellent Offer	185
V	Elsie Accepts of a New Situation	194
VI	A Letter from Australia for Francis, which Causes Surprise in an Unexpected Quarter	199
VII	Harriett Phillips Does a Little Bit of Shopping, which is Somewhat Fatal to her Projects	210
VIII	Francis Makes a Favourable Impression on Harriett Phillips	218
IX	A Bonnet Gained and a Lover Lost	227
X	A Seance	232
XI	Spiritualism, Love, and Politics	239
XII	Chiefly Political	244
XIII	Good-Bye	251
XIV	Francis Hogarth's Canvass and Election	260
XV	Mrs. Phillips's First Grief	277
XVI	Another Good-Bye	286

Volume Three

I	Mr. Brandon's Second Proposal to Elsie, and its Fate	297
II	Mrs. Peck	304
III	Raising the Wind	315
IV	Miss Phillips Meets with a Congenial Spirit in Victoria	326
V	Dr. Grant Prosecutes his Suit with Caution and Success, and Brandon Finds his Love-making All to Do Over Again	332
VI	Mrs. Peck's Progress	344
VII	Business Interrupted by Love	350
VIII	Mrs. Phillips is Relieved	367

IX Mrs. Peck's Communication 373
X Mrs. Peck's Disappointment 385
XI Elsie Melville's Letter 396
XII What Can be Made of it? 402
XIII Not so Bad, After All 414
XIV Meeting 421
Epilogue 428

INTRODUCTION

Catherine Helen Spence was an unusual Australian pioneer. Arriving from Scotland to the new, fast-growing township of Adelaide in 1839, she stayed all her life in the town, leaving bush hardships to others, and instead became South Australia's first 'career woman', despite contemporary male prejudice and determination that women had no place in public life. So successful was Spence in her varied occupations and achievements, as novelist, journalist, preacher, public-speaker, electoral candidate, that at a public celebration of her 80th birthday she was described as 'the grand old woman of Australia'.

Spence was a feminist long before the term was coined. Her liberation began with what appeared to be the disastrous loss of her family's fortunes and consequent emigration to Australia. Arriving on her fourteenth birthday, the well-educated, ambitious and sensitive girl sat down and cried in the hot Australian sun and wind. She was not then to know that in this colonial society the rigid constraints of class and gender would lose much of their power to compel women into permanent economic and social dependency.

When her father died a few years later, Catherine found she had not only herself, but also her mother to support. This was the first

lesson revealing to her the falsity of the complacent male assumption that only men were family bread-winners. It became the central theme of *Mr. Hogarth's Will.* The wealthy Mr. Hogarth, who has given his two orphaned nieces Jane and Alice Melville thoroughly 'masculine' educations, afraid they will fall prey to fortune-hunting husbands, leaves his estate to an illegitimate son, Francis Hogarth. On pain of forfeiting his inheritance, Francis is forbidden by the Will from marrying or assisting either of his cousins. They, because they were not provided with desirable female accomplishments by their odd education, are precluded from teaching, and search in vain for respectable work. They find temporary asylum with their washer-woman, Peggy Walker, a remarkable woman who has spent some years in Australia but returned to Edinburgh to bring up her five orphaned nieces and nephews. Ultimately, after the working out of a complicated plot, all the main characters in the novel end up in Australia, where less harsh social conditions promise a happy future for them all.

Catherine Spence's own experience of emigration had not been easy at first. After her father's death the Spence family might almost have starved without the financial assistance of their Scottish aunts, until Catherine acquired a steady income. How many similar, but publicly unacknowledged female support-systems must have existed in a world which pretended all economic resources were in the hands of men?

By the age of thirty Spence had published her first two novels, *Clara Morison: A Tale of South Australia During the Gold Fever* (1854), and *Tender and True* (1856), written letters and articles for the press, and exchanged the gloomy Calvinism of her Presbyterian childhood, with its fatalistic determinism, for the intellectual freedom of Unitarianism. She had also refused two offers of marriage and cheerfully accepted that she was 'booked for a single life', as she records in her *Autobiography.*

In *Clara Morison* the heroine, a middle-class female emigrant to Adelaide, finds that she must descend to domestic service to survive, and in a book distinguished by its domestic realism, she is restored

to her original social position only through the accidental discovery of cousins, and marriage to the man she loves. If Cinderella can be described as a female archetype, then here it is. However Spence also stresses—and she was already a loyal Australian by choice—that such happy endings were more likely in an egalitarian colonial setting where social mobility was the norm rather than the exception.

Tender and True is an examination of sexual politics within marriage, making it clear that male selfishness is destructively exacerbated by the masculine requirement of female selflessness. But in *Mr. Hogarth's Will* (Spence's third novel, published in 1865), while its major plot follows the conventions of the romantic novel of the time, with its resolution in happy marriages for the two heroines, Spence also provides us with two alternative heroines, both of whom are unmarried, no longer young, and not only self-supporting but also bringing up dependent nieces and nephews. All of these characteristics, not co-incidentally, were also true of Spence herself. Alice and particularly Jane Hogarth are admirable in their resolute courage in the face of adversity, but it is the washer-woman Peggy Walker and the farmer Miss Thomson (based upon a real aunt of Spence's), who are the more memorable. Their portraits owe nothing to the conventions of fiction, and, because of their dependants, they make a much stronger plea for female employment as a necessity, not a luxury. How often must this have been the case for the unmarried in a society which saw so many children orphaned? Spence herself brought up three different families of orphaned children.

Spence wrote six novels and two other fictional works, and the story of her efforts to find publishers and the very modest remuneration she received is a depressingly familiar one. She faced the added disadvantages of distance from London's literary market, and the problem of a limited demand for colonial themes. *Mr. Hogarth's Will,* like most of her novels, tries to overcome the latter disadvantage by having its setting in both the old and the new countries. Her loyal identification of her own interests with those of

South Australia make inevitable the novel's very partisan comparison between the two societies. Spence's commitment to realism had more to it than the literary conventions common to all mid-nineteenth-century fiction. She was also scrupulously honest about the experience of emigration. Australia was no El Dorado where fortunes could be guaranteed even for the most unsatisfactory of younger sons. Nor, in Adelaide at least, was it merely the repository for Britain's criminal overflow. But its overwhelming advantage was its far less rigid class structure, an egalitarianism which rewarded hard work and merit and therefore presented unique opportunities for women to advance themselves as well as men.

Spence was shrewdly aware of how the class structure particularly disadvantaged women. Female occupations were ruthlessly restricted to exclude the middle classes. A woman might work, if she had to, but she could not also retain respectability. So it is that Alice and Jane Melville, unable to find respectable employment in any way equal to their social position or expensive education, finally find shelter and even food from the washer-woman Peggy Walker. The one 'professional' position Jane applies for, as superintendent matron at an asylum for the insane, is shamefully remunerated simply because there are so many applicants for it. The market-place was a male domain, and respectable women came very cheaply.

The uncle whose Will is the cause of all the Melville sisters' troubles, is an eccentric and a radical. Convinced that 'the minds of men and women are radically the same', he educated his nieces accordingly, making no concessions on the grounds of sex. Spence is perfectly fair in showing us that while book-keeping, the classics, Euclid, chemistry and mineralology suited Jane's talents admirably, Alice's more literary sensibility is sadly neglected. Mr. Hogarth also claimed 'he never saw a woman take up man's work without succeeding in it'— brave words which almost qualify him as a feminist—but his Will puts this theory to the test in the real world, and it is not the theory which fails, but nineteenth-century society.

Jane's unsuccessful search for work reveals the full extent of

masculine prejudice, and her rational replies to the transparently chauvinist arguments offered as reasons for not giving her a job as a book-keeper, a position for which she was eminently qualified and suited, show only too clearly the weakness of her antagonist's case. But she is finally routed by the familiar notion that jobs must go to men in order that they may marry and support women, despite its patent inadequacy in a society with a statistically proven surplus of unmarried women.

This is not, however, a novel which preaches to us. Catherine Spence does use the conventional novel form as a means of expressing her many opinions and ideas, particularly on contemporary women's problems. But she dramatises them through conversations, shows how progressive and radical ideas develop in different characters, and subtly breaks with certain stereotypes in her characters. Francis Hogarth, the fortunate legatee, has a sensibility which in many ways is more 'feminine' than Jane's 'masculine' propensities for mathematics and political reform. He has more imagination, a love of poetry and very good taste. His trip to France educates him in politics and social life, and in this we find evidence of Catherine Spence's own knowledge of French ways, another legacy of her Scottish Enlightenment background. Jane in turn, living with Peggy and her family, develops a new sympathy for the working class and a respect for the intelligence possessed by children like the nephew Tom, who in Australia will undoubtedly rise to great things.

Spence's own most important public activities were associated with the proportional representation cause which aimed to reform the electoral system to guarantee the representation of minorities. As early as 1859 she had published a booklet on the Hare system of proportional representation, which won her the admiration and friendship of John Stuart Mill. She did not take up the issue of female enfranchisement until quite late, but it is nevertheless an issue in this novel. Francis Hogarth becomes a supporter of voting reform, in which Australia is seen, quite accurately, as being ahead of England, having already introduced manhood suffrage and the

secret ballot. As yet Spence was no suffragette, but she does have Francis ask how the interests of women and children are to be looked after by male voters. And he takes up the issue which is the novel's main concern: 'The difficulties which are thrown in the way of the weaker sex, in their attempts to earn a livelihood, by law and by society, are very unworthy of the age we live in.'

As well as the liveliness of the novel's conversations, there is considerable wit to be found in them. Spence had an excellent sense of humour and was quite free from bitterness or shrillness, however strongly she felt about feminist issues. Her satirical description of the popularity of the fashionable 'religious' novel ridicules that particular popular taste as well as showing just why Alice Melville's literary attempts are doomed to failure. She is equally satirical about the need for a hypocritical strategy for women in social life. Jane Melville expresses herself intelligently and forthrightly, just like a man in fact. The neighbourhood young ladies know how fatal this is to social success for a woman: 'Even if she does know a thing very well, she should keep her knowledge in the background; there is a graceful timidity that is far more attractive than such unladylike confidence.' Spence's irony here doesn't contradict the truth of the observation and in the character of William Dalziel, the shallow suitor for Jane's hand who is indirectly responsible for Mr. Hogarth's Will, and even Alice's suitor William Brandon to a lesser degree, she shows just how easily men are threatened by intellectual strength in women.

Yet Brandon admits that from Peggy Walker's courage, self-denial and truthfulness, he learned to think more highly of women, and it is obvious that contempt for women often derives from contemptible women. Harriet Phillips' egotistical snobbery is a case in point, and in Mrs. Phillips there is a truthful tribute to the power of beauty even when unredeemed by intelligence or breeding.

Francis Hogarth's social reformist activities and his political education actually stem from Jane Melville's ideas, and it is she who urges him to stand for Parliament. The political discussions between the cousins, as they then think themselves, reveal a

cautious conservatism behind Spence's ideas for electoral reform. She shared, with George Eliot, the same initial reasons for not joining the movement for women's suffrage, although she was later to redeem herself thoroughly after meeting activist women in England and America. At this stage however, she sees her scheme of proportional representation as a way of mitigating the danger of the enlargement of the franchise—namely that the new voters would be ill-educated and could swamp the polls. Women, so poorly educated in general, were thought to be a bad risk for the same reason.

Yet, after all, this is a novel with a number of heroines who tend to throw the conventional heroes into the shade. Francis Hogarth is admirable not only because of his sympathetic sensitivities, but because before he inherits Mr. Hogarth's fortune he has patiently worked his way up in the world from poverty to respectability. He is of course Spence's ideal colonist, exactly the kind of immigrant needed by Australia. It is Francis who maintains that only the best of Scotland emigrates, providing a nice rejoinder to the notion that only the second-rate go to the colonies. William Brandon and Arthur Phillips are lesser men whose weaknesses are redeemed by other strengths: one has married a woman only for her remarkable beauty, but he remains loyal and devoted to her, while the other is attracted to Alice Melville because of her 'femininity' and weakness, but before he finally wins her he concedes her moral and artistic superiority. For such women as Alice marriage was itself a vocation. Jane Melville also finds her happiness and fulfilment in marriage, but it is clear from her earlier urging of Francis into public life, that much of her energy and intelligence will find vicarious expression through her husband's activities. Spence points out that in a fairer world, one less structured to exclude women from the exercise of their talents, Jane would have been an outstandingly successful professional woman, and this is made quite explicit in the novel's final pages.

Spence's two unmarried 'career' women, Peggy and Miss Thomson, constitute the strongest strand of Spence's feminist

arguments. Despite a social system stacked against them, one which added insult to injury by its derogation of the 'spinster', they are the novel's most admired characters and therefore deserve to be called its heroines, too. Peggy Walker, without any of the benefits of education or social position, possesses extraordinary moral courage and intelligence which mock the lowly title of 'washer-woman' and demonstrate Spence's admiration for the Scottish peasantry. Miss Thomson has become the most successful farmer in the district, and her lack of social pretension is another reason for the superiority of the Scots as colonists: 'It is better to be at the head of the commonalty than dragging in the rear of the gentry' she tells Alice Melville. Furthermore, spinsters they may be, but Spence makes sure they miss out on none of the pleasures of motherhood, as well as the responsibilities. Their dependent nieces and nephews respect and love them quite as dearly as they could their real mothers, and the novel's final scene of the Christmas gathering of friends and extended family emphasises this.

By the end of *Mr. Hogarth's Will* we have not only the conventionally happy resolution of the novel's plot, but a final and definitive conversation about women's rights. It seems entirely appropriate in its context, and this is an indication of how, throughout the entire novel, Spence has woven strands of opinions and ideas which stretch its range far beyond the conventionally domestic sphere thought appropriate for women's fiction as well as their lives. She has interpolated Peggy's story of emigration, Madame de Vericourt's letter with its contrasting picture of French social customs, some experiments with the spiritualism so fashionable at the time, theories of agricultural reform, political reform, and the thorny subject of illegitimacy. Her well-educated characters have quoted various contemporary writers and discussed all manner of topics of public interest such as the Married Women's Property Act, in which Spence herself was vitally interested.

In an Australian literary context this novel has an importance which for too long was obscured by more fashionable male stereotypes in fiction, the myths of mateship and the bush which

persist to this day. Spence transcended the idiosyncratically national, exclusively male picture of Australian life and showed instead the reality. Colonial lives were lived much as English lives were, and the same intellectual currents flowed through both societies, but there *were* more opportunities for the talented individual, of either sex. Catherine Spence was herself living proof of it. Quite as much a heroine as any of her fictional creations, she provided a real-life example of triumphant female excellence.

Helen Thomson
Monash University

VOLUME ONE

MR. HOGARTH'S WILL

I

THE WILL

In a large and handsomely-furnished room of a somewhat old-fashioned house, situated in a rural district in the south of Scotland, was assembled, one day in the early summer of 185—, a small group in deep mourning.

Mr. Hogarth, of Cross Hall, had been taken suddenly ill a few days previously, and had never recovered consciousness so far as to be able to speak, though he had apparently known those who were about him, and especially the two orphan nieces whom he had brought up as his daughters. He had no other near relations whom any one knew of, and had never been known to regret that the name of Hogarth, of Cross Hall, was likely to become extinct. He had the reputation of being the most eccentric man in the country, and was thought to be the most inconsistent.

With the highest opinion possible of women, and the greatest pleasure in their society, he had never married; and with the greatest affection for his nieces, and the greatest theoretical confidence in them, he had hedged them about with countless laws and restrictions, and had educated them in a way quite different from the training of young ladies of their rank and prospects. He had succeeded two childless elder brothers in the possession of the

estate; and Jane and Alice Melville were the only children of his only sister, who had been dead for fifteen years.

The funeral had just taken place, and the two girls had been summoned into the drawing-room to hear the will read by Mr. MacFarlane, the Edinburgh lawyer, who had drawn it out. They found in the room Mr. Baird, their uncle's medical attendant, and a stranger whom they had never seen before—a tall, grave-looking man of about thirty-four, whose mourning was new, and who showed a deep interest in what was going on.

Both the man of law and the man of medicine looked nervous and embarrassed, and delayed proceeding to business as long as they possibly could; fumbling with knots of red tape; opening the closed curtains to admit a little more light, and then closing them again, as if the light was too strong; so that the sisters had time to look at the stranger, and to wonder who he was and what his business could be there. He also seemed to be taking notes of the young ladies in a quiet, timid manner.

At last the will was opened, and after the usual preamble, the lawyer's voice seemed to break a little. He cleared his throat, and continued in a lower tone—

'As I have come to the conclusion that the minds of men and women are radically the same, and as I believe that if the latter are trained in the same way as the former they will be equally capable of making their own way in the world, I have acted upon this principle in the education of my two beloved nieces, Jane and Alice Melville, the only surviving children of my sister Mary Hogarth; and as I foresee that if I were to leave them wealthy heiresses my purpose would be completely thwarted, by Jane losing her independent character, and Alice sinking into a confirmed invalid, and by both being to a dead certainty picked up by needy spendthrifts, who will waste their fortunes and break their hearts, as their father, George Melville, served my poor foolish sister, I hereby convey and dispone all my property, whatsoever and wheresoever, heritable and moveable, to Francis Ormistown, otherwise Hogarth, at present head clerk in the Bank of Scotland, who is my son by a private

irregular marriage contracted with Elizabeth Ormistown, on the ninth day of July, 18—, and who is my heir-at-law, though he would find it difficult to prove his claim, as he knows nothing of the relation between us, and as the only party besides myself cognizant of the marriage dares not come forward to prove it, but whose progress I have watched with interest, who has made an honourable position for himself, without any assistance from me beyond a good education, who has served faithfully, and who is likely to rule uprightly, who has raised himself from nameless poverty, and whom, therefore, I judge to be worthy of wealth and honour: Provided always, that he shall pay to Jane and Alice Melville, my beloved nieces aforesaid, the sum of twelve pounds a year each, in quarterly payments in advance, for three years following my decease, when such payments shall cease, as by that time I believe they will be independent in circumstances: Provided also that he shall give to the said Jane and Alice Melville, the furniture and personal effects belonging to them, as mentioned more particularly in the schedule marked A, appended to this instrument; and that he shall give to the said Jane and Alice Melville no further assistance either in money or in money's worth, directly or indirectly, whatsoever: Also providing that the said Francis Ormistown, otherwise Hogarth, shall not marry either of his cousins; the marriage of such near relations being mischievous and improper.

'In case of any of these provisions being disregarded by the said Francis Ormistown, otherwise Hogarth, all my heritable and moveable property shall be divided among certain benevolent institutions, in the order and manner set forth in the schedule marked with the letter B.

'All these provisions I have made, as being the best for my surviving relatives; and I believe they will eventually acknowledge them to be such.'

It would be hard to say which of the three parties interested, felt most astonishment at this extraordinary will. Jane Melville stood rigid and silent, with her face flushed and her eyes filled with tears, which she would not let fall. Alice's face lost all colour, and she

seemed ready to faint. But the greatest excitement was shown by the fortunate legatee. He shook from head to foot, steadying himself on the table—looked from the two girls to the two gentlemen with bewildered eyes—and said at last with difficulty, in a low, soft, tremulous voice—

'Was Mr. Hogarth in his senses when he made this will?'

'A little excited, but indisputably in full possession of his senses, strange as the will appears,' said Mr. MacFarlane, the lawyer; 'and Mr. Baird will corroborate my opinion.'

Mr. Baird bowed his head affirmatively. 'Quite true—his head was quite clear at the time. The will was made six weeks ago, and you, Miss Melville, know how well he was then. Very grieved, indeed—most inconceivable conduct—cruel—inconsiderate. I feel deeply for your disappointment. Try not to give way, Miss Alice—or perhaps you had better give way, it may relieve you. Mr. MacFarlane tells me that he remonstrated with Mr. Hogarth. Most painful duty—must obey instructions, of course. Your uncle seemed like adamant. I pity you with all my heart.'

'And so do I, with all my heart,' said Mr. MacFarlane.

'And does no one pity me?' said the low voice of the heir to all; but it was unheeded, for Alice had fainted. Her sister and Mr. Baird laid her on the sofa, and applied the usual restoratives.

Mr. MacFarlane began to speak in an undertone, to the new master, of the extent and value of the property he had thus suddenly come into possession of, and congratulated him rather stiffly on the turn of fortune that had raised him from a life of labour and comparative poverty to ease and affluence; but his embarrassment was nothing compared to that of the man whom he addressed. Francis Hogarth looked round the spacious room, and out of the window to the pleasant shrubbery and smooth-shaven lawn, and shuddered when he thought of the two young cousins, brought up apparently in the lap of luxury, who were to be turned out upon the world with £12 a-year for three years. The elder sister seemed to have a vigorous and robust constitution, but the younger looked delicate. He saw, in his mind's eye, two governesses, dragging out a weary and monotonous existence, far from each

other, while he, possessed of superabundance, was debarred from helping them.

He advanced timidly to the sofa. Alice, who had recovered consciousness, covered her face with both her hands, and sobbed aloud. Jane turned towards him a glance, not of reproach, but of pity. He felt it, and took her hand.

'Believe me, Miss Melville, no one can regret this extraordinary will as I do. I will overturn it, if I possibly can.'

'You cannot,' said Jane; 'it is quite in keeping with all my uncle's ideas—quite consistent with all he has told us over and over again. He had many strange notions, but he was generally in the right, and it *may* prove to be so now.' The sigh that accompanied these words told how faint her hopes were.

'It has been positive unkindness to bring you up as he did, and now to throw you upon the world. My beginning was different. How could he expect the same success for you—women, too?'

'And are women so inferior, then? It was my uncle's cherished belief that they were not. He said he never saw a woman take up man's work without succeeding in it. I must try to show that I will be no exception. He was not unkind to take us on our mother's death from a careless and unprincipled father, to bring us into a quiet and happy home, to educate us to the best of his judgment, to be always kind, always reasonable. Ah, no, my dear uncle, though this seems very hard, it was not meant for unkindness!'

'It is cruel, cruel,' said Alice. 'He must have been mad. What will become of us? What will become of us?'

At this burst of despair from Alice, Jane's courage gave way, and the heavy tears rolled down her cheeks. 'Elsie,* darling, at the worst we can only die, and we are not afraid of death. But no, we shall live to conquer all this yet.'

'You cannot as yet lay any plan,' said Mr. Macfarlane. 'Mr. Ormistown—Mr. Hogarth, I should say—is in no hurry to take possession. You can have a month to look about you, and there is no saying what may turn up in a month.'

*Elsie is Alice's pet name; Jane is sometimes called Jean.

'Certainly,' said the new cousin; 'I am sure I should be most happy to give the young ladies accommodation in this large house for as long as they please, if that is not forbidden by the will.'

'A permanent residence is clearly forbidden; for no assistance, beyond the small money payment specified, can be offered or accepted; but I think a month to remain and to collect all their wardrobe and personal property may be permitted.'

'I ought to return to the bank, and work till they find a substitute, and will leave my cousins the undisturbed possession of Cross Hall for a month. In the meantime, I feel as if my presence must be a painful intrusion. I must leave you.'

'Perhaps,' said Jane, 'though you cannot give us money, you may be able to give us advice. You are going to Edinburgh; you may see or hear of something we could do.'

'I should be most happy to do so. What line of life should you like to enter on?'

'Anything we could make a living by.'

'Then I suppose a governess's situation?'

'I might teach boys, but I have not learned what would qualify me to instruct girls. But I do thoroughly understand bookkeeping, write a good hand, have gone through Euclid, and know as much of the classics as nine out of ten young men in my rank of life. But my uncle cared very little for the classics. I know a good deal of chemistry and mineralogy, but uncle was most pleased with my bookkeeping. How did you get on when you began to work for yourself?'

'I entered the bank as a junior clerk, at the age of sixteen, and got £30 for the first two years. An unknown friend—I know now who he was—who had paid for my education and all other expenses previously, sent me £12 a year for three years to help out my earnings.'

'And you could live on that?' said Jane.

'I did live on it somehow,' said Francis. 'My coats were very threadbare and my meals scanty, but I weathered these three years, and then I got a good step, and crept up gradually. I have been now

in this same bank for seventeen years, and am at present in the receipt of £250 a year, thinking myself rich and fortunate;—now I am rich and unfortunate. Why did not my father leave me to the career I had made for myself, and you to the inheritance you had been brought up to expect?'

'Thirty pounds a year to begin with,' said Jane, half aloud; '£250 after seventeen years' work. Very sweet—all one's own earning. I am not afraid, only let Elsie keep up heart.'

'I cannot,' said Elsie; 'I'll be dead long before seventeen years are over.'

'I will take good care of you,' said Jane.

'How are you to take good care either of yourself or of me if we are starving?' said Elsie, with a fresh burst of tears.

'We will do our best. So you are going, Mr. Hogarth. Write to me if you can hear of anything for me. I will be much obliged to you. Good-bye.'

Jane shook hands with her cousin kindly, and soon after Mr. MacFarlane, and Mr. Baird also, withdrew, leaving the sisters alone. Elsie wept till she was completely exhausted, while her sister sat at the table with pen and ink and paper before her, but writing nothing.

After a while Elsie started up from the sofa. 'Jane,' said she, 'if we were to marry, it would put an end to all this perplexity. It was strange that uncle put in the clause forbidding us to marry that man. Neither of us would demean ourselves so much, but uncle disliked the marriage of near relatives. How strange that so little is said about the mother. I could not look at him, but you did. Is he like his father? My uncle was a very handsome man; I fancy this man is plain.'

'I see little or no likeness to my uncle, but he is by no means plain-looking.'

'Will he get into society? Do they consider such people legitimate?'

'The marriage was irregular, but legal,' said Jane. 'I see now the cause my uncle had to dislike the Scotch marriage law. He must

have been made very miserable from some unguarded words spoken or written; but this does not prevent his son taking the position of a legitimate heir. He is quiet and unassuming, and will take a very good place in society.'

'It was well,' said Elsie, with a faint laugh, 'that this clause was inserted, for you seem to be in some danger.'

'Not at all; but we were thrown together in very extraordinary circumstances, and I could not help feeling for his position as he felt for ours. Nor could I help asking for advice from him. I agree with my uncle about cousins. He was right there, as he always used to be. At least, he brought me up to think like him, and I can scarcely believe that what he has now done is wrong.'

'But, Jane, setting this cousin out of the way, what do you think of William Dalzell?'

'I was just thinking of him when you spoke,' said Jane, resolutely. 'Uncle must have had him in his mind when he mentioned fortune-hunters in his will, for he never seemed to like him coming here so often; and just six weeks ago I had been going out riding with him every day. You said you were not well, and would not accompany us. I suppose I was giving him what people consider a great deal of encouragement. If my uncle had said plainly that he disapproved of the intimacy, I wonder if I would have given it up? Perhaps not—one does not like to be dictated to. It appeared to myself so strange that he should prefer me to you. And now I recollect that my uncle must have paid his last visit to Edinburgh just before he made his will; and there he would see this young man filling his place in the world so well, while I was behaving so foolishly. The contrast must have struck him, and he certainly has put an end to everything between Mr. Dalzell and myself.'

'Oh, Jane, he is no fortune-hunter; this will make no change. If you marry him you must take me home with you, and tell him it is what I deserve for standing his friend so well.'

'My dearest Elsie, you have talked a great deal about Mr. Dalzell, and I have rather foolishly listened to it, but that must be stopped now. I know he is poor; he thought to better himself by a wealthy

marriage; and perhaps if I had been left now with £20,000, with nothing to do and nothing to think of, his agreeable qualities—'

'Well, you own he has agreeable qualities.'

'Yes; I have always owned it—they might have induced me to marry him; and you, as the possessor of other £20,000, would have been a most welcome inmate of our house until you chose for yourself your own home. But now, Elsie, I know William Dalzell is not the man to encumber himself with a penniless wife and a penniless sister-in-law.'

'He is not mercenary—I am sure he is not,' said Elsie with animation.

'Perhaps he is not positively mercenary; but after all am I worthy of the sacrifice? Look at me, Elsie; even your sisterly partiality cannot make a beauty of me. My turn of mind is not suited to his; I have always felt that; and, above all, I am not very fond of him.'

'Not very!'

'No; I have liked him a good deal; but now in this crisis, when we have to begin life in earnest—when I am puzzling myself how to find food and clothing and shelter for you and me—I feel as if Mr. Dalzell's past attentions belonged to another world altogether, so I am putting them aside completely.'

'Ah! but Jane, only listen to me. If he were to come now, and lay himself and all that he has at your feet, that would prove that he was no fortune-hunter, but a real true lover, as I always believed him to be.'

'He will not do it,' said Jane, quietly; and she now began to make some memoranda.

'We have no ornaments, Elsie,' said she, sadly.

'No; I never heard you regret the want of them before.'

'I should like to have something to sell. Emilia Chalmers has £200 worth of jewellery, most of it left by her aunt. If we had so much, we might convert it into money, and might stock a little shop.'

'A shop!' said Elsie, shuddering.

'Why not? One is more independent keeping a shop than in a

governess's situation, and there my business knowledge would be of use. It is wrong and absurd to have a terror of a shop.'

'I cannot help feeling a great repugnance to shopkeeping.'

'Then would you rather be a governess, supposing you were capable?'

'Oh, Jane, that is such a hard life. I should be separated from you; and then one is worried by the children, and snubbed by the parents, sneered at by servants, and ignored by visitors.'

'Then dressmaking? You work beautifully.'

'The late hours, and the close rooms; do you think I could stand it?'

'I am a little afraid for you,' said Jane, thoughtfully. 'What would you like to do?'

'Why, I have never thought of doing anything but being with you, working a little, reading a little, going out a little, and having nobody over me but you, my own darling sister. It stuns me to be told that I must go to work for a livelihood.'

'I hope we may be able to live together as you hoped, eventually; but in the meantime we must both put our shoulders to the wheel.'

'Have we no friends who would give us a home—at least for a while, till we get accustomed to the thought of hard work?' said Elsie.

'We have no relations, and we have made but few friends. I fear no one would come forward to help us now that we need help so much. It is a pity that my uncle kept us so much to himself, and that we were so fully occupied with our own home duties that we had little or no time for society. Now we have no capital for a start, and no friends to help us on, only our talents and our education—a small stock-in-trade, I fear.'

In the course of the afternoon the man-servant, James, announced that Mr. Dalzell was below, and that he sent his compliments and wished to know how the young ladies were.

It was not the first visit since Mr. Hogarth's death. He had paid a visit of condolence on the following day, and had never been so affectionate or impressive in his manner to Jane as on that occasion.

'Show Mr. Dalzell upstairs, James,' said Jane; 'I think I should like to see him.'

The man looked somewhat intelligent, and obeyed.

'I cannot see anybody—I am not fit to be seen,' said Elsie, retreating in haste from the room; 'and indeed, Jane, I wonder at you wishing to see him so soon after this dreadful news.'

'He has been at the funeral, I suppose. It is very proper of him to inquire for us, and very imperative that we should understand each other;—the sooner the better. But do not stay if you do not like. I should prefer to see him alone.'

Mr. Dalzell was shown into the darkened drawing-room, where he was some time in discovering that Miss Melville was alone. A few of the kind commonplaces which had been so successful on his previous visit—remarks on the loss she had sustained, on the excellent character of her deceased uncle, and on the necessity of bearing the blow with fortitude, which her strong mind was quite capable of—were made by Mr. Dalzell in unconsciousness that they fell very differently on Jane's ears now. Jane asked for his mother, and heard that she was very well, and sent her kindest regards and condolences, and hoped that the Misses Melville would be able to see her on the following day.

'Were there many people at the funeral?' asked Jane.

'Oh yes, a great many; Mr. Hogarth was so extensively known, and so much respected.'

'Were there any strangers?'

'Several—to me,' said Dalzell.

'Did you observe no one in particular?'

'Yes, a gentleman from Edinburgh, said to be a *protegé* of your uncle's, who took rather a prominent place on account of there being no male relative surviving.'

'Have you heard,' said Jane, with an effort—'have you heard anything of the will?'

'Nothing whatever—did not think it proper or delicate to inquire, though I saw Mr. MacFarlane after it had been read. It is a matter of no consequence to me how Mr. Hogarth has left his

property. My feelings will be quite the same towards—'

'Stop,' said Jane; 'my uncle has left his entire fortune to this stranger from Edinburgh, who is his son by a private marriage. Elsie and I have had an education, and must make the best we can of it.'

'Miss Melville, this is incredible—quite incredible. You are merely trying me. Mr. Hogarth was incapable of such madness and injustice. It is not treating me well to play upon me in this way.'

'In proof of what I say, here is a certified copy of the will—the final will—executed six weeks ago, when, as you know, my uncle was perfectly well both in body and mind. It is incontestable.'

The bewildered young man tried to read the paper put into his hand, but he could not follow the written words. Jane's sad face and her manner convinced him, however, that she was telling him the truth.

'Now,' said Jane kindly, 'you have talked a great deal of nonsense to me when my position was very different; but I am quite aware that things are altogether changed. I will not feel at all hurt or angry about it. We part perfectly good friends. But you cannot afford to marry a wife without money, and I should be sorry to be a burden to any man.'

William Dalzell looked at the girl he had fancied himself in love with for the last few months, and felt that his love had not been of a very deep or absorbing character. If the two girls had been equal favourites of their uncle's, his choice would have fallen on Elsie, who was prettier, more elegant, more yielding, and, as he thought, more affectionate. Her impulsive and confiding manner, her little enthusiasms, her blunders, were to him more charming than Jane's steady good sense and calm temper. Jane never wanted advice or assistance; she was too independent in mind, and too robust in body, to care much about little attentions, though she had become accustomed to his in the course of time, and as there was no other person to compare him with, had allowed herself to think a good deal of him. Mr. Hogarth had always shown so marked a preference for Jane, and had so often expressed displeasure and impatience at

Elsie's deficiencies; his property, not being entailed, was entirely at his own disposal, so that it was probable that Jane would be left the larger share of it, while if he made love to Alice it was quite possible that she would be disinherited altogether, for he knew that he was not a favourite with the old gentleman. He did not think that anything could shake Mr. Hogarth's confidence in Jane, and he had been very careful in feeling his ground sure before he made a formal proposal. He had tried to persuade himself that Jane's face was charming, though not regularly handsome; so it was to some people, but he had not eyes to see the charm. Her figure was undeniably fine, her temper good, her principles to be depended on. Her education had been peculiar, and singularly secular—his mother had felt a little shocked at her want of religion—but then Mr. Hogarth was very odd, and when she was married she would see things differently; and on the whole Mrs. Dalzell felt that her handsome son had chosen with great prudence and good sense in fixing his affections upon the elder and the favorite niece. His small property was heavily encumbered, and such a marriage would make him hold up his head again in the country. Mrs. Dalzell's attentions to Jane had been nearly as assiduous as her son's, and to the motherless girl they were quite as welcome; and she had shown so much affection for Alice, too, that both sisters had been very much captivated with her.

William Dalzell felt Jane's kindly-meant speech as a sort of reproach. He would have preferred to make a speech himself, and to have seen her more agitated. Though he had never thought himself very much in love, he believed he had inspired a strong love, and that it would be very hard for Jane to give him up. But things were completely taken out of his hands; she did not even now, in the first pain of parting, dream of breaking her heart. She was his superior, painfully his superior, and he did not like it.

'You are quite right, Miss Melville,' said he; 'what you say is quite true. I am involved and embarrassed, and could not offer you anything worth having.'

'And I will make my own way in the world,' said Jane; 'and,

William Dalzell, do not be hurt if I give you one friendly piece of advice on parting—try to make your own way in the world too. Shake yourself clear of your own embarrassments by your own industry—a far better way than by marrying a rich wife.'

She looked very kindly at the young man as she spoke, but he did not take the advice in the friendly spirit in which it was given. He answered rather shortly, that he dared to say he would do as well as other people, and then began to ask what she knew about the heir, if she had ever seen him before, or heard Mr. Hogarth speak of him. She answered—

'No, never; but I cannot answer questions. I cannot converse rationally any longer. You had better go away, Mr. Dalzell, and let me have a little rest, for I am rather weary.'

The young gentleman stumbled down stairs, and rode home ruminating over the downfall of all his cherished expectations; while Jane said to herself, 'It is over, and it is better so. He really is a smaller character than I thought he was.'

II

DISAPPOINTMENT AND HOPE; PROSE AND POETRY

When Jane Melville told her cousin that her uncle had been always kind and always reasonable, she expressed her own opinion, for she had loved and honoured him so much that she felt no hardship in doing everything he wished; but no one else in the house or in the neighbourhood would have endorsed that opinion. When the rumour spread far and wide that he had disinherited his nieces, in the expectation that the education he had given them would enable them to provide handsomely for themselves, the servants and workpeople about shook their heads, and said it was 'aye weel kenned that the auld laird had a bee in his bonnet;' while the class with whom Mr. Hogarth associated on more equal terms declared; that this last eccentricity of affection (for it was all done out of pure love), surpassed all his other oddities with regard to the girls, which had long been the talk of the whole country.

They had, as Jane sadly confessed, made but few friends. Their uncle's reasonable prejudices extended to morning visits, which he called a frivolous waste of time; and he had a similar dislike to evening parties; not on account of a puritanic disapproval of dancing, or of young people of different sexes meeting and having opportunities of getting acquainted with each other, but the hours

were so irrational, and the conventional dress so unbecoming and dangerous to health, that he had prohibited Jane and Elsie from accepting the invitations that were showered on them when they had given up lessons and were supposed to be ready to come out. If people would meet at six, and break up before twelve, and wear dresses fashioned like their ordinary attire, Mr. Hogarth saw no objection to evening parties. He had invited the neighbours to such a party, and mentioned in his note of invitation the conditions on which it was to be attended. A good many had accepted, partly from curiosity, and partly from a wish to be friendly; but, in spite of really good arrangements and an excellent supper, the party was not such a success as to be repeated often by Mr. Hogarth, and was never imitated by any of his guests.

The Misses Melville danced well, walked well, and rode admirably; they spent several hours every day in the open air; had learnt to swim, and to shoot both with bow and arrow and with rifle. Their physical education had been excellent, and had probably saved Elsie's life, for she was extremely delicate when young, but had gained strength as she grew up.

Their book education had been chiefly conducted by an old gentleman, who had lived for eight years in their house as tutor, and they had spent several winters in Edinburgh, to attend classes and lectures. No money, no care, and no time had been spared on their education, so that it was rather a pity that, in the eyes of the world, it was so unsatisfactory when completed. Both had gone through the same routine; for Mr. Hogarth seemed to think that education made characters, instead of merely drawing out what there is in the original material, and he was disappointed that the uniformity of the training had not produced two characters more similar than those of Jane and Elsie. Jane's tendencies were to the practical and the positive; and she gladly availed herself of her uncle's whim to educate her like a man of business, regretting none of the accomplishments and showy acquirements which are too apt to be considered the principal part of female education. Expecting that she would be left in possession of considerable property, and

virtually the guardian of her younger sister, she saw a fitness and propriety in her being taught the management of money, the science of agriculture, the care of an establishment, and the accurate keeping of accounts.

Elsie would have preferred another training, but it was not given to her; and though she made but a lame attempt to follow Jane's footsteps, and acquired only a superficial knowledge of what her sister was the perfect mistress of, her uncle believed that, bad as she was, she would have been much worse if she had not been forced into rational studies. Though she was not a marvel of solidity, she still had as good a knowledge of accounts, general information, history, and science, as is possessed by many boys who get on very well in business or in professions, when once set fairly to work.

Mr. Hogarth had no great opinion of the value of teaching languages, and thought that a knowledge of things was of far more importance than a knowledge of the names of things. The girls had learned, however, a good deal of Latin and Greek from Mr. Wilson, their tutor, who thought it a pity that Jane's fine abilities should not have a classical education; and he had induced Mr. Hogarth to agree to it by the argument that these languages are invaluable for the ready and correct understanding of all scientific terms. French and Italian the girls themselves were anxious to learn; and as they had been promised a continental tour some fine summer, their uncle thought they might be useful acquirements then, so they had lessons from the best masters in Edinburgh, and profited by them. And here for the first time Elsie's progress had been far greater than Jane's. Mr. Hogarth had himself spent a good deal of time in his youth in France; but he had a higher opinion of French society than of French literature, and he thought that from the lips of brilliant Parisian women they would learn more of the spirit of the language and of the people than from the books they studied in classes or read at home.

Elsie had a natural taste for music, and a remarkably sweet voice in speaking, which, if it had been cultivated, would have made her an excellent singer; but her uncle was sure that to indulge her with

a musical education would only weaken her mind. Mr. Hogarth had seen no good come of music. A taste for singing and a fine voice had been the ruin of thousands—they had been most mischievous to Elsie's own father, and they had been the chief fascinations which had won upon his dear sister Mary. She and George Melville had sung duets together, and from that had been led to try a duet through life; and a very sad and inharmonious life they had made of it.

So poor Elsie's natural tastes were discouraged and thwarted; and after the positive lessons were over, and her education was said to be finished, she felt vacuity and *ennui* when Jane rejoiced in full employment. The housekeeping was ostensibly taken by the sisters in alternate weeks; but though Jane relinquished the keys for the stated period, she never relinquished the superintendence. She remembered what Elsie forgot; she looked forward where Elsie would have scrambled in the best way she could through the passing hour, and constantly thinking for her and remedying her blunders. Elsie was apt to forget that any responsibility rested on herself.

Nothing in their singular training was considered odder than that, while they were educated in a more masculine manner than most boys, they were obliged at the same time to make a greater proportion of their own clothes than any girls of their own rank or circumstances, and that they had been carefully and systematically taught to make them in the best manner possible. The only instructions which they had received from one of their own sex had been given to them by an excellent plain needlewoman, a first-class dressmaker, and a fashionable milliner; and in the last two branches Elsie's taste had made her excel her sister even more than in French and Italian.

At the time of their uncle's death, Jane was twenty-three years old, and Elsie two years younger. They had but very recently given up regular study, for their uncle thought girls were far too soon 'finished', as it is called, and turned out in a very incomplete state of mental and moral development. He would not let them think

themselves educated till they had seen more of the world than could be done in Edinburgh, which was a city he had rather a contempt for, as a mere provincial capital, too superstitious and narrow-minded for his taste. Paris and London were the schools for men, and therefore, according to his notions, for women also; but when the time arrived for the tour on the Continent and the winter in London, which had been promised to the girls, he felt his health had given way, though he had no positive illness, and delayed leaving home till the following year, when he hoped to be able to enjoy it, and to show all he meant to show to the girls without fatigue or indifference. If he had been able to go with them on the previous year, as had been arranged, he would probably have left his fortune otherwise, for Mr. Dalzell's attentions had only been of recent date.

As the news of the will spread, every one said they really ought to call on the Melvilles, poor things; but no one was in a hurry to perform so disagreeable a duty. Mrs. Dalzell was so astounded by the change that was made in her son's prospects, and so embarrassed lest she should be looked to for assistance in the present urgent necessities of the girls, that though she had been by far the most intimate and cordial of their friends, she was not the first to visit them. Three or four matrons had come and gone, who had made but short calls, and who had taken refuge in commonplace inquiries as to how and when Mr. Hogarth had been first taken ill, and at what hour he died, but had given very little sympathy, and no advice. The minister of the parish had called, as in duty bound, on the day after the funeral, and suprised both Jane and Elsie by a style of conversation very different from any they had ever heard from his lips. In his previous visits to Cross Hall he had never talked of anything but the weather, and crops, and the news of the neighbourhood. His tastes, his studies, his politics, and his faith were so opposite to those of Mr. Hogarth that there was no safety, and likely to be no pleasure, in conversation that left the neutral ground he took. But now, when the eccentric and sceptical Mr. Hogarth had crowned all this sins by an act of such injustice to his

nieces, and they were in affliction from bereavement and poverty, he wished to give them spiritual comfort, and to teach them something that he knew had been omitted in their education; but he couched his consolation in language that seemed strangely unfamiliar to the girls he addressed, and when he spoke of crosses to be borne, that God has made crooks in every lot that no man may make straight—when he dwelt upon the temptations of riches, and the difficulty with which the rich can enter the kingdom of Heaven, and hoped that his young friends would see the hand of God in this trying dispensation, and would follow humbly His leading—Jane, who hoped to conquer her difficulties, and did not mean to succumb to them, did not feel much comforted or edified by the well-meant exhortation. Both girls felt pained, too, by the reflections he cast on their late uncle, and by the warning to be prepared for sudden death, as this had been an instance of the Master coming when no one was looking for Him, and when the loins were not girt, nor the light burning. Both girls had loved their uncle; and even though Elsie felt that he had been often hard to her, and that the will was not a just one, she could not bear the idea that Mr. Herries suggested of his probable place in the future state, while Jane felt indignant.

They had both hoped for some help and comfort from Mrs. Dalzell; but when her visit was so long delayed, their expectations fell considerably. Jane had become so tired of the useless kind of condolence that was offered, that she determined to ask for advice from the next person who came, and that happened to be Mrs. Dalzell. She spoke a little more freely and kindly to the girls than other people had done; but still she was keeping serious difficulties at arm's length, when Jane turned rather sharply round on her with the abrupt question—

'What do you think we ought to do, Mrs. Dalzell?'

'Indeed, I cannot say, Miss Melville. This most unaccountable conduct of Mr. Hogarth's has taken us all by surprise, so much that I can think of nothing but overturning the will. I am sure when William told me of the extraordinary disposition of the property, I

felt—I cannot tell you how I felt. Such a shocking thing to leave all to a son whom nobody ever heard of before, and to leave his sister's children destitute. You certainly have a claim on the heir, for a maintenance at least. He should be made to refund a part of the spoil.'

'He would if he could, but it is forbidden. There is no help in that way,' said Jane. 'But employment, Mrs. Dalzell; can you suggest any employment for us?'

Mrs. Dalzell hesitated. 'Mrs. Chalmers is in need of a finishing governess for Emma and Robina; but I am afraid neither of you two young ladies would suit her, for we cannot get music-masters here, and one must have a governess who has a good knowledge of music. If Mr. Maxwell had not just engaged a tutor for his boys, you might have perhaps undertaken that place, Miss Melville.'

'I think I might,' said Jane.

'Would it not be pleasanter, if we have to take situations, to go to a distance,' said Elsie. 'I do not think I could I bear you or myself to be near Cross Hall when everything is so changed.'

'It would be more agreeable, I have no doubt, Miss Elsie; and I cannot help thinking that in such a place as Edinburgh or Glasgow, where there are masters and mistresses for everything, you could get on by having classes, or engaging as teachers at some institution. In the country we want governesses and schoolmistresses to know everything a girl ought to learn.'

'Is there nothing but teaching that we can do?' said Jane.

'Well, you know there is nothing that a gentlewoman can turn to in such circumstances as yours but teaching, and I would be very glad indeed to see you both in nice comfortable situations. By-the-by, Miss Elsie, I copied into my album the very sweet verses you sent me, and have brought them back to you. Are they really your own? WIlliam says he thinks they are.'

'Yes,' said Elsie, 'they are original.'

'Well, I could not have thought it; they are extremely pretty.'

'By-the-by,' said Jane, 'do you not know Miss Thomson, Mrs. Dalzell? My uncle always spoke of her with respect and admiration,

as an instance of the skill and success with which a woman can conduct masculine avocations. A gentlewoman-farmer, and a thriving one. I wish we had known her.'

'Oh, yes. I do know Miss Thomson. Of course we are not exactly in the same position, we being proprietors, while she is only a farmer; but she is a most excellent and estimable woman in her way, though she is a bit of a character. She is now growing old, and not so active as she has been.'

'She is said to be a benevolent and a kind-hearted, as well as a clever woman,' said Jane.

'Oh, yes; and well she may be liberal, for she has made money, and has not the status to keep up that old country families must maintain.'

'I wonder if she would engage me as her helper, and teach me farming. I know a good deal of theoretical agricultural chemistry. Will you be so good as give me a letter of introduction to her; I should feel greatly obliged to you.'

Mrs. Dalzell willingly granted this small request, and felt much disposed to magnify its importance. It would be a good thing if, without any trouble or sacrifice on her own part, she could aid her dear young friends by bringing them into contact with a person who was more able to further their views than herself. She was sure that Miss Thomson was the very person to apply to, for of course she would take an interest in a young lady so unfortunately situated. It was so well thought of on Miss Melville's part; but then Miss Melville was always so quick and sensible. The letter of introduction was written, and then Mrs. Dalzell took leave.

Next day Elsie was languidly reading the local weekly journal, when she came upon a paragraph which related to themselves. Mr. Hogarth's will was described and commented on. There was congratulation for the heir and commiseration for the nieces.

'Oh, Jane,' said she, 'is it not dreadful to be brought before the public in this way; everybody must be talking about us, and of course everybody has got hold of the story of William Dalzell and you too. I am glad they did not put that in the newspapers, at any

rate. Every one will think that he gave you up, and will fancy you are so distressed about it.'

'We cannot help either what people think or what they say. I do not wonder at the *Courier* making a long paragraph on the subject, for they have not had such an interesting piece of local news since Mr. Fisher committed suicide.'

'I do not like the appearance of my own name in print,' said Elsie.

'It is a very pretty name, nevertheless, and would look as well on the title-page of a book as any I know—only in a newspaper you do not like it,' said Jane. 'I must bid you good-bye for a few hours now, for I am going to Miss Thomson's. I am going to ride, and will not be very long.'

Miss Thomson had just taken up the local newspaper after her morning ride over the farm, and had read the peculiarly interesting paragraph relating to Mr. Hogarth's will, when Mrs. Dalzell's note was put into her hands, and Miss Melville was announced.

Miss Thomson was a very fine-looking old lady, with keen, though also kind grey eyes, looking out from rather shaggy eye-brows, and an open frank smile on her mouth. The colour of health still bloomed on a cheek that had seen sixty summers and winters, and the elasticity of youth had only been transformed into the dignity and repose of a green old age. It is better to be at the head of the commonalty than dragging in the rear of the gentry, and for substantial comfort, liberal housekeeping, generous almsgiving, and frank hospitality, the farmhouse of Allendale was out and out superior to the mansion of Moss Tower, where the Dalzells had lived for at least two centuries.

As Mrs. Dalzell's note had been introductory and not explanatory, Miss Thomson could not guess the cause of the unexpected visit. She, however, kindly welcomed Miss Melville, and asked her to sit down, which Jane did with an ease and youthful dignity that was as suitable to her time of life as Miss Thomson's at three-score.

'I have called, madam,' said Jane, 'because I have always admired you, and wished to know you; and also because at this critical

juncture I have thought that your advice would be far more valuable to me than that of people who have never made an effort or conquered an obstacle. You know our position'—and she glanced at the open newspaper.

'Yes, I do. I feel both surprised and grieved at your uncle's extraordinary settlement,' said Miss Thomson.

'My uncle always used to point to you as an instance of what women could do if they tried, and I am sure he must have had you in his eye when he felt so sure of my success in life. Could you, would you teach me to farm, and I will keep your books, write your letters, manage your household, be your factotum, if you will allow me. I have studied agricultural chemistry, and if you would permit me to learn from you the practical details of farming operations, I might really be of use to you.'

Miss Thomson shook her head. 'My dear girl, you do not know what you ask. Without capital, and a large capital, no one need think of taking a farm in Scotland; and all those things that you offer to do for me are precisely the things that I can do for myself, and I hope will be able to do for the next ten years. I should be better for an assistant, it is true, but it must be some one who can ride to market, buy stock, sell to butchers, take or let grass parks, and oversee my working farm steward, for I am getting rather old for such long rides as I have been in the habit of taking on the farm. And, my poor girl, anxious as I am to befriend you in your straits, and to encourage your honest ambition, I have nephews and nieces, and grand-nephews and grand-nieces of my own, who have all claims upon me. My two married sisters have large families, and not very much to keep them on, so I have to help in various ways. Do as you like, the burden of bringing up the next generation is pretty equally divided among us, and I am only thankful that Providence has so prospered me that I can be of use of the young people. I have arranged that my nephew, John Forrester, is to come and do for me what I cannot so well manage without help; and as I have no idea of falling behind the high farming of the times, I have given him a thorough course of the agricultural chemistry, so much

in fashion, before he tries the practical branch of the science. I hope he will not be too new-fangled and upsetting altogether with his theories; but he is a good lad in the main, and I think he will do. Besides John, I have to help his brother James to begin business, and I have two nieces whose education I am making more thorough than their parents could afford to do.'

'So you have no room for me,' said Jane. 'I should have known it. I have no claim on any one, not a relation in the world but a sister, less fit to cope with it than myself, and a cousin, newly found under sad circumstances, and tied down not to assist us. But could you not give us any encouragement, for that is what I want most? Your own experience—'

'My own experience is very different from what yours can be. My father died in the early years of a long lease of twenty-one years, when he had laid out several thousands, all the capital he had, and all he could raise, upon the land, hoping to get it out again with interest and a large profit, for the farm was a fine one, though it had been badly managed before. He had no son to take up the lease; and had things been wound up, and the lease sold, there would have been a heavy loss. I believed that I could manage the concern, and got leave from the landlord, rather as a favour, to continue on Allendale. I was industrious and methodical, and reduced the expenses of management below what they had been in my father's time, and consequently made more money than even he could have made of it. My landlord willingly took me again for a tenant when the lease was expired, particularly as I offered as much as any one for it. The value of the lease, stock, and crop, that I began business with, could not have been less for me to keep than £5,000, though if they had been sold they might have brought only half that amount. You see I had a good start. I like the work, and it likes me. I am a richer, a happier, and a more useful woman, than I could have been if I had had £20,000 all left me in a lump.'

'This is very different, indeed, from our case,' said Jane. 'It is the want of capital that I feel so very hard. I could make something of capital.'

'I suppose that for you, Miss Melville, with nothing but youth, health, and a stout heart, there is nothing but a governess's situation to be thought of. Society seems to say to gentlewomen who have not enough to live on, "Teach or marry;" and the governess market and the marriage market are both sadly overstocked. People have not all got a taste for either alternative. Here am I, a sensible, well-disposed woman, but yet I never could teach in my life, and I never had any wish to marry.'

'The world is large,' said Jane; 'there are thousands of fields of labour. Uncle did not wish us to be governesses, I am quite sure; he did not educate us for it; and I do not think he wished us to marry either.'

'He should have left you a small competence—not enough to tempt others, but to save you from being tempted yourself,' said Miss Thomson.

'I dare say he made a great mistake; but I think he fancied that the strong necessity for effort would stimulate us to exertion. To vegetate on a small annuity would not be so pleasant as to earn even the same income for ourselves,' said Jane.

'Well, my dear girl, I do not fear for you, though things look so very gloomy at present. You have got the stuff in you. There is promise of success in your step and voice—in your quick eye and honest smile. Is your sister like yourself?—no; you said she was less fit for the life that is before you; that is a pity.'

'It is; but we love each other so dearly—we are all the world to each other.'

'Well, that is good for both of you; love is just as great a necessity as air or food. I cannot help thinking that you should try your luck in Edinburgh; you are more likely to find what will suit you there than in a country side, like this of Swinton. Have you any friends there?'

'None to rely upon,' said Jane.

'Your cousin that has come into such an inheritance, does he seem friendly?'

'Very much so, but he is forbidden to give us help.'

'In money, perhaps; but it would be only right if he would take some trouble to make inquiries, and speak for you to any one he thinks could employ you. It would be a satisfaction to his own mind, besides.'

'I have a letter from him this morning, saying that he has heard of something that he fears is not good enough for me, or either of us, and urging me to come to Edinburgh, to see for myself, offering me or both of us, if we are so inclined, the hospitality of his humble home, as he calls it. I cannot afford to go to a hotel, and we have no friend to whose house we could go uninvited, so I feel inclined to accept the invitation.'

'You had better do so, Miss Melville; and as it may be a while before you meet with work, and as travelling about to look for it costs money, you will be so good as to take this, with my best wishes,' said Miss Thomson, opening her desk and taking out a five-pound note and handing it to Jane, who, though she had fancied she never could have accepted money from a stranger, felt this to be offered so frankly and kindly, that she thanked Miss Thomson and took it.

'This is the best sign of you yet—no foolish pride—no flying in my face with indignant disclaiming of what people call charity, and throwing the bit of paper on the carpet for the lass to sweep out, but a sensible and reasonable way of taking from a fellow-creature what she would take as pleasantly from you if she needed it and you had it to spare. You will do, Miss Melville; only mind, as the old Scotch proverb has it, "You must set a stout heart to a stey brae".'

On Jane's return to Cross Hall she found her sister in very much better spirits than when she set out for Allendale. An idea had struck Elsie, consequent partly on the remark Jane had made about her name looking well on the title-page of a book, and partly on her seeing in the Poet's Corner of the *Swinton Courier* some verses very inferior to her own which Mrs. Dalzell had returned to her. She was a poet; and what was there to hinder her from distinguishing herself in the literary world by thoughts that breathe and words that burn; and also from earning in this pleasant way a

handsome income. Hope arose out of the vision; the fanciful and fragile mind that every one had depised and undervalued might, perhaps, do greater things than Jane's clear head and busy hands. Never had her ideas flowed more rapidly, or her words arranged themselves so well. She began by bewailing her own sad fate, the loss of fortune, and the desertion of friends; and the sincerity of her feelings made it feel like an inspiration. Things that appeared to her to be new thoughts crowded on her, and before Jane's return she had finished a short poem very much to her own satisfaction.

She would scarcely wait to hear the result of her sister's visit to Miss Thomson, but impetuously and affectionately made Jane sit down to listen to her lay.

'I wish I were a good judge, Elsie. It seems to me to be very pretty. Here and there I would alter a word; but, on the whole, I think you have succeeded,' was the welcome criticism.

'You think so; and you are so prosaic. I feel as if I could go on for ever writing. Don't you think you have seen worse verses printed, not in a newspaper, but in a book?'

'I read so little of that kind of literature; but I am sure you often read pieces to me, from both newspapers and books, that do not interest me half so much.'

'Oh, Jane, I count so much on your good opinion, because I know that you will give it honestly, and because I think if I can please you I may please anybody.' And Elsie looked so animated, so joyous, and so spiritual, that Jane's hopes rose. She, indeed, was no judge of poetry, but anything that could give courage and hope to her sister's mind must be a good thing.

'You must persevere, my dear. It will do yourself good, if no other good comes of it,' said she.

'But other good is sure to come of it, Jane. Do not such things get printed, and of course the writer is paid for them? I can write so fast; and now I know some of the real trials of life, I can speak from experience.'

'And you are the type of the bulk of the poetry-reading public,' said Jane thoughtfully. 'The lady readers, I mean; generous,

impulsive, and romantic; you ought to know what will suit the public taste. I wish you all success. But I have failed in my object, and have been advised to go to Edinburgh. You saw I had a letter this morning from Mr. Hogarth, with an invitation for both of us to come and live at his house, and look about us. You would not like to go?'

'No, Jane, I would far rather stay here and write; but it would be uncomfortable for you to go by yourself. I will go, if you very much wish it.'

'No, my dear, if you think this writing is to be your vocation, it is not necessary for you to look for a situation, and I do not mind going by myself, only I feared you would be unhappy alone.'

'I will be quite happy. I must have something better than this done while you are away.'

'I must write to my cousin, accepting the invitation, and telling him when to expect me. The sooner I can go the better.'

III

CLOSED DOORS

Francis Hogarth was waiting for Jane at the railway station, and as they walked together to his house in the outskirts of the town, she eagerly asked him about the situation he had heard of that he feared would not suit.

Her cousin hesitated a little, for it seemed so far below her deserts and her capabilities; but Mr. Rennie, the manager of the bank in which he had so long been employed, had told him that the — Institution, the principal asylum for the insane in Scotland, and an admirably managed establishment, wanted a second matron; and that from the accounts he had heard of Miss Melville's practical talents, it was probable that she would be the very person to fill the situation well. Jane eagerly asked after the duties and the salary, but Francis could not give her all the particulars she desired. Mr. Rennie was to see one of the Directors of the — Institution on that evening, and was to make inquiries; he had some influence with one or two of the directors, and would use it in Miss Melville's favour if she was disposed to apply for it. It was expected that there would be at least fifty applications for it, and a little interest was a good auxiliary even to the greatest merits in the world. The duties, so far as Francis knew them, were the active superintendence of a

large number of female servants, and the charge of all the stores, both of food and clothing, required for a household of several hundreds, who could none of them think for themselves. He did not know if she would come much in contact with the patients; he hoped not, for he thought it would be a sufficiently exhausting and anxious life without that. He had heard that the institution parted with the present occupant of the situation for incompetence—that there had been both waste and peculation.

'I feel sure that my superintendence of my uncle's household, and my knowledge of accounts, should enable me to fill such a situation well, and from the number of applications, and the responsible nature of the duties, the salary should be handsome,' said Jane. 'I think I should send in an application, and I feel obliged both to Mr. Rennie and you for the suggestion. The establishment is well managed; you know it is one of those to which my uncle's property was to go in case you disobeyed his injunctions. He had a high opinion of the kind and rational treatment of the patients there. I do not see any objection to mingling with them either. I might be very useful.'

'It seems a throwing away of your talents and acquirements, to make a mere housekeeper of you,' said Francis.

'It is not such an insignificant office after all. What contributes to the comfort and happiness of a family every day, and all day long, is surely as valuable a thing as much book-learning; and to keep such a large establishment going smoothly and satisfactorily requires much care and thought, and a particular kind of talent, which I think I possess, and which such a life will develop. When can I see Mr. Rennie, and when can I send in my application?'

'Mr. Rennie particularly desires to see you to-morrow morning; and if you like the prospect he holds out, your application can be sent in immediately.'

When they reached the small but prettily situated cottage occupied by Francis, Jane was agreeably struck with the comfort and neatness of everything about it. The furniture, without being costly, was good of its kind; the very excellent collection of books was

methodically arranged in ample book-shelves, and carefully preserved by glass doors; the bright fire in the grate—for though it was called summer, it was but a bleak cold day in Edinburgh; and the respectable-looking middle-aged woman who had just laid the cloth for dinner, and now brought it in; all gave an air of comfort and repose to a dwelling much humbler than she had been accustomed to live in, but far better than any she could hope for a while to occupy. There were on a side table a few costly articles of *vertu*, and a magnificent folio of engravings, which had been bought by Mr. Hogarth since his accession to fortune; but substantial comfort had been attained long before.

Jane was rather surprised to see the large proportion of poetry and fiction that filled the book-shelves. Little did Mr. Hogarth the elder suppose that the bank clerk, whose outer life was so satisfactorily practical, had an inner life whose elements were as fanciful and unreal as poor Elsie's. His taste was certainly more severe and fastidious than hers, for he was older, and had read more; but his love, both of art and poetry, was very strong, and had been to him in his long solitary struggle with fortune a constant and unfailing pleasure. He had found in them some amends for the want of relatives and the want of sympathy; and now his heart turned with strong affection to both of his cousins, and especially to the one who treated him with so much delicacy of feeling and such generous confidence. It was like finding a long-lost sister; there was so much to ask and to answer on either side. Jane liked to talk of her uncle; and Francis' curiosity about his unknown father, whom he had only occasionally seen at long intervals as a stranger who took a little interest in him, was satisfied by her clear and graphic descriptions of his opinions, his talk, and his habits; whilst she, beginning a new life, and doubtful of the issue, eagerly asked of his early experiences, and liked to chronicle every little step in a steady and well-deserved progress.

Though Jane had such a practical turn of mind, and such an excellent education, it must not be supposed that she knew much of the world. Educate women as you will, that knowledge is rarely

attained at twenty-three; and she had lived so much in a Utopia of her own, fancying that things that were right were always expedient, and that they should always be valued for their intrinsic worth, that she did not see the difficulties of her situation as clearly as many people who had not half her understanding. She and her uncle had been too apt to talk of things as they ought to be, and not as they actually were. With all Jane's quiet good sense, there were points on which she could be enthusiastic, and on this evening the successful cousin was struck by the warm expressions of an optimism in which he could not share, uttered by one who had good cause for complaint and dissatisfaction.

When the cousins went together to the Bank of Scotland on the following day, and were shown into Mr. Rennie's private room, Jane's hopes were somewhat damped by the details she received about the situation. The duties were even greater than she had supposed, consisting in the active and complete superintendence of a great many female servants, and a slighter control over a still larger number of female keepers, who also acted as housemaids and chambermaids; the control of the workroom, so as to see that there was no waste, extravagance, or pilfering there; the arrangements necessary in the cooking and distribution of such large quantities of food, so that each should have enough, and yet that there should be no opportunity of theft; and the watchfulness required to prevent any of the girls employed in the establishment from flirting with any of the convalescent gentlemen. The wages given by the directors had been too low to keep servants long in the place, or to secure a good class of girls who would be above dishonesty or other weaknesses; and this made the duties of their superintendent particularly irksome; while there was a good deal to be done for the patients themselves, though not so much by the second as by the upper matron.

All this seemed a formidable amount of work for one head and one pair of eyes to do; and when Jane was told that the salary was £30 a-year, and that so many applications had been and were likely to be sent in, that great interest was necessary for success, she was

by no means so decided on sending in hers. Even the privileges annexed to the situation, of a small bedroom for herself, and a parlour shared by two others, with a fortnight's holidays in the year, though very necessary to prevent the second matron being removed speedily into one of the wards, did not seem so tempting as to revive Jane's last night's enthusiasm.

'Surely,' said she, 'the payment is very small for the work and the responsibility.'

'There is so much competition for a thing of this kind,' said Mr. Rennie. 'There are so many women in Scotland who have too little to live on, or nothing at all, that they will gladly snatch at anything that will give them food and lodging, and the smallest of salaries. I know of a situation of £12 a-year that received forty-five applications from reduced gentlewomen. The payment is never in proportion to the work.'

'But the work has been badly done hitherto, I understand,' said Jane. 'It is not having too little to live on that makes a woman fit for such a situation as this. Why do not they raise the salary and insist on higher qualifications?'

'I cannot tell why they do not, but so it is,' said Mr. Rennie.

'Is there any chance of rising from second to first matron?' asked Jane. 'That is worth £90, you say.'

'In the course of fifteen or twenty years, perhaps; but the duties are very distinct at present, and require different kinds of talent.'

'Yes,' said Jane; 'and great interest with the directors might get a new person in, and fifteen or twenty years' services would have less weight. I do not feel inclined to work twenty years for £30 even with a better chance of £90 at last than is offered here. It is at best a prison life, too; not the life I had hoped for, nor what I am best fitted for. My cousin's place is filled up here, I understand.'

'Every one below Mr. Ormistown has got a step, and we only want a junior clerk. No doubt we will have plenty of applicants.'

'Will you take me?' said Jane. 'Do not shake your head, Mr. Rennie. Cousin Francis, speak a word for me; I am quite fit for the situation.'

'If you could do anything to further Miss Melville's views in any way you would lay me under a deep and lasting obligation, Mr. Rennie,' said Francis. 'I have most unconsciously done both of my cousins a great injury, which I am not allowed to repair. My late father had as much confidence in this young lady's talents and qualifications as he had in mine. I know she is only too good for the situation she asks for.'

Mr. Rennie was disposed to try to please Mr. Hogarth. He had always had a high opinion of him, and had great confidence in his judgment and integrity. He was to take the chair at a dinner given to the whole bank staff by this man who had advanced all his subordinates one step, and left them pleased and hopeful; and he could make the usual complimentary speeches with more sincerity than is common at public dinners. He had also introduced the new laird of Cross Hall to his wife and family on equal terms, and they had been very much pleased with him. But when Miss Melville again gravely asked for the vacant clerkship, his habitual courtesy could scarcely prevent him from laughing outright.

'It would never do, my dear madam,' said he; 'young ladies have quite a different sphere from that of ledgers and pass-books."

'But I would do the work,' said Jane, opening a ponderous volume that lay on the manager's table, and running up a column of figures with a rapidity and precision which he could not but admire. Then on a piece of loose paper she wrote in a beautiful, clear, business-like hand an entry as she would put it in the book, showing that she perfectly well understood the *rationale* of the Dr. and the Cr. side of the ledger; and then gravely turning to Mr. Rennie, she asked him why she would not do.

'It is not the custom, my dear young lady; I can get young men in plenty who want the place.'

'I have no doubt that you can, but I want it too; and, in consideration of the prejudice against my sex, I will take the place, and accept the salary you would give to a raw lad of sixteen, though I am an educated and experienced woman of twenty-three. I want something that I can rise by. I could be satisfied with the career of

my cousin, without the fortune at the end. Young women in Paris are clerks and bookkeepers; why should they not be so here?'

'France is not Scotland, or Auld Reekie Paris. We consider our customs very much better than the French. Why, you know quite well it would never do. You would turn the heads of all my clerks, and make them idle away their time and neglect their work. You do not see the danger of the thing.'

'No, I do not,' answered Jane. 'Do I look like a person who would turn any man's head? If I do such mischief, turn me off; but I ask, in the name of common sense and common justice, a fair trial. If I do not give satisfaction I will stand the consequences.'

The serious earnestness with which Jane pleaded for so strange an employment—the matter-of-fact way in which she stood upon her capabilities, without regarding suitabilities—impressed Francis Hogarth while it embarrassed Mr. Rennie. It was impossible to out-reason so extraordinary an applicant, but it was still more impossible to grant her request. Skilled as the banker was in the delicate and difficult art of saying 'No,' it had to be said oftener and more distinctly to Jane Melville than to the most pertinacious of customers, to whom discount must be refused.

'I admire your spirit, Miss Melville. If one thing cannot be accomplished you must try another. But in an establishment like this, you see, I could not possibly take you in. A private employer might admire your undoubted ability; but I am responsible to a Board of Directors, and they would decidedly oppose such an innovation. Your sex, you are aware, are not noted for powers of secrecy. I dare say it is a prejudice; but bank directors and bank customers have prejudices, and no one likes any additional chance of having his affairs made public.'

'You know you are talking nonsense, my good sir,' said Jane. 'It is because women have never had any responsibilities that they have been supposed to be unworthy of trust. Where they have been honoured with confidence they have been quite as faithful to it as any men.'

'But, my dear madam,' said Mr. Rennie, 'what would be the

consequence if all the clever women like yourself were to thrust themselves into masculine avocations? Do you not see that the competition would reduce the earnings of men, and then there would be fewer who could afford to marry? The customs of society press hard upon the exceptional women who court a wider field of usefulness, but I believe the average happiness is secured by—'

'By a system that makes forty-five educated women eager to give their life's work for £12 a-year, and fifty applying for the magnificent salary of £30 for a most exhausting and responsible situation. These are not all exceptional women, Mr. Rennie, but many of the average women whose happiness you are so careful of. You know there are enormous numbers of single women and widows in this country who must be supported, either by their own earnings or by those of the other sex, for they *must* live, you know.'

Mr. Rennie smiled at Jane's earnestness.

'You smile, "*on ne voit pas la necessité*," said Jane. 'I dare say it would really be better for us to die.'

'I am sure nothing was further from my lips than either the language or the sentiment. I think your case especially hard—*especially* hard.'

'I thought it was, till I heard of these numerous applications; and the sad thing to me is, that it is *not* especially hard. Some innovation must be made: have you and your directors not the courage to begin? I am willing to endure all the ridicule that may be cast on myself.'

'There are other departments of business where your unquestionable abilities and skill might be employed and well paid for; but here, I must repeat, it is impossible—impossible—perfectly impossible. Mr. Hogarth is going to favour us with his company this evening, and Mrs. Rennie and my daughter Eliza would be most happy to see you. I would like to introduce my daughter to a young lady who knows business so well. You will be good enough to pardon my necessary incivility: most painful to me it has been to refuse your request, backed by such excellent reasons,—but you will accompany Mr. Hogarth, and show you are not unforgiving.'

Jane accepted the invitation willingly. Francis was not pressed for time; the bank had released him without the usual notice, so he offered to accompany his cousin wherever she chose to go to.

'Do you think,' said she, when they were again in the street, 'that I could get employment with any bookseller or publisher? I will try that next. Will you go with me to a respectable house in that line of business?'

There was no situation vacant for any one in the first two establishments they called at. In the third there was a reader wanted to correct manuscripts and proofs, and as Mr. Hogarth was supposed to be the person applying for the employment, he was asked his qualifications. When he somewhat awkwardly put forward Miss Melville, the publisher respectfully but firmly declined to engage her.

'Whatever I could or could not do—whatever salary I might ask—you object on account of my being a woman?' said Jane.

'Just so,' said the publisher; 'it is not the custom of the trade to employ *Ladies of the Press*. You do not know the terms or the routine of the business.'

'I suppose I could learn them in an hour or two; but I see you do not wish to employ me, even if I had them at my finger-ends. Do you employ women in no way in your large establishment?'

'Yes, as authors; for we find that many books written by ladies sell quite as well as others.'

'But in no other way?'

'Only in this,' said the publisher, taking the cousins into a small room at the back of his large front shop, where eight or ten nice-looking girls were busily engaged in stitching together pamphlets and sheets to be ready for the bookbinder. 'It is light work; they have not such long hours or such bad air, nor do they need much taste or skill as dressmakers do.'

'So their wages are proportionally lower,' said Jane.

'Just so,' said the publisher; 'and quite right they should be so.'

'Of course; but do they not rise from stitching to bookbinding?'

'Ah! that is man's work. I have bookbinders on the premises, to

finish the work that the girls have begun.'

'And they spend their lives in this stitching—no progress—no improvement—mere mechanical drudgery.'

'Yes; and in time they get very expert. You would be amazed at the rapidity with which they turn the work out of their hands. The division of labour reduces the price of binding materially.'

'No doubt—for you have girls at low wages to do what is tedious, and men at higher to do what is artistic; that is a very fair division of labour,' said Jane, bitterly.

'Nay, nay; I believe our profession, or rather trade, is more liberal to the sex than any other. Write a good book, and will give you a good price for it: design a fine illustration, and that has a market value independent of sex.'

'I can neither write nor draw,' said Jane, 'but I would fain have been a corrector of the press; from that I might have risen to criticism, and become a reader and a judge of manuscript; but I see the case is hopeless. I suppose it is not you, but society who is to blame. Perhaps I may be reduced to the book-stitching yet; if so, will you give me a trial? In the meantime, I wish you good morning.'

The publisher smiled and nodded. 'A most eccentric young woman, and, I daresay, a deserving one; but she takes hold of the world at the wrong end,' said he, as she went out to pursue her inquiry elsewhere.

'Now,' said Jane, 'I can release you, for I will make my next application myself. If I fail here I really will be surprised, for I make it to one who knows me.'

Mrs. Dunn, the head of the dressmaking and millinery establishment where the Miss Melvilles had been initiated into these arts, had been very handsomely paid for instructing them, had always praised Jane's industry and Elsie's taste, and had held them up as patterns for all her young people. Of course she knew, as all the world knew, that they had been disinherited by their uncle, but she fancied they had other influential friends or relatives; so when Miss Melville was announced, she thought more of an order for mourn-

ing then of a request for employment. But the young lady, in her own plain way, went at once to the point.

'You were accustomed at the time I was with you to have a bookkeeper, who came regularly to make up your bills and your accounts. Have you the same arrangement still?'

'Yes, and the same gentleman; a first-rate hand at his figures; employed by many beside me,' said Mrs. Dunn.

'Then he cannot miss one customer. Will you give the business to me on the same terms, for the sake of old times?'

'To you, Miss Melville! it is not worth your having. It is only by his having so many that he makes it pay, though he is as good an accountant as any in Edinburgh.'

'I might in time get a good many too. Surely women might put all their work in the way of their own sex. I am quite competent; I convinced a bank manager to-day that I was fit for a situation in his establishment, but he did not like the idea of taking a young woman amongst his clerks. You can have no objection on that score. You know I will be quiet, careful, and methodical.'

Mrs. Dunn was very sorry, but really nobody ever thought of having young ladies to make up their books. It was not the custom of any trade. A gentleman coming in gave confidence both to herself and to the public; and she had no fault to find with Mr. McDonald—a most gentlemanly man, with a wife and family, too—it would not be fair to part with him without any cause. And, indeed, the business was not what it used to be—it needed the most careful management to get along, and she could not risk having a change in her establishment just at present; perhaps by-and-by.'

'While grass grows horses starve,' said Jane. 'If I establish a reputation and get employment from others you could not object to me. Everyone is alike; neither man nor woman will give me a chance. I cannot blame you, Mrs. Dunn, for thinking and acting so much like other people.'

'I am sure it would be better for you to take a nice comfortable situation; but I thought you had friends. If there was any other way that I could serve you in I would be so happy. If you had asked to be

taken into the work-room—but I suppose you look higher.'

'I do not know how low I may look ere long, Mrs. Dunn. It is quite possible I may trouble you again, but in the meantime—'

'In the meantime I want you to come into the show-room and see the new sleeve just out from Paris—it would improve the dress you have on amazingly. I suppose that was made in Swinton. And you must see Mademoiselle; she is with us still, and as positive as ever; and many of the young people you will recognise. How we have all talked about you and Miss Alice lately. It was such an extraordinary settlement!'

Jane forced herself into the show-room, listened mechanically to the exclamations and remarks of Mademoiselle, the forewoman, shook hands with all the work-girls she had known, looked with vacant eyes on the new sleeve, and heard its merits descanted on very fully; then went back into Mrs. Dunn's parlour, and had a glass of ginger wine and a piece of seed-cake with her; after which she took leave, and Mrs. Dunn felt satisfied, for she had paid Miss Melville a great deal of attention in spite of her altered circumstances.

'Where am I to go to now?' said Jane to herself as she again trod the pavement of Princes Street and walked along it, then turned up into the quieter parts of the town where professions are carried on. She passed by shops, and warehouses, banks and insurance companies' offices, commission agencies, land agencies, lawyer's offices.

'Every one seems busy, every place filled, and there appears to be no room for me,' she said to herself. 'I must try Mr. MacFarlane, however; he knows something of me, and will surely feel friendly. I hope he will not be so much astonished at my views as other people have been.'

Mr MacFarlane, however, was quite as much suprised as Mr. Rennie, or the publisher, when Jane asked him for employment as a copying or engrossing clerk, either indoors or out of doors. He was quite as much disposed to exaggerate the difficulties she herself would feel from not understanding the forms of law, or not being

able to write the particular style of caligraphy required for legal instruments. He had heard of the singular education Henry Hogarth, an old crony and contemporary of his own, had given to his nieces, and as his own old-bachelor crotchets lay in quite another direction, he had never thought of that education doing anything but adding to their difficulties, and preventing them from getting married. When the girls had been left in poverty he only thought of their trying for the nice quiet situations that every one recommended, but which seemed so hard to obtain, and then sinking into obscure old maidenhood in the bosom of a respectable family. When Jane mentioned the matronship, Mr. MacFarlane strongly advised her to apply for it, for the salary was more than she could look for in a situation, and she would probably be more independent. But as for him employing a girl as a law-writer, what would the profession say to that? It was quite out of the question.

'I fear I have no turn for teaching, but I suppose I must try for something better than a situation. Could I not get up classes?'

'Oh! yes, certainly—classes if you feel competent.'

'Not quite for French or Italian. My uncle was never satisfied with our accent; and we must advertise French acquired on the Continent now-a-days, if we want to succeed in Edinburgh. The things I could teach best—English grammar and composition, writing and arithmetic, history, and the elements of science—are monopolized by men; but I must make an effort. I am sorry my dear old friend, Mr. Wilson, is no more, he would have recommended me strongly; but I will go to Mr. Bell. I studied under him for four winters, and though I am threatening him with competition, I know I was his favourite pupil, and I hope he will help me. I never would encroach on his field if I could find any elbow-room elsewhere.'

This was another long walk, and to no purpose, for Mr. Bell was away from home, in bad health, for an indefinite period, leaving his classes in the care of a young man, who had been strongly recommended to him.

The other masters she had had were not likely to take nearly so

much interest in her as Mr. Bell; but she was resolved to leave no stone unturned, and went to see several of them. They gave Miss Melville very faint hopes of success. Edinburgh was overdone with masters and mistresses, rents were very high, and classes the most uncertain things possible. But she might apply at one of the institutions. Thither she went, and found that her want of accomplishments prevented her from getting a good situation; and her want of experience was objected to for any situation at all. With a few more lessons, and a little training, she might suit by-and-by.

She was glad that those long walks and many interviews occupied the whole day till the time Francis had appointed for dinner; she had not courage to face the empty house and the respectable woman-servant till she was sure her cousin would be at home to receive her. Heartsick, weary, and footstore she felt, when she reached the cottage where Francis was standing at the door to welcome her return.

'Well, friend,' said he, 'what news?'

'No good news. I suppose I must advertise. Perhaps there is one person in England or Scotland who would fancy I was worth employing, even though I am apparently very much at a discount.'

'Are you much disheartened?'

'I am very tired,' said she; 'Rome was not built in a day. I was a fool to expect success at once.'

'You are not too tired to go to Mrs. Rennie's with me this evening. I have ordered a carriage to call for us.'

'Thank you, I will need it, and my dinner, too, in spite of the wine and cake at Mrs. Dunn's.'

Her cousin's quiet sympathy and kindness soothed the girl's aching and anxious heart; she told him her experiences; and though he was not very much suprised at the result, he felt keenly for her disappointment. She had brought a little piece of needlework to fill up vacant hours, and after dinner she took it out, and soothed her excited feelings by the quiet feminine employment. There was an hour or more to be passed before the carriage came for them, and Francis sat on the other side of the fire cutting the leaves of a new

book, and occasionally reading a passage that struck him. Had any one looked in at the time, he could not have guessed at the grief and anxiety felt by both of the cousins. No; it was like a quiet domestic picture of no recent date, not likely to be soon ended. Jane's sad face lighted up with an occasional smile at something said or something read; and Francis Hogarth saw more beauty in her countenance that evening than William Dalzell had ever seen in all the days he had spent with the supposed heiress whom he meant to marry.

IV

AN EVENING AT MR. RENNIE'S

After an hour spent in this quiet way, Jane Melville was sufficiently rested and tranquillized to go among strangers, in spite of her knowing the idle curiosity with which she was likely to be regarded. There was a small party at Mr. Rennie's; but excepting herself and the ladies of the family, it was composed entirely of gentlemen. Now that Mr. Hogarth had come into a good landed property, he had spent more than one evening in the family of the bank manager, and had been discovered to be presentable anywhere; that he had very tolerable manners and good literary taste; and both Mrs. and Miss Rennie recollected well how often papa had spoken highly of him when he was only a clerk in the bank. Miss Rennie was about nineteen, the eldest of the family, rather pretty, slightly romantic, and a little fond of showing off her extensive acquaintance with modern literature. Her interest in Mr. Hogarth was great, though of recent date; and now to see one of the cousins whom he was forbidden to marry, on pain of losing all his newly-acquired wealth and consequence, was an exciting thing to a young lady who had suffered much from want of excitement. Her father had been able to tell her nothing of Miss Melville's personal appearance, though he had dwelt upon her abilities and her

eccentric character, and told her age. Among the party was the publisher to whom Jane had applied for a situation, who had contributed his share of information about her; a young Edinburgh advocate, who had not very much to do at the bar; a Leith merchant, an old gentleman of property in the neighbourhood of the city, and two college students, all anxious to see people who were so much talked about.

'Decidely plain and common-looking, and looks twenty-seven at least,' was Miss Rennie's verdict on seeing Miss Melville.

'Plain, but uncommon-looking,' was the opinion of the gentlemen on the subject. The open, intelligent, and womanly expression of countenance—the well-turned neck and shoulders—the easy, well-proportioned figure—though not of the slight ethereal style which Mr. Hawthorne admires, but rather of the healthy, well-developed flesh-and-blood character of British feminine beauty—might redeem a good deal of irregularity of features.

Though her self-possession had been sorely tried on this day, though she had been disappointed, and was now worn out and perplexed, and though her faith in human nature had been shaken, she made an effort to recover the equanimity necessary for such an evening as this, and succeeded. Her quiet and lady-like manner surprised Mr. Rennie; he had thought her masculine in the morning. She listened with patience and pleasure to Miss Rennie's playing and singing, and then looked over some books of engravings and prints with the old gentleman, who was a connoisseur. And when the advocate and the publisher, between whom there seemed to be a good understanding, entered into conversation on literary matters, and successful and unsuccessful works, she, thinking of her sister and her hopes, listened most attentively.

'Well,' said the legal gentleman, 'I like smart, clever writing, and don't object to a little personality now and then. It pays, too.'

'Those things certainly take well,' said the publisher, 'but there are other things that take better.'

'What are they?'

'Not at all in your way, Mr. Malcolm; but yet at the present time

there is nothing that pays so well as an exciting religious novel on evangelical principles. Make all your unbelievers and wordly people villians, and crown your heroine, after unheard-of perils and persecutions, with the conversion of her lover, or the lover with the conversion of the heroine—the one does nearly as well as the other; but do not let them marry before conversion, on any account. Settle the hero down in the ministry, to which he dedicates talents that you may call as splendid as you please; make your fashionable conversation of your worldly people slightly blackguardly, and that of your pets very inane, with spots of religion coming out very strong now and then, and you will have more readers than Dickens, Bulwer, or Thackeray. Well-meaning mothers will put the book without fear into the hands of their daughters. It is considered harmless Sunday reading for those who find Sunday wearisome, and it is thought an appropriate birth-day present for young people of both sexes. I dare say these books are harmless enough, but their success is wonderfully disproportioned to their merits. They must be such easy writing, too, for you need never puzzle yourself as to whether it would be natural or consistent for such a character to steal, or for another to murder. "The heart is deceitful above all things, and desperately wicked," and the novelist at least takes no pains to know it.'

'You fire me with a noble zeal and emulation,' said Mr. Malcolm. 'Is it true that the trumpery thing my sister Anne tormented me to order from you last week has gone through five editions?'

'Just about to bring out a sixth,' said the publisher; 'and the curious thing is that it is not at all exciting: but these American domestic quasi-religious novels (though novel is not a proper term for them) are the rage at present. If one could trust to their details of every-day life being correct, they might be useful as giving us the Americans painted by themselves; but there is so much that is false and improbable in plot and character, that one is tempted to doubt even the cookery, of which we have *quantum suff.*'

'The conversation is the greatest twaddle I ever saw,' said Mr. Malcolm. 'If the American people talk like that, how fatiguing it

would be to live among them! I could not write so badly, or such bad English. I must take a successful English novel as my model.'

'Mr. Malcolm is literary himself,' said Miss Rennie, who had left the two students to amuse each other, and now joined the more congenial group. 'He writes such clever things in magazines, Miss Melville, I quite delight to come on anything of his, they are so amusing.'

'Miss Rennie, I am overwhelmed with gratitude for your good opinion. Then you like my style? Do you hear that, you ogre? Publishers, you know, Miss Melville, are noted for living upon the bones of unfortunate authors, and never saying grace either before or after the meal. This Goth, this Vandal, this Jacob Tonson, has had the barbarity to find fault with the last thing I put into the "Mag".'

'Well, I thought you had never done anything so good. It was so funny; papa laughed till he shook the spectacles off his face, and then all the children laughed too.'

'Listen, thou devourer of innocents, thou fattener on my labour and groans. My work was good, and my style better, fashionable as Miss Rennie's flounces, and piquant as the sauce we will have from our host at supper.'

'The style has been fashionable,' said the publisher, 'but it is getting overdone. Everybody is trying the allusive style now, and wandering from the subject in hand to quote a book, or to refer to something very remotely connected with it. Every word or sentence is made a peg to hang something else on. Our authors are too fond of showing off reading or curious information; the style of the old essayists—'

'Bald and tame, with very little knowledge of the finer shades of character,' interrupted Mr. Malcolm. 'I wonder why you, as a critic, can compare our brilliant modern literature to such poor performances.'

'They have their deficiencies, certainly; but there was a simplicity and directness in these old writings that we would do well to imitate.'

'I had better imitate the style of the paying article at present, and write an evangelical novel. I had better read up in it; but the unlucky thing is that they invariably put me to sleep; so perhaps I would do better to trust to my own original genius, and begin in an independent manner.'

'Is it not a treat,' whispered Miss Rennie to Jane, 'to get a peep behind the scenes in this way? Mr. Malcolm is quite a genius. I am sure he could write anything; but he really ought not to go to sleep over those charming books. He is such a severe critic, I am quite afraid of him.'

'Then you write yourself?' said Jane.

'Oh! how foolish of me to let you know in such a silly way. I write nothing to speak of. I never thought any one would take me for an authoress. But I do so doat on poetry, and it seems so natural to express one's feelings in verse—not for publication, you know—only for my friends. Once or twice—but this is a great secret—I have had pieces brought out in the "Ladies' Magazine." If you read it, you may have seen them; they had the signature of Ella—a pretty name, is it not?—more uncommon than my own.'

'Is it a fair question,' said Jane, anxiously; 'but did you receive anything for your verses?'

'You have such a commercial turn of mind, Miss Melville, as papa says, that you really ought to be in business. No; I did not receive or, indeed, did I wish for any payment. I would mix no prose with my poetry.'

'You are not in need of money,' said Jane, with a slight sigh; and she turned to the publisher, and asked if he brought out new poems as well as new novels.

'Poetry is ticklish stuff to go off, particularly in Edinburgh,' said he. 'I am very shy of it, except in bringing out cheap editions of poems of established reputation, or reprints of American poets.'

'Where there is no copyright to be paid for,' said Mr. Malcolm; 'I know the tricks of the trade.'

Mrs. Rennie had asked Jane to play and sing, which she could not do, and then had engaged in conversation with Mr. Hogarth for a

considerable time. Now she supposed Jane must fancy she was not receiving sufficient attention from her hostess, considering that she was the only lady guest, so she came forward, and withdrew her from the animated conversation of the gentlemen, and proceeded to entertain her in the best way that she could. Her younger children (not her youngest, for they were in bed) were gathered around her, and the conversation was somewhat desultory, owing to their interruptions and little delinquencies. It was now getting time for them, too, to go to bed, and it was not without repeated orders from mamma, supported at last by a forcible observation from papa, that they bade the company good-night, and retired. They were all very nice-looking children, and not ill-disposed, though somewhat refractory and dilatory about the vexed question of going to bed.

Talking to them and about them naturally brought up the subject of education; and Jane timidly inquired if Mrs. Rennie was in want of a governess, or if she knew any one who was.

'No; the children are all at school or under masters—the best masters in Edinburgh—for Mr. Rennie is extravagant in the matter of education. The children get on better—there is more emulation; and then there is such a houseful of ourselves, that we would not know where to put a governess, though it might otherwise be an economy,' said Mrs. Rennie.

'I should like to have classes,' said Jane—trying to speak boldly for herself; 'to teach what I have learned under the same masters whom you are so pleased with—English philologically, with the practice of composition, writing, arithmetic, and mathematics. I can get certificates of my competency from the professors under whom I have studied. I must leave the neighbourhood of Swinton, where there is no field for me, and start in this line; my sister can assist me, I have no doubt.'

'I never heard of such a thing, Miss Melville; you had much better take a situation. The worry and uncertainty of taking rooms and paying rent, when there are so many masters that you cannot expect but a very few pupils, would wear you out in a twelvemonth.

If I were to send you my two girls—and I am sure I have every reason to be satisfied with their present teachers—what would they do for you? Oh, no, Miss Melville. Take my advice, and get a nice quiet situation, or go into a school, where you might take music lessons in exchange for what you can teach now.'

'I am too old to learn music,' said Jane, 'and I have no natural talent for it. As for a nice quiet situation, where am I to get it?'

'Surely, Miss Melville, you must have many friends, from the position you have held in —shire; you must know many leading people. Consult with them. I am sure they would never advise you to take such a risk; I cannot conscientiously advise you to do it myself. Mr. Rennie was telling me about the matronship of the — Institution. Don't you think that would be better? The salary is not high, but there is no risk. I know one of the house-surgeons very well, and I know he says everything is very comfortable, and he is one of the pleasantest men I know.'

'I am reconsidering the matter,' said Jane. 'I suppose if I make up my mind to it, the sooner I apply the better.'

'I should say so,' said Mrs. Rennie. 'I am sure Mr. Rennie will give you all his influence, for he says you appear to be such a capable person. He told us all about your turn for figures and ledgers, and that sort of thing.'

'I have naturally strong nerves, too,' said Jane.

'Oh, they say it is nothing being in such a place, when you once get used to it.'

'But what would become of my poor sister?' said Jane. 'We did so much wish to be together; and in such a situation I could see so little of her.'

'That would be the case in any situation; and what is there to prevent her from getting one for herself?'

'Just as much and more than prevents me. Still, twenty-four and thirty pounds a year would keep her tolerably comfortable till she can get employment or meets with success otherwise,' said Jane, half thinking aloud. 'I think I will write out my application when we get home to-night.'

'Where are you staying—in Edinburgh?' asked Mrs. Rennie.

'At my cousin's.'

'At Mr. Hogarth's?—you do not mean to say so!'

'He asked me to come and stay with him while I inquired about this situation, or anything else that might appear to be better. You know I cannot afford to take lodgings or live at a hotel, and no one else thought of offering me a home.'

'It was very kind and well-meant on his part, no doubt; but it was scarcely advisable on yours to accept it.'

'I spoke to Miss Thomson about it, and she saw no objection.'

'Miss Thomson of Allendale: very likely she did not—she is used to do just as she pleases, and never minds what the world thinks.'

'She was the only person who gave me either help, encouragement, or advice. I thought all she said was right and reliable. You do not know what it is to me, who have no relation in the world but Elsie, to find a cousin. He seems like a brother to me, and I know he feels like one. If it had been in his power to give me money to engage a lodging, perhaps he would have done so, but it is money assistance that is so strictly forbidden by the will.'

'If he had only spoken to some experienced friend on the subject—if he had only spoken to *me*—I am sure it could have been better managed. In the meantime, if you have no objection to sharing Eliza's room, we will be glad to keep you here for the remainder of your stay in Edinburgh. You had better not go home with your cousin to-night.'

Jane paused for a few minutes—many bitter thoughts passed through her mind. 'I am much obliged to you for your kind offer, but I do not think I can accept it. If I have made a mistake, it has been committed already, and cannot be undone. To-night, I will write my application to the directors of the — Asylum; to-morrow I will be on my way to Cross Hall. I cannot, after such a day as this, collect my thoughts sufficiently in a strange house, among strangers, to do myself justice in my application, nor can I

bear to let my cousin know that his brotherly kindness, and my sisterly confidence, may be misunderstood and misinterpreted. I have no mother, and no adviser. I had feared that perhaps the direct or indirect assistance of food and lodging for two days might peril my cousin's inheritance,—though Miss Thomson thought there was no danger of that either,—but I never imagined that any one would think the less of me for accepting it. If you do not tell him, he need never know it; for I am sure it was the last idea he could have entertained.'

What sad earnest eyes Jane turned on Mrs. Rennie!—she could not help being touched with her expression and her appeal. A vision of her own Eliza—without friends—without a mother—doing something as ill-advised, and feeling very acutely when a stranger told her of it, gave a distinctness to Jane's present suffering that, without that little effort of imagination, she could not have realized. Besides, she had a great wish to think highly of Mr. Hogarth, and to please him; and the certainty that he would be extremely pained and, perhaps, offended by her suggestion that he had compromised his cousin's position by his good-natured invitation, had its influence.

'What you say is very reasonable, Miss Melville, but you forget that to-morrow is Sunday. You would not travel on the Sabbath, I hope?'

'I seem to have forgotten the days of the week in this terrible whirl,' said Jane. 'I would rather not travel on Sunday, but this seems a case of necessity.'

'Not so,' said Mrs. Rennie, kindly. 'Come and go to church with us to-morrow forenoon, and dine with us; if you feel then that you would prefer to stay here, you can easily manage to do so without making your cousin suspect anything. If you still are anxious to go home, you can do that on Monday morning; but I fancy Tuesday is quite early enough to send in your application.'

'Thank you, Mrs. Rennie,' said Jane. 'I am very much obliged to you indeed for your kindness, and I think I will avail myself of it; but to-night—to-night—I must have some quiet and solitude.'

'I have been somehow or other separated from you all the evening,' said Francis, as they were on their way home. 'Have you enjoyed it at all? It was hard for you to have to see so many strangers after so trying a day.'

'Rather hard,' said Jane, with quivering lips. 'Life altogether is much harder than I had imagined it to be. I want Elsie very much to-night; but I will see her as soon as I can possibly get home.'

'You do not mean to go so soon? you have done nothing satisfactory as yet. We must make attempts in some other direction.'

'I have made up my mind,' said Jane; 'I will apply for the situation I despised this morning. People outside of asylums seem to be as mad and more cruel. I will write my application to-night, and it will go by the first post.'

'Do not be so precipitate; there is no need to apply before Tuesday, and I believe even Wednesday would do. Spend the intervening days in town; something suitable may be advertised in newspapers. You have not yet applied at any registry offices. You said Rome was not built in a day, yet a day's failure makes you despair. Do not lose heart all at once, my dear cousin. Though I never had anything half so hard to bear or to anticipate as you have now, I have had my troubles, and have got over them, as you will in the end.'

The tone of Francis' voice gave Jane a little courage; but she was resolute in writing out her application before she went to bed. It was beautifully written and clearly expressed. She asserted her qualifications with firmness, and yet with modesty, and gave satisfactory references to prove her own statements. Of all the applicants, she was the youngest; but Francis was sure that her letter would be the best of the fifty.

Though Jane thought this decisive step would set her mind at rest, sleep was impossible to her after such excitement, fatigue, and disappointment; and the solitude she had longed for only gave her leave to turn over all the painful circumstances of her position without let or hindrance. Never had she felt so bitterly towards her

uncle. In vain did she try to recall his past kindness to soften her heart towards him; for all pleasant memories only deepened the gloom of her present friendless, hopeless poverty; and the prospect of her inevitable separation from Elsie, which had never been distinctly apprehended before, was the saddest of all the thoughts that haunted the night watches.

Francis had been invited with Jane to spend the day with the Rennies, and the cousins went to church with the family. Jane heard none of the sermon nor of the service generally. She had not been in the habit of paying much attention at church, and there was nothing at all striking or impressive in the preacher's voice or manner, or in the substance of his discourse, to arrest a languid or preoccupied listener. Jane was thinking about the Aslyum, and about how much or how little it needed to make people mad—if they were often cured—and if they relapsed—a great part of the time; and when Miss Rennie asked her how she liked the sermon, Jane could not tell whether she liked it or not. Mr. and Mrs. Rennie confessed that Mr. M——was nothing of a preacher, but he was a very good man and a private friend. They liked to go to their own regular parish church, and did not run after celebrated preachers; though Eliza was a great admirer of eloquence, and was very often straying from her own place of worship to go with friends and acquaintances to hear some star or another, quite indifferent as to whether he were of the Establishment or of the Free Kirk, or of some other dissenting persuasion.

The conversation at Mr. Rennie's all Sunday afternoon was much more on churches, sermons, and ministers, than any Jane had ever heard before. She had never seen anything of the religious world, as it is called, and felt herself very much behind the company in information. Her cousin Francis was much better acquainted with the subject; he seemed to have heard every preacher in Edinburgh, and to know every one of note in the kingdom.

Mrs. Rennie, apparently in a casual manner, asked Jane to make her house her home while she remained in Edinburgh; and the invitation was accepted with the same indifferent tone of voice,

which concealed great anxiety at heart.

'I should like my cousin to accompany me to my unfashionable chapel,' said Francis. 'Will you either join us or excuse us for the evening, as it is the only opportunity I may have for a long time to take Miss Melville there? Miss Rennie, you are the only one likely to have curiosity enough to try a new church.'

'I am sorry I cannot go this evening, for I have promised to go to St. George's, to hear Mr. C—, with Eleanor Watson and her brother. You had better come with me; it is the last Sunday he is to preach in Edinburgh,' said Miss Rennie.

'You must excuse me this once,' said Mr. Hogarth; 'I have a great wish that Miss Melville should hear my minister. At any other time I will be at your command.'

Miss Rennie could not disappoint either Eleanor or Herbert Watson, or herself; so Francis and Jane went alone to the little chapel. 'It will do you good to hear a good sermon, and I expect that you will hear one.'

The idea of getting any good at church was rather new to Jane; but on this occasion, for the first time in her life, she felt real meaning in religious worship. Never before had she felt the sentiment of dependence, which is the primary sentiment of religion. She had been busy, and prosperous, and self-reliant; all she said and did had been considered good and wise; her position was good, her temper even, and her pleasures many. Now she was baffled and defeated on every side—disappointed in the present, and fearful of the future.

Prayer acquired a significance she had never seen in it before; the tone of the prayer, too, was different from the set didactic utterances too often called prayer, in which there is as much doctrine and as little devotion as extempore prayer is capable of. It was not expostulatory either, as if our Heavenly Father needed much urging to make Him listen to our wants and our aspirations, but calm, trusting, and elevated, as if God was near, and not far off from any one of His creatures—as if we could lay our griefs and our cares, our joys and our hopes, at His feet, knowing that we are sure

of His blessing. Was this union with God, then, really possible? Was there an inner life that could flow on smoothly and calmly heavenward, in spite of the shocks, and jars, and temptations of the outer life? Could she learn to see and acknowledge God's goodness even in the bitterness of the cup that was now at her lips?

It was no careless or preoccupied listener who followed point after point of the sermon on the necessity of suffering for the perfecting of the Christian character. The thoughts were genuine thoughts, not borrowed from old books, but worked out of the very soul of the preacher; and the language, clear, vigorous, and modern, clothed these thoughts in the most impressive manner. There were none of the conventionalisms of the pulpit orator, who often weakens the strongest ideas by the hackneyed or obsolete phraseology he uses.

'Thank you, cousin Francis,' said Jane, as they walked back to Mr. Rennie's together. 'This is, indeed, medicine to a mind diseased. I will make my inquiries as I ought to do tomorrow; but if I fail I will send in my application; and if I succeed there, I will go to this asylum in a more contented spirit. It appears as if it were to be my work, and with God's help I will do it well.'

Jane began her next day's work by calling on her Edinburgh acquaintances, and then went to the registry offices; but Monday's inquiries were no more successful than Saturday's; so she dropped her letter in the post, and felt as many people, especially women, do when an important missive has left them for ever to go to the hands to which it is addressed. It seems so irrevocable, they doubt the wisdom of the step and fear the consequences.

When Jane reached home and told her sister of the application she had sent in, Elsie was horrified at the prospect, and shook her sister's courage still more by the pictures she conjured up of Jane's life at such a place, and of her own without the one dearest to her heart; but after she had said all she could in that way, it occurred to her that if her poems succeeded, as she had no doubt they would, Jane's slavery need but be shortlived. Her work had made great progress during the short time of her sister's absence, and she

continued to apply to it with indefatigable industry. Scarcely would the ardent girl allow herself to think of anything but what to write;—the tension was too severe, but Elsie would take nothing in moderation.

V

A HUMBLE FRIEND

The last week of the Misses Melville's stay at Cross Hall had begun before Jane heard of the result of her application for the matronship of the — Institution. Mr. Rennie then wrote to her that the directors had appointed a widow, very highly recommended, and apparently very well qualified. Miss Melville's letter had received careful attention, and had favourably impressed all the directors; but her youth and her being unmarried were great objections to her, while the kind of housekeeping she had conducted at her uncle's was not likely to be the best school for the management of an establishment of this kind. Mr. Rennie was very sorry for Miss Melville's disappointment, but he could not suggest any other situation likely to suit her.

Elsie jumped for joy when she heard of Jane's rejection, and kissed her sister over and over again. 'We shall not be parted, darling; you will not go to slave among strangers and to be terrified by mad people. I cannot—really, I cannot do without you— you are my muse and my critic, as well as my best friend and adviser.'

Jane was not quite so much exhilarated by her failure as her sister; but Elsie's extravagant delight comforted her not a little. While they were talking over this matter, Jane was called away to

receive the linen from the laundress for the last time, and to bid her good-bye. Peggy Walker was somewhat of an authority in the district—a travelled woman, who had been in Australia and back again, and was now living with a family of orphan nephews and nieces, and an old man, their grandfather. Public rumour pronounced her a niggardly woman, for though she had property she worked as hard as if she had nothing, and took the bread out of other folk's mouths; but as she was really an excellent laundress, she had the best custom in the neighbourhood, and her honesty, her punctuality, and her homely civility, had made her a great favourite with Jane Melville.

'I fear it must be good-bye this time, Peggy,' said she; 'next week's washing must be given to other hands.'

'Eh, now, Miss Jean, ye dinna say so. I heard the new man was coming to the Hall, but no just so very soon as that. But ye are no going out of the place for good?'

'For good or ill, Peggy, we leave Cross Hall next Thursday.'

'And where are you going to?'

'I wish I knew.'

'Preserve us, Miss Jean! Are you and Miss Elsie, poor bit thing, unacquainted with where you are going to?'

'It is only too true.'

'Well, I am going to leave the place too; but I ken well where I am going, and that is to Edinburgh.'

'Why are you leaving Swinton? I thought you were doing very well here.'

'I don't say that I have any cause to complain of my prosperity here; but, you see, Tam is wild to learn the engineering, and he wants to go to Edinburgh, where he thinks he will learn it best; and I don't like to let him go by himsel', for though he is no a bad laddie, he is the better of a home and a head to it, and I would like to keep my eye on him. Grandfather makes no objections, and the bairns are all keen for Edinburgh, so I am going to flit next week. As for leaving this place, I am sure I have been growled at quite enough about coming from Australia and taking work away from

my old neighbours, so I will try my luck where I don't know who I am taking custom from. I've been in and got a house and a mangle in a nice quiet part of the town, no owre far from Tam's place where he is going to work, and a healthy bit it looks, too.'

'Peggy, I wish I had your confidence and your reason for confidence. I, too, want to go to Edinburgh to try my luck there; but though my uncle spent quite a fortune on my education, and though I did my best to profit by it, I really can see no way of making my living.'

'Hout tout,' said Peggy, 'no fear of you making a living, you could do that as well as me; but it is more than a living for yourself you are wanting; you are thinking of Miss Elsie, poor bit lassie, and would fain work for two. I mind well when my sister left the bairns to my care with her dying breath, I felt my heart owre grit. It was more than I, a single woman, with but seven pounds by the year of wages, could hope to do, to keep the bit creatures; but yet it was borne on my mind that I was to do it, and God be praised that He has given me the strength and the opportunity, and it is little burden they have been to any other body; and in due time, when they have got learning enough, and are come the length to get the passage, I will take them back with me to Melbourne, where their prospects will be better than in the old country.'

'Oh, Peggy! would Australia suit us? Would you advise us to go there?'

'No, Miss Melville, I scarcely think so. For the like of me it is the best place in the world; for the like of you I cannot be at all clear about it. I'll tell you my story some day, but not now, for I am pressed for time, getting everything in readiness for the flitting; and I want time to collect my thoughts; my memory is none of the best. But, Miss Melvile, if I am not making too free, I have a little room in my new house that I would be blithe to let you and Miss Elsie have, and you could stay there quietly till something turns up for you.'

'If we can afford the rent.'

'Oh, the rent!' said Peggy; 'you need not think about the rent, if

you could only give the lasses a lesson in sewing (for I'm no very skilful with the needle, and my hands are so rough with the washing and dressing that the thread aye hanks on my fingers), and make out my washing bills for my customers that are not so methodical as yourself. As for writing and counting, it is my abomination. There need no rent pass between us.'

'Thank you, Peggy, thank you; that will suit us nicely. But tell me, can we—that is, Elsie and me—can we live in Edinburgh on twenty-four pounds a-year?'

'I have known many a family brought up decently on as little, or even less,' said Peggy; 'but then they were differently bred from you and could live hard. Porridge and potatoes, and muslin kail, with a salt herring now and then.'

'Well, porridge and potatoes it shall be,' said Jane, 'for three years, and then starvation, if the world pleases.'

'If God pleases, Miss Jane; the chief thing is for us to place our trust in Him,' said Peggy.

'You are right, Peggy, I suppose; but it is hard to unlearn so much old schooling and to accept of new teachings. Did your faith support you when you were perplexed and disappointed—when friends were unfaithful, and the world hard and cruel?'

'My trials have not been just like yours; but whatever God sent, He gave me strength to bear; and it will be the same with you, Miss Jean, if you put yourself humbly in His hands. But the auld laird cared for none of these things; though I am sure when he left you so poorly provided for in this world, he behoved to have given you a good hold of the hope of a better;—besides that, it makes us contented with a very humble lot here below. I am, maybe, too free-spoken, Miss Jean, but I mean no disrespect.'

'No offence can be taken where none is meant, Peggy; and friends are too scarce with us now for us to reject any good advice . I am very glad to know that we can subsist on our income, for I have not been accustomed to deal with such small sums.'

'You have wealth of clothes, no doubt; enough to last you for a while; so there need be no outlay for that.'

'And we have our own furniture—too much, I suppose for your little room. We can sell the overplus when a push comes. I do not think anything could suit us better than your kind offer.'

'I have heard,' said Peggy, 'that the folk hereabouts think you will be getting up a subscription.'

'They are very much mistaken,' said Jane; 'the hardest living is preferable to that. I wish you could say that Melbourne, or any part of Australia, would do for us. Everybody was surprised when you returned to Swinton so suddenly.'

'Well, I could send the bairns more money from Melbourne than I can make for them here, and no doubt the folk thought me foolish to leave such a place; but what good was the money to the poor things when there was no management, for the old man is but silly, and the bairns had mostly the upper hand of him, though whiles they did catch it. I have had my own ado with Tam for the last two years. I think I have got the victory now; but I must try and keep it. So, as grandfather dreads the water, I think I will stop in this country while he is to the fore, and meantime the lads and lasses must have their schooling and Tam his trade. But I keep on clavering about my own concerns, while you are in doubt and difficulties about yours. When do you leave Cross Hall?'

'I should like to leave on Wednesday, for my cousin comes to take possession on that day, and Elsie cannot bear any one to see us bidding farewell to our dear old home.'

'I cannot just flit before Thursday.'

'Well, I suppose we must stay to welcome the new owner; I have no objection to doing so.'

'It may be painful to your feelings, Miss Melville, but yet I think it would be but right. There are things you may mention to the new man that would do good to them that are left behind you. That poor blind widow, Jeanie Weir, that you send her dinner to every day, would miss her dole if it was not kept up; and I know there are more than her that you want to speak a good word for. I hear no ill of this Maister Francis; and though we all grudge him the kingdom he has come into, it may be that he will rule it worthily.'

VI

A BUNDLE OF OLD LETTERS

Elsie had a headache when Francis came to take possession of his new home, and scarcely made her appearance; but Jane, who felt none of her sister's shrinking from him, showed him over the house, and told him how it had been managed, hoped he would keep the present servants, and particularly recommended to his care the gardener, who, though rather superannuated and rheumatic, had been forty years in the service of the family, and understood the soil and the treatment of it very well.

He was not only glad to hear what she said, but was resolved to be guided by it, and took a memorandum of her poor pensioners, that they, at least, should not suffer by Mr. Hogarth's will.

Then she walked with him over the grounds, and pointed out what improvements her uncle had made, and what more he had contemplated making. She was rather deficient in taste for rural beauty. She loved Cross Hall because it was her home, and because she had been happy there, rather than because she fully appreciated the loveliness of the situation and the prospect. Her cousin, townsman as he was, had far more natural taste. It was romantically situated, and the grounds were beautifully laid out; there were pretty hamlets in the distance, gentlemen's country seats embowered

in trees, green cornfields, merry brooks, and winding valleys. Francis' eyes and heart were filled with the exceeding beauty of the landscape.

'You must be very sorry to leave all this Jane,' he said.

'I believe that is the least of my troubles. I am more sorry to leave these;' and she led him to the stables, and showed him the two beautiful horses she and her sister had been accustomed to ride. 'You will be kind to them for our sakes, and the dogs, too. I am—we are both—very concerned to part with the dogs.'

'Should you not like to take any of them with you?' said Francis, eagerly.

'No, no; dogs such as these would be a nuisance in a crowded little room in Edinburgh, and I do not think they would like such a life, for their own part. You will take better care of them than we could possibly do. But I forget: you have, perhaps, as little affection for animals as I have taste for scenery.'

'I am not naturally fond of pets—which is rather strange; for my solitary life should have made me attach myself to the lower animals. But perhaps I am not naturally affectionate. I must cultivate this deficient taste, however; and be assured that anything you have loved will always be cherished by me; and every wish that you may express, or that I can even guess at, that I am allowed to gratify, I will be only too happy to do so. It has been a strange and stormy introduction we have had to each other; but I am so grateful to you for not hating me, that I chafe still the more at the cruel way in which my hands are tied. I have consulted several eminent lawyers in the hope of being enabled to overturn my father's will, but without success. If a man is not palpably mad he may make as absurd a settlement of his own property as he pleases; and your assertion of your uncle's peculiar opinions tends to support the validity of the testament. Though no one thinks that the disposition of the money will serve the end Mr. Hogarth intended, yet he believed it would, and the spirit and intention of the will must be carried out. Oh, my father! why did you not give me a little love in your lifetime instead of this cursed money after your death?'

'Cousin,' said Jane cheerfully, 'I believe you will make a good use of this money. As my uncle says, you have served well, and should be able to rule justly and kindly. I do not think so much about the improvement of the property by your taste as of the care you will take of the condition of the people upon it. This last month has been a hard, but a useful school to me. I have thought more of the real social difficulties of this crowded country than ever I did before. Bringing my own talents and acquirements into the market, and finding myself elbowed out by competition, I think of those who have to do the real hard necessary work of the world with more sympathy and more respect. Not that I ever despised them—you must not imagine me to be so hard-hearted as that; but my feeling for them is deepened and heightened wonderfully of late. Now they are apt to say that *parvenus* are of all men the most exacting and the most purse-proud; and that a mistress who has been a servant is harsher to her female dependants than one who has been accustomed to keep domestics all her life. It is difficult for me to conceive this; but there must be truth in it, or it would not be a proverb in all languages. You will be an exception, Francis. You will have my uncle's real kindness without his crotchets and his dictatorial manner. You must not be offended if I call you a *parvenu* in spite of your birth. You have come suddenly into wealth that you were not brought up to expect.'

'If I do not recollect my past life, I will certainly remember your present advice whenever I am tempted to think too much of myself and too little of others.'

'Everything is to lead to the perfecting of your character, you see,' said Jane.

'I cannot bear even improvement at the expense of any one's suffering but my own,' said Francis.

'I have been thinking so much about that sermon I heard at your church. I do not know that the preacher brought out the particular point; but we are made such dependent beings, not only on God, but on each other, that we do indirectly profit by what we do not purchase by our own effort or pains. We would not choose to have

it so; but when Providence brings on ourselves or others sorrows we grieve for, we are right to draw from them all the good we can. It is something if my uncle's rather unjust will has given you property with a sobered sense of its privileges and a strong sense of its duties—something to set against Elsie's sufferings and mine. And, besides, the loss of it has done me one great benefit.'

'Tell me what,' said Francis, eagerly.

'It is quite possible, though I cannot tell how probable, that I might have married a man to whom I am not well suited in any respect, and who was still less adapted to make me happy if I had not been disinherited. I am thus frank with you, cousin Francis, for I should like to give you all the consolation I can.'

'And you have been deserted by a lover, as well as impoverished; and you ask me to take consolation from it.'

'No, no; nothing so bad as that. I only explained matters to him, and we parted. I am very glad of it. Be you the same,' said Jane, looking frankly and cheerfully in her cousin's face, and the cloud passed off it.

'Your sister has no affair of this kind?'

'No; nothing,' said Jane.

'And yet she seems to suffer more.'

'Not now; she is busy writing a volume of poems that is to make our fortune. Dear Elsie! I hope it may.'

'Poems—well, she may succeed; but I have more hope of you than of her.'

'Because you know me better; but yet my efforts have all been very fruitless. I am not a judge of poetry, though I like what Elsie writes. I wished her to consent to my taking your opinion as to her verses, but she shrank from it with most unaccountable and, as I thought, unreasonable fear. I wonder how she can bring her work before the public if she dreads one critic.'

'It is very natural, Jane. Among the public there may be some to admire, and some to depreciate; but the one critic to whom the author submits his work may be of the latter class, and there seems to be no refuge from him. It is curious to see the revelations of the

inner self that some authors make to the world—revelations that they would often shrink from making to their nearest friends. They appeal to the few in the world who sympathise with them, and disregard the censure of all the rest. And recollect that, though to you I am a friend, your sister has seen very little of me, and her first impression was exceedingly painful. If you have told her I am a good judge of poetry, she will be all the more averse to submit her compositions to my criticism, for my opinion might bias yours, and yours is her greatest comfort and encouragement. No one can wish her success more earnestly than I do. But for yourself, what are your present intentions?'

'If it were not for leaving Elsie, I might try for a situation as housekeepter in a large establishment; I know I am fully competent for that. I should prefer something by which I could rise, but the choice may not be given to me. We go to Edinburgh to-morrow. I do not think the small room we are going to will hold all the furniture we are entitled to, so will you be good enough to let what we cannot accommodate remain at Cross Hall till we can send for it?'

'Certainly; you had better lock up your room with your own things in it, and take the key,' said Francis.

'No, no; I am housekeeper enough to know that all rooms must have occasional air and sunshine. I can trust either yourself or the housemaid with the key, knowing well that everything will be kept safe.'

'Where are you going to live?'

'With a very humble friend in — Street.'

'That is very near where my earliest recollections of life in Edinburgh found me situated.'

'Do you remember your mother at all?'

'I am not quite sure; but I think I have some shadowy recollection of a place before I came to Edinburgh, where I think I was with my mother.'

'Do you think she is alive now?'

'Mr. MacFarlane says he believes she is. Do you think I should try to discover her?'

'Alive all these years, and never taking any care or notice of you! Very unmotherly on her part!' said Jane, thoughtfully.

'No one knows how she may be situated—her relations with my father must have been very miserable. I cannot tell who was most to blame—but if she were in distress, and I could help her, I am not forbidden to do that, though Mr. MacFarlane strongly advises me to make no inquiry.'

'I think, if she hears of your inheriting Cross Hall, she is likely to come forward if she needs assistance, and you certainly should give it.'

'I wish very much to look over Mr. Hogarth's private papers. Mr. MacFarlane has given me the keys of all his repositories. I particularly wish you to go over them all with me, as there may be many that concern you far more than myself. Could you spare me a few hours to-day for that purpose? I am in hopes that we may find some clue to this marriage, and perhaps some hint that might guide me in my conduct to my mother, supposing she is still alive. If I could find anything that would upset or modify the will, I am sure your happiness in the discovery would be less than mine.'

The long and patient search which extended over the greater part of two days discovered nothing whatever at all definite with regard to Francis' birth. No scrap of writing could be found that could be supposed to be from his mother. An old bundle of papers marked outside, 'Francis' school bills, &c.' was all that rewarded their search, and they gave no information except that his education had cost his father a considerable sum of money.

A packet of letters in a female hand, with a French post-mark, was eagerly opened by the cousins, and contained a number of long and confidential letters from a Marguerite de Véricourt, which extended over a number of years, and stopped at the year when Jane and Elsie came to live with their uncle. Jane's knowledge of French was better than her cousin's, and the sight of the words '*le pauvre Francois*' arrested her attention in the first she opened. 'We have come to something at last,' said she, and she translated the passage, '"I am glad to hear that the poor Francis is doing so well at

school—surely you must learn to love him a little now. My Arnauld grows very intelligent; and Clemence, with no teaching but my own, makes rapid progress." That is all; your name is not mentioned again in this letter. We must go on to the next.'

Letter after letter was glanced over, and then translated, because though there was little mention of the poor Francis, but such a short allusion to something Mr. Hogarth had written about him as was found in the first letter, there was much that was very interesting in them all. They were written with that curious mixture of friendship and love, so natural and easy to Frenchwomen, and so difficult to Englishwomen. Madame de Véricourt appeared to be a widow with two children, a boy and girl. Her letters showed her to be a capable and cultivated woman, passionately attached to her children, living much in society for part of the year in Paris, but spending the summer in a country château, where she became a child again with the little ones. She wrote about her affairs, and her children's, as if she were in the habit of transacting business, and thoroughly understood it, and as if she knew Mr. Hogarth's whole history and circumstances, and took a very affectionate interest in them. She reminded him frequently of conversations they had had together, of long walks and excursions they had taken in company; her children sent messages to her good friend, and she took notice of expressions in his letters which had pleased or disappointed her.

For herself, she had been unhappily married when extremely young; but before the correspondence had begun she had been for some years a widow, and she was fully aware of the position of Mr. Hogarth. The most interesting letter of all was the last, which appeared to have been written in answer to his, telling of his resolution to adopt his sister's children; and she seemed very much delighted at the idea.

'Since you say that you cannot bring yourself to love the poor Francis, whom, nevertheless, my heart yearns after, and of whom I love to hear even the meagre details you give to me, I rejoice, my friend, that you have made a home for your sister's sweet little girls.

You must have something to love. Ah! to me my Arnauld and my Clemence brought unspeakable comfort. I do not think of them as Philippe de Véricourt's children; they are the children whom God have given to me. I do not watch fearfully, lest his ungovernable temper and his selfish soul should be reproduced in them. I trust that God will make them good and happy, and aid me in my efforts towards that end. You cannot separate the idea of Francis from that of the woman who cheated you, and did not love you; who has blighted your hopes of domestic happiness; and who still, even from a distance, has the power to threaten you with exposing the disgrace that you are connected with her. I am sorry that you cannot feel as I do; but if you can love these little girls, it may make you softer towards him. When you wrote to me of your poor Mary's sad death, and of the sadder life that had preceded it, I began to wonder whether, after all, your system of free choice in marriage produces greater happiness or greater misery than ours of a marriage settled by our parents.

'I recollect how bitterly I felt that I had been made over, without my wishes or tastes being consulted, to a man who cared so little for my happiness; but at least I had no illusion to be dispelled; I did not marry as your sister did, hoping to find Elysium, and landing in hopeless misery; and yet my parents loved me after their fashion. I have often thought that those whom we love, and who love us, have far more power to injure us than those who hate us; but, alas! neither friends nor enemies can injure us more than we do ourselves. Your sister Mary had the disenchantment to go through; I had to chafe at the coercion; while you, my friend, had to muse bitterly on the consequence of one rash speech of your own, which chained you to an unworthy and detested wife.

'I think we need a future state that we may do justice to ourselves in it quite as much as to repair the wrongs we may have done to others. Which of us has really made the best of himself or herself? I really try now for the sake of my children to be cheerful; but sad and bitter memories are too deeply interwoven with my being for me to succeed as I should wish. If I live, I hope that the fate of my

Clemence may be happier than her mother's, so far as the state of society in France will allow of it: I will give her a choice, and, at any rate, a power of refusing even what appears to me to be a suitable marriage; for no doubt it is better for an intelligent and responsible human being to choose its own destiny, and to run its own risks. I fancy that the mistake in your English society is, that your girls have apparently the freedom of choice without being trained to make good use of it. If your sister Mary was as inexperienced and as ignorant as I was at the time when my parents gave me to M. de Véricourt, she could not distinguish between the selfish fortune-hunter and the true lover; the conventional manners were all the same, and she chose for herself a life of misery. Your interference only roused the spirit of opposition, and without preventing the marriage, made your brother-in-law regard you with more dislike and suspicion. Ah! my friend, when I see a young girl about to be married, my heart is full of anxieties for her—I know the risk she runs. But I did not feel them much for myself. I grew into the knowledge of my unhappiness as I grew in knowledge of what might have been; but the recluse life of a French girl prevents her from expecting much from marriage but an increase of consequence. With us it is a step from tutelage to liberty—from nonentity to importance. It cannot be quite so much so in England; but, from the greater prevalence of celibacy, it has even more *éclat* and prestige than here, where marriage is the rule. The *trousseau,* the presents, the congratulations, the going into society under the interesting circumstances of an engagement, must divert a girl's attention from the really serious nature of the connection she is forming.

'You will have pleasure in educating your little girls. Make them strong in body and independent in mind if you can. They are likely to be handsome, intelligent, and, if you continue to be prejudiced against poor Francis, rich. Give them more knowledge and more firmness than their poor mother had. I have no doubt that they will grow up good, for you will be kind to them. Girls all turn out well if you give them good training in a happy home; but as for happiness,

that depends so much on their choice in marriage, that all you have done for them may be thrown away, if you do not educate them to be something more than amiable and pleasing companions. They must be trained to feel that they are responsible beings: let their reading be as various, their education as comprehensive, as you would give to boys of their rank. You know that ignorance is not innocence, and that some knowledge of the world is necessary to all of us if we are to pass safely through it. I am glad to hear that Jane so much resembles you, and that Alice is so like her mother, and that you find their dispositions amiable and remarkably sincere.

'I have told you that I have difficulties with Clemence in the matter of truthfulness. She cannot bear to say or to do what she fancies will be disagreeable or painful to any one. She fears, if she does so, that she will not be loved; but I think I am succeeding in convincing her that we must learn to bear pain, and occasionally to inflict it. When I stood over her last night with a cup of bitter medicine she drank it like an angel, and I said to her, "My love, I taste this bitter taste with you, and would rather that I had not to give it to you; but if I, or any one whom you love, needs it, you must learn the courage to present it."

'Arnauld disobeyed my orders one day last week, and played with his ball in the drawing-room, and broke a vase that I prized highly. Clemence took the blame on herself, for she thought I should be less displeased with her than with her brother; but she was not sufficiently skilful to hide the truth. Her *bonne* was enraptured with her generosity, and embraced her with the *empressement* which is so ridiculous to your insular ideas; but Clemence saw that I was not pleased.

'"Mamma," said she, 'is it not right I should bear something for Arnauld? I thought you would be so angry with him."

'"More angry than he deserves?" said I.

'"No, mamma; but I thought he would feel it so much: and even if you were as angry with me, and punished me as severely as you would have chastised him, I should have felt that I did not deserve it."

'"And that, on the contrary, you were very generous?"

'"Yes, mamma."

'"Then Arnauld would have escaped altogether, and you would have borne any pain like a martyr?"

'"But would not Arnauld have loved me for it?"

'"I do not know, Clemence,' said I, 'He knew, when he did the mischief, that I would be displeased, and it is just and right that he should take the consequences. A noble soul feels a certain satisfaction in bearing deserved punishment, but it can never rejoice in the punishment of another for its fault. I know you meant kindly; but, my love, you should make no unnecessary sacrifices. Providence will bring to you many opportunities of giving up your wishes, and of bearing a great deal for others, but it must never be done at the sacrifice of truth."

'Clemence was much impressed with what I said to her; and Arnauld, too, seemed to feel that it would have been mean to have taken advantage of his sister's mistaken generosity. I labour to make them think for themselves, for I often fear that my life will not be spared to guide them much longer. When you come again to France, bring with you your little girls. I have spoken to my children about them, and they are eager to become acquainted with them.'

At the end of this letter was written, in Mr. Hogarth's handwriting, 'Died, October 14th, 18—,' shortly after the date of the letter.

'I wish,' said Jane, 'that my uncle had shown me these letters; but I suppose there are some things that one cannot tell to another person.'

'There is no encouragement here to induce me to make inquiries about my mother,' said Francis. 'I think, for the present, I will let the matter rest.'

VII

UP AND DOWN

When Jane had spoken of £20,000 each, as the probable fortune of herself and her sister, if their uncle had made his will in their favour, she rather under than over estimated the value of Mr. Hogarth's property. She had expected that many legacies to old servants and bequests to several charitable institutions might have been left, and there still would have been that handsome sum for his adopted children. Francis Hogarth found that he had come into possession of a compact little estate in a very fine part of the country, a small part of which estate had been farmed by the proprietor, who had tried various experiments on it with various success. There was also money invested in the funds, and money laid out in railway shares, as well as a considerable sum in the bank for any present necessity, or to be spent in the improvement of the property.

Elsie had expressed a doubt of her cousin's getting into society; but there appeared to be no likelihood of any of the country gentry looking down on the new laird of Cross Hall. The visiting acquaintance of people of sufficient standing in and about Swinton had consisted of twenty-four marriageable ladies and only four marriageable gentlemen, even including William Dalzell, who was

known to be both poor and extravagant, and an old bachelor-proprietor, nearly as old as Mr. Hogarth, senior, and as unlikely to marry. Parties in the country were greatly indebted to striplings and college students home for holidays to represent the male sex. They could dance, and could do a little flirtation, and thought much more of themselves than they ought to do; but as for marrying, that was out of the question. An exchange of two heiresses for one heir of Cross Hall could not but be considered to be an advantageous one. It was not in human nature that the young ladies themselves, and their fathers and mothers, and party-givers generally, should not be eager to know Francis Hogarth, and be more than civil to him. The court that is paid to any man who is believed to be in a position to marry, is one of the most distressing features in British society; it is most mischievous to the one sex, and degrading to the other. Long, long may it be before we see anything like it in the Australian colonies!

No doubt, if it is excusable anywhere, it is so in country or provincial society in Scotland. 'We cannot help spoiling the men'—says a distressed party-giver in these latitudes, conscious that this state of things is not right, and half-ashamed of herself for giving in to it—'there are really so few of them.' The sons of families of the middle and upper classes as they grow up are sent out to India, to the army, to America, or to the Australian colonies. Even when they do not leave the kingdom, they leave the neighbourhood, and go to large towns, where they may practise a profession or enter into business with some chance of success. Their sisters remain at home with no business, no profession, no object in life, and no hope of any change except through marriage. Many of their contemporaries never return, but settle in the colonies or die there; but, if they do return with money—perhaps with broken constitutions and irritable tempers from India—they still consider themselves too young to look at the women with whom they flirted and danced before they left the old country, and select some one of a different generation, who was perhaps a baby at that time. Fathers and mothers see too clearly the advantages of an establishment to

object to the disparity of years and the state of the liver, while the girl, fluttered into importance (as Madame de Véricourt says) by presents, and jewels, and shawls, thinks herself a most fortunate woman, particularly if she is not required to go to India, but can have a good position at home.

So when a young man, not more than thirty-four, rather handsome, of good character, and apparently good temper, intelligent and agreeable, who went to church the first Sunday after he came to Cross Hall, and who was the legitimate heir to the old family of Hogarth, came to settle in the county as a neighbour, his having been clerk in a bank for eighteen years was not looked on as a drawback. He was all the more likely to take good care of his money now he had got it; and calls and invitations came from every quarter. Mr. and Mrs. Rennie, who had had visions of his being exactly the person to suit their Eliza, had a month's start of the country neighbours; but they feared the result of his being thrown among such families as the Chalmerses, the Maxwells, the Crichtons, and the Jardines. He had asked the Rennies to pay him a visit at Cross Hall in the autumn, when they always took a run to the country or to the seaside, and had accompanied his invitation with a request, that if his cousins came to Edinburgh, the Rennies would show them some kindness and attention, which they readily promised to do.

If Mrs. Rennie had known his secret feelings towards the country families, she might have set her mind at rest as to their rivalry; but Francis was very reserved, and his training had not led him to place confidence in any one, till his heart had recently opened to his cousin Jane. He received the visits of his new neighbours civilly, and accepted their invitations; but the conduct of these people towards the disinherited girls made him secretly repel their advances towards his prosperous self. It appeared to show such barefaced worldliness and selfishness, that he shrank from the most insinuating speeches and the most flattering attentions.

He did not know how much of the coldness of Jane and Elsie's old neighbours proceeded from the dislike and suspicion with which

Mr. Hogarth's religious opinions, or rather his religious scepticism, was regarded in a particularly orthodox district. They had exchanged formal visits, and had invited each other to large parties, because not to do so would have been unneighbourly; but with none of the people about Swinton had there ever been any familiar intimacy. Jane and Elsie were supposed to be deeply tinged with their uncle's heresies, and they were such very strange girls, having been so strangely brought up; and having no mother or female relative to exert any influence, their uncle had brought them up like boys, which everybody thought very improper. Emilia Chalmers, who was musical, could not get on with them at all; the three Miss Jardines, who were very amiable girls, with nothing in them, could not tell whether to call them blues or hoydens; their Latin and algebra on the one hand, and their swimming-bath, and their riding about the country without a groom on the other, made them altogether so unfeminine. Their uncle thought they were quite able to take care of themselves and of each other, and fancied more mischief might arise from the attendance of a groom than could result from his absence; and the girls cared for no company in their rides till William Dalzell had offered his escort and made himself so agreeable.

Miss Maxwell and the Crichtons had failed to make either Jane or Elsie take any interest in a theological dispute on a point of doctrine between some neighbouring ministers which was agitating all Swinton at the time; and when at last Jane was forced to give an opinion on one side or the other, she gave it quite on the contrary side from the right one, so that they were sure the girls were quite as bad as their uncle. Both girls had been educated to express themselves very clearly and decidedly; whereas, as Emilia Chalmers says, whenever a young lady gives an opinion it should always be delivered *sotto voce*, that is, under the powers of the performer's voice, to borrow an image from her musical vocabulary. Even if she does know a thing very well, she should keep her knowledge in the background; there is a graceful timidity that is far more attractive than such unladylike confidence.

'Depend upon it, gentlemen do not like it,' Miss Jardine would say. 'If Jane Melville were not an heiress, do you think William Dalzell would submit to her airs? I know him better than that.'

But, yet, when the girls were shown to be no heiresses, every one was very sorry for them. If a subscription had been got up to assist them in their difficulties, there was no one who would not have given something. Even the Misses Crichton and Miss Maxwell would have subscribed as much as they did to the Foreign Missions, and that was no inconsiderable sum; and if Jane and Elsie had thrown themselves on the compassion of the neighbourhood, there were many who would have offered them a temporary home. But they preserved their independent spirit even though they were not heiresses, and could not sue *in formâ pauperis.* It was a subject of much conversation that the Misses Melville had preferred to go with Peggy Walker, the laundress, to some poor place in the old town of Edinburgh, to making any application for assistance to people of their own sphere. What they could do under Peggy's auspices was not likely to be of a very brilliant description.

It is not to be supposed that Peggy Walker was not as good a judge of orthodoxy as the Misses Crichton and Miss Maxwell, but she had not so great a horror of the family at Cross Hall as they had; she had been for several years out of her own parish and country, and had learned some toleration. As she said, the old laird was a just man and a kind one, and until he made his will she had no fault to find with him; and as for the young ladies, they were just the cleverest and the tenderest-hearted to the poor of all the gentry in the country-side. Many a tale of distress had Peggy told them, and had never failed to find the girls open their purses, or go to see the poor people. They had a liberal allowance, and had no extravagant tastes in dress; but their charities had been so extensive that at the time of their uncle's death, there was no great balance in either girl's hands. They knew that Peggy was no niggardly woman, but a most liberal one according to her means and her opportunities—that she gave personal services out of a very busy life, and money, too, out of an income that had many claims on it.

The house-servants and the labourers in Mr. Hogarth's immediate employment were very sad at parting with the young ladies, who had always been so kind and so considerate. If the neighbours had thought the girls proud, none of the servants did. If Francis had not tried hard to please them all, and to make them feel that he regarded them for the sake of those who had been before him, it would not have been likely that he would have gained their good opinion; but he succeeded in doing so.

Peggy Walker thought she had got into a very snug and comfortable dwelling in a flat in — Street, and when she gave what she considered the most cheerful-looking apartment to the young ladies as their sleeping-room, she certainly did all she could for their accommodation. The old man, Thomas Lowrie, was particularly pleased with the look-out to the street. He could sit in his own chair and see all the bustle of life going on below, and made little complaint of the noise at first. The five children thought there was nothing so charming as running up and down the common stair, and were quite proud of their elevated position in the world; but the Misses Melville could not but feel an immense difference between their own ideas of comfort and those of the humble family with whom they lived. The floors were clean, and the stairs, too, after a fashion; but the coarse dark-coloured boards could not be made to look white. The walls which Peggy's own hands had sized of a dark-brown colour looked rough, and cracked, and gloomy. They were aware that their scanty means did not allow them to indulge in any separate meals or attendance, and Jane and Elsie began as they meant to go on, and shared the homely meals in the homely home. They had never thought that they had any luxurious tastes; but the very plain fare and the inelegant service seemed to take away even the natural healthy appetite of youth. The noise of the children, and the querulous voice of their grandfather, with Peggy's sharp, decisive remarks, were all different from the respectful silence with which they had been attended at Cross Hall. Peggy was anxious to make the girls as happy as she could, and feared that they must feel this a downcome; but her

hands were full of work, and her head of cares. She had made her venture in the world, too, and, with so many dependent on her, it was a considerable risk. They could not help admiring the wonderful patience which she had with the old man, who was not her own father, but merely the father-in-law of her dead sister. She allowed him a weekly modicum of snuff, and was particular that Tom, or one of the others, should read the Bible or the news to him in a clear, distinct voice, that the old man might be able to hear all of it. In all little things she gave way to him, but in all great and grave matters she judged and acted for herself, whatever grumbling might follow. Over the children she kept a very careful watch; and even when she was absent on necessary business, her influence was felt in the household.

After the first day was over, and the girls had gone to their own room for the evening, Elsie broke out with—

'Jane, this is dreadful! How different from what I imagined poor people's lives to be! Nothing beautiful or graceful about it. Poets and novelists write such fine things about poverty and honest toil, and throw a halo of romance about them.'

'Yet Peggy is above the average—far above the average,' said Jane, thoughtfully; 'these children are better taught and better mannered than three-fourths of the peasantry in Scotland, but yet it is a great change to us, a very great change.'

'I am sure they might be a great deal better than they are. Oh, Jane, I really can eat nothing served up as it is done here; and that grumbling old man's Kilmarnock nightcap, and his snuff, are enough to disgust one. Even at tea did you notice Peggy stirring the teacup with such vigour, and balancing her saucer in the palm of her hand?'

'I never fancied there was so much in little things,' said Jane; 'but we must get over our fastidiousness—we must indeed. It is a pity we were brought up so softly and delicately, though we thought we were so remarkably hardened by our uncle's training.'

'I cannot even write to-night,' said Elsie. 'Everything looks so sordid and miserable, and the town here is so dirty and mean.'

'We must walk out to-morrow a good long way—you know what beautiful walks we used to have all around Edinburgh. We must breathe fresh air and poetical inspiration.'

'I wish I could write,' said Elsie, turning over her sheets of manuscript. 'I have been able to write a little every day since I began, no matter how grieved or anxious I have been. Who is it says that genius is nothing but industry? and I have been so industrious! I must try to write to-night; we are settled as far as we can expect to be settled for some time, and I ought to begin as I mean to go on.'

'No, my dear, you feel disappointed and disenchanted to-night; do not think of writing. Your work ought to be done at your best moments. To-morrow is a new day, and I believe it will be a fine one: sleep till to-morrow.'

'But I cannot sleep either.'

'Rest, then, as I mean to do.'

A little tap at the door announced Peggy.

'Is there anything I can do for you, young ladies?'

'Nothing, thank you, Peggy, but come in,' said Jane.

She entered, and found Elsie hurriedly gathering together her manuscript, with a heightened colour and some agitation. Love letters were the only conceivable cause of a girl's blushing over anything she had been writing, to Peggy's unsophisticated mind. 'I should not interrupt you, Miss Elsie; I did not know you had letters to write.'

'It is not letters,' said Jane; 'she is writing a book.'

'A book! Well, that is not much in my line; but no doubt books are things that are wanted in the world, or there would not be such printing-houses and grand shops for making and selling them. And you are expecting to get a price for that, Miss Elsie?'

'I hope so.'

'Well, it is more genteel work than what I have been used to; but the pen was always a weariness to me. I thought shame of myself when I was in Australia, that I could write nothing to the bit creatures that I was spending my life for, but just that I was weel,

and hoped they were the same, and bidding them be good bairns, and obedient and dutiful to their grandfather and grandmother, and that they should mind what the master said to them at school; and then I would send kind regards to two or three folk in the country-side, and signed myself their affectionate aunt, Margaret Walker. But, dear me! I should have said fifty things forbye that senseless stuff. I am thinking, Miss Jane and Miss Elsie, that if they had been your nephews and nieces, and you had been parted from them by all these thousands of miles of land and water, that your letters would have been twice as often and ten times as long, full of good advice and loving words. I have heard bonnie letters read to me. I marvelled greatly at them—everything so smooth and so distinct, just as if the two were not far apart, but had come together for an hour or so, and the one just spoke by word of mouth all that the other wanted most to hear. I would like the bairns learned to write well and fast, for when the pen is slow, the heart cannot find utterance. I have heard worse letters even than my own, full of repetitions and stupid messages, and nothing said of what the body that got the letters wanted most to hear. There is a very great odds in letters, Miss Melville, and mine were so useless and so bare, that I thought it better to sacrifice a good deal of money and come home to attend to the bairns myself, and to counsel them by word of mouth.'

'Peggy, you have had adventures,' said Jane. 'I wish you could tell my sister and me all that happened to you when you were in Australia. Your life may be useful to us in many ways.'

'Not to put into a book, I hope,' said Peggy suspiciously. 'I have no will to be put into a book.'

'No fear of that,' said Elsie.

'It's poetry you're writing, like Robbie Burns's. I can see the lines are different lengths. I'm thinking you'll have no call to make any poetry on me, so I may tell you my story. It may make you think on somebody or something out of your own troubles.'

'It was a great wonder to the Swinton people that you returned a single woman,' said Jane. 'They say Australia is the country to be

married in.'

'I might have been married over and over again, up the country, and in Melbourne too,' said Peggy; 'but you see I had the thought of the bairns on my head, and I did not feel free to change my condition. Some of them said if I likit them well enough I could trust to their doing better for the young folk than I could myself; but I never let myself like them well enough to trust them so far, though one or two of them were very likely men, and spoke very fair.'

'Perhaps when you return to Australia you may make it up with one of them yet,' said Elsie, who, in spite, of her depression, felt some curiosity as to Peggy's love passages.

'The best of them married before I left Melbourne, like a sensible man, who knew better than to wait on my convenience. I see, Miss Elsie, you are wondering that the like of me, that never was what you would call well-favoured, should speak of offers, and sweethearts, and such like; but in Australia it's the busy hand and careful eye that is the great attraction for a working man. I never had much daffing or nonsense about me, and did not like any of it in other folk, but I had lots of sweethearts. But I'll tell you the whole story, as neither of you look the least sleepy, and if I am owre long about it ye may just tell me so, and I'll finish it up the morn's night.'

So Peggy sat down to tell her tale, while Elsie crept down on a little footstool, and laid her head in her sister's lap, glad to receive the fondling which Jane instinctively bestowed on her dependent and affectionate sister.

VIII

PEGGY WALKER'S ADVENTURES

'You see, Miss Jean and Miss Elsie, that my sister Bessie and me were always very much taken up with one another; she was a good bit aulder than me, and as my mother died when I was six years old, she was like a mother to me. I'll no say that she clapped and petted me as you are doing to your sister, Miss Jean, nor that she had the gentle ways of speaking that gentlefolks have; but verily to use the words of Scripture, "our souls were knit together in love," and we thought nothing too great to do or to bear for one another. Bessie was far bonnier than me, but scarcely so stout; and Willie Lowrie, that had been at the school with her, and a neighbour's son, courted her, when they came to man's and woman's estate, for a long time. My father was a cotter on Sandyknowe farm, a worthy, God-fearing man, but sore distressed with the rheumatics, that came upon him long before he was an old man, and often laid him off work. His sons went about their own business; and he used to say that though they might help him in the way of money nows and thens, it was from his two lasses that he had the most comfort. Bessie waited till I was grown up and at service in a good place, where I pleased the mistress, before she married Willie. My father went home with her, and lived but three years afterwards, saying always that Bessie and

Willie were good bairns to him, and his grey hairs went down to the grave in peace.

'But, wae-sakes! bairns came to Bessie thick and fast, and Willie took a bad cough, and fell into a decline. He just wasted away, and died one cold winter day, leaving her with four young things, and another coming. Bessie did not fold her hands in idle lamentation when the desire of her eyes was removed with a stroke. No, she went to the outwork, and wrought double hard; owre hard, poor thing, for after little Willie was born she never looked up. And then and there I vowed to God and to her that I would do a mother's part by her orphans as long as life was vouchsafed to me.

'Willie's father and mother had left Sandyknowe, and gone to a place about forty miles off. They were living poorly enough, but they came to me in my desolation, and offered to take the bairns if we—that is, my brothers and me—would help whiles with money to get them through. But, you see, James and Sandy were married men, with families of their own, and Robert and Daniel were like to be married soon, and it was borne on my mind that I was to be the chief person to be depended on.

'I went home to my place at Greenwells. It was a big farmhouse, and I was kitchenmaid, and had the milking of the kye, and the making of the butter and cheese to do, and such like, and Mrs. Henderson said that I was a faithful industrious lass. But, dear me! what was seven pounds by the year to maintain the bairns? I thought over it and over it on the Sabbath night after I came home. I tried to read—the 14th of John's Gospel—but my heart would be troubled and afraid in spite of those bonnie consoling words. I knew the old people, the Lowries, were not the best hands for bringing up the bairns, for they were so poor. I had no money—not a penny—for you may guess that in my sister's straits I kept none in the shuttle of my chest, and no way of keeping a house over their heads by myself could I see. Mrs. Henderson came into the kitchen with Miss Thomson. You know Miss Thomson of Allendale. She was on a visit to the mistress; they are connections, you know.

'"Well, Peggy," said Mrs. Henderson, "I see you are just fretting,

as usual."

'"I'm no fretting, ma'am, I'm praying," said I.

'"The best thing you can do," said Miss Thomson.

'"Of course it is,' said Mrs. Henderson, "provided it does not hinder work, and Peggy is neglecting nothing."

'"I wish, ma'am, that you would let me take the housemaid's place, as well as my own; I can do more work if you would raise my wages."

'"Nonsense, Peggy," said the mistress, "you are busy from morning till night; you cannot possibly do more than you are doing now. You cannot be in two places at once."

'"No, ma'am, but I could take less sleep. I am stronger than ever I was; and I have so many to work for. The bairns-maid and me could manage all the housework."

'Mrs. Henderson shook her head, and said it was not to be thought of, but she did not mind raising my wages to eight pounds by the year, for I was a good servant; and with that I had to be content—at least, I tried.

'Next day a fat turkey had to be killed and plucked, and I had an old newspaper to burn for singeing the feathers. I could not but look at the newspaper, when I had it in my hand, and the first thing that struck my eye was, that domestic servants, especially if they were skilful about a dairy, might get a free passage to Melbourne, by applying to such a person, at such a place, and that their wages when they got out to Australia would be from sixteen to twenty-five pounds by the year. It was borne on my mind that I should go to Australia from the moment I cast eyes on that paragraph in the paper. I did not just believe everything that was in print, especially in the newspapers, even in those days; for I knew the real size of the big turnip that was grown in Mr. Henderson's field, and it was not much more than half what the "Courier" had it down for, but I felt convinced that I should inquire about this matter of free passage to Australia. It was a providence that Miss Thomson was stopping in the house at the time, for she was a woman of by-ordinary discretion and great kindness; so I opened

my mind to her, and she said I was right, and gave me a letter to the agent, who was a far-away cousin of her own, and three pounds in money forbye, to buy fitting things for the voyage; and she told me how I was to send money home for the youngsters, and wrote a line to a friend of hers that lived close to the Lowries, asking her to look whiles to see that the bairns were well and thriving.

'It is not often that I greet, Miss Jean, but Miss Thomson twice brought the tears to my eyes, first with her kindness when I left Scotland, and again with her kindness when I came back, and brought her, no the silver—I would not shame her with giving back what had really been life and hope to myself and five orphan bairns—but some curious birds that I had got up the country, that she sets great store by. I told her how I had got on, and what had induced me to come back; I told her that I never could pay back my debt to her, and would not try to do it, but that if we prospered, there had been much of it her doing; and she said she admired nothing so much as my resolution and courage in going to Australia, until she admired still more my resolution and self-denial in coming back. I do not think much of flattery, Miss Elsie—they say it is very sweet to the young and the bonnie—but these words of praise from a good woman like Miss Thomson made my heart swell and my eyes overflow. You have been at Allendale, Miss Jean; you must have seen the birds in the lobby.'

Jane had been too much engrossed with her own affairs during her only visit to Miss Thomson to observe Peggy's birds, but she drew a good omen form the coincidence of Miss Thomson's assistance being given so frankly to two women both in distress and in doubt.

'How did you like the voyage, Peggy?' asked Jane.

'It is queer how that voyage has faded out of my mind, and yet it was a long one—over five months; they know the road better now, and do it quicker. I was not more than four months coming back in a bigger ship. I mind we had a storm, and all the women on board were awful feared, and a boy was washed overboard, and there was some ill-blood between the captain and the doctor; but all that I

could think on was to get to the end of the voyage, and make money to send home to the bairns.

'Well, to Melbourne we got at last, and a shabby place I thought it looked; but the worst of all was, that such wages as had been spoken of in the papers were not to be had at all, for if ever the folk there are in great want of anything, there seems to be abundance of it before it can be sent out; so I could not get the offer of more than thirteen pounds, and I mourned over the distance, and the five months lost on the passage, with such small advantage at the end of it. I said I wanted a hard place. I had no objections to go to the bush—I dreaded neither natives, nor snakes, nor bushrangers, but I behoved to make good wages. I was explaining this at the Agency Labour Office, when a gentleman came in—an Englishman I knew him to be by his tongue—and he said—

'"Like all new comers, this young woman is greedy of filthy lucre."

'"I have come here to better my condition," said I.

'"And so you will, in time," said the gentleman, "but you must not expect a fortune all at once."

'"Are you in want of a servant, sir?" said I.

'"Very much; but I don't know that you will suit me."

'"I'm thinking," said I, "that if the mistress were to see me she would be of a different opinion, sir."

'"Very likely she would. I dare say Mrs. Brandon would highly approve of you. Perhaps, after all, you will do. What are you?"

'"Plain cook, laundress, and dairymaid," said I.

'"Age? Mrs. Brandon would like to know."

'"Twenty-five. I have got five years' character from one place, and three from another, and a testimonial from the minister. I may look rough, with just being off the sea, sir, but I think the mistress will find out that I am fit for any kind of work. I am not afraid of work or distance, or solitude, or anything."

'"You are a trump," said he, "a regular brick; but confess that you are greedy. If I say thirty pounds a year, you will go more than a hundred miles up the country?" That was a great distance from

town in those days, Miss Jean, though they think nothing of it now. All my fellow-passengers objected to such distances, but I had no objection.

'"Yes, sir," said I, cheerfully, "I will go, and be much beholden to you for the offer."

'"And start to-morrow, wages to commence then?" said he.

'"The sooner the better," said I. "Only, if I want to send siller to my friends I may not be able to do it from such a wild place."

'"I will manage all that for you," said the gentleman. "I am accustomed to do it for one of my shepherds. But recollect you will have to do a great deal of work for your high wages. The cows are wild, and must be bailed up and foot-roped. You may get an ugly kick or butt"—

'"As if I had never seen Highland kyloes! I am not at all feared. Providence will protect me on land, as it has protected me by water. After five months of the sea, with only a plank between me and eternity, you cannot terrify me with kye."

'"We have few conveniences for saving labour; but I see I need not explain anything to you; you can think of nothing but your thirty pounds a year; so, Mr. What's-your-name, draw up the agreement for a year."

'The agreement was drawn out and signed Walter Brandon and Margaret Walker, and the next day I was on the road, if road you could call it, for the like of it you never saw—sometimes rough and tangled, sometimes soft and slumpy, sometimes scrubby and stony. I marvelled often that they kept in the tracks. I rode on the top of a dray through the day, and slept under it at night. There were four men with us; two of them were inclined to be rough; but I soon let them see that they would need to keep a civil tongue in their heads to deal with me. We were nigh a fortnight on the road, but somehow I did not weary of that as I did of the voyage, for my wages were going on, and something making for the bairns of that journey.'

IX

PEGGY WALKER'S ADVENTURES

'It was near dark on a Saturday when we got to Barragong, which was the name of Mr. Brandon's station. The master had got home long before us, for he had gone on his horse.

'"Well, Peggy," said he, as I got off the dray, "how do you like bush travelling? Slow, but sure, is it not?"

'"Uncommonly slow," said I.

'"Why, you have got worse burnt on the top of the dray than even on shipboard. Spoiled your beauty, Peggy."

'"My beauty is of no manner of consequence," said I, "it has not broke my work arm, and that is more to the purpose. Will you please, Sir, to ask the mistress to show me the kitchen?"

'"You ask to see what is not to be seen," said the master. "There is no kitchen to speak of, and as for the mistress, it is a pure invention of your own."

'"No mistress?" I gasped out; "ye spoke of Mrs. Brandon."

'"It was you that spoke of her, Peggy; and as I hope in time to have such a person on the premises, I made bold to say that you would suit her, and in the meantime I dare say we will get on very well. You will be really the mistress here, for there is not another woman within twenty miles."

'I started back, fairly cowed at the thought of being in that wild place alone, among I knew not how many men of all sorts of characters.

'"It was not fair of you, Sir," I said; "I never thought but what you were married when you took me up so natural."

'"But really, Peggy, you are the very person we want here, and I can make it worth your while to stay. You want good wages, and you will get them; you are not a child, and you can take care of yourself. It is hard that because I am so unlucky as to have no wife, I am to have neither cleanliness nor comfort. Make the best of a bad bargain, Peggy; I confess that your eagerness after good wages led me too far, but I felt the temptation strong. Try the place for a week, and if you do not like it, you can go back. Mr. Phillips's drays are going into town, and if you cannot make up your mind to be contented here, you can return to Melbourne with them."

'I took the measure of Mr. Brandon that week, and I came to the determination that I ought to stay. To be sure it was wrong of him to fetch me out on false pretences, as it were, but I had walked into the trap myself, and, as he said, he was in great need of a servant. He might be weak, but he was not wicked; at least, I felt that I could hold my own. It was a rough place for a gentleman to live in. Am I wearying you, young ladies? I could leave off now, and go on the morn's night.'

'"I am interested very much in your story," said Elsie.

'"And so am I," said Jane. "I know not where fortune, or rather, as you more properly call it, Providence may send us; and your experience has a peculiar fascination to me. Do, pray, go on.'

'Well, as I was saying, it was a rough place, and he was a gentleman in his up-bringing and in many of his ways. You would not have believed, if you had seen him in Melbourne, and heard him speak such English, that he could go about in an old ragged, dirty shooting-coat, with a cabbage-tree hat as black as a coal nearly—that he could live in a slab hut, with a clay, or rather, a dirt floor, and a window-bole with no glass in it—and that he could have all the cooking and half the work of the house done at the

fireside he sat at, and sit down at a table without a table-cloth, and drink tea out of tin pannikins. The notion of getting such wages in a place with such surroundings quite dumb-founded me; and he had the things too; for by-and-by I found napery and china in a big chest that I used for a table out of doors; and bit by bit I made great improvements at Barragong. He gave me one of the huts for myself, and I was a thought frightened to sleep there my leafu' lane at first, but I put my trust in my Maker, and He watched over me. I cooked in my own hut, and settled up the master's. He began to think that a boarded floor would be an improvement, and he got the men to saw them up. Hard work it was for them; and ill-coloured boards they made; but when they were laid down, and a glass window put in, the master's hut looked more purpose-like.

'I was not feared for the wild kye when I saw that the stockkeeper would help me to get them into the bail; and when we got a milk-house dug out of the hill-side, I made grand butter. I'll not soon forget the day I had my first kirning. The stockkeeper—George Powell was his name—had got into the dairy, as I thought, to lick the cream, for he was an awful hand on it; but he kept hanging about, and glowering at the milk-pans, and then looking at me, till at last he said some nonsense, and I told him to be off with his daffing; I would tell the master if he said an uncivil word.

'"I don't mean to be uncivil, Peggy; quite the contrary," says he.

'"Then what do you mean?" says I, taking his hand off my shoulder, and driving it bang against the stone slab we put the milk-pans on.

'"I mean, Peggy, will you marry me?" says he; "that's civil enough, surely."

'"No I won't," says I. "Thank you for the compliment, all the same, but I have no wish to change my condition."

'"Tell that to the marines," says he. "If you don't like me, tell me so; but none of that nonsense."

'"I like you well enough; but what I say is no nonsense. I do not wish to change my condition."

'"It would be a good change for you," says he. "I wonder you are not frightened to stay here a single woman. Now, if you were my wife, I could protect you;" and he flourished the arm I had given the bang to—and a goodly arm it was.

'I told him about the bairns, and he just laughed at me. "We'll see," says he. "We'll see. Wait a little."

'Well, every kirning that he was not out at a distance on the master's business, did that man Powell come into the dairy and ask me the same question, and get the same answer; and three of the shepherds, and a little imp of a laddie that looked after the horses, made up to me too, and seemed to think it was not fair that I would choose none of them. Any woman with a white face might have had as many sweethearts; but I think it was my managing ways that took Powell's fancy. If a fairy could only move a lot of the women from the places where they are not wanted, and put them where they are, there would be a wonderful thinning taken out of Scotland and planted in Australia. But ye see there are no fairies; and at such a distance, it costs a lot of money to move such commodities as single women. I have puzzled my brains whiles about the matter, Miss Jane, and many a time I have repented coming back to a place where hands are many and meat is scarce; but it will not be for long; and in the meantime I try to help all the distressed bodies that I know about; and that I have kept my five bairns from being a burden to anybody, is enough work for any woman either here or in Australia. I'm going off of my story; but the marvel to me that I was so beset with sweethearts that did not want them, while so many lasses here never can see the sight of one, always makes me think that there should be a medium, and that lasses should neither be ower-much made of or neglected altogether. But to go back to the bush. I had to rule with a high hand at Barragong, and really to demean myself as if I were the mistress, to keep folk in their place. But the worst was to come.

'The master had not been well for a week or so, and I had taken especial care of him, and got him gruel and such like, that he seemed very glad of; and he was getting better, and was sitting by

the fire while I was setting down the supper, when he said—No, I cannot tell you what he said. No; he was not well, and may be did not know exactly what he was about. I cannot tell his words, though they are burned into my memory as clear and distinct as though I had heard them but yesterday, but they were most unbefitting words for him to say or for me to hear.

'I stood still for a whole minute or more, and looked him in the face. He did not like the fixed steady way I kept my eyes on him.

'"Say such a thing again if you dare," said I. "You had no such thought in your head or your heart when you brought me out to Barragong. I knew that by your eyes. You must treat me respectfully if you mean to call yourself a gentleman."

'"Don't be so very hot, Peggy. You have made a fellow so comfortable, that he may be excused for thinking more of you than he used to do," says he.

'"Think more of me!" says I; "you think less of me, or you would not dare—"

'"What was I to fancy," says he, "when you refuse Powell so pertinaciously, but that you are looking higher?"

'"Mr. Brandon," says I, "George Powell is high enough for me, for he would make me his wife; and if I was free to marry, I would look for no higher match. But to think that what you offer is higher!—May God forgive you for the thought!"

'"Why, Peggy, perhaps I may offer higher yet; you are a good and a clever girl, and will make an admirable wife."

'"Not to you, sir; nor to any one out of my own station. Do not think of making a fool of yourself, just because there is nobody here to compare with homely Peggy Walker."

'He looked at me more particularly than he had ever done before. I leaned my hands on the table, and squared my elbows, and spread my great browned hand and red arms before him. He laughed, and said, "Peggy, you are right; you are a worthy girl and a clever, and in the sight of God are worth ten of me; but when I think of taking you home and presenting you to my mother and sisters as Mrs. Brandon, it is rather comical. As for anything else, you are too good

a girl, and I will say no more about it, only I wish you would marry Powell and be done with it."

'Well, Miss Jean, this was the beginning and the end of it with the master; but I think that man Powell was my greatest tempation, especially after Mr. Brandon's words. He really was a protection to me, for he was always civil and respectful in his language to me, and there was not one of the men who dared say the thing that would anger him. But it fell out that I was removed from Barragong before I had given in to Powell, though I'm not saying what might have happened if I had stopped there for six months longer.

'The master had a friend, a Mr. Phillips, who lived twenty miles off, who had more stock and more men on his station than we had at Barragong;—a nice quiet gentlemanly man, who had done as silly a thing as Mr. Brandon had half evened himself to. He had married out of his degree, though he had more temptation to it than the other, for the lassie was very bonnie, and very young, and I dare say he thought he could learn her the ways of gentlefolks.

'Be that as it may, the lady, Mrs. Phillips, was expecting her inlying, and her husband had trysted a skilled nurse from Melbourne, for a doctor could not be had; but when the appointed time came, the nurse had made some other engagement, and could not or would not come; nor did she send a fit person in her place. There was not time to get any one from Melbourne, and Mr. Phillips came to Barragong and entreated me to come to his wife, and Mr. Brandon to spare me. I said I had but little skill, but that I would do the best I could for the poor lady in her straits, and the master said he would let me go with pleasure if I would only promise to come back when Mrs. Phillips was well and about again.

'I thought I had been rather deceived in this instance too, for I fancied there was no woman about the place but the mistress herself; but I saw a well-grown strapping lass in the kitchen, and I thought she might have answered as well me; but I soon found out that though the woman (Martha they called her) had legs and arms and a goodly body of her own, she had no more head than a bairn,

and would have been a broken reed to trust to in any time of peril or difficulty.

'It did not seem to me at first that Mrs. Phillips was so unlike a lady, for she had an English tongue, and she was very well-favoured, and sat quiet in her seat, and ordered folk about quite natural. She had been married now well on for a year, and had got used to be the mistress. But I had not been long there ere I found out her faults and her failings; and to my mind her husband had but a poor life with her, though he did seem to be very fond of the young creature, with all her deficiencies. You see she had not an atom of consideration either for him or for any other body on the station; she was either too familiar or too haughty to the girl Martha; as for me, I knew my place better, and if she did not keep me at my distance, I could mostly keep her at hers.

'Not many days after I went to the Phillips's, she was taken ill and safely delivered of a fine lassie. I have seen women make a great fuss about bairns, till I cannot be surprised at anything they say or do, but the joy of the father over the wee Emily was beyond anything I ever saw. To see the great bearded man taking the hour-old infant in his arms, kissing it over and over again, and speaking to it in the most daft-like language, and calling on every one to admire its beauty! No doubt the bairn had as much beauty as a thing of that age can have, but I don't think any of the men he showed it to admired it much. I know Powell, for one, when he came with his master's compliments to inquire for Mrs. Phillips, and may be to have a crack with myself, was not much taken up with the brat, as he called it. I had it in my arms, and it was greeting, poor thing, so I had no time to give Powell a word, except just the message for Mr. Brandon.

'Mrs. Phillips was by no means an easy lady to nurse. I knew well how strict old Tibbie Campbell, who used to nurse Mrs. Henderson, used to be about what a lying-in woman should have to eat and drink, and what care she took that she could catch no cold, and I thought I behoved to be as particular with Mrs. Phillips; but she would not hear reason. She said that such a climate as Scotland

should be no rule for treatment in Australia, and she thought she should know her own constitution best, and what was likely to agree with her; so she would take no telling from me. As for Mr. Phillips, he would always give her what she wanted if she teased for it long enough, or if she began to greet, so she carried her point in spite of my teeth. And, poor thing, she suffered for it; for she first took the cold, and then the fever; she was out of her senses for five weeks, and barely escaped with her life. It was a weary nursing. Mr. Phillips was wonderful in a sick-room, and relieved me greatly; but I had such an anxious life with the bairn as well as the mother. He used to beg me, with tears in his eyes, to save the bit lassie, if it was in my power, and the man's life seemed to hang on the little one's. His eye was as sharp as a mothers'—sharper than most mothers'—to notice if Emily looked worse or better. It was a novelty to me to see such care and thought in a man, not but what it is well a father's part to care for his own offspring, and to take trouble and fatigue for them.

'Mr. Brandon, all the time that the mistress was lying between life and death, was wondrous patient, and never made a complaint for the want of me, though I am sure things were at sixes and sevens at Barragong; but when Mrs. Phillips had got the turn, and was able to move about again, he sent me a message to come back. Well, I had promised, no doubt—and I had a far easier life at Mr. Brandon's than where I was, and nothing had ever been said about wages by Mr. Phillips to me—but then the poor little lassie, it seemed as much as her life was worth to leave her to her mother and the lass Martha, for they had not the sense of an ordinary woman between them, and my heart clung to the bit bairn with great affection.

'One day Powell came over with the spring-cart to fetch me home, and I was in a swither what to do, for ye don't just like to press services on folk that do not want them; but by that time Mr. Phillips had got to know the necessity of the case, and it was only because he wanted the offer to come from his wife that he had not asked me before; but she was unreasonable, and he had to do it

himself. She did not see why she and Martha could not manage the baby; she was sure Peggy was no such marvel; that there was no difficulty in feeding the child; that it was cruel to put a strange woman over to give her orders, for Peggy was far too independent for her place; and then Emily would love her nurse better than her own mother. I know that was the way she went on to Mr. Phillips, but on this point he was unmovable. When he asked me as a great favour to stay, I consented for the sake of him and of Emily.

'Powell was very angry at me for stopping, and took quite a spite to the little lassie that caused my stay. The way he spoke of that bairn decided me. If he could not be fashed with one, how could he be fashed with five? I was determined on one thing, that I should not have a house of my own unless there was room in it, and a welcome in it, for Bessie's orphans; so it was settled in my mind that day that I never could be Mrs. Powell.

'I stopped at the Phillips's for more than eighteen months. The mistress got used to me, and the bairn Emily was as fond of me as bairn could be. I had more freedom from sweethearts there at first, for the men were greatly taken up with Martha; but by the time I had been three months there I had nigh hand as many followers, as she called them, as she had herself. And followers she might well call them. I could not go out with the bairn for a walk, or out to the kye, or turn my head any way, without one or other of them being at my heels. And when Martha got married to one of the men on the place, which happened ere long, I seemed to have the whole station bothering me; but I would have nothing to do with any of them. Mr. Phillips gave more credit than any of the folk I had ever seen to my yearnings after Bessie's orphans, and my resolutions to live single for their sake; but he never could see that they would be such a drawback to any decent man that liked me; but I knew there were few men so taken up with bairns as he was.

'Well, as I said, Mrs. Phillips, finding I did my work well and quietly, gave over interfering with me, and seemed to get to like me; but when her time was drawing near again, she was not disposed to trust herself to my care altogether, nor, indeed, was I

very keen of the responsibility. She wanted to go to Melbourne, but the master would not hear of it; and not all her fleeching, nor her tears, nor three days' sulks, in which she would not open her mouth to him, would make him give in to that.

'He seemed to have the greatest dread of parting with her, particularly to go to Melbourne; and it was a busy time of the year, so that he could not stay with her there. But he said he would go and fetch a doctor, if one was to be had, and keep him in the house till he was needed, and for as long as she was in any peril; and with that she behoved to be contented. He was as good as his word, for he fetched one from the town. I did not much like the looks of the man, but I said nothing, and the mistress seemed quite satisfied.

'But Mr. Phillips took me by myself, and says he to me, "I believe this man is skilful enough and clever enough, but he has one fault—we must keep drink from him and him from drink, or we cannot answer for the consequences. But for this fault he would have had too good a practice in Melbourne for us to be able to have him for weeks here. There is no place near where he can get drink, so I think we can easily manage to keep him all right. We need not tell Mrs. Phillips, Peggy."

'Well, I kept watch over this Dr. Carter very well for a fortnight or more, and he seemed to go on all right; but after that time he got very restless, and I used to hear him walking about at night as if he could not sleep, and through the day he could not settle to his book as he used to do at first, or go to take a quiet walk, or ride not over far from the house, but took little starts and turned back, as if something was on his mind.

'I misdoubted him, but with all my watching I could see nothing. As ill luck would have it, the night the mistress was taken ill, and I went to call him up, there I found this man Carter as drunk as he could be, to be able to stand, with an empty brandy bottle beside him that he had knocked the head off. The keys were in my pocket, and not a bottle missing out of the press. There never was much kept in the house, for Mr. Phillips was a most moderate man, and tea is the great drink in the bush; but in case of sickness we aye had

some brandy by us. But the poor deluded man had got one of the men about the place to ride forty miles to get him this brandy that had just come at the time when he was especially needed to be sober. I told him the lady was wanting him, and Mr. Phillips and me shook him up; and he half came to himself; and if the mistress had not smelt the drink so strong upon him, she might not have known: She had another fine lassie, and all was going on very well, for the mistress was more reasonable. She had bought her experience very dear the time before, and would take a telling. When the doctor had got over his drinking fit he was very penitent, and spoke quite feelingly on the subject. Mr. Phillips turned off the man that had fetched him the brandy, and told all the men on the station the reason why. The man Carter did not want for skill, nor for kindness either, when he was sober; so, as we were more fearful for the fortnight after than the fortnight before the birth, we just kept him on. Little Harriet was a fortnight old, and the mistress was doing so nicely that Mr. Phillips thought he might leave us for one of his out-stations, where he was wanted, and said he would not be home for two or three days. And then the poor demented creature of a drunken doctor contrived again to get hold of drink, and was far more outrageous this time. Mrs. Phillips was lying on the sofa in the parlour, when he came in and terrified her by roaring for more brandy; and when I came in to settle him, he grippit me by the arm and threatened me with I don't know what, if I refused him. The mistress entreated me to turn him out of doors—and so I did. He got on a horse of the master's—I marvelled how he kept his seat—and set off, and I felt easy in my mind.

'But I had just got the mistress quieted down, when the native boy Jim, that was always doing odd jobs about the place, came running past the window with such a look of terror on his face that I saw something was wrong. I ran out quick but quietly, to ask what was the matter.

'"Fire! Peggy," says he; and then, sure enough, I looked out, and the grass was on fire, but very far off, and a strong wind blowing it right to the slab huts on the head station with their thatch roofs.

Nothing could save us if it came near, and as I have told you it was a busy time, and the men were all hither and thither, and nobody left on the place but Martha, and Jim, and myself, and the mistress ill, and two infants, as I may say, for Emily was not thirteen months old. The only thing that could be done was to burn a broad ring round the houses, as I had seen done at Barragong; but that craved wary watching. By good luck the bairns were both sleeping, and Mrs. Phillips resting quiet, so I called Martha and Jim, and said we must take wet bags and green boughs and beat the fire out as we burned. Jim was as quick and clever as need be, and set about in earnest; but Martha said she could do nothing for terror, and prayed me to remember her situation.

'"Your situation," says I, "will be far worse if you don't bestir yourself for your own safety. If you won't lend a hand for the sake of your poor helpless mistress and the innocent bairns, you behove to do it for the sake of your own four quarters." So she got more reasonable, and helped us somewhat, but it was close work, for the fire was near. It was all that poor wretch of a doctor's doing, too, for he had been trying to smoke, and had dropped his lighted pipe in the dry withered grass, and it blazed up like wild; he got out of it, for he was travelling against the wind, while we were in full waft of it. I thought the wind and the fire would beat us, and was like to throw up the work in despair, when I saw a man on horseback galloping for dear life. I thought it was the master at first, but it was Mr. Brandon, and he was nigh hand as good, for he fell to, and worked with all his might, and with his help we saved the house, and all the precious ones in it. In time the men dropped in, and they set about working to save the run, but if the wind had not providentially changed at night, they would scarcely have been able to save it. As it was, there was thousands of acres of land laid bare, and a flock of sheep killed; the poor beasts have not the sense to run away out of the fire.

'Oh! the appearance of the place that night was awful to behold; and just before the wind chopped round the master came home, riding like fury.

'"We are all safe," said I, as I ran to meet him, and I saw his face by the light of the blazing fires around us was as pale as death. "Mrs. Phillips and the bairns are not a hair the worse. Thank God for all his mercies!"

'"Thank God!" said he, "thank God! Now they are preserved, I can bear the loss of anything else!"

'He came to his wife, and kissed her and the bairns with solemn, and, as I thought, with pathetic thankfulness. I was afraid she would be sorely upset with the terrible events of the day, and I never closed my eyes that night, but sat up by her bedside lest she should take a bad turn; but she did not seem any the worse of it, and both her and the bairns got on brawly. The loss of the sheep was no such great matter in these times, for there was so little market for them, that we had to boil them down for the sake of the tallow—that could be sent to England. Times were changed before I left the colony, for the diggings made a great demand for sheep and cattle to kill; but when I was up the country the waistrie of flesh was sinful to behold. I have many a day sinsyne thought on the beasts and the sheep that were slaughtered there for the working men, and how the bits that they threw about or left on their plates might be a good dinner for many a hungry stomach in Scotland.

'Well, after I had been more than a year and a half at Mr. Phillips's, my wages just running on as they had done at Mr. Brandon's, and five pounds sent every quarter, as opportunity offered, for the bairns, I heard word of a cousin of William Lowrie's coming out to Melbourne, to follow his trade of a stone-mason there, and I had a strong desire to see him, to ask after my orphans; for if my letters to them were but poor, the letters I got back were no better, so my heart was set on seeing Sandy Lowrie, who had lived close by, and knew the bairns well. It chanced that Mr. Phillips had a man and his wife on the station at the time that had no family. The man was nothing of a hand at work, but the wife was one of those bright, clever, cheery little Englishwomen that can turn hand to anything, and had such a fine temper—nothing ever could put her out. So, as she could do for the mistress as well as

myself, I asked leave from the master and Mrs. Phillips to go to the town and see Sandy. The mistress was fashious, for she did not like anybody about her to please themselves, and she had got used to me, as I said before; but the master was as reasonable as she was the contrary.

'He said to me, the day before I left, "Peggy, I owe you a great debt. You have saved the life of my wife and children."

'"Under Providence, sir," said I.

'"Under Providence, of course," said he; "but I fear Providence would have done little for them if Martha had been the only instrument Providence had at hand to use, so I am over head and ears in debt to you."

'"No, Mr. Phillips," said I, "my work you have paid me well for; my kindness you have returned with kindness and consideration such as I never hoped to meet with in a strange land. If I have nursed and cared for your children you have comprehended my love for my own poor bairns; and this permission to visit Melbourne, that I may hear about them, is a great favour, and one I will never forget to be grateful for."

'"You are not to let me off in this way," said he. "You will find a hundred pounds lying in the bank to your credit, which, as you are a prudent woman, you may be trusted to invest yourself in any way that you may judge best for yourself or the orphans. My idea is that you may take a little shop, and this sum would stock it. I could assist you with my name further than the sum of money I have given to you, if it is necessary."

'It flashed on my mind that this was a grand opening; but it seemed so selfish and greedy-like to take advantage of his kindness, and to leave him, and Mrs. Phillips, and the bairns, to further my own plans. I said as much to him, but he would not hear of a refusal.

'"You never can manage to do much for the children at service, for all your wages, except your own necessary expenses, goes home and is spent; but by having a little business, you may save more than you could send to them now, and get them a better education,

and give them a better start. No doubt we will miss you here; but Mrs. Bennett is a very excellent person, and now I hear that Dr. Grant is going to buy Mr. McDougall's station, only fifteen miles off, we can get him to come on an emergency, though he says he would rather not practise. I will not say that we can do very easily without you, but we must not keep you always here."

'The kindness of Mr. Phillips I will never forget. Well, it was done all as he planned it. I went to Melbourne and saw Sandy Lowrie, and he gave me good accounts of the bairns, as growing in stature, and Tam and Jamie keen of their learning, but the old woman, their grandmother, he said was sore failed, and no likely to be long spared.

'I took a little shop at a low rent, in a little village, a bit out of the town, for I was frightened to incur much risk, and I set up on my own footing, with "M. Walker, general store," over my door-cheek.

'I was doing a decent business, in a small way, among poor people mostly; and I set my face very steady against giving credit, for two reasons—first, that I was not clever enough to keep accounts; and besides that, it just does working folk harm to let them take on. At a time of sickness I might break through my rule, but at no other time. All the folk about me called me Miss Walker, very much to my surprise; and as I was thought to be making money, I had no want of sweethearts. After I had gone on for some years the diggings broke out, and there was an awful overturn of everything in Melbourne. I made a lot of money, and I bought the shop from the landlord, and was very proud to get my title-deed written out on parchment, and to see myself a woman of landed heritable property; and then I made my will, too, for I had something to leave. I never was doing better in business in my life than when Robbie Lowrie, a brother of Sandy's, came out to go to the diggings, and maybe with an eye to make up to myself; but the news he brought me made me change all my plans and return to Scotland. He told me that the grandmother was dead, and that the old man, who never had half the gumption of his wife, was not able

to control the five youngsters; so that they were getting out their heads at no allowance. Tam, in particular, he said, was a most camsteery callant; but the old man, he said, was fairly off all work, and not one of his own bairns were either able or willing to help him, and I knew that he had an awful horror of the sea. So I let my shop, and sold the stock for time; and indeed the payments have no been owre regular, and the man that took it is still in my debt. I found the grandfather and the bairns were really as Robbie had said, and I have had my own work to set things to rights. They were in debt, too, though I had sent them double the money after I had the shop than before; but they just thought that a rich auntie in Australia was a mine of wealth, and the folk very unwisely gave them trust whenever they asked it. But they were doing very weel at the school, and I find it a hantle cheaper to give them learning here than in Melbourne; so it answers me better to bide here than to take them out, even if grandfather would agree. He was good to me and mine in my straits, and I cannot think to leave the old man now.

'But what with the rent and the schooling, and one thing and another, I found that the rent of my bit shop would not pay all expenses, so I took in washing and dressing for the folk about Swinton. I was aye clever at it, and I got a great inkling about clear-starching and fine dressing from that Mrs. Bennett, at Mr. Phillips's station, for she was a particular good laundress. A body learns at all hands if one has only the will. And ye see, now, it seemed better for Tam and the rest that I should try my luck in a bigger place, and I hope I may not repent of it.

'That's all my story. It's no much tell; but yet, ye see that none of my brothers have been burdened with my bairns. I have done it all myself.'

Jane sat silent a few moments after Peggy had finished her narrative, and then thanked her gravely and earnestly for it. Elsie, too, had been much interested in the advertures of this clever, upright woman, and was only sorry it could not be available—neither incident nor sentiment—for her poetry.

'Now, I have kept you up long enough, young ladies. If what I have said gives you any heart, I will be glad. I hope you will sleep well, and have lucky dreams; so good-night.'

X

ELSIE'S LITERARY VENTURE, AND ITS SUCCESS

Elsie Melville found the second day in —— Street better than the first. An early walk with Jane restored her to her equilibrium, and she sat down to write in her own room with more rapidity than before; while Jane went out and made inquiries at registry offices, or anywhere else that was likely to lead to employment; but day after day passed without success. Rather than do nothing, she assisted Peggy in the lighter parts of her work, made clothes for the children, and helped them with their lessons in the evening. Peggy was astonished at the progress which they all made with such assistance, and particularly delighted with the great influence Jane had over Tom. As she grew accustomed to the ways of the house, she learned to endure the noise patiently, and she found these five young Lowries really interesting and remarkably intelligent. Tom especially was eager for knowledge, and his trade, which he entered into with all his heart, was calling out all his abilities and all his ambition. There were many things that he had difficulty in getting information about, for he was but a young apprentice, and the journeymen and older apprentices wanted him to wait on them rather than to learn the business. But he was not to be kept back in that way; he was determined to find things out for himself, and in

every difficulty he found help and sympathy from Jane Melville. Her out-of-the-way knowledge made her a most useful auxiliary, and she rejoiced that there was one person in the world that she could assist with it. She did not forget Peggy's wish about the quick writing, and taught those peasant children to express themselves fluently on paper. Their manners were improved under her influence, and what was still uncouth or clumsy she learned to bear with.

Another resource to lighten the weight of anxiety and disappointment was found in Peggy's extraordinary gift in finding out distressed people, which even in her new residence, did not desert her. Jane, who had been accustomed to put her hand in her purse for the benefit of Peggy's protégés, felt at first very grieved that she had nothing to give, but she learned that a great deal of good can be done with very little money, and satisfied herself by giving sympathy, personal services, and advice. It was astonishing what good advice she gave to other people for bettering their prospects, while she seemed quite unable to do anything for herself. But so long as Elsie was busy and hopeful with her poems, Jane could not bear to leave her; if they failed, they must try what they could do separately. In the meantime, she was more disposed to try classes than anything else, for her experience with the Lowries proved to her that she could teach clever children, at any rate, with success; but as she could not get the promise of any pupils of the rank and circumstances that could make them pay, she hesitated about incurring any risk.

Elsie had completed poems sufficient to fill a small volume before her sister had seen any opening for herself. It was with some strong agitation on Jane's part, and still stronger on Elsie's, that they presented themselves to the publisher who had said he would give a good price for a good book written by a woman, and offered him the manuscript for publication. Alas! tastes differ as to what is a good book, and in nothing is there so much disparity of opinion as in the article of poetry. He did not give much encouragement to the sisters, but said he would read over the manuscript and give an answer in ten days. Any one who has ever written with the hope of

publishing can fancy Elsie's feeling during these ten days. Her own verses rang in her ears; she recollected passages she might have altered and improved, and wondered if they would strike the critic as faulty; then again she recalled passages which she fancied could not be improved, and hoped he would not skip them; now she would sit idle in the thought that, until she saw there was a market for her productions, there was no necessity for multiplying them; then again she would work with redoubled industry to see if she had not quite exhausted her fancy and her powers.

The final verdict was unfavourable:—'There is some sweetness of versification and of expression in Miss Melville's poems, but they are unequal, and want force and interest. They never would become popular, so that I feel obliged to decline the publication. Poetry is at all times heavy stock, unless by authors of established reputation.'

Elsie sat sad and dispirited at this her first failure, but her sister comforted her by saying that Edinburgh was not the best market for anything new—London was the place where a new author had some chance. Elsie easily caught at the hope, and retouched some of her most imperfect pieces before sending them to a great London house. To publisher after publisher the manuscript was sent, and after due time occupied in reading it, the parcel returned with the disappointing note—

'Mr. B——'s compliments, and he begs to decline with thanks Miss Melville's poems, as, in the opinion of his literary adviser, they could not answer the purpose of publication.'

Or—

'Messrs. H——, B——, & Co.'s compliments, and though they are overstocked with poetry, they have read carefully Miss Melville's poems, but find them of the most unmarketable kind, so beg to decline publication.'

Or—

'Messrs. S——, E——, & Co.'s compliments, and they regret that the subjective character of all Miss Melville's poems will make them uninteresting to the general reader. They therefore regret that they cannot bring them out.'

When the notes were as brief as the foregoing samples, the pain was not so severe as in the last which Elsie received, in which a careful but most cutting criticism accompanied the refusal. There is no doubt that Elsie's poems were crude, but she had both fancy and feeling. With more knowledge of life and more time, she was capable of producing something really worth reading and publishing. If there had been no talent in her verses, she would not have had a reading from so many good publishing houses; but she did not know enough of the trade to know this, and her humiliation at her repeated disappointments was exceedingly bitter.

There is no species of composition that should be less hurried than poetry. Even if it is struck off in a moment of inspiration, it should not be published then, but laid aside for alteration and polishing after a considerable time has elapsed; and much of our best poetry has been very slowly composed, even at first. Our poor little Elsie had prepared by great industry her volume of poems in less than four months, and had not taken time to reconsider them. They were not narrative pieces, in which the interest of the story carries you along in reading, whether the diction is perfected or not, but mostly short lyrical poems, and contemplative pieces, which are always much more effective when found amongst other descriptions of poetry or in a magazine, than when collected together in a volume. They were generally sad, a common fault with poetesses; but poor Elsie had more excuse for taking that tone than many others who have done so.

She had to mourn the loss of fortune and the coldness of friends; the conduct of William Dalzell to her sister had made a deeper impression on her mind than on that of Jane. She had more capacity of suffering than Jane had, and when she took the pen in her hand, she felt that her life—and all life—was full of sorrow. Jane had induced Elsie to accompany her to the chapel, where she herself had learned her first lesson of submission and of Christian hope; but even in religion Elsie inclined to the contemplative and the tender rather than to the active and the cheerful side of it. She looked with far more intense longing to the Heaven beyond the

earth than Jane did, and had not the interest in the things about her to make the dreariness of her daily life endurable. Her poetry had been her one resource; and that appeared to be very weak and contemptible in the opinion of those who ought to know.

Whether the literary taster for the publisher last applied to was less engrossed with business than the others, or whether he thought it would do the aspiring poetess good to show her her faults, I cannot tell, but he wrote a long letter of critical remarks. There was one ballad—an idealization of the incident in Jane's life which had so much impressed Elsie, in which William Dalzell was made more fascinating and more faithless, and Jane much more attached to him than in reality—which this correspondent said was good, though the subject was hackneyed, but on all the others the sweeping scythe of censure fell unsparingly. 'Her poems,' he said, 'were very tolerable, and not to be endured;' mediocrity was insufferable in poetry. The tone of them was unhealthy, and would feed the sentimentalism of the age, which was only another name for discontent. If poetesses went on as they were doing now-a-days, and only extracted a wail from life, the sooner they gave up their lays the better. The public wanted healthy, cheerful, breezy poetry, with a touch of humour here and there, and a varied human interest running through it—a fit companion to the spirited novels of Charles Kingsley, then at the height of his fame. If poets were to teach the world, as they boasted that they were, they should not shut themselves up, and practise variations on the one poor tune, 'I am miserable; I am not appreciated; the world is not worthy of me;' but go forth to the world and learn that there are nobler subjects for poetry than themselves. Then, with regard to Elsie's diction and rhymes, this critic selected a number of the most faulty and imperfect verses for censure, and Elsie had the miserable satisfaction of having to acknowledge that they deserved it. I have little doubt that the critic thought he was giving the poetess a good lesson; but if he had seen the suffering that his letter caused, and the youth and inexperience, and the sad circumstances of the poor girl who received it, he would have repented somewhat of his very

clever and satirical letter.

Heartsick and humbled, Elsie lost hope, and health, and spirits. She wrapped the rejected manuscript in brown paper, and put it in the farthest corner of one of her drawers. She was only prevented from committing it to the flames by Jane's interference.

'Now,' said she, 'I must be as busy as you. Peggy must teach me to iron—surely I can learn to do that—and let me make Nancy's frock. But, after all, Jane, this will not do for a continuance; we must seek for employment somewhere. I have spent a good deal of time over this useless work, and postages have come heavy on our small means. I must try to earn something.'

The heavy tears fell fast on the frock as the girl worked at it; the listless hands dropped their hold of it occasionally, and she was lost in bitter thoughts. She however finished it, and then busied herself with a new bonnet for Peggy, which was to be made not at all fashionable, but big and rather dowdy. Elsie's taste rebelled a little at the uncongenial task; but she was doing her best to please Peggy when the postman delivered two letters to Jane—one from Francis, and the other from Mrs. Rennie. Francis' letters had been frequent, and had been a little interesting even to Elsie, and this one was more so than usual. He was coming to Edinburgh for a week or two, and meant to see them as much as possible during his stay. He was to be at a party at the Rennies' on New Year's Day, and his cousins were to be invited also; he trusted to meet them there. The Rennies had occasionally called, and shown the girls more kindness than any of their Swinton friends, or their other Edinburgh acquaintances. They had spent a fortnight, in autumn, at Cross Hall, and had enjoyed it very much.

The note from Mrs. Rennie contained an invitation for both sisters to this party; and to girls who had been shut up so many months with no society but that of Peggy and her relations, the prospect of spending one evening among their equals in social position was very pleasant. Jane anticipated pleasure, besides, from seeing and talking with her cousin about everything and everybody in and about Cross Hall, as well as about a tour on the Continent

which he had taken. Even Elsie's face brightened a little as she gave the last loving touches to her sister's dress, and said that she had never seen her look better, though she was a little thinner and paler than she used to be—to Elsie's eyes she was quite as pretty.

XI

SOME GRAVE TALK IN GAY COMPANY

Francis had hoped to see his cousins before he met them at the party, but when he called at Peggy Walker's he found that they were out taking their customary long walk, so he met them in Mrs. Rennie's drawing-room for the first time. Certainly the two girls in mourning were not the plainest-looking in the room. Neither sister was beautiful, but Elsie was very nearly so, and her recent suffering had thrown more intensity into her expression, and made her look more lovely than ever. But it was to Jane that Francis' eyes turned affectionately and anxiously, and he grieved to see the traces of weariness, of care, and he even thought, of tears, on the face which to him was the most interesting in the world. He shook hands with her warmly, and looked inquiringly in her face, and then drew her into a quiet corner in a window-seat, where they could talk without being much observed. Elsie did not sit beside them, but left them to their own conversation, assured that she would hear all that she cared to know by-and-by; yet she was not neglected, for Miss Rennie had taken a great fancy to her, and was determined, if possible, to get her partners. At Mrs. Rennie's parties there never was any scarcity of gentlemen, for they had an extensive family connection, and Mr. Rennie was a kind and hospitable man,

who had a large acquaintance in the city. Miss Rennie had judged hardly of Jane's personal appearance at first sight, but she thought Elsie a most elegant and interesting creature.

'We have written so often and so fully to each other that I fancy that we have little to say now we meet,' said Jane, smiling.

'We have written so much to each other that we have all the more to say, Jane,' said her cousin. 'I never get a letter from you without its making me wish to talk over it with you. You have no news, however, I suppose?'

'No news,' said Jane. 'I wrote to you of Elsie's last bitter disappointment. It was a cruel letter; she felt it all the more, because she says it is all true. But, really, Francis, I think her poetry did not deserve it. She has never mentioned her verses since.'

'And for yourself, you can see no prospect?'

'It seems impossible to get up the classes that I hoped for. I think I must take to Mrs. Dunn's and the dressmaking, for we cannot go on as we are doing.'

'Ah! Jane, my cup of prosperity has very many bitter drops in it.'

'And mine of adversity has much that is salutary and even sweet in it. Do not think me so very unhappy. If any one had told me beforehand of these months that I have passed since my uncle's death, I should have thought them absolutely intolerable, and would have preferred death. But there is no human lot without its mitigations and ameliorations. God tempers the wind to the shorn lamb. I am not happy, perhaps; but I am not miserable. I have not to live with people whom I despise, for there never was a more estimable woman than Peggy Walker, or more promising children than her nephews and nieces. You cannot fancy what interest I feel in Tom, and how I am ambitious for him. He will make a figure in the world, and I will help him to do so. We women have no career for ourselves, and we must find room for ambition somewhere. I have no brother and no husband, and I find myself building castles in the air for Tom Lowrie and for you, Francis; for you are proving yourself the good master, the conscientious steward of the bounties of Providence that I hoped you would be; and is that nothing to be

glad of? I know I look sad, but do not fancy me always in this mood; if you saw me in the evenings with Tom, and Nancy, and Jamie, and Jessie, and Willie, you would see how cheerful I can be. Here, I am reminded too painfully of what I have lost; there, I feel that I have gained somewhat.'

'You want to relieve my mind, my generous cousin, by making the best of your very hard lot.'

'Every lot has its best side,' said Jane, 'and it is only by looking steadily at it that one can obtain courage to bear the worst. I see this in visiting the very poor people whom I wrote to you about. Some people are querulous in comparative comfort; others have the most astonishing powers of cheerful endurance. I have learned upon how very little the human soul can be kept in working order from a poor rheumatic and bed-ridden old woman, who is so grateful for the use of one hand while she is helpless otherwise, and who has had a very bad husband, and several very careless and cold-hearted children; but she has one son who comes to see her regularly once every three months, and brings her the scanty pittance on which she subsists; and surely I, with youth, and health, and work to do, should try to be cheerful, even though the work is not such as I could prefer. —And you have been in France as well as England since I saw you last in August. I want to hear further particulars of your travels, since you say that you have more to give. They interested you very much, particularly those in France.'

'Very much, indeed; all the more as I acquired the language. I wrote to you that I met with Clemence de Véricourt, now Madame Lenoir.'

'Is she handsome?' asked Jane.

'No; I thought her almost ugly till she opened her mouth, and then I forgot it, and felt the charm of the most winning manner and the most brilliant conversational power in the world. Frenchwomen are not to compare with Englishwomen for beauty, but they can be irresistible without it.'

'How did you get an introduction to her?' asked Jane.

'French society is more accessible than it is here; but I met with a

French gentleman in a *café* who had known my father, and who recongized my name, who introduced me to a good many very pleasant salons, and to Madame Lenoir's among others. Arnauld is dead; he fell in Algeria. His sister speaks of him with the tenderest affection.'

'Is she happily married? After all her mother's solicitude, it would be hard if she too were sacrificed.'

'So far as I can see, she appears to be happy. The husband is of suitable years and good character; not so brilliant as his wife. But really what Madame de Girardin says appears to me to be true, that French women are superior to their so-called lords and masters. It is strange to me, who have been always so shy, and so shut out from society, to be introduced—or rather plunged—into so much of it.'

'Had you not society of your own when you were in the bank—your fellow-clerks and their wives and sisters?'

'I had little intimacy with any of them, and was particularly in want of acquaintances among the other sex. A man with no relations who recognized his existence, and who is conscious of the doubtfulness of his birth, as I was, does not like to push himself into society in a country like this of Scotland, where family connections are overrated. Now, every one seems to think that being owned by my father in his will quite sufficient, while I am more ashamed in my secret soul of my birth than I ever was.'

'Indeed!' said Jane, 'I thought it would have pleased you to be acknowledged.'

'*You* should see, if the world does not, that if one party has juggled the other into a marriage, without any love on either side, it may involve legal succession to property, but does not make the birth a whit more respectable. I had a mother who did not care for me, and a father who did his duty, as he fancied, by me, but who disliked me, and they appear to have hated one another.'

'You extorted respect and regard from your father, and you have cause to be proud of that. If mutual love between parents is to be the great cause of pride of birth, I, too, have reason to be ashamed

of mine, for I think my mother's love was worn out before many years of married life were over, and my father's never was anything but self-love and self-will. But whatever our birth may be, we are all God's children, and equal in His eyes, in that respect at least. —Did Madame Lenoir speak to you of her mother?'

'Yes, she did, and recollected that my name was the name of an old and dear friend of her mother's; so she was especially kind to me for my father's sake. I saw Madame de Véricourt's portrait, too. She was prettier than her daughter, at least in repose; but neither of them were at all like my ideal; for I forgot the French class of face, and embodied my fancy portraits in an English type.'

'You enjoyed French society, then?'

'Very much, indeed. The art of conversing these French people carry to great perfection. It is not frivolous, though it is light and sparkling; it is still less argumentative, but it has the knack of bringing out different opinions and different views of them. We pity the French for their want of political liberty, but the social freedom they enjoy is some compensation. —But what interested me still more than these brilliant salons, was the tour that I took through the country, and the careful observation of the condition and prospect of the small proprietors so numerous in France and Flanders. The contrast between the French small landowner and the English agricultural labourer is very great. Nothing has struck me as so pathetic as the condition of the English farm labourer—so hopeless, so cheerless. Our Scottish peasants have more education, more energy, and are more disposed to emigrate. Their wages are fixed more by custom than by competition, and their independence has not been sapped by centuries of a most pernicious poor law system; yet, though I think their condition very much better than those of the same class south of the Tweed, it is nothing like that of the peasant proprietor.'

'They say that small holdings are incompatible with high farming,' said Jane, 'and that such a crowded country as Britain must be cultivated with every advantage of capital, machinery, and intelligence.'

'So they say here; but the small proprietors of France and Flanders will tell another story, for they will give a higher price for land than the capitalist, and make it pay. The astonishing industry of the Flemish farmers in reclaiming the worst soil of Europe, and making it produce the most abundant crops, shows me the fallacy of our insular notions on that head. I cannot but regret the decrease of the yeomanry class in Great Britain, and the accumulation of large estates in few hands. Scotland, for instance, is held by 8000 proprietors or thereabouts, of whom I am one. I should like to try an experiment. You know that sand flat, that is worth very little but for scanty pasture, at the back of the Black Hill, as it is called. I would divide it into allotments among the most industrious and energetic of my farm-labourers, and show them the method pursued by the Flemish farmers, and see if in the course of ten years they are not growing as good crops as in the most favoured spots on the estate. "Give a man a seven years' lease of a garden, he will convert it into a desert; give him a perpetuity of a rock, he will change it into a garden." Your uncle did not think it would pay to reclaim that piece of land; I will try if our peasants have not the stuff in them to make the most of the land.'

'What an excellent idea!' said Jane.

'I knew you would sympathize with this plan, and with another which I have also in my head—to build new cottages for all the agricultural labourers on the estate. It is shameful that while the proprietors' houses, and the farmers' houses, have been enlarged and improved so much during the last century, the cottage of the hind and the cotter should still be of the same miserable description; the partitions to be made at the labourer's own expense, and too generally done by the enclosed beds, which are not right things in a sanitary point of view. The money value of the rent is increased, too, for so many weeks of reaping in harvest time is worth more now than a century back. I have got plans for the cottages which I wanted you to look at this morning; I think they will do.'

'You must let Peggy see them; she was brought up in one of

those cottages you speak of, and will know all their deficiencies. It will set a good example to the neighbourhood,' said Jane.

'And, after all, it will not cost me more to build these cottages, and make thirty families more comfortable and more self-respecting, than it would to enlarge Cross Hall, as Mr. Chalmers advises me strongly to do—by building a new wing and adding a conservatory in the place of your modest little greenhouse. Every one knows I have come to the estate with money in hand instead of encumbrances to clear off, as so many proprietors have, so they can think of my spending it in nothing but in increasing my own comfort or importance. Another reason for my trying these experiments and improvements is to see if we cannot keep some of our best people in Scotland. Our picked men, and many of our picked women, emigrate to America and Australia. The recent emigration to Australia since the gold-diggings were discovered has been enormous. It must hurt the general character of the nation that we lose our best and our ablest as they grow up. I confess that if I were in their place I should do the same; but let my experiment succeed, it may be imitated.'

'Whether it is imitated or not, it is right to try it. I will watch the result with the greatest interest. You know nothing could give me greater pleasure than your success in such a noble work,' said Jane, with sparkling eyes. 'My uncle's will is to turn out no mistake.'

'We must go over together the names of those I mean to give the allotments to. You know the people better than I do,' said Francis.

'It is not fair that the commonages should be enclosed to enlarge great estates; the waste lands should belong to the nation, and be given to the class that needs them most, and that could, perhaps, make most of them,' said Jane. 'You are bringing my uncle's theories into practice. If it were not for Elsie I should have nothing to regret in the settlement that my uncle made; and, perhaps, there is something brighter in store for her.'

'Has she none of the alleviations that you are so good as to make the very most of?' asked Francis.

'She has more pleasure naturally in books and in nature than I have, but at the present time she appears to have to have lost her relish for both. She has felt that her estimate of her powers has been too great, and now it is far too humble. For myself, I think just as highly of my own abilities and acquirements as ever I did. I am sorry that your minister has left his church, for I hoped to become acquainted with him; and he looked so cheerful that I thought he might do Elsie good. This new clergyman does not strike me as being so genial or kindly, though I certainly like his sermons and his devotional services very much. It is certainly not the least of the blessings of my adversity that I have learned to place myself in God's hands, and to feel that he will do all things well for me.'

'Can you not place your sister in the same care?' asked Francis.

'It is easier to trust God for yourself than to trust Him for those whom we love,' said Jane; 'but I try hard for that amount of faith. Elsie is so weary of her life sometimes, it is difficult to give her courage. This is grave conversation for a dancing party; but you do not see the incongruity. If we cannot carry our religion into our amusements, and into our business, it will not be of much use to us.'

The sound of a well-known voice arrested Jane's attention: it was that of William Dalzell, who was shaking hands with Mr., Mrs., and Miss Rennie very cordially, and then, in an embarrassed manner, doing the same with Elsie.

'How did our friends get acquainted with Mr. Dalzell?' said Jane.

'When they were visiting me at Cross Hall, we had a gathering of the neighbouring families, and Mrs. Rennie did the honours for me. Mr. Dalzell, with his mother, and two young lady cousins, were of the party. I thought the county people would have held themselves aloof from the more plebeian society of an Edinburgh banker, but he at least has condescended to accept Mrs. Rennie's invitation to her own house. The exclusiveness of classes, and sects, and cliques, is extremely amusing to me. But I am engaged to dance this dance with Miss Rennie, so you must excuse me.'

As Francis went up to claim Miss Rennie's hand, a gentleman was in the act of asking it—'I am engaged to Mr. Hogarth—see my

card—but as you are a stranger in Edinburgh, you will be obliged to me for introducing you to his cousin, one of the sweetest girls in the world, and one whose story is the most interesting and the most romantic I ever heard. Oh! Mr. Dalzell, I forgot you.'

'This is sad, to be so easily forgotten. I had hoped that my requests had made more impression,' said he.

'I do not think Laura is engaged for this dance. Excuse me a moment till I ascertain.' Miss Rennie walked across the room, leaving William Dalzell and the stranger together, but she presently returned, with the assurance that Miss Wilson was disengaged, and would be happy to be introduced to Mr. Dalzell. Miss Wilson was ward of Mrs. Rennie's, as Jane had heard, a West Indian heiress, somewhat stupid, and very much impressed with her own wealth and importance. Miss Rennie had a pitying sort of liking for her, though sometimes Laura's airs were too much for her, and they would not speak to each other for a week at a time. She had just left school, having made all the progress which money without natural ability or any of the usual incentives to application could attain, and was to live at the Rennies', which she thought a very dull place. This large party was the brightest thing in her horizon at present, and she was looking her best, and took her place in the dance with one of the handsomest men in the room, with much more animation than was usual with her.

'Now,' said Miss Rennie, 'I have done my best for Mr. Dalzell. I must attend to my other stranger before I fulfil my engagement to you, Mr. Hogarth, and I hope you will excuse me, when it is to get a partner for Alice. Miss Melville, I suppose, does not care about dancing, she is so dreadfully matter-of-fact. I know you have been talking politics, or something as bad, in that corner all this evening.'

So Miss Rennie led the stranger across the room, and introduced Miss Alice Melville to Mr. Brandon, from Australia.

XII

MR. BRANDON IN EDINBURGH

'You must excuse any blunders I may make in my dancing, Miss Melville, for I am an old bushman, and have been out of practice for many years,' said Mr. Brandon.

In spite of Elsie's being an admirable dancer, she was too much excited to do her best, and the stranger made no great figure in his first *débût* in that line. Miss Rennie was inwardly rejoicing that she had herself got rid of him.

'What part of Australia do you come from?' asked Elsie, in the first pause.

'From Victoria, as it is called now. It was called Port Phillip when I went there.'

'Have you been long in the colony?'

'A long time—long enough for all my friends to forget me. But yet I need make no complaint; they have all been very kind; but I think I am entitled to a spell now.'

'To a what?' asked Elsie, to whom the term was new.

'To a rest, or rather a fling—a holiday. Ah! Miss Melville, you can have no idea what a rough life I have led for many years. You cannot fancy how delightful, how perfectly beautiful it is to me to be in such society as this after the Australian bush.'

Miss Melville had a better idea than he fancied. It is curious to meet people as strangers of whom you know a great deal, and when Elsie looked at the very gentlemanly man beside her, whose dress was perfectly fashionable, whose air and mien were rather distinguished, and whose language, in spite of a few colonial colloquialisms, had the clear, sharp tone and accent which agreeably marks out an educated Englishman among an assembly of Scotchmen, and recollected the description of his dress and habitation which Peggy had given, and the scenes and conversation which she had narrated, she was almost afraid of betraying her knowledge by her countenance.

'Have you been long home from Australia?' she asked, as a safe question.

'A few months, and am enjoying it intensely.'

'And what brings you to Scotland? I suppose your relations are all English?'

'Oh, an Australian thinks he ought to see the whole of Britain, when he can visit it so seldom. A man is treated with contempt on his return if he has not seen the Cumberland lakes and the Scottish Highlands. But I have relations in Scotland besides;—the old lady sitting by Mrs. Rennie in black *moiré* (is it that you call it?) is a sort of aunt of mine, and is connected in some inexplicable way with the Rennies. Your Scotch cousinships are an absolute mystery to me; it is a pity I cannot understand them, for I am indebted to them for a great deal of hospitality and kindness, of which this is one of the most agreeable instances;'— and Mr. Brandon looked at Elsie as if he meant what he said.

'It does one good to see a man enjoying a party; our fashionable style is for the indifferent and the done up,' said Elsie, with a smile. 'I do not know if gentlemen enjoy life in spite of that nonchalant or dismal manner; but I know it is not pleasant for the lookers on.'

'I cannot see why they should assume such a disagreeable style of conduct. To me, you English and Scotch people seem the most enviable in existence—amusement after amusement, and education, elegance, and refinement to heighten every enjoyment. I often say

to myself, "Walter Brandon, my good fellow, this will not last; you must go back to your stations and your troubles in a few months;" but for the present I am in Elysium.'

By this time they had finished their dance, and were standing beside Jane. She looked up at him with her steady eyes—'The happiness is in yourself—not in the country, in the amusements, or in the society. You have earned a holiday, and you enjoy it.'

'All Australians feel the drawbacks of the colonies when they come to visit England,' said Mr. Brandon.

'It depends on their circumstances, whether they do or not. I often wish that I were there,' said Jane.

'And so do I,' said Miss Rennie, who with Francis had just joined them. 'There must be a grandeur and a freshness about a new country that we cannot find here; and those wonderful gold diggings, too, must be the most interesting objects in nature.'

'The very ugliest things you ever saw—and as for grandeur or freshness, I never saw or felt it. The finest prospect I could see in Victoria is the prospect of getting out of it, particularly now that the diggings have spoiled the colony. We cannot forget Old England.'

'Oh! of course I like patriotism,' said Miss Rennie; 'no country can be to us like the land of our birth.'

'But I think we should try to like the land of adoption also,' said Jane. 'The Anglo-Saxons have been called the best of colonists, because they have adapted themselves so well to all sorts of climates and all sorts of circumstances.'

'True—true enough,' said Mr. Brandon. 'The Adelaide men who came across to the diggings used to talk with the greatest enthusiasm about their colony, their farms, their gardens, their houses, their society. I fancied that it was because they left it for a rougher life, and that Adelaide was like a little England to them; but, perhaps, the poor fellows really liked the place. At any rate, almost all of them returned, though Victoria appeared to be by far the most prosperous colony. But I made an excellent colonist, in spite of my never becoming much attached to the place. I adapted myself to

sheep wonderfully, and to black pipes and cabbage-tree hats, and all the other amenities of bush life; and now, Miss Rennie, will you be good enough to adapt yourself to me for a quadrille?'

Miss Rennie was not engaged, so she could not refuse. Elsie saw that her cousin wished to talk to her; she feared it was to be on the subject which was the most painful of all—her unfortunate poems. She fancied that he must think her presumptuous in her old ambition, and dreaded his condolences; so she made some pretext to move away out of hearing of his conversation with Jane, and stood by the hired musicians, who were the most unlikely persons in the room to know anything about her or her disappointment. Standing there, with her slight and graceful form stooping slightly, and her face cast down, Miss Rennie again pointed her out to Mr. Brandon, of whose dancing she was tired, and to whom she wished to talk, asking him if he did not think her a lovely creature, and explaining the very peculiar circumstances in which the two girls were placed.

'They have been well educated, papa says, but very peculiarly, so that their prospects are not the better for it. We live in a frivolous age, Mr. Brandon. I do not take much interest in Jane, but Elsie is a very sweet girl.'

The Australian settler looked again more closely at Elsie, and acknowledged to himself, as well as to Miss Rennie, that she was certainly elegant.

'Shall we go to her now? she looks so deserted, Mr. Brandon. Oh! Mr. Malcolm, I must introduce you to Miss Melville's sister.'

'And co-heiress in misfortune,' said the young lawyer, shrugging his shoulder.

'She is lovely—come,' said Miss Rennie. She took both gentlemen across the room. Elsie started when she saw them coming close up to her.

'Miss Alice Melville—Mr. Malcolm—a successful author. Your sister saw him here some months ago.'

The sight of a successful author was rather too much for Elsie's present feelings. Her eyes filled with tears, but yet she must speak.

'Yes, Jane told me she had that pleasure,' said she.

'Miss Melville is here also, I hope,' said Mr. Malcolm.

'Yes, she is talking to—to Mr. Hogarth.'

'To Mr. Hogarth? Yes, I see—very good friends they appear to be, in spite of circumstances. Two superior minds, you see.'

'He takes such care of your horses and dogs, Miss Alice; and as for your room, when mama proposed making it into a card-room, as it was larger than the library, he looked as black as thunder, and said he never would have cards played there. It was a Blue Beard's room, so we got no access to it.'

'I thought he would be kind to the animals; he promised as much to Jane.'

'Oh! indeed, he is as good as his word, then,' said Miss Rennie. Then, recollecting that this talk must be painful to the girl, she turned to Mr. Malcolm, and asked how his evangelical novel was getting on.

'Finished, and in the press by this time.'

'Will it be a success? But everything you write is a success, so I need not ask,' said Miss Rennie.

'The pub. says it has not exactly the genuine twang, but I hope no one will observe that but himself. I have more incidents in it than usual in works of the class—an elopement, a divorce, a duel, a murder, and a shipwreck.'

'I must have a first reading, recollect. It must be so interesting,' said Miss Rennie.

'Thrilling, I should say,' said Mr. Brandon. 'Well, to me there is a deep mystery in bookmaking. How one thing is to follow another—and another to lead to another—how everything is to culminate in marriage or a broken heart, and not a bit of the whole to be true, I cannot conceive; and as for poetry, it seems to me an absolute impossibility to make verses rhyme. Can you tell me how it is done, Miss Melville?'

Elsie started. 'No, I cannot—I cannot tell.'

'You must ask Miss Rennie about poetry,' said Mr. Malcolm; 'she does some very excellent things in that way.'

'You perfidious creature, I see I must never tell you anything, for you are sure to come out with it at all times and all places,' said Miss Rennie.

'It is a true bill then,' said Mr. Brandon, bowing to the tenth muse. 'I cannot help wondering at you. I must not approach so near you, for you are so far removed from my everyday prosaic sphere. I must take shelter with Miss Melville, who knows nothing about the matter. I cannot comprehend how people can make verses; it cannot be easy at any time.'

'It is sometimes easier than at other,' said Miss Rennie. 'If the subject is good the words flow correspondingly fast.'

'And what do you consider the best subject,—marrying or burying, love or despair? I suppose you have tried them all.'

'Oh, no. Do not imagine me to be a real author—only an occasional scribbler. Mr. Malcolm can tell you that I do not write much.'

'You must show Mr. Brandon your album,' said Mr. Malcolm, 'and let him judge for himself.'

'Will you let me see it too?' said Elsie eagerly; 'do let me see it.'

'You may look over it together,' said Miss Rennie good-naturedly, 'though I do not show it to every one. It will perhaps convince Mr. Brandon that it is nothing so wonderful to write verses, and make him less distant in his manner. My own pieces are signed Ella.'

Miss Rennie's album contained a number of selections from her favourite poets, but except her own there were no original verses in it. Her friends preferred copying to composing, and among a very large circle she was the only one who had tried any independent flight into the regions of poetry; so that it was natural she should think a good deal of herself, for every one begged for something of her own to put into their albums, though they could not reciprocate in kind. Mr. Malcolm contributed some smart prose pieces; Herbert Watson was clever at caricatures; Eleanor painted flowers sweetly; while Laura Wilson, ambitious to have something to show in Miss Rennie's album, had copied a number of riddles in a very angular hand, which was illegible to an unpractised eye.

Elsie and Mr. Brandon, however, had got the album to see Ella's verses, and they turned to them with curiosity and interest. Her quicker eye and greater experience, both in poetry and in ladies' handwriting, made her read each piece in less than half the time taken by Mr. Brandon, and she re-read and scanned every line and weighed every sentiment and simile while he was making his way to the end.

'Well, really this is remarkably good,' said he. 'I wonder Miss Rennie does not publish: she could fill a nice little volume. I am sure I have seen far worse verses printed. Have not you?'

'Yes,' said Elsie. 'I believe Miss Rennie has had pieces published in periodicals, but it is not so easy to get a volume printed.'

'Of course, there is a risk; but then the pleasure, the fame, should count for something. To have one's name on the title-page of a pretty little volume must be very gratifying to the feelings.'

'Oh no, not at all. I do not think so; but I do not know anything about it. I should not speak.'

'You shrink from any publicity; well, I suppose that is very natural, too, yet I should not think that Miss Rennie does so; and as she is the author, I am imagining her feelings. What is this other piece called?—"Life's Journey." What can Miss Rennie know of life's journey— staying at home with her father and mother all her short life?'

'If she had been to Australia and back again, she would have been entitled to speak on the subject,' said Elsie.

'But really it is a very pretty piece, after all,' said Mr. Brandon, after he had read it.

'Though written by one who has never been further from home than Glasgow in her life,' said Elsie.

'I do not mean that Miss Rennie's never being out of Scotland should make her know little; but you young ladies are taken such care of, that you know very little of what life really is.'

'It must be a disadvantage to all female authors,' said Elsie, 'to know so little of business and so little of the world. I do not wonder at men despising women's books.'

'Now, Miss Melville, have I really said anything that you should put such a construction on? If I have, I must ask pardon. I am only astonished at the extraordinary talent which your sex show in turning to account their few opportunities; and for my part, I should not like them to have greater means of knowing the world. I am not a reading man, by any means. My remarks about books are perfectly worthless, but I can only say that I think these verses very pretty. I don't know whether they are subjective or objective—transcendental or sentimental. In fact, between ourselves, I do not know what the three first words mean. I can give no reason for my liking them.'

'But they please you,' said Elsie; 'and that is all a poet can wish.'

'Oh, I thought the poets of this age gave themselves out as the teachers of the world; but you take a lower view. I am glad to meet with some one who is reasonable. The young ladies have all got so clever, so accomplished, and so scientific since I left England, that I am a little afraid of them. I hope you are not very accomplished.'

'Not at all,' said Elsie.

'Don't you play the most brilliant music with great execution?'

'I do not play at all.'

'Nor sketch from nature—nor draw from the round—nor paint flowers?'

'Nothing of the kind.'

'Then you must have gone in for science, and you are more formidable than any of the sex.'

'My uncle wished me to go in for science, but unluckily I came out without acquiring it.'

'How glad I am to hear it! I can talk to you without being tripped up at an incorrect date, or an inaccurate scientific or historical fact. You can warrant yourself safe to let me blunder on?'

'Is it not very good of the young ladies to set you right if you are wrong, and if they are able to do so?'

'It may be very good for me, but it is not at all agreeable. I cannot help wondering very much at the industry and perseverance that young ladies show in becoming so very accomplished. I am sure that

many a lady spends as much time and energy in learning music as would, directed otherwise, realize a fortune in Australia.'

'Yes, many men in Australia have got rich with very little toil,' said Elsie; 'but women cannot make fortunes either here or there, I suppose.'

'So they content themselves with making a noise,' said Mr. Brandon. 'I like some music, Miss Melville; but not the brilliant style. It shows wonderful powers of manual dexterity, but it does not please me.'

'My sister says, she wonders why so many women spend so much time over the one art in which they have shown their deficiency—that is, music.'

'Their deficiency? I think they show their proficiency, only that I do not care about it; that is probably my fault, and not theirs.'

'But Jane says, that as so many thousands—and even millions—of women are taught music, and not one has been anything but a fourth-rate composer, it shows a natural incapacity for the highest branch of the art. In poetry and painting, where the cultivation is far rarer, greater excellence has been attained by many women. Their inferiority is certainly not so marked as in music.'

'That is rather striking, Miss Melville; but I did not expect such an admission from such a quarter. I see you are not strong-minded. My aunt, Mrs. Rutherford, and her daughters, have rather been boring me with their theory of the equality of the sexes: this is a first-rate argument. Will you take it very much amiss if I borrow your idea, or rather your sister's, without acknowledgement? I have felt so very small, because they were always bringing up some instance or other out of books which I had never read, that to bring forward something as good as this, might make them have a better opinion of me.'

'I am sure neither Jane nor I would care about the appropriation of the idea, though it seems rather treacherous to put ours into our enemy's hands.'

'Your enemy's!—that is hard language for me. I trusted to your being friendly.'

In spite of Mr. Brandon's expressed admiration for Miss Rennie's verses, he got soon tired of reading them, and preferred the intervals of conversation between the pieces. Before they had looked through more than half of the album, which was a very large one, he proposed to return to the dancing-room, and Elsie reluctantly left the book on the library table, hoping to snatch another half-hour to finish it. Miss Rennie's verses were decidedly inferior to her own;—even her recent humiliation could not prevent her from seeing this, and she felt a good deal inspirited.

Several times during the evening, she was on the point of mentioning Peggy Walker's name to her old master, but she knew too much about them to be able to do it with ease; she, however, ascertained that he was to be some time in and about Edinburgh, and learned from Miss Rennie where Mrs. Rutherford lived, so that she could tell Peggy where she might find him, if she wished to see him.

In the quadrille which Elsie danced with Mr. Brandon, William Dalzell and Laura Wilson were at first placed as *vis-à-vis*, but they moved to the side, and Elsie had the pleasure of seeing her sister and cousin instead. But both sisters could not but hear the familiar voice making the same sort of speeches to Miss Wilson that he had done a few months ago to Jane. How very poor and hollow they appeared now! Elsie thought Miss Wilson would just suit him. She was rich enough to make him overlook her defects of understanding and temper, and what was even harder to manage, her very ordinary face and figure. There was an easy solution of Mr. Dalzell's cultivating the acquaintance of the Rennies in this wished-for introduction to the wealthy ward.

Mr. Dalzell thought he ought to ask Jane to dance once, just to show that he did not quite forget his old friends. He tried Elsie first, but she was fortunately engaged to Mr. Malcolm, so he walked slowly to Miss Melville, and asked her hand in an impressive manner. She willingly accepted, and spoke to him as she would to any ordinary acquaintance. He was piqued; he had hoped to have made her a little jealous of his attentions to Miss Wilson, and tried

to get up a little sentimental conversation about old times, and the rides they used to have, and the romantic scenery about Cross Hall and Moss Tower, but not the slightest sigh of regret could his ear catch. He apologized for not having been to see her, and said his mother regretted that her last visit to Edinburgh had been so hurried that she had no time. Jane said quietly that she had not expected to see either of them. Had she not found it dull living in the Old Town with Peggy Walker?—No, she had never felt it dull; she had always plenty to do. Was Peggy as much of a character as ever?—Yes; she was glad to say, Peggy was the same admirable woman she had always been, and on nearer acquaintance her character became still more appreciated. The children must be a nuisance?—The children were particularly fine children, and a great resource to her. He thought Miss Alice was not looking well. Had she felt the want of the fresh country air?—For a moment this arrow struck her; a painful expression passed over her face, but she subdued her feelings quickly.—Yes, perhaps Alice did suffer from the change; but they were going to have a week's amusement while their cousin was in town, and she hoped her sister would be the better for it.

Neither Mr. Dalzell nor Jane were sorry when the dance was ended and they were relieved of each other's company; and he returned to Miss Wilson, while she joined Elsie in the library, where she was finishing her critical reading of Miss Rennie's album, with a better coadjutor than the Australian settler, in the person of her cousin. She was rather afraid of him at first, but she found that in general their opinions were the same as to merits and demerits, and she could not help owning that it would have been well to have taken him into her counsels before she tried the public.

'I have been telling Francis,' said Jane, 'that I am making up my mind to go to Mrs. Dunn's.'

'Then I will go with you, Jane; we must go together; you are not to have all the drudgery.'

'I say I am only making up my mind; it is not made up yet. I will wait another week before I decide. You are to be in town for a few

days, Francis, and you will see us every day before we go. I wish to have a little amusement before I settle; so, Elsie, let us arrange. The theatre to-morrow night, the exhibition on Thursday morning, a concert on Thursday evening, and on Friday an excursion to Roslin; Saturday I am not sure about, but we will see when the time comes.'

Elsie stared at her sister; it was so unlike Jane to be pining for amusement. 'I do not care for going out, I am so unfit for it. I would rather stay at home till the time comes to go to Mrs Dunn's.'

'No, we will not let you stay and mope at home. If it has somewhat unsettled my strong nerves to be living as we have done, so that I feel I must have a change, what will be its effect on you to stay at Peggy's without me?'

'Your sister would rather not go out with me,' said Francis.

'No; I have been unjust and uncharitable to you, but I hope I will not be so again. Forgive me for the past, and I will promise good behaviour for the future.'

'If you are not too tired in the morning, would not a walk be pleasant?' said Francis. 'I want to show you what strikes me as the finest view of Edinburgh. I do not expect Jane to appreciate it; but from your remarks on these verses, I am sure you have an eye for nature, and a soul for it.'

Elsie was pleased, and felt more kindly to her cousin than she had ever done before. There are times when a little praise, particularly if it is felt to be deserved, does a sad heart incalculable good. She agreed to the walk with eagerness, and looked forward to it with hope.

XIII

PEGGY'S VISITORS, AND FRANCIS' RESOLUTION

The girls were somewhat later in rising on the morning after the party than usual, and when they got up, they found that Peggy was out on one of those errands that Jane and Elsie had been accustomed to do for her. She had got into very good custom, from her real skill and punctuality, even in the short time that she had tried her luck in Edinburgh; and this week she had had more work than she could manage. On these occasions she used to get the assistance of a very poor woman who lived at a considerable distance, who had once been a neighbour of her sister Bessie's, and had been kind to Willie when he was in his last illness. Jane, sometimes with and sometimes without Elsie, had always gone to tell this woman about the work, but on this occasion Peggy had to take the long walk herself—not that she grudged it—for to put half-a-crown in poor Lizzie Marr's pocked was worth a good deal of trouble and fatigue.

She had returned about twelve o'clock, when the girls were getting ready to join their cousin in their promised walk, and just as she got to the top of the stairs, a man's foot was heard at the bottom. They were going for their bonnets, when a sharp tap was heard at the door, and Peggy opened it, and they beheld, not Francis, but Mr. Brandon.

'Well, Peggy,' said he, 'how are you? I thought I could not be mistaken in those elbows. I have followed you from Prince's Street all this long way, but you would never turn round, and I could not outstrip you, for you know we bushmen are no great walkers, and you always were a wonderful 'Walker' in every sense of the word. And how are you again, Peggy?'

Peggy shook hands with her old master, and gazed at him with great surprise.

'Surely, these are not the bairns you used to speak of?' said Mr. Brandon, looking at the Misses Melville with astonishment quite equal to hers.

'No; the bairns are all at the school—all but Tam— and he's at his trade, but they will be here for their dinners directly. These are two young ladies that have taken a room off me. They are no so well off as they should be, more's the pity,' said Peggy, lowering her voice.

'I met them last night at a party. How do you do, Miss Melville?' said he, shaking hands with Elsie first, and then with Jane.

'But what brought you here on this day?' said Peggy.

'Just your elbows, Peggy. I was coming to see you at any rate, but I did not think you were here. You must have shifted your quarters. Here is your address,' said Mr. Brandon, taking out his pocket-book—'"Peggy Walker, at Mr. Thomas Lowrie's, Swinton, —shire." I was going to see you to-morrow, but you have saved me a journey to no purpose.'

'I brought the bairns into the town for better schooling, and on account of Tam; and grandfather finds it agrees brawly with him, too. Grandfather,' said Peggy, raising her voice, 'this is Master Brandon that you have heard me speak about whiles—the first master I had in Australia.'

Grandfather expressed his sense of the politeness of Mr. Brandon in coming all that way to see Peggy. Not but what she was a good lass, and worth going a long journey to have a crack with.

'Well, Peggy,' said Mr. Brandon, taking a seat near the fire, 'and how do you like this cold country after so many years in a hot one?'

'The winters are not so bad, but the springs are worse to stand. But if a body's moving and stirring about they can aye keep heat in them.'

'If moving and stirring can keep you warm you will never be cold. But, Peggy, you will want to hear the news.'

'Indeed do I,' said Peggy; 'the diggings are going on as brisk as ever, I suppose?'

'Just as brisk, and sheep as dear, and wool steady; so, you see, I've taken a holiday.'

'But you're going back again?'

'I must go back, for I have not made my fortune yet. But, by-the-by, it is a great pity that you left Melbourne when you did. You would have been a wealthy woman if you had stayed. There's Powell—was he married before you went?'

'Ay, he was. I heard word of it in Melbourne.'

'Well, he's as flourishing as possible; he will soon be richer than me. On his own account now. Bought a flock and run, for an old song; cured the sheep; and is now on the highway to wealth. Ah! Peggy, why were you not Mrs Powell?'

'It was not to be,' said Peggy, calmly; 'but has he any bairns?'

'Two, Peggy; and he is very proud of them.'

'Ay, ay; a man has need to be proud and pleased with his own. And the wife?'

'Oh, she's a nice enough person. Getting a little uppish now; but not the manager you are,' said Mr. Brandon. 'More given to dress and show, and that sort of thing. But I have a message for you from Mr. Talbot, the lawyer, you know, though I dare say he has written to you on the same subject.'

'My man of business,' said Peggy, with a little pride. 'I have not heard from him for a long time.'

'He is very sorry indeed, that you let the tenant have a right of purchase to your shop.'

'Oh, it is not of much consequence—he never was a saving body; I don't think he will ever raise the £250.'

'Will he not?—when the place is worth £2,500 now; if he

borrows the money, he will carry out the purchase, and thus you lose the chance of making a little fortune. He, of course, will keep it on till the end of the lease, at the low rent he has it at, and then take it up for the price specified. You cannot think how vexed I felt to hear you had let this property slip through your fingers.'

'It is a pity,' said Peggy. 'It would really have been a providing for the bairns; but they must just provide for themselves. I am, at least, puting them in the way of doing it. The rent comes in regular enough, and is a help; and the £250 will come in some time, and set us up in some way of doing.'

'£250 is not the sum it used to be,' said Mr. Brandon; 'but, in your hands, I have no doubt it will be turned to good account.'

'Here come the bairns now,' said Peggy, as the quick, noisy steps of the heavily-shod children were heard clattering up the stairs.

'I will now see what you have made so many sacrifices for. Name them as they come in.'

'Tom, Jamie, Nancy, Jessie, Willie.'

'A fine lot of youngsters, upon my word, and sure to make good colonists.' And, as he said this, Mr. Brandon saw a tear stand in the eye of the devoted aunt at his praises of her orphan charge.

'God be praised, they have their health; and on the whole they are good bairns, though a thought noisy whiles,' said she.

'There's a gentleman at the stairfoot,' said Tom. 'He says he has come for you and your sister, Miss Melville, and as it was our dinner-time, he would not come up.'

'Bid him walk upstairs, for the dinner's no ready. Mr. Brandon was aye rather an off-put to work, and ye'll no get your dinner for a good quarter of an hour yet.'

'We are quite ready,' said Jane; 'We will go at once. It is our cousin, who was to call for us.'

'We may go out to play then for a bit?' said Willie.

'If ye'll no go far, and be sure to be in time for the school.'

Francis came up, to be surprised at the sight of Mr. Brandon, and to receive a hurried explanation of his presence at Peggy Walker's, and then they went for a walk. By daylight he was struck more with

the change that had shown itself in both of his cousins, and with the poor home they had to live in. Jane's proposal on the previous night to go to Mrs. Dunn's had distressed him more than any other of her projects, and yet he could do nothing to prevent it, unless by making the sacrifice which my young lady readers think he should have made long ago, and given up the estate to marry his cousin. 'All for love, and the world well lost,' is a fascinating course of procedure in books and on the stage, but in real life there are a good many things to be considered. It was only lately that Francis had discovered how very dear Jane was to him. If such a woman had come across his path when he was in the bank with his 250*l.* a-year, with any reasonable chance of obtaining her, he would have exerted every effort and made every sacrifice to gain such a companion for life. He would have given up all his more expensive bachelor habits—his book-buying, and his public amusements, and thought domestic happiness cheaply purchased by such privations. And if Jane could have shared his brighter fortune, he would have offered his hand and heart long before. But now, even supposing that he had contracted no expensive habits, and he found that he had—that he liked the handsome fortune, and the luxuries annexed to it—it was not his own personal gratification that he was required to give up, but the duties, and the opportunities for usefulness that Jane so highly prized for him. He could not even expect to take as good a position in the world as he had quitted. His place at the Bank of Scotland was filled up, and the quixotic step he thought of taking was not likely to recommend him to business people. And he must prepare not only for providing for a wife and family, but for Elsie, too; and until this day Elsie had shrunk from him, and he had rather despised her; but during their walk he saw the affectionate and sincere nature of Jane's sister. He thought that he could not only offer her a home, but that he had some prospect of making it a happy one, which is by far the most important thing in such matters, and he gradually brought himself to believe that it was right he should make the sacrifice. Other opportunities of usefulness might open themselves in some other sphere; he would

give up Cross Hall to the benevolent societies if Jane would only consent to be his wife. The cousinship he thought no objection; they were both very healthy in body and in mind, and as unlike each other in temperament and constitution as if they were not related. Neither Jane nor Elsie was likely to keep her health at a sedentary employment; it was the daily long walk that had kept them so well as they were. It was not right to undervalue private happiness, after all, for any public object whatever. Here was the best and dearest woman in the world suffering daily, both in herself and through her sister, and he could make her happy; he knew that he could do that. If she refused, however, it would interfere with the warm friendship that he knew to be her greatest comfort and his own most precious possession; but she could not, she would not refuse him. He saw the kind look of her eyes; and felt convinced that though Jane believed it was only friendship, the knowledge that she was all the world to him would change it into love. And then to begin life afresh; no longer solitary; no longer unloved; could he not conquer difficulties even greater than he had ever to contend with? He did not pay proper attention at the theatre that night. Jane and her sister were delighted with the performance, and forgot their daily life in the mimic world before them; but he was building such castles in the air all the time that he was not able to criticise the play or the acting, but left that to Elsie, who certainly did it very well.

XIV

GOOD NEWS FOR FRANCIS

When the children went out, and the young ladies had gone with their cousin, Mr. Brandon took the opportunity of asking how it happened that the Misses Melville were staying with her. She explained their position in a more matter-of-fact way than Miss Rennie had done on the preceding night, and then dilated on their virtues, particularly on Jane's.

'So clever, and so sensible, and so willing! There's nothing she does not understand, and yet, poor thing, she says she must go to the dressmaking, for with all her by-ordinary talents and her by-ordinary education, there is not another hand's turn she can get to do. I'm sure the pains she takes with the bairns at night, I just marvel at it. There's Tam, she can make him do anything she likes. It is a grand thing for a laddie when he is just growing to be a man to have such a woman as Miss Melville to look up to—it makes him have a respect for women.'

'He need look no higher than you, Peggy,' said Mr. Brandon.

'Ah! but you see I am not quick at the book learning. I'll no complain of Tam for want of respect to myself, for he is a good lad, take him altogether; but then, Miss Jean, she helps him with his problems and his squares, and runs up whole columns of figures

like a lang-legged spider, and tells him why things should be so and so, and seems as keen to learn all about the engineering as himself; and she helps Jamie with the Latin, that he craikit on so lang to let him learn, though for my part I see little good it will do him, and him only to follow the joinering and cabinet-making trade; and Tam, he will no be behind, and he must needs learn it too; and as for her writing, ye could read it at the other end of the room. And in her uncle's house there was such order and such government under her eye as there was not to be seen in another gentleman's house in the country. And yet, poor lassie, she says there's nothing but the dressmaking for her. And Miss Elsie, too, writing day and night, and cannot get a bode for her bit poems and verses, till now she is like to greet her een out over every letter she gets from London about them. I can see Miss Jean has been egging up Mr. Hogarth, as they call him—I'm no wishing him any ill, but I wish the auld laird had made a fairer disposition of his possessions—well, Miss Jean has been stirring up this Mr. Francis to take them out for the sake of Elsie, for she is just fading away.'

'I like her the best of the two, and she is certainly far the prettiest. The eldest one is a little too clever for me, and too much disposed to preach, even in a ball-room.'

'Well, I dare say she saw you had had rather little preaching in the bush, and I am sure you were none the worse of all said to you. But it makes us the more vexed at losing the real value of my bit property, for if I had had the twenty-five hundred pounds you speak about we could have begun business in Melbourne together. She can keep books, and Miss Elsie has a clever hand at the millinery;—we could have got on famously. I must let you see the bairns' writing-books, and the letters she learns them to write, and their counting-books, too.'

Mr. Brandon looked and admired quite to Peggy's satisfaction; and then he spoke to the old man in a kindly way, calling him Mr. Lowrie, and saying he had often heard Peggy speak of him at Barragong. How much pleasure little courtesies like this give to poverty and old age! The old man's face brightened when he heard

that he was known at such a distance by such a gentleman as this, and he answered Mr. Brandon's inquiries as to his health and his hearing with eager garrulity.

'Well,' said Peggy, 'I am no poorer than I was if I had not known about the bit shop being worth so much; but when I think on Miss Jean and her sister, and the lift it might have been to them, I think more of it than I would otherwise do. And now, Mr. Brandon, I'll trouble you to move from the fireside; I must put out the kail. But you were aye fond of being in a body's way.'

'I have it,' said Mr. Brandon; 'it will do.'

'What will do?'

'You remember the Phillipses?'

'What should ail me to remember them? But I have such a poor head, I forget to ask the thing I care most about. How's Mr. Phillips, and how's Emily?'

All well, and the other four, too.'

'And Mrs. Phillips?'

'As well as ever, and handsomer than ever, I think.'

'Oh! her looks were never her worst fault. But what did you mean by saying it would do?'

'The Phillipses came home in the vessel with me, and are settled in London for good. I think the eldest Miss Melville would be exactly the sort of person they want to superintend the household, for Mrs. Phillips has as little turn for management as ever, and there is a considerable establishment. And, also, she might make Miss Emily and Miss Harriett attend to their lessons, for, though they have masters or some such things, they are too much the mistresses of the house to be controlled by anybody.'

'Their father was always very much taken up with these lassies—Emily used to be like the apple of his eye; and the mistress is too lazy to cross them either, I'm thinking,' said Peggy.

'Just so. If Miss Melville's preaching in season or out of season can give her a little more sense, I think Phillips will be all the better for it. She can keep house, admirably, you say; and that she is able to teach, these children's books testify. Tell Miss Melville to

delay her resolution about the dressmaking till I communicate with Phillips, which I will do by to-day's post. He is talking of coming up to the north shortly, principally to visit you, I think, so he may see her, and can judge for himself. Your account of the young lady seems everything that can be desired, and Mr. Phillips has such a high opinion of your judgment that your recommendation will carry great weight.'

'He'll bring Emily with him to see me,' said Peggy. 'Tell him to be sure and bring Emily with him. I cannot ask you to take pot-luck with us.'

'No, I thank you; I have just breakfasted. I do not keep such early hours as I did at Barragong. We turn night into day in these lands of civilization, and for a change it is remarkably pleasant. But how do you take to Scotch fare after Australia?' asked Mr. Brandon, eyeing with astonishment the infinitesimal piece of meat which made the family broth.

'I did not take quite kindly to the porridge at first, and missed the meat that we used to have in such abundance; but use is second nature, and though I whiles look back with regret to the flesh-pots of Eygpt, I have my strength, and I have some prospect of getting back to the land of wastrie and extravagance, as I aye used to say it was at Barragong; and Mr. Phillips's place, at Wiriwilta, was worse still. And Mr. Phillips has made his fortune with all that waste, and with all his liberality, and a foolish wife, and an expensive family, and is living in London like a gentleman as he is,' said Peggy. 'And you really think he would be glad to have Miss Jean?'

'I have not a doubt of it; but good-bye for the present. I hear your youngsters rattling upstairs. I will see you again ere long, and must get better acquainted with them. Good-bye, sir,' said Mr. Brandon, to Thomas Lowrie, who having never been called either Mr. or Sir in his life before, was lost in astonishment at the remarkably fine manners of Peggy's old master.

'A very civil-spoken gentleman, Peggy,' said he. 'It must have been a pleasure to serve a gentleman of such politeness.'

'What a pity,' said Peggy to herself, 'that I ever should have told

the young ladies that daft-like story about me and the master. I wish I had bitten my tongue out first. But who was to think of him turning up like this? And he's just the man for Miss Elsie; but I have made her laugh at him, and I misdoubt if her proud spirit will bend to him. And after all, what the worse is he, if she had known nothing about it. And I dare say all young men are alike; and he's better than the most half of them. There was Elsie so taken up with that lad Dalzell, that came courting Miss Jean, and if she had heard half that was said about him, poor Mr. Brandon would have been a saint in comparison. But an opening for Miss Jane is aye worth something. To think of her being put under the like of Mrs. Phillips; and it's like I'll see Emily—a spoiled bairn, no doubt—but she had naturally a fine disposition, at least humanly speaking.'

It was not in human nature, however, that Peggy should quite lose sight of her own concerns in her pleasure at the thought of Miss Melville having something better to do than dressmaking. The recollection of the years of hard work that had converted her little shop into a freehold, her old pride in having her title made out on parchment, the hurry she had been in to get it let, to go home by a particular ship, and the obstinate way in which her tenant's wife insisted on a right of purchase, and her own reluctant admission of the clause, thinking that as the house was not new, 250*l.* was an outside value for it, and now to think of its being such a kingdom. The town had run up to her little suburban shop, and far past it; on every side the monster, Melbourne, had been adding to his extent, and now, on account of the bit of garden and large yard, that she had thought would be so nice for the children, when she had them out, and that she had bought very cheap, the value of her property was increased tenfold—but she was none the richer. The sacrifice she had made had turned out even greater than she had expected, and now she could not help thinking of how she would miss Miss Melville, and what a loss it would be to her bairns; and how she was to keep Miss Elsie in tolerable spirits without her sister was another perplexity.

The duties of the day were gone through as usual, however; but

when the children and the old man had gone to bed, Peggy made up her mind to make a martyr of herself, and to sit up for the young ladies, who had not been home all day, and with a piece of mending in her hands, which got on but slowly, she mused on her ill luck. Very tired and sleepy, and a little out of humour, she was when she opened the door for Jane and Elsie.

'Well, well! I just hope you're the better of your late hours, though they are not just what I approve of.'

'Only once in a way, Peggy; our holiday will soon be over. But you should not have sat up for us—promise not to do it again. We have enjoyed the theatre to-night, have we not, Elsie?'

'Yes, but the disenchantment comes so soon again.'

'I have no great opinion of theatres and play-acting, and such like. I was once in a theatre in Melbourne, though,' said Peggy.

'With one of your sweethearts, Peggy?' asked Jane.

'Whisht with your nonsense, Miss Jean; don't be talking of sweethearts to a douce woman like me,' said Peggy, who, nevertheless was rather proud of her Australian conquests, and liked to hear them alluded to now and then.

'But how did you like the play?'

'I cannot say I did. To see folk dressed up and painted, rampaging about and talking havers, just making fools of themselves. A wee insignificant-looking body setting up to be a king! and the sogers—you should have seen the sogers, as if they could ever fight.'

'It is likely there was nothing very first-rate on the Melbourne boards at that time, but our play to-night was perfectly well got up,' said Elsie, 'and the acting was admirable.'

'I'm no clear that at its best the theatre is a fit place for Christian men and women to frequent,' said Peggy.

'You prefer the stern realities of life to its most brilliant illusions,' said Jane.

'Speaking of the realities of life, Mr. Brandon says he knows of something likely to suit you, Miss Jane,' said Peggy.

'Indeed!' said Jane, with an incredulous smile.

'At least, he says you must resolve on nothing till you hear from him. He is going to write to London to Mr. Phillips.

'Your Mr. Phillips—is he in London?'

'Yes; and Mr. Brandon says they are sorely in need of somebody to keep the house—for I fancy everything is at rack and manger if Mrs. Phillips has the management—and to make Emily and Harriett mind their books, for they are such spoiled bairns. I was showing Mr. Brandon what you could do with Tam and Nancy and the others, and he says you are exactly the person that they need; and I can see that it is wondrous feasible.'

'What salary should I ask?' said Jane; 'or should I leave it to Mr. Phillips?'

'You had better leave it to him; he is not such a skinflint as our benevolent associations. I always found both him and Mr. Brandon open-handed and willing to pay well for all that was done for them. To me, Mr. Phillips was most extraordinary liberal.'

'Then you think it likely I will get this situation at a respectable salary?'

'I think you are almost sure of it.'

'What good news for Francis, to-morrow!' said Jane.

END OF VOL. I.

VOLUME TWO

MR. HOGARTH'S WILL

I

HOW FRANCIS RECEIVED THE GOOD NEWS

When Francis, after a night's rest disturbed by thoughts and calculations as to ways and means, had arrived at the definite resolution to ask Jane Melville to marry him, he recalled a thousand signs of her affectionate regard for him—of her understanding his character as no one ever cared to understand it before—of her sympathy with all his past life and his present position, which left him no doubt that she would return his love and accept of him. The home and the welcome he was prepared to offer to Elsie would plead with her own heart in his favour. All her theoretical objections as to cousins marrying (which after all is a very doubtful point, and has much to be said on both sides); all her ambition for himself would melt away before the warmth of the truest love and the hope of the happiest home in the world. And yet she was not to be won entirely, or even chiefly, by personal pleadings for happiness, or by the feeling that her life and Elsie's might go on smoothly and cheerfully with him. She was to be convinced that it was right that she should marry him, and then the whole of her affectionate and ardent nature would abandon itself to the pleasure of loving and being beloved. It was because she had no husband to occupy her heart that she dwelt so fondly on those abstractions of

public duty and social progress, and he would convince her that out of an aggregate of happy homes a happy people is composed. She had found opportunities both of gaining knowledge and of doing good in the most unfavourable circumstances, and she would have more chances as his wife, with his co-operation and sympathy.

She was not the sort of woman his poetical and artistic dreams had been wont to draw as the partner of his life; not the lovely, clinging, dependent girl who would look up to him for counsel and support, but something better, both in herself and for him, than his fancy had ever painted. Her powers of sympathy had been increased by her knowledge; she was as just as she was generous. There was no corner of his heart he could not lay bare to her; no passage of his past life that he could not trust to her judging fairly and charitably. Whether he rose or fell in the world; whether he gained social influence or lost it in the career that he had again to begin, her foot would be planted firmly beside his; her insight and sympathy would heighten every enjoyment and fortify him for every trial. That he felt her to be beautiful, perhaps, was more in his powers of seeing than in her positive charm of countenance; but so far as the soul looked through her eyes and breathed from her lips, she had a sort of beauty that did not weary any intelligent gazer, and at all events, which could never weary Francis Hogarth. After all the flattery he had met with since his accession to fortune, and the conventionalisms of society in which he had been plunged, he felt the transparent sincerity of Jane's character something to rest in with perfect confidence and perfect satisfaction. The most brilliant Frenchwomen had not her earnestness or her power, though they had far more vivacity, and made their interlocutors more satisfied with themselves. And Francis felt that he ought to be married; and how could he ever attach himself sufficiently to any other woman and not draw comparisons between her and the woman whom his interest—his wordly interest alone—forbade him to make his wife? He must learn to love Jane less, or obtain from herself leave to love her more.

Jane's joyous greeting, when he came to Peggy's for his cousins,

to take them to the Exhibition, startled him not a little; and when she eagerly told him of Mr. Brandon's views for her future advancement; and that both he and Peggy had no doubt that she would suit the Phillipses; and that an answer was sure to be had in a few days, and demanded his congratulations on her altered prospects; then asked him to submit his plans for cottages to Peggy's inspection, as she was by far the most competent judge as to their merits or deficiencies. Old Thomas Lowrie was also taken into council, and his wondering admiration of the bonny slated houses was something worth seeing. Peggy's suggestion of the addition of a little storeroom, in which milk and meal and potatoes could be kept, was put and carried unanimously. They then went into the allotment questions, and Jane, Elsie, and Peggy, offered their opinions as to the fittest persons for the boon, and then began to wonder how many years it would be before they could make the land pay. All this, which ought to have gratified Francis—for every man should be glad when people take an interest in his plans—struck a chill to his heart, for it boded no good to his new visions.

'You seem to be in great spirits altogether, to-day, Jane,' said he.

'How can I help it? The prospect of a situation of fifty or sixty pounds a year is something overpoweringly delightful to me. If I had heard of such a thing six months ago, I should have been glad, but now that I have felt the difficulty of getting any employment whatever, and feel quite sure that I am fit for this, my only dread is lest Mr. Phillips may have got another person, or may not like my appearance; but if he is satisfied to engage me I am determined to save money to start in business. By and by we are going to join Peggy in Melbourne.'

'But your sister—how do you feel about leaving her?'

'I was quite aware that I must leave her if I meant to do anything of any value for myself.'

'I am never going to stand in Jane's light any more,' said Elsie. 'I am not so selfish as to regret any piece of good fortune that comes to her alone.'

'And I think of inquiring a little further as to her poems,' said Jane.

'Oh, no! that is altogether useless,' said Elsie.

'You promised yesterday to let Francis see them to-day, Elsie. We must have his opinion on this subject. I certainly think I could do more personally, than by letter, to get them published.'

'And Jane always wished so much to see London,' said Elsie. 'I am so glad to think she has such a prospect, and from all Peggy's accounts of Mr. Phillips, he is everything that could be wished. How little we thought when we listened to her long tale about her taking such care of Emily and Harriett Phillips, the first night we came to live here, that she was saving pupils for Jane. It seems like a fate.'

'Then what are *you* going to do?' said Francis, who did not seem so much delighted with Jane's good news as she had expected. 'Are you to live here with Peggy, as before?'

'Not just as before. I am going to Mrs. Dunn's through the day, and Peggy is good enough to say she will be glad to keep me, though I lose my better half in Jane. I think I really have some taste and talent for millinery, and I mean to try to cultivate it; for if we begin business together in Melbourne, it may be very useful. Jane and I lay awake half the night, talking over our plans, and I do not see why we should not make our way in time.'

'Then, you are going to forget the Muses altogether, and give your whole soul to business?'

'Did you not do that every day, cousin Francis, when you were at the Bank?' said Elsie.

'Perhaps you may write better poetry when you do not make it your day's work. Do you not think she may, Francis?' said Jane.

'Very probably—very probably she may;' said Francis, thoughtfully, as if he were weighing the advantages of literature being a staff, over its being a crutch, but in reality he was not thinking of Elsie or her verses, at all.

He had prepared himself to make a great sacrifice—to do something very generous and Quixotic—not altogether uninfluenced by

the wish for personal happiness of the highest kind; but yet he believed that his chief motives for taking the resolution were the forlorn and hopeless situation of the two girls. Now they were no longer forlorn or hopeless. If this situation for Jane was obtained, and Elsie persevered in her determination to work hard at the perfecting of her taste for making caps and bonnets, they had a definite plan of life, likely to be as prosperous as that he could offer to them. And Jane would not accept of him to-day, though she would probably have done so yesterday. His plans, his ambitions, were too dear to her to be thrown away lightly, and he could see nothing but sisterly affection in her eyes. If she took the position she was entitled to at Mr. Phillips's, she was likely to meet with some society there, and Mr. Brandon, or some other Australian settler, not so shy of matrimony without a fortune on the lady's part, as the middle-class Englishman of this century is, might see some of the virtues and attractions which he had learned to love—no one could see so many of them as himself—and might win the best wife in the world, without being fully conscious of the blessing. He knew the real strength of his love, when he tried to fancy Jane the wife of any one else. He almost wished she might fail in her object, and that Mr. Phillips would decide that she would not suit. He was selfish enough to hope that she might not be happy there. They must continue to correspond as frequently and as openly as hitherto. He would watch for any turn that might offer him hope, and he must be all the more careful to disguise his real feelings, lest it might prevent her from expressing herself as frankly as she had done. When a blessing appears to be lost its value is greatly enhanced, and all the comforts, and privileges, and opportunities, of his present situation, that he had made such an effort to give up, seemed to shrink into insignificance, compared with the domestic happiness that was now eluding his grasp.

'There was great lamentation among the bairns this morning when I said something about Miss Jean maybe leaving us; but they took great comfort from the recollection that they had learned to write so well that they might send real post letters to her—not

mere make-believes—and she promised to answer them. Tam says if she goes to London she must keep on the look-out for anything that is in his line, and indeed Miss Jean said she would. It is a real blessing that penny post. In my young days, to think of writing back and fore to London about anything ye wanted to know would have been out of the question for poor folk,' said Peggy.

'You must write to me, too,' said Francis, 'about all the things and all the people you see, and how you like them, and if you tire of London or of teaching—just every mood as you feel it. I do not think it was quite fair in you always showing me the brightest side of your life. I do not mean to show you always mine.'

'When you are disappointed because the workmen will not build the cottages fast enough, or because the inhabitants do not keep them as clean as your fastidious taste thinks necessary, or because the dull Scottish brain will not readily take up the Flemish or French ideas you want to engraft in them, you will write all your indignant or disgusted expressions to me, rather than lose patience with the people themselves—it is safer. I am prepared for some disappointments, but I will wait patiently and in hope for the end.'

'Did you always have this large amount of public spirit, Jane? It struck me very forcibly the first evening you spent with me at my house.'

'I think it lay dormant for a few months before my uncle's death,' said Jane, laughing; 'but it came out stronger than ever afterwards. Francis is very grave to-day. I would not trust him with your verses, Elsie; his criticisms will be far too severe in his present mood.'

'But I will trust him just at this very time,' said Elsie; 'for if this dull morning has made him a little depressed, perhaps he may feel a little for me sitting in my cheerless room, without hope and without society. I beg your pardon, Jane, you are always good and kind, and so was Peggy, and every one; but it was so dull—so very dull. But what I mean is, that if Francis is moody and dispirited, as a great many people are at times, my verses will not seem to him such a wail as to the busy, merry world we live in. I never saw a more favourable-looking critic.'

Elsie then went to her drawer, and for the first time since she had tied up her manuscript touched it without a sick pang at her heart. The very sight of the enveloping brown paper had been odious to her: but to-day she felt courage enough to untie it, and to select a few of what she considered her best pieces for her cousin's perusal.

Much depends on the mood of the reader of poetry. Francis did not find Elsie's sad views of life at all overdrawn, and he pointed out both to her and to Jane many fine passages, and what he considered to be pretty images. Here and there he found fault; but, on the whole, he said Elsie's verses were full of promise, and she only had to wait patiently for awhile—to observe as well as to reflect, and not to be quite so subjective—to attain to excellence.

At the Exhibition and at the concert in the evening, Francis had again to admire the naturally fine taste of his younger cousin, and to lament with her that none of her talents had been cultivated. According to all his preconceived fancies, he should have fallen in love with Elsie; but it was not so. She was a sweet, amiable girl, with a great deal of quickness and undeveloped talent, but she was chiefly dear to him as Jane's sister. Elsie felt for the time restored to a better opinion of herself, and was grateful to the person who thought well of what the world seemed to despise. She was disposed now to do Francis justice, and more than justice. Never had she talked with a man of finer taste or more admirable judgment. She caught another glimpse of William Dalzell, who was at the concert with the Rennies and Miss Wilson, and contrasted her old favourite with her new, very much to the disadvantage of the former.

Francis was aware that this was the person from whose attentions Jane had been in such danger. He could scarcely conceive the possibility of a woman of such admirable sense and such penetration as Jane forming an attachment to one so shallow and so unheroic. He felt himself scarcely worthy of Jane Melville, and he would never compare himself with the Laird of Mosstower. But the young people had been thrown together, and had spent much of

their time of meeting in the open air. William Dalzell was a good rider and a fearless sportsman; he rode a beautiful horse, and was very careful of it. He appeared to have a good temper, and his mother worshipped him, while Elsie was never weary of sounding his praises. Mr. Hogarth was in indifferent health, and was somewhat exacting at all times. He had not the sympathy with the high spirits of youth that he had had in former years, so that Jane had enjoyed the animated rides, where she did most of the talking to a listener, young, handsome, and determined to be pleased with everything she said and did. She thought she interested him in her favourite subjects; he had said that she improved him, and his mother said the same; so that she rejoined in her influence, which seemed to bear such good results.

Miss Rennie, who had heard when in —— shire, a somewhat exaggerated account of young Dalzell's attachment to Miss Melville, was very much disgusted with his conduct, and though his attentions to Laura Wilson amused her very much, she had a grudge at him for their mercenary motives. Laura was evidently captivated at first sight; she could speak of nobody but Mr. Dalzell, and Mr. Rennie as her guardian was a little alarmed, but on inquiry he found that Moss Tower was not very deeply dipped after all; Mrs. Dalzell had her jointure off it, but he was an only son, and any little wildness or extravagance of youth was likely to be put an end to by marriage. Laura was a somewhat troublesome ward, so passionate and so self-willed that even at school she had carried her point against him by sheer determination over and over again, and he wished heartily to be well freed of her by marriage with a tolerably respectable man. Her fortune he would secure her future husband from making ducks and drakes of by settlements, which are generally in Britain framed as if the future husband was an enemy to be dreaded, and not a friend to be trusted. For the law as it stands puts such enormous power, not only over happiness (which is inevitable), but over property and liberty, into the hands of the husband, to be used against as well as for the advantage of the wife, that it is only by taking power from both, and vesting it in trustees,

that money can be saved for the wife and children. In the cases where the marriage is a happy one, the settlement is a hindrance and a nuisance; but in such cases as that of William Dalzell and Laura Wilson, it would be prudent to evade the law of the land, and to preserve the property of the heiress by such means.

II

JANE'S SITUATION

In an almost incredibly short time, Mr. Brandon called at Peggy Walker's to say that he had had a letter from Mr. Phillips, who thought very favourably of Miss Melville from his description, but who would come to Edinburgh himself in a day or two and see the young lady, so as to judge for himself.

He came accordingly, but, to Peggy's great disappointment, without Emily or Harriett. They had both bad colds, and he could not make them travel in the depth of winter even to see Peggy. Jane and Elsie could not but admire the kindly greeting to gave to his old and faithful servant, and the interest he took in her affairs and her children, which was even more strongly expressed than Mr. Brandon's; and as for grandfather, he could not tell which of the two Australian gentlemen was the most polite.

The manners of the younger sister took Mr. Phillips's fancy more than those of the elder, but he saw that Jane would suit him best; so, in a much shorter time than she could have conceived possible, she found herself engaged to accompany him on his return to London, as housekeeper and governess, at a salary of £70 a year.

'We mean to come to Edinburgh next summer, when we will probably take a tour in the Highlands, so that you have a prospect

of seeing your sister then,' said Mr. Phillips: 'but I must have you with us as soon as possible, so I hope you will be ready the day after to-morrow.'

'Yes, I will be quite ready then,' said Jane. 'I have not much to do, except to part from Elsie, and that will be hard to do at last as at first.'

While Mr. Phillips talked to Peggy about his children, and especially of Emily, the girls both examined his countenance and drew their conclusions as to his character. He was not so handsome as Mr. Brandon, being smaller and more insignificant-looking, and his fair complexion had not stood so well the constant exposure to the weather under an Australian sun as Mr. Brandon's dark one, but his smile was remarkably bright, and though his manner was very gentle and pleasing, he did not seem to want for decision of character.

'I doubt Emily is changed out of my knowledge. I have not seen her since she was four years and a half old, when you brought her to Melbourne for me to see, and when she coaxed me out of far more lollies than were good for her.'

'I will bring her up in summer, and you will acknowledge that you would know her anywhere. As for you, she will know you quite well, for did not we get your likeness taken at the time, and she shows it to every one as that of her dear old nurse.'

'I hope you're no spoiling the bairn.'

'Oh! no, not much—at least, if we are, we will get Miss Melville to counteract our bad treatment.'

'You're no to make Miss Melville a terror—that's no fair. But the wee things after Harriett, how do you call them?'

'Constance, Hubert, and Eva.'

'Well, they should save the eldest from being destroyed by foolish indulgence, for Emily and Harriett should be learned to give way to them.'

'Everybody gives way to all of the five—but you must not say they are spoiled, either. Harriett and Emily, too, learned a lot of monkey tricks on board ship. The gentlemen took so much notice

of them, and encouraged a good deal of impertinence in the children.'

'A ship is a bad school for bairns,' said Peggy. 'Mine will be come some length before we go on board, and are not like to be so much taken notice of. Does Mrs. Phillips like England?'

'Very much, indeed. She will not go back with her own goodwill, and I hope not to need to return.'

'All your friends are in this country,' said Peggy, 'and Mrs. Phillips will have so much new to see here that she will not regret the station. And how's Mrs. Bennett, is she still with you, and Martha, Mrs. Tuck they call her now?'

'They are both on the station yet, Peggy; Mrs. Bennett the same admirable woman she used to be, but one cannot advance her any way with such a poor creature of a husband. There is no rise in him; he is a shepherd, and a shepherd he will remain to the end of his days, spending his wages in an occasional spree, and then coming back to us to work for more; while that poor silly Martha happened on one of the best men about the place, and I have left him an under-overseer. If the two men could only have exchanged wives, things would appear more equitably arranged.'

'Well,' said Peggy, when Mr. Phillips had gone, 'people can see other folks' blunders, but the man that I thought worst mated on the station was the master himself. You'll have to take high ground with Mrs. Phillips, Miss Melville, for if you give her an inch she will take an ell. As for him, he is everything that is reasonable; and the bairns, you must just make them mind you. But she is the one that will give you the most trouble.'

When this engagement was entered into Jane accompanied Elsie to Mrs. Dunn's, who readily took her into her work-room, and was very much pleased to hear that Miss Melville had got such a desirable situation. The Rennies were also full of congratulations, and felt that their invitations and their getting the sisters an introduction to Mr. Brandon, had secured such a magnificent salary from another Australian millionaire. Miss Rennie was particularly pleased that she had dwelt so much on the misfortunes and talents

of the sisters. The last evening Jane spent in Edinburgh was passed at the Rennies'; Mr. Brandon was asked to meet the girls he had been of such service to, and though Mr. Hogarth was rather dull, and Laura Wilson in a particularly unamiable mood, the liveliness of the Australian settler made it pass off very pleasantly.

Jane had not only Mr. Phillips, but Mr. Brandon also as travelling companion. Australians in England have a great tendency to fraternise, even though they were not much acquainted in the colony, and when his old neighbour returned to London, Brandon thought he could not do better than go with him, and go back to the north when it was not quite so cold. The gentlemen had a great deal to say to each other on matters both colonial and English. In English politics they took quite as great an interest as if they had never been out of Britain, and in Continental politics they took a greater interest than is usual with English people. Jane was occupied with her own thoughts. The parting from Elsie had been a sad one, so had the good-bye to Francis, who had said so much about her writing if she was unhappy, or if she did not think she could keep her situation with a lady of such a peculiar temper as Mrs. Phillips, that she could not help fearing herself for the permanency of the situation.

Nothing that had fallen from Peggy, or from Mr. Brandon either, had prepared Jane for the exceeding beauty of Mrs. Phillips. Jane never had seen a woman so strikingly handsome before. When she spoke the charm was somewhat broken, for her ideas were not brilliant, and she expressed herself in indifferent English; but in repose she was like a queen of romance. Tall and large, but exquistely formed, with a soft creamy complexion, with a slight faint rose colour on the cheeks, and a more vivid red on the pouting lips, finely-shaped brown eyes, and a profusion of rippling dark brown hair, she certainly offered the fairest possible excuse for her husband's marrying beneath his rank—both social and intellectual. Such beauty as Mrs. Phillips's is a power, and Jane felt how difficult it would be to take high ground with so exquisite a creature. As Mr. Brandon said, she was handsomer than ever; the girlish beauty of

sixteen, which she possessed when she captivated Mr. Phillips, had matured into the perfect beauty of womanhood. Though the mother of five children, she was not, and certainly did not look, twenty-seven. Emily was not so regularly handsome as her mother, but had more animation and more play of feature. Harriett would have been considered a pretty child in any other family, but she was quite a plain one in this.

No sooner had Mr. Phillips entered his house than Emily clung round his neck; Harriett mounted on one knee and played with his hair; Constance got on the other to have a little similar amusement with his beard and whiskers; Hubert clamoured for a ride on papa's foot; and little Eva cried to leave her nurse's arms to be taken up by him too.

'I was very glad to hear from Mr. Phillips, that you was coming, Miss Melville; the trouble of the house and the row of the children make it far too much for me, and when one comes home to England for a holiday, they want to have some peace,' said Mrs. Phillips. 'Now, Miss Emily, you must be on your good behaviour, now Miss Melville's come to be your governess.'

'I'm sure I shan't behave any better to her than to my own dear papa,' said Emily, with a storm of kisses.

'You're getting up to be a great girl. I'm sure Miss Melville will be quite shocked at your backwardness.'

'She is a bush child,' said Mr. Brandon, 'and has been running wild all her life; you must excuse her for the present, but we hope to see great improvement.'

'I am much afraid you will be disappointed, you dear old boy,' said Emily, who had left her father and come up to Mr. Brandon, who was her particular favourite. 'Keep your spirits up as well as you can; I am not going to be like your wonderful nephews and nieces at Ashfield. I never saw such ignorant children; they did not know how to make dirt pies, nor could they jump across the ditch, or get up by the trees to the top of the garden wall. Harriett and I had such a beautiful race round that garden, and they looked on so terrified.'

'They could take the shine out of you at lessons, however,' said Mr. Brandon, 'and I won't take you there again to have another such spirited race till I hear satisfactory accounts of you from Miss Melville.'

'Oh! the race was well enough, but the visit was very slow upon the whole, so I don't think I will break my heart if I never see the place again. Harriett may try to deserve it, but I will not take the trouble.'

'I hate books,' said Miss Harriett, 'except picture books, and the fairy tales papa reads to us.'

'You must not mind what they say, Miss Melville,' said Mr. Phillips.

'I do not intend to do so. I hope to make them like their lessons by and by, and in the meantime they must learn them whether they like them or not.'

'You would be astonished, Lily,' said Mr. Phillips, addressing his wife, 'to see what a clever, intelligent family of nephews and nieces Peggy has got. Miss Melville has been good enough to give them some extra instruction, and they certainly have profited by it; but even without that, Peggy has given them every advantage that she possibly could.'

'Oh! Peggy had always very uppish notions,' said Mrs. Phillips, 'it will be a pity if she educates these children above their position.'

'No one knows what position they may not take with such abilities and education in such a colony as Victoria. I may have to stand cap in hand to Tom Lowrie yet,' said Mr. Phillips.

'You, Stanley!' said his wife; 'you are so fond of saying absurd things.'

'Don't you know the insecurity of runs? And who knows but Tom may be Prime Minister or Commissioner of Public Lands or Public Works, or the chief engineer on a new railway, that may go right through my squatting rights? My dear Lily, I have a respect for incipient greatness, and when I stood among these young people, I felt they would be rising when I was perhaps falling.'

'Were these your motives?' said Mr. Brandon, laughing. 'I admired the young Lowries for what they were in themselves, and did not go so far into the future as you. I hope, Emily, that in time, Miss Melville will make you what Peggy calls keen of your learning, as well as her bairns.'

'Did you like learning when you were a little girl?' asked Emily of Miss Melville.

'Very much, indeed.'

'So mamma says, but then she did not have to learn very much. If I had not such a horrid lot of tasks, perhaps I might like some of them.'

'But, my dear, you are so very ignorant, you have everything to learn now that you have come to England,' said her mamma.

'But I hope not everything at once,' said Jane.

'Not quite,' said Mr. Phillips; 'but perhaps too much so. You will see the list of the girls' studies to-morrow, and judge for yourself.'

Mrs. Phillips was favourably impressed with Jane. She was well born and well educated, but she was plain looking. She had heard of her sudden and sad reverse of fortune, and felt disposed to take her up and patronise her. She had suffered from the want of a domestic manager and house counsellor; even the very good temper and great forbearance of her husband had given way at the small amount of comfort that could be obtained with such a lavish expenditure of money as his had been since they came to London; and he had spoken more sharply to her about her mismanagement than about anything else, so she felt that now he had a housekeeper of his own choosing, she should escape from all responsibility. Her manner to Jane was exceedingly kind, and Jane's hopes rose at her reception.

Mrs. Phillips always went to bed early, unless she was kept up by amusement and gaiety; her style of beauty was of the kind that suits best with plenty of sleep and few cares—so at ten o'clock she said she could sit up no longer, and left Mr. Phillips to explain all the duties expected of Miss Melville, so that she need not be disturbed by any inquiries in the morning.

Mr. Phillips did so with a clearness and precision that showed he had been often obliged to see to the disbursement of the money as well as the earning if it. He gave Jane the keys and the house-books, showed her what he thought was the sum he could spend on family expenses, and hoped that she would make it suffice.

'I wish you to be one of the family, Miss Melville; to visit and go to public places with Mrs. Phillips. I think we may dispense with all the masters for my little girls, except for music, and I hope that you will succeed in making them like both you and their lessons. I also hope, in a short time, to give you still more difficult and delicate work to do, and if you can be successful there, I will be most grateful to you. Mrs. Phillips has had a very imperfect education; she was born in the colonies, and was married when a mere child, and since her marriage she has had few opportunities of improving herself either by books or society. I think she feels her deficiencies; so if you could ingratiate yourself with her—she appears to be most favourably disposed towards you at first sight—and induce her to learn a little from you, you would add very greatly to our happiness and comfort, and I should be infinitely your debtor.'

Mr. Phillips hesitated, and coloured a little while he made this suggestion. Jane said she would do what she could, and would be most happy to further his views in this and in every other way; but she felt not a little fearful at the idea of having to ingratiate herself with the woman she had been exhorted to take high ground with, and to teach, probably in the most elementary branches, the most lovely creature she had ever seen, the mistress of the house, and a person several years her senior. Still, no difficulty—no honour. She had wanted full employment, and here she was likely to get it.

Jane did not think she had naturally any great turn for children, but the little Phillipses had been so accustomed to have people pet and yield to them that they actually seemed to enjoy the repose and happiness of obeying, and obeying at once, their calm, grave governess, who never asked them to do anything unreasonable, but yet who always insisted on implicit acquiescence. They were

indebted to her for the shortening and simplifying of all their lessons in the first place, and that called out a considerable amount of gratitude. She had a clear way of explaining things to them, and she had such a large information on all subjects that she filled out the dry skeletons of geography and history which children are condemned to learn, and made them look living and real to them. Their father had taught the two elder girls to read, and to read well and fluently; but they had had no other lessons till they had come to London, and found their hitherto unexercised memories quite overtaxed by masters, who saw that the girls were quick, intelligent, and observant, with a great deal of practical knowledge quite unusual in England at their years, but absolutely devoid of all school acquirements. They found their lessons much more interesting to learn and much better retained when learned under Miss Melville than under their masters; and though they were not particularly fond of her, they were very happy with her.

Mrs. Phillips's only objection to Miss Melville was her Scotch accent; but, before six weeks had passed she had got over that, and thought being in London had softened it down very considerably, and she did not think the children were at all inclined to pick it up. She began to wonder if the governess would not give her some help or some hints, for she was going to visit her husband's relations in Derbyshire for a second time—her first visit had not been very long—and she hoped and wished that she might get on better than she had done before. Her husband had never found any fault with her in the bush of Australia; but her blunders before his father, brother, and sisters had distressed him so much that he had spoken to her many times rather sharply in private about them. Though she was a woman of a very indolent character, now that Jane managed all her housekeeping and her servants, wrote all her notes—that, however, was a saving of time to her husband rather than to herself—and relieved her a good deal from the worry of the children, she felt that she had some time on her hands, in spite of her going out a good deal to see and to be seen. She was no reader, and had no taste for needlework; but she had the gift of being able

to sit in an easy chair thinking of nothing in particular, and doing nothing at all, but looking so beautiful that one might have fancied her thoughts to be of the most elevated description.

One day, while in this state of luxurious ease, she asked Jane how long she had been at school, and opened her eyes a hair-breadth or two wider when she was told of the education so peculiar, so protracted, that Mr. Hogarth had given to his nieces, and that even after she had left off regular study, Jane had never ceased to be learning something. Even now she was keeping up, partly for Tom Lowrie's sake, and partly for her own gratification, some of those branches of learning that were likely to be useful to him, and corresponding with him every week on those subjects.

Mrs. Phillips sighed, and said she had been married at sixteen, and had been very little at school all her life. She had always been moved from place to place when she was a girl, and there were no schools in the colony that were fit to teach young ladies then. Even now, it was the children's education that had been Mr. Phillips's great inducement to come to England, and she liked it very much herself, there was so much to see in London. But would Miss Melville think it very absurd if she were to propose to take lessons now? Jane said she would not think it at all absurd; she was sure Mrs. Phillips would find it very pleasant. But she was rather perplexed when the lady said that her chief ambition was to learn the pianoforte and how to make wax flowers. She had no particular taste for music, and no artistic taste at all; but music and wax flowers were expensive, fashionable, and showy accomplishments, and these Mrs. Phillips desired to acquire.

'These are things, unfortunately, that I cannot give you any assistance with,' said Jane, recovering her presence of mind, 'and perhaps you would not like to have masters and mistresses coming in for yourself. Any other branch of study we could go on with together, and that would be pleasanter. Music demands so very much time if you wish to make rapid progress.'

'Emily only practises an hour and Hariett half an hour a day now, and though their master wished them to practise twice as long, they

seem to get on much better since you said they should not be so long at the piano.'

'Because it is practising, not amusing themselves or dawdling, and because it is an hour and half an hour, neither more nor less, and not an uncertain time, which is left to the performer's pleasure. To make any progress with music after you are grown up, you must give three or four hours a day to its acquirement, and that you would find it difficult—almost impossible—to keep up. But, as I said before, music is a thing I am so ignorant of that I can give you no assistance and no advice on the subject.'

'I would like your assistance,' said Mrs. Phillips, 'for the children do get on with you, and they say that you make their lessons an amusement.'

'Should you not like to be with us while we we are at study, and see if you think you could derive any benefit from my method? Come into the schoolroom to-morrow with us?'

'Mrs. Phillips agreed to this, and thought the lessons were very pleasant. Sometimes Jane made the little girls repeat their lessons to their mamma, still exercising the supervision which made them feel they must be as careful as heretofore. The oral instruction which accompanied the lessons studied from the book, seemed to Mrs. Phillips as well as to the children, the most interesting part of it, and as the language was simplified for the comprehension of the little pupils, it was not at all too abstract for their mother. She declared herself delighted with the morning at school, and tried to persuade herself that she was only going there to see how her governess did her duty by her children. In this way, by sitting two hours every forenoon with Miss Melville, she contrived to pick up something, and though both her husband and Jane would have been glad if the studies had been prosecuted a little futher, they were very much pleased with so much improvement.

The idea of learning music still haunted Mrs. Phillips, and she obtained her husband's consent to her having lessons from Emily's master; but her progress was so slow that she tired of it in a month, and blamed her teacher for his stupid dry way of setting her to

work. If Miss Melville had only understood music, she knew she would have got on ever so much better, for she had such a knack of teaching people. On the whole, Jane was satisfied with her situation, and with the manner in which she filled it, and when Mr. Phillips paid her her first quarter's salary, he expressed himself in the highest degree satisfied with everything she had done. If she could only have felt that Elsie was well and happy, she would have been perfectly happy herself, but the letters from Edinburgh were not at all cheerful. Elsie's account of herself, and Francis's accounts of her, were unsatisfactory, and even Peggy had written a few lines recently to say that she was uneasy about her, and did not think the situation at Mrs. Dunn's agreed with Miss Elsie at all.

It was still months before she could hope to go to Edinburgh to see her sister; but she wrote, urging her to give up her employment, and to take as much open-air exercise as possible, and also to take medical advice on the subject; but Elsie did not agree to this. The family plans were all laid for a visit to Derbyshire, and Mr. Brandon, who seemed always to be on the move, when his old neighbours were leaving London, seeing Jane's distress about her sister, ventured on a good-natured suggestion in her behalf.

'I think you might go up now and see Peggy before you go to Derbyshire; you know she is anxious to see Emily and the other children. I could go with you. I wish so much to see the meeting between them.'

'We cannot go to Scotland so early in the season. Autumn is the time when it is pleasant to travel in the north.'

'But then I cannot be a witness to Peggy's delight, for if you delay so long I will have to be off to Melbourne before that time. I thought if you went now you might leave Miss Melville with her sister while you pay your visit. You do not mean to take her there, and the servants here will, I suppose, be put on board wages during your absence, so that she need not remain in London.'

'We hope and expect that Miss Melville will accompany us to Derbyshire, that the children may go on with their lessons, and not get into as much mischief as they did on their last visit,' said Mr.

Phillips.

'I am sure their aunts made great complaints of them,' said Mrs. Phillips, 'and I do not wish to give room for so much complaint again. I hope Miss Melville will come with us.'

'I would have escorted Miss Melville to Edinburgh before I went to Ashfield, for I must see that worthy Peggy again before I leave England, and visit my Edinburgh relatives again, too, and my time is getting short,' said Mr. Brandon; 'but if you cannot spare her, I cannot do anything but go to see her sister, and report myself on her appearance; perhaps your letters are duller than the reality.'

'Did you not tell me your sister was a milliner, Miss Melville? What a sad thing. I am sure you are such a treasure to us that I wish some other family would take your sister,' said Mrs. Phillips.

'She thinks millinery preferable to idleness; but the long hours, and the cold rooms, and the solitary life are too hard upon her.'

'It must be dull for her to have no other society but that of our good Peggy and her bairns after a long day's work. Don't you think, Lily, that it would be a pleasant change for her to come and spend a few weeks with us after we return to London, as her sister cannot yet go to her?' said Mr. Phillips.

The idea of befriending Jane's sister in this way was not disagreeable to Mrs. Phillips. The invitation was given, and joyfully accepted. Mr. Brandon would delay his visit to the north till it was about the time for Elsie to come down, and would take care of her on the way.

Jane felt happy in this new proof of the kind feeling of the family towards her, and accompanied them to Derbyshire with a lighter heart.

Mr. Phillip's father was a medical man, with an excellent country practice, intelligent, chatty, and hospitable. He had married a Miss Stanley, who was not only of very good birth, but who had a considerable fortune, which was settled on her children. Her eldest son's portion of it had been the nucleus of the handsome fortune he had realised in Victoria. The old gentleman had been long a widower, and his two unmarried daughters lived with him, and kept

his house, while his younger son had been brought up to assist his father in his profession, and eventually to succeed to the practice, but he, seeing how well his brother Stanley had got on, had a great hankering after an unlimited sheep-run in Australia.

The Misses Phillips were not young, but they were well dressed, well mannered, and good looking. There was a happy, prosperous, confident air about both of the sisters, and especially about the younger of the two. They were the darlings of their father, the first in their own set of acquaintances, a great deal taken notice of, on account both of their mother's social position and their father's professional talent, by county families; successful in domestic management, successful in society, of good understanding, and well educated, the Misses Phillips were looked up to very much, and felt that they deserved to be so. They were much disappointed in their brother's wife; from his letters, and the likenesses he had sent home, they were prepared for a romantic and interesting, as well as beautiful woman, but her want of education and of understanding, which they soon discovered on personal acquaintance, was most mortifying to ladies who thought they possessed both in a high degree, and they were quite distressed at having to introduce her into society. The husband saw and felt their coldness towards his wife, while Mrs. Phillips filled his ears with complaints of their uppishness, and their disagreeable ways.

Mr. Phillips had been so proud and so fond of his sisters, and had talked so much to her about their beauty, their cleverness, and their goodness, that she thought she too had a right to be disappointed. Their beauty had diminished during his fourteen years' absence in Australia; their cleverness only made her uncomfortable; and their goodness did not seem to extend to her. What right had a couple of ordinary-looking old maids to look down on her, a married woman of so many years' standing, so much younger and handsomer? She liked Jane Melville far better than either of her sisters-in-law, for, with more real mental superiority, there was an inferiority in position that set her at her ease.

Mr. Phillips was a little disappointed with his sisters, though he

would scarcely own it to himself. The blooming girls of twenty-one and seventeen whom he had left were somewhat faded in the course of the many years' absence; and the very different lives that they had led made them take different views of most subjects. Their opinions had hardened separately, and when they met again they did not harmonize as they had done. His sisters were more aristocratic in all their tastes and feelings than the Australian squatter; they had scarcely mixed at all with children, and had no patience with his wild bush children, whose frankness and audacity were so terribly embarrassing; and they had shown their disappointment at his *mésalliance* very decidedly.

But on this occasion things went on much better; both Mrs. Phillips and the children were decidedly improved, and the sisters-in-law gave Miss Melville the credit of it, and liked her accordingly.

Miss Melville was presentable anywhere, though she was only a governess. The tale which Mr. Phillips told of her reverse of fortune interested them all, particularly the old gentleman.

He had met with Jane's uncle when he had been studying in Paris, who was then only a younger son, and had been just released from the strict discipline of a Scotch puritanical home, and not being ambitious of filling the subordinate office of 'Jock, the laird's brother,' wished to learn a profession, and thought he might try medicine as well as anything else. He was then clever, idle, and extravagant, but a great favourite with everybody. Jane questioned Dr. Phillips about the date of this acquaintance, but it had occurred before the supposed time of Francis's birth, so that he could throw no light on that question. Still she wrote to Francis on the subject, though she had thought his letters lately had been colder than before, and feared that his friendship for her was not so deeply seated as hers for him. Willing to show that her feelings towards him were unchanged, she entered into the same minute description of the family she was at present living with as she had done of the pupils, and the employers, and the visitors in London. She was at this time more interested in Dr. Phillips and his younger son Vivian than in any of the ladies of the family, and felt particularly

puzzled to explain the desire of the latter to leave the country and his profession, when he had talents quite sufficient to make a good figure, for such a life as Mr. Brandon's had been in the Australian bush. He was the most scientific man whom Jane had met with in society; and, as he met with very little sympathy from either of his sisters in his chemical experiments or his geological researches, he appreciated her intelligent and inquiring turn of mind. There were many things he could throw light on which would be of service to Tom Lowrie, and were mentioned in her letters to him. Young Dr. Vivian Phillips had submitted to a great deal of the inevitable spoiling which an only brother at home receives. Georgiana was very strongly attached to him; and though Harriett had always said that she preferred Stanley, yet, when he came back, with his uncongenial wife and large family of young children to engross nine-tenths of his heart, her partiality for him seemed to fade away, and she felt that Vivian was far better than the other—at least, more clever and more English in his ideas; but Stanley was more liberal, and had a better temper. Vivian had fits of bad temper which no one could conquer, and his sisters found it was the only plan to let him alone.

Vivian would never think of falling in love with his brother's governess—he knew his own position too well for that: so that his sisters had no fear of his being in any danger when Jane joined him in his experiments in the laboratory, or went out with him and the children geologising. And they were perfectly right in that surmise. He liked Jane because he felt her to be a perfectly safe person—just a little more interesting than a companion of his own sex, and one to place rather more confidence in, for she had more sympathy and more enthusiasm; but she had excellent sense, and did not appear to be at all impressible.

Jane described the beautiful country walks she took, which she was sure Francis or Elsie would appreciate far better than she could do. She contrasted the activity and full life of the gentlemen of the house with the languid idleness of Mrs. Phillips and the busy idleness of her sisters-in-law, and thought it very unjust that all the work of the world should be done by the one sex and so little left

for the other. She had thought the Misses Phillips superior to the Swinton young ladies at first; but on closer acquaintance, she found it quite as difficult to grow intimate with them. She thought she would prefer the High Church, and almost Puseyite, tendencies of the English women to the narrow and gloomy views of her Scotch neighbours; but her independent turn of mind, her eager love of inquiry and her thirst for truth, were as much cramped by the one as the other.

An enormous part of the Misses Phillips' lives was occupied in visiting and receiving visitors. Their superintendence of their father's household was very different from what had been expected from Jane and Elsie at Cross Hall. They had old and faithful servants, who knew their work and did it, and rarely troubled their mistresses for orders. They did not take the same interest or trouble about the poor which the Misses Melville had done. If Dr. Phillips mentioned any case of distress, the cook was directed to send broth, or wine, or they might even give a little money; but there was no personal inconvenience suffered or sacrifice made for the relief of want or the comforting of sorrow. The charity was given with the smallest amount of sympathy, and accepted with the smallest amount of gratitude.

In public matters, in social progress, in sanitary reforms, all the gentlemen took a lively interest; but the ladies considered these things quite out of their own line. There was this difference, however, between the sisters, that Georgiana (the eldest) could make any sacrifice cheerfully for any member of her own family, but Harriett was disinclined to make any, even for them. It is not to be supposed that the world in general saw all these traits as Jane, in her peculiar circumstances, and with her observant powers, had so much opportunity of doing. They were considered to be very superior and very amiable young ladies, and Mr. Brandon had been rather surprised at himself for not fixing his affections on Harriett, who, as the favourite sister of his dearest friend, would be suitable in every respect, and who appeared to have all the qualifications to make a good wife.

III

ELSIE'S SITUATION

It was not mere fancy on Jane's part that Elsie was ill and unhappy. She had magnanimously made up her mind to go to work with industry and spirit, and Mrs. Dunn was perfectly satisfied with her. But she missed Jane's society far more than her sister could miss hers. Jane was constantly employed in occupations that demanded intelligence and thought. She had access to books; she went to theatres and places of public amusement even more than she cared for; she had the society of Mr. Phillips constantly, and that of Mr. Brandon and several other Australians, who were either retired on a competency or home on a visit, very frequently, and she certainly thought them generally pleasant and intelligent, and more agreeable company than the provincial people in and about Swinton. Their frank acknowledgment of the early struggles which they had had with fortune, the hearty manner in which they enjoyed the prosperity they had earned, and their kindly feeling towards each other, made Jane have a favourable impression of colonial people. Mr. Phillips had become acquainted with several people from other colonies than Victoria, partly on board ship, and partly from other introductions. A curious and ignorant suspicion that somehow all Australians have a sort of convict origin, made it more

difficult at that time for them than for retired Indians to get into general society. There was no nice distinction drawn between the different colonies; between New South Wales and Victoria, or South Australia and Tasmania in those days—a slight savour of Botany Bay was supposed to hang about them all. But they formed a pleasant little clique of their own, less exclusive than most cliques, and generally disposed to hold up each one his own particular colony as preferable to the others. They might contrast it unfavourably with Britain, but as compared with the other colonies, it ought to bear the palm.

Elsie felt the want of this intelligence and this variety of character that Jane described to her so minutely in her frequent letters, and regretted that she could write nothing interesting in return. When she came home after a long day's work, she thought she ought to try to keep up a little of her sister's discipline with the Lowries, and went over their lessons with them.

Tom used to bring to her the most puzzling questions, which she thought she ought to be able to answer, and made great efforts to do so; but instead of the intellectual work refreshing her after the sedentary needlework, she felt all the more exhausted by it. As for her poetry, she appeared to be unable to write a line, and though she sometimes could read an old book, she seemed quite unfit to pay attention to anything new.

She missed the long walks she had daily taken in Jane's pleasant company. It was not far from Peggy's house to Mrs. Dunn's place of business, and it was a very monotonous walk. The white regular houses, all of one size and height, with their thousands of windows exactly on the same model, seemed always staring her out of countenance, and made her feel depressed even in the early morning. She felt the keen piercing east winds of an Edinburgh spring as she had never done at Cross Hall, where they were sheltered from them by a beautiful plantation of trees; and the continued poor living and the hurried meals began to tell upon a constitution naturally much less robust than Jane's, so that she began to look pale and thin, and coughed a good deal, and lost her appetite.

With all these drawbacks she improved so much in taste and skill that Mrs. Dunn raised her wages—or salary, as she genteelly called it—and put her at the head of the department in which she so much excelled, so that she could not bear to give up her contribution to the little fund that Jane was putting into the Savings Bank.

Miss Rennie had persuaded her mamma to try Mrs. Dunn's establishment, and had told that lady that it was all on Miss Elsie Melville's account, so she often saw her and Laura Wilson there, and made bonnets for both of them with her own hands; and the Chalmerses and Jardines had also come to see how Elsie got on, and other people from the neighbourhood of Swinton. Elsie would rather not have had dealings with so many old acquaintances, but Mrs. Dunn thought it was a just reward for her kindness that she had this increase of custom.

One day, about four months after she had been engaged in this business, Miss Rennie and Miss Wilson came in with most important-looking faces. While Miss Wilson was busied turning over the fashion-books, her friend whispered to Elsie:

'It is really a case; Laura is engaged to Mr. Dalzell, your old friend and neighbour, and she is going to give one of her wedding orders here. Mrs. Dunn should be greatly obliged to you, for we never would have come to the house but for you. But this marriage amuses me a good deal. I'm sure your sister was fifty times too good for him, and Laura and he will just suit each other. He is very much attached to her fortune, and she will have it settled upon herself; at least, papa will see that is done as tightly as she could wish, and Laura has a sharp eye to number one, I can assure you. She is quite delighted at the idea of being married at eighteen, to such a handsome man, of such a good family. Mrs. Dalzell has been to see us, and been so gracious. After all, what better luck could she look for than to be married for her money? with such a temper as she has, too. He certainly is handsome; but for my part, I would rather have a man who is downright ugly than one who grins and bows like William Dalzell. I will be quite glad when this affair is over.

Lovers are very tiresome when one does not quite believe in the love.'

'Well, Laura dear, have you made up your mind about the dresses?' continued Miss Rennie, in a louder voice.

'You had better go to Mademoiselle Defour about the dresses,' said Elsie. 'I must keep to my own department.'

'Oh, Laura wants your taste to help us to decide; you know better what suits than mademoiselle,' said Miss Rennie.

'But I am going to be busy here,' said Elsie, who never felt much disposed to wait on Miss Wilson, and at this time less than ever; and she turned to an elderly lady, of a very pleasing countenance, who, with a pretty girl of thirteen, entered the showroom at that moment.

'Oh, Miss Thomson,' said Miss Rennie, shaking hands with the new comer, 'how do you do? Are you in Edinburgh just now? You must come to see mamma; she will be so disappointed if you leave her out. Have you come to hear Dr. B—? He preaches for the last time in Edinburgh on Sunday.'

'I am to be in Edinburgh for a few days,' said Miss Thomson, 'and will certainly call on your mother.'

'This is one of your nieces, I suppose?' said Miss Rennie.

'Yes, this is Grace Forrester, my youngest niece, who has been doing so well at school, and been such a good girl altogether, that I must needs give her a new frock for a party she is invited to next week, and get it fashionably made, too, no doubt.'

'This is not the dressmaking-room—Miss Melville is the milliner. We must go to the next room for Grace's frock,' said Miss Rennie.

'But I am in want of a new cap and bonnet for myself, and I must teach Grace that old people must be served first, and that young folks must wait with patience,' said Miss Thomson, looking very kindly on the girl. 'Miss Melville can take my order, I suppose? You are the sister of the young lady who called on me some time ago?'

'Yes, ma'am,' said Elsie.

'I can see a very slight likeness. I was very glad to hear such good

accounts of your sister getting a situation with some rich colonial people in London; and I hear, too, that you are a remarkably good hand in your own line, so I have come to ask you to make me a cap and a bonnet that will keep on my head; and that is what I cannot get the fashionable milliner I have employed so long to make me this year back.'

'I can make to please Peggy Walker,' said Elsie, smiling; 'but you will wish for more style—a compromise between fashion and comfort.'

'With a decided leaning towards comfort,' said Miss Thomson. 'Are you still living with Peggy Walker? An admirable woman she is, and one whom I have the greatest respect for; but does she take good care of you? You look thin and ill.'

'I am not very well, but Peggy is everything that is kind and careful. I have missed my sister, sadly. I hope, however, to see her soon, for Mrs. Phillips has been so good as to ask me to spend a few weeks in London, and Mrs. Dunn is going to spare me.'

'Well, I am glad to hear it,' said Miss Thomson, 'for it seems to me you want a change and a rest. Your cousin is making great alterations at Cross Hall.

'Alterations for the better,' said Elsie. 'He told us about them.'

'Well, I'm not clear about the allotments; but the cottages I do most highly approve of, and I am coming upon my landlord to build me eight or nine, after the same plan, as near as may be. The Allendale cot-houses are very old, and I will never consent to have my work-people as badly lodged as they have been. If I asked for five hundred pounds to add to the farm-house, I would get it at once, for I am a good tenant; but my landlord demurred at such an expenditure for cot-houses. I think I will carry my point, however.'

'You know,' said Miss Rennie to Miss Thomson, 'of the new neighbour you are likely to get at Moss Tower? Mamma wants to have a talk with you about Laura's marriage, as you know the Dalzells.'

'Oh, yes, certainly, I'll call on your mother. I don't forget any of my cousins, though they are a few times removed. But, dear me,

Eliza, that poor girl Melville looks ill; the brae she has had to climb has been owre stey for her. I must look in on Peggy Walker, and hear what she says about her,' said Miss Thomson, as they moved into mademoiselle's department and gave orders about Grace's frock, while Miss Wilson looked over dresses, made and unmade, and received hints and suggestions from any quarter she could.

Elsie wished that she could be out of the establishment before Miss Wilson's wedding order came to it; so she was very glad when, after a longer day than usual, in which she had exercised her utmost skill for Miss Thomson's behoof, and certainly pleased herself with her work, she returned home and found Mr. Brandon sitting talking in his usual cheerful way to Peggy and the old man.

Dr. Phillips had wished that Elsie should join her sister before she left Derbyshire, and spend a week or so at his house, for he had been so delighted with Jane that he had a desire to become acquainted with Elsie also; so that Mr. Brandon had come sooner than he had intended, and proposed an early departure. Elsie looked so glad, so very glad to see him; expressed herself so grateful to him for all the trouble he was taking for her; and after asking for Jane and the Phillipses, began to inquire about his own relations, and how he had enjoyed his visit to Ashfield, with so much interest, that Mr. Brandon thought her manner more pleasant than ever.

IV

ELSIE REFUSES AN EXCELLENT OFFER

Mr. Brandon had come home with the intention of marrying, and had flirted a good deal during the six or eight months of his stay in England, but he had seen so many young ladies that one had driven another out of his head. He thought he might have fallen in love with Miss Harriett Phillips, who, though not very young, would in all other respects be very suitable, and who, he had no doubt, would accept him; but still he could not manage to cultivate an attachment strong enough to warrant such a desperate step as a proposal. Ever since he had seen Elsie Melville at Mrs. Rennie's party, her face and form, and her pleasant voice with its Scotch accent, recurred more frequently in his thoughts than those of any woman he had seen. Her elegance, her gentleness, her sprightliness, had struck him at sight, and her forlorn condition was very interesting. Her poetical talents, of which he had heard from Peggy, impressed him a good deal, and the manner in which she had taken so industriously to the only means of earning a livelihood open to her, though one which was so far beneath her, had certainly called forth his respect.

The sight of Elsie again, though in diminished beauty, revived all those sentiments of compassion and protection that he had felt for

her from first hearing of her misfortunes. Yes, he would marry her, and then she would grow rosy and happy; and he would get her poems published at his own expense, and have such a splendid copy for herself to lay on her drawing-room table—for she should have a drawing-room at Barragong, and every comfort, and even luxury, that Victoria in those days could afford. He never would be ashamed to take Elsie to see any of his friends or relatives, for she was a gentlewoman born and bred. As for her being a milliner for the present, it was only so much the more to be proud of.

These thoughts lay in Brandon's mind, and strengthened every day of his short stay in Edinburgh; his strong-minded cousins thought Walter Brandon was more contemptible than ever, for he did not seem to have an idea in his head; whereas it was because he had one idea very strongly in his head and heart that he was so disinclined for argument or discussion. Peggy, who perceived Brandon's evident admiration, again regretted her own burst of confidence in her autobiographical sketch, but thought that now Miss Elsie was so downcast and so miserable, that she would never think of refusing so excellent an offer as her old master could make. She began to praise Mr. Brandon—to whose character, however, she never did full justice, from not understanding many of its best points. She liked Mr. Phillips much better, who was graver. Her Scotch phlegmatic temperament could not appreciate the fine spirit and unvarying good humour of Brandon, and his random way of talking she thought flighty and frivolous. But yet she could, and did, praise him for his kindness of heart and his want of selfishness, which he had shown on many occasions, great and small, at Barragong. These panegyrics were bestowed with discretion, not being told to Elsie herself, but brought out incidentally in conversation with grandfather, who thought highly of Brandon, and never ceased to extol his politeness.

Elsie and Brandon had a railway carriage to themselves for a considerable part of the way; and he thought he never could have a better opportunity of declaring himself; so, with rather less stammering and hesitation than is usual on such occasions—for he

had not the least doubt of a favourable answer—he made Elsie understand that he loved her, and asked for her love in return.

'No, no—oh, no!' said Elsie, covering her face with her hands.

'Why "No," Miss Alice? "Yes" sounds a great deal prettier. I'll take such good care of you, and I am sure you will like Australia. Peggy has not given you a very dismal account of Barragong, and I have had it very much improved since her time, and I will have a great deal more done to it; and before we go I will have your book printed——'

'My book,' said Elsie; 'what book?'

'Your poems—I know they are beautiful—Peggy told me about them; and we will have them brought out in the very best style, and I will be so proud to think what a genius I have got for my own darling.'

Elsie sighed deeply; tried to speak, but could not. It was a good sign, Mr. Brandon thought—a sigh was ten times more encouraging than a smile. He knew he had hit upon the right thing when he had spoken of her poems; it was wonderful how discerning love had made him.

'You are mistaken, Mr. Brandon,' said she with difficulty, scarcely daring to raise her eyes to the level of his waistcoat; 'I am no genius, and my poems are not worth printing—poor, crude, empty productions. I believe I can make caps and bonnets, but that is all that I can do.'

'That is only your opinion of yourself. But with my will, you shall make no more frippery of the kind. It is quite beneath you.'

'It is not beneath me to earn an honest livelihood.'

'No; but it was cruel to make you have to do it. I have been so sorry for you all these months, when Miss Melville told me how you were employed.'

'Do not say anything more about your pity for me; it pains me.'

'It is not pity; it is love,' said he, stoutly.

'Love born of pity; that will die when—I mean if—but it cannot be; I never can be your wife—the most unsuitable, the most wrong thing that I could do. Do not speak any more about it.'

Elsie's real distress convinced Mr. Brandon of her sincerity, but it set him on a wrong scent. There must be a rival; no doubt she must love some one else, or she would have given him a hearing. It was not possible that a girl would prefer poverty, solitude, and a position like that which she held at Mrs. Dunn's, to marriage with a good-looking, good-tempered fellow like himself, who would deny her nothing, and who intended to be the kindest husband in the world—if her heart was disengaged. Now poor Elsie was as heart-whole as a girl could be, but her manner of refusing made him think of a number of little signs which looked as if she were the victim of a hopeless attachment. Her sadness, her poetry, her little sighs, her diffidence, her pining away, were all due to the shameful conduct of one who in happier days had sought her hand, and had deserted her when fortune changed. His pity for her increased, but his love did not. If she had the bad taste to prefer a sad memory to a living lover, she might do so. He did not care to inquire as to the particulars of her unhappy love, even if he had thought it honourable to do so. The truth is, that Mr. Brandon did not love Elsie very much, though he thought he did so when he asked her. If she had said yes—if she had looked at him with grateful eyes, and told him that she would try to do her best to make him happy, his love would have become real, and would have surprised both himself and her by its strength and its steadiness. But he had never dreamed of such a thing as a refusal, and he had hastened his proposal, not from any feeling of insecurity, but from a desire to make Elsie very happy, and to do it as soon as possible.

But he had been refused—positively refused. Elsie might have said more of the obligation to him—might have been more grateful for the compliment which he had paid to her—Walter Brandon thought it would have been graceful to do so; but she said nothing of the kind. She sat in a rigid, painful silence till they reached the next station, where other passengers joined them, and put an end to a *tête-à-tête* which was rather awkward for both parties. She felt that she had given pain and mortification to a man who had meant well by her, and she did not dare to open her lips in consolation or

extenuation. She could not trust herself to speak; she would not venture to renew any solicitation. Forlorn and humbled as she was, she felt that she was in the greatest danger; that it was a tremendous bribe that was offered to her. She had Peggy's story ringing in her ears, and thought of Peggy's insight and Peggy's courage. The weak and facile Mr. Brandon was apt to fall in love, or to fancy that he did so, with any woman he came in much contact with, and she was as unsuitable for him, even more unsuitable, than Peggy was. The discipline of the last ten months had been too severe for her; it had crushed her spirit, and injured her health. She felt alarmed about her cough, and recently had been thinking more of the blessedness of an early death than the happiness of an early marriage. She felt herself to be sickly, low-spirited, wanting in energy, no fit companion for any colonist, and especially unfit to be the wife of a man of so little force of character. His offer appeared to her to be rash and imprudent. What did he know of her to warrant him in risking his life's happiness in such a way? But yet, though it was foolish in him to ask her, and though it would have been very wrong in her to accept of him, she was grateful, *so* grateful. How little Walter Brandon could guess how grateful she felt, when, after their journey was over, he took her cold, trembling hand, and placed her in the carriage that was to take them to Dr. Phillips's.

'You seem afraid of me, Miss Alice,' said he. 'Do not think that I will say another word on the subject, if it is painful to you. I know better than to persecute a woman with my addresses, if I see she does not like them. But do you *really* not like them?'

'No, I do not,' said Elsie, abruptly. 'You will see hundreds of other women who would suit you far better than I could do.'

'If you would only love me, I should be quite satisfied with your suiting me—but if you cannot, there need be no more said about it.'

Jane was engaged with her pupils when her sister arrived, and Mrs. Phillips, who had not been very regular in her attendance at school lately, stayed in the room this morning in order to see and remark upon Miss Melville's pretty sister. She could see little beauty in the sad face, with the weary look about the eyes, and the lines

round the mouth, that had been the result of Elsie's real experience of life. The figure, Mrs. Phillips confessed to her husband and to Mr. Brandon, was rather good, but wanted development; it was too much of the whipping-post order. The Misses Phillips said they really thought Jane the better looking of the two girls, for she had such a beautiful expression; while Mr. Phillips said that Elsie had fallen off sadly since he saw her in Edinburgh at the new year. She had struck him then as being very pretty, but he did not think so now, and, of course, in every other respect but personal appearance she could not be compared with her sister. Dr. Phillips said he must have her examined about her cough, for it should not be trifled with. He hoped that it had not been too long neglected. All these remarks, coming immediately after his refusal by the object of them, made Brandon somewhat reconciled to the circumstance, though if he had had a kinder answer, they would have made no difference in his feelings towards Elsie, but would probably have made him love her all the more.

When Harriett Phillips spoke in warm praise of Miss Melville's excellent understanding, and her fine, open, intelligent, expression of countenance, he thought he never saw her own countenance look so open or so attractive. He felt disposed to be consoled, and he was very sure that she was quite willing to console him.

Jane saw much amiss with her darling sister at the first glance, but hoped that the change, and Dr. Phillips's advice, which he had said would be at her service, and her own society, would benefit Elsie greatly.

Elsie did not muster courage to tell Jane of the incident of the railway journey till they had retired for the night.

'You know I could not answer otherwise, Jane; I did not love him; do not be angry with me,' said Elsie, apologetically.

'Angry with you my dear child! No, I honour you,' said Jane.

'You see Jane, I have been so unhappy, so ill, and so low-spirited, that I could easily have snatched at an escape from this dreary life, and said I would marry him; but he would have been so disappointed when he came to know me.'

'You do not love him now, Elsie, but could you not have learned to love him? It is not to be supposed that a girl has a ready-made attachment to be given to the first man who sees fit to ask her; she must take a little time.'

'But, Jane, though he has been very kind to us, you know—you remember Peggy, and what she said about him?'

Jane nodded assent.

'I know I have been rude about it. I ought to have said much that I felt, but when girls say such things they either give more pain afterwards, or get committed. Oh! Jane, tell me again that I have been right.'

'Right? yes,' said Jane, thoughtfully. 'Perhaps you ought to have a man of more fixed principles, if he could he had. But Elsie, my darling, it is not who we ought to have in the world, but who will have us; reflect that you may never have such an offer, or, indeed, another offer of any kind, again. I do not mean to bias your judgment, my own dear sister. Only think—he has, as you say, been very kind. He is not faultless; but who is? As for Peggy's story, that was many years ago; and, so far as I can judge from our friends here, he bears an excellent character. We should not condemn a man for life on account of something wrong done, or, as in this case, only purposed, when very young, and in circumstances of temptation which you and I, perhaps, can scarcely appreciate. He took Peggy's first answer in a right spirit, and you can see how he respects her. All I have seen of him since I came to London, has disposed me to think favourably of him. His temper is the finest in the world, I think.'

'Finer than Francis'?' said Elsie, who knew her sister's very great regard for her cousin, and never fancied she could think any man his superior in any point.

'Yes, sunnier than Francis'.'

'But he is not half so clever or so cultivated,' remonstrated Elsie.

'His cleverness lies in a different direction.'

'I think him inferior to Francis in every way,' said Elsie, 'and that weighed with me in giving my answer. You should think your husband the very best person you ever saw.'

'Perhaps when he is your husband you may, but I fancy that a girl who has a good father and brothers, does not at once give a man this preference when he asks for her hand. As I said before, he is not faultless, but would not life with him be preferable to life as it is for you now?'

'Don't, Jane; don't side with my cowardly self. To marry him, not loving him, as he perhaps deserves to be loved—not honouring him as I know I should honour my husband—but merely because I am miserable—how cruel to him, how base in myself! I know, besides, that he only pities me. Oh! Jane, if it were only life with you I could bear it better, but I am so weary of that workroom at Mrs. Dunn's, and of seeing people there whom I used to know, and getting a pitying sort of recognition from them. The very girls in the workroom pity me, and Peggy pities me, and even the children and their grandfather pity me. Oh! Jane, Jane, I am tired, tired to death of all this pity. Nobody ever thought of pitying you in your hardest times; you could hold up your head, and mine seems as if I never could raise it more. It must have been only pity in Mr. Brandon's case—what did he know of me to make him love me?'

'Have you forgotten that you are a very sweet, charming girl, Elsie—that your eyes are both bright and true—that your voice is pleasant, both in itself, and for the very pleasant things you can say? My darling, you must not lose all pride in yourself in this way. I wish half the offers of marriage that are made were founded on as much respect as Mr. Brandon felt for you. Though he talked slightingly of your work at Mrs. Dunn's, do not fancy but that he honours you for doing it. Besides, though he is not very literary, he may admire your talents. He meant to please you by speaking about your poems.'

'If he thinks I could be brilliant in society, or do him any credit in that way, he would be sure to be disappointed, and what a terrible thing it must be to disappoint a husband! It is not so much his deficiencies as my own, that weigh upon me. And, besides, Jane, I am not well; I really think I am going into a consumption—the sooner the better, if it were not for you, my dearest—and to marry

any one with such a conviction, would be positively wicked.'

'Oh, you are not going into a consumption, Elsie, I hope and believe,' said Jane, as cheerfully as she could. 'Your apprehension of such a thing shows that you are in no danger. You will see Dr. Phillips to-morrow morning, and get something to set you to rights. I am glad you are joining us here, for the sake of his advice. I like him so very much, and I think him clever—perhaps not naturally so acute as Dr. Vivian, but he has had a large practice so long, and so little wedded to routine, and so willing to accept of any new light that can be thrown on medicine, that his greater experience more than counterbalances his son's greater talent. And he is cheerful, too; the sound of his voice, and even of his step, is like a cordial to the sick and the depressed, I think. I know it does me a great deal of good, and it must benefit you.'

'You are very happy here; honoured, and useful, and well paid,' said Elsie.

'Oh! yes, dear; I have a great deal to be thankful for, and in time we will be able to be together always. In the meantime your holiday must be enjoyed to the utmost.'

So the sisters talked of their plans for the future, and of the routine of their past life, as cheerfully as they could, and tried to banish Mr. Brandon from their thoughts. Elsie was asleep first, and then Jane anxiously lay awake, weighing the probabilities about her health and her recovery, and also thinking with approval, but certainly with regret, of Elsie's conscientious refusal of so excellent an offer as she had that day received. Her own opinion of Mr. Brandon had risen since she had known him better, and she believed that Elsie would have suited him extremely well. She only hoped that he would not accept her sister's answer as final, at least, if Dr. Phillips pronounced favourably on the subject of her health.

V

ELSIE ACCEPTS OF A NEW SITUATION

When Dr. Phillips had asked Elsie a great number of questions on all sorts of subjects, that seemed but remotely connected with the cough that she was so alarmed about—had sounded her chest, and gone through the several forms of examination—

'Now,' said she, 'Doctor, tell me the truth; I am not at all afraid to hear it. I have no dread of death; indeed, I rather desire it than otherwise.'

'I am sorry to hear it, my dear girl; for I do not see any chance of it. There is nothing organic the matter with you—nothing whatever—only a nervous affection that a little care will overcome. You have been overworked and underfed. You have been out of doors only in the early morning and the late evening, and have scarcely seen the sun for months. You have had a great deal on your spirits, and been exceedingly dull. You have missed your excellent sister, and I do not wonder at it. It would have been a miracle if you could have kept your health this unkindly spring, with all these drawbacks. But you have nothing whatever alarming in your case.'

'My dear Miss Meville,' continued he, turning to Jane, 'I assure you that your sister only wants what she has come to England to

obtain—change, cheerful society, sunshine, and generous diet—to restore her to perfect health.'

Elsie gave one sigh at this verdict.

'Do not think me ungrateful, Dr. Phillips; I should be thankful to be restored to health; but life has been so hard for me lately, that I felt almost glad to think that, without any fault of my own, God was going to take me away, and that Jane would join me by and by, when her work was done. She is fit for the work she has got to do, and I appear to be so unfit for it. I suppose we ought to love life—'

'It is a sign that one is out of health when one does not,' said Dr. Phillips. 'Your depression of spirits is more physical than mental; but then it reacts upon your health. You used to be cheerful before you left that place—what do you call it?—where my old friend Hogarth brought you up.'

'Yes, quite cheerful,' said Elsie; 'but things have gone very differently with me since.'

'Well, you must regain your old spirits, if possible; and in the meantime, get on your bonnet and have a little drive with me while Miss Melville is busy with her pupils. If you won't mind a few stoppages, we will have a pleasant round, through as pretty a part of the country as England can boast of.'

Jane asked privately for Dr. Phillips's opinion, being sure that he gave Elsie his brightest view of her case.

'There is nothing positively wrong with her at present, Miss Melville; but she has got into such a low tone of health that she needs care. She must never return to such a life as she has had lately; she must have a lighter employment, more open air, and better food.'

'It is so difficult,' said Jane, 'to get employment. I am sure there are a thousand chances against my finding such an excellent situation as I have with Mrs. Phillips.'

'And a thousand chances against their meeting with such an excellent governess and housekeeper. The pleasure is mutual, I am sure. I must see what your sister is fit for, when she is a little stronger.'

Both Elsie and Jane saw at once that Mr. Brandon was disposed to take Elsie's rejection as a final decision, and that he would have no difficulty in transferring his attentions, if not his affections to Miss Harriett Phillips. Elsie felt that she could not have been much admired or loved, when he could so soon attach himself to a woman so very different from herself. Here it certainly might be love without any mixture of pity. He made himself very agreeable, and Miss Harriett was not so much flattered as gratified. All his homage was received by her as her due; there were no quick flushes of pleasure or surprise at any little mark of kindness or attention; no disclaiming of any compliment which was paid her as exaggerated or undeserved; the smile of perfect self-complacency sat on her face, and gave ease to her every action and every speech. She never hesitated in giving her opinion; she never qualified or withdrew it when given. She knew herself to be perfectly well-informed and perfectly well-bred. She felt herself to be Mr. Brandon's superior in every point—in natural ability, in education, in acquired manner, in social position, and, of course, in moral character also, for she had no faith in the goodness of the other sex. She saw many of their faults, and guessed at many more, and she did not see or understand their virtues; and Brandon made no pretence to being particularly good, and spoke slightingly of her favourite clergyman, who was rather too High Church in his notions to please the latitudinarian ideas of an Australian bushman. Her connection with the county Stanleys gave her a prestige that Mr. Brandon never could have, for his family were only middle-class people, not at all intellectual or aristocratic. Her brother was astonished to see how much more Georgiana and Harriett spoke of their relations by the mother's side, who had never done anything for them, than those good uncles and aunts Phillipses, who had invited them for the holidays, and given them toys and books without number; but all his laughing at his sisters could not alter their views, and his own wife sided with the ladies, and was very proud of her husband's aristocratic name and relations, though she had none of her own.

Though in all these respects Harriett Phillips was so much Mr. Brandon's superior, she was disposed to accept of him when he asked her, as he was sure to do. It was so difficult for her to meet with her equal, either social, intellectual, or moral; and a husband, even though an Australian, began to be looked upon as a desirable thing at her time of life. And though Brandon was not fascinated by her, though he was not interested in her, though he felt no thrill in touching her hand, no exquisite delight in listening to her voice or her singing, he began to feel that this was to be his fate, and that the quiet, pale girl who had refused him would not make so suitable a wife for him as Harriett Phillips, after all.

He was somewhat astonished, however, when he heard from this last-named lady, about a week after Elsie Melville's arrival, that her sister-in-law had engaged her services as lady's-maid. A lady's-maid was what Mrs. Phillips had long desired to have, and now, when she saw Elsie's excellent taste, both in dressmaking and millinery, she thought that with a few lessons in hair-dressing she might suit her very nicely, and it would be quite a boon to the poor girl, whom Dr. Phillips had forbidden to return to her situation in Edinburgh. Mr. Phillips, though he thought that a lady's-maid was rather beyond his circumstances and his wife's sphere, hoped such good things from her associating constantly with two such women as Jane and Elsie Melville, that he readily gave his consent. Elsie as readily agreed to serve in this inferior capacity. The pleasure of being near her sister was not to be refused on account of being so far subordinated to her. She was deeply impressed with her own inferiority, and fell into her place at once.

Harriett Phillips could not help a slight sneer at her sister-in-law's assumption in this new step towards gentility; but as she was going to London with the family, she had no doubt that Elsie would be glad to be of service to her too, as she appeared to be very good-natured, and willing to oblige a family who had been so very kind to her sister and herself. There were so many things that were secured for Elsie by this arrangement which were imperatively necessary for her health, that Jane submitted to it as the best possible under the

circumstances, though she feared that Mrs. Phillips would show to Elsie the caprice and bad temper which she dared not show to herself. And in this she was not mistaken; for Elsie was so yielding and so diffident, that her new mistress exercised a great deal of real tyranny over her, varied by fitful acts of liberality and kindness. Peggy Walker opened her eyes very wide when she heard of both the young ladies, whom she had been accustomed to look up to, being dependent in this way on Mrs. Phillips, whom she had always looked down upon; but she knew that the sisters were together, and that that was a happiness to both that outweighed many other drawbacks. She herself was very much engrossed with the care of grandfather, who, as well as Elsie, had felt the ungenial spring very trying, and who did not seem to rally as the season advanced; so she was thankful that Elsie was otherwise bestowed than in her house of sickness.

Dr. Phillips had the satisfaction of seeing a considerable improvement in Elsie before she left Derbyshire, and used to have her company in his morning drives to visit his patients, when her pleasant conversation and winning manner made him ere long prefer her to her graver and less pliant sister. He missed both the girls when they went to London, and even Dr. Vivian paid Jane the compliment of regretting her society a little for a week.

VI

A LETTER FROM AUSTRALIA FOR FRANCIS, WHICH CAUSES SURPRISE IN AN UNEXPECTED QUARTER

A few weeks after the return of Mr. Phillips with his family, his sister Harriett, and our friends Jane and Elsie to London, where the courtship, or rather dangling, of Mr. Brandon was going on in the same uninteresting manner, but with no apparent jar to prevent its leading to matrimony at last, Jane was surprised by the sight of her cousin Francis, who said he had come to the metropolis, chiefly for the purpose of seeing her.

'I called at Peggy Walker's, before I left Scotland;' said Francis, 'but the family write to you so frequently that I suppose you know all the news. The old man is looking very ill, however; I was quite struck by the change in his appearance. I do not think that situation healthy; I feel very glad you and Elsie have both left it. How is Elsie getting on with Mrs. Phillips?'

'Tolerably—only tolerably. But her health is better—decidedly better.'

'And you, Jane, you are looking much better than when I saw you in Edinburgh last.'

'You have not written to me at such length about your cottages and your allotments as I expected, Francis. I suppose you are too busy to have time to write, but now you have come; we can talk over all these matters.'

It had not been voluntarily, or without a great effort, that Francis had so much slackened his close correspondence with Jane; but her letters were so cheerful, she seemed so busy and hopeful, she saw so many people, and appeared to be so much appreciated by Mr. Phillips and by all his family, that he had no hope of her allowing him to make the sacrifice he longed to make, and he thought he must try to accustom himself to look on her as lost to him.

'I have been busy,' said he, 'but I do not attempt to excuse myself by such a reason. I have not given you answers at all worthy of your letters.'

'I have always thought that it is considered the great art in a gentleman's letter that he should put a great deal of matter in few words, while a lady piques herself on making an excellent letter out of nothing. If your letters were shorter than mine, they were not, on that account, unsatisfactory,' said Jane.

'Your observation of character and manners is so much more acute than mine, that you can see and hear nothing which you cannot photograph faithfully, and make an interesting picture of, and you seem to have interesting people to write about,' said Francis.

'I do not think that if I had been at Cross Hall, and you in London, my letters would have been the longest. Our old neighbours were very uninteresting—do you not find them so?'

'All except Miss Thomson, whose acquaintance I have recently made, and who has enough of originality and goodness about her to give some salt to the district. She is much interested in both of you; especially in Elsie, whom she saw at Mrs. Dunn's, and got to make something for her, which has given the greatest satisfaction.'

'I must tell this to Elsie,' said Jane; 'she needs a little praise, and it does her good.'

'But I want first to consult you about a letter I received the day before I left home,' said Francis. This was his excuse for exposing himself to Jane's influence again. The thing might have been done by letter, but he scarcely though it could be so well done; so he had first seen Mr. McFarlane in Edinburgh, and then hastened to

London to ask the advice of the dearest friend he had in the world on the subject of this ill-written and ill-expressed letter.

It ran as follows:

'Melbourne, 20th April, 185—.

'My Dear Son Frank,

'I have heard that you are come into the property at last. I knew he could not keep it from you, though he wanted to, for you was the hair, and had the rights to get it. I hope you will not forget a mother that has always remembered you, though I was forced to part from you when you was very little, so you will scarce know my face again. I would not stand in your light, and it has turned out all right for you.

'I had an allowance of a hundred and fifty pounds a year from him as long as he lived, and when it stopped I made some inquiry, and found that you had got Cross Hall and all that he had. I think that I should have got some notise of his being dead, but I am quite used to being neglected. I hope you will not let me be any poorer, but the contrary, for I have been a better mother to you than many a one as makes more fuss. It was him as would not let me keep you, and drove me away to Australia. I would come to see you now that he is out of the way, but I cannot afford the expense. If I had not met with shuch ungrateful conduct from them as ought to have provided for me, I might have been rich enuf; but it is a bad world, and the longer I live, I see that it gets worse and worse. It will be for your advantage to keep friendly with me, and at any rate you will do as much as your father did, which was little enuf, God knows. But I expect as the baby that I loved so dear will be a good kind son to me now you have come into the property.

'Address to Mrs. Peck, care of Henry Talbot, Esq., solicitor, — Street, Melbourne. I was not allowed to keep my own name or to take his, and so everybody knows me by the name of Mrs. Peck, but I am really and truly your afexionate mother.

'Elizabeth Hogarth.'

'P.S. Send me an answer and a remittance by the first mail. I am very badly off and need money.'

Jane read this letter twice over, and looked at the address and the postmark carefully.

'What do you think of it?' said he, anxiously.

'Have you asked Mr. McFarlane if he thinks this letter genuine?'

'He never saw any of Elizabeth Hogarth's writing. Any communication which my father received from her, he must have destroyed at once.'

'Did he know anything of the £150 a year?'

'He thought it probable some money was paid to keep her at a distance, but did not know anything as to how much it was, or when it was sent.'

'Is there any trace in the banking transactions of my uncle of such a payment being remitted regularly to Australia?'

'I can see nothing of the kind. I looked over some old books with that intention, but your uncle's books were not by any means so minute and methodical as yours. He drew large sums and did not record how he spent them, whereas your housekeeping books are models of accurate accounts. I hope Mr. Phillips appreciates your talents in this line?'

'Quite sufficently, I assure you. But with regard to this letter—what was Mr. McFarlane's advice on the subject?' asked Jane.

'To take no notice whatever of it; for that it would only bring trouble and discredit on me if she was no impostor, and be a very foolish thing if she was. He says that he had mentioned to my father, when he was making his will, that in all probability the widow, if left out of the will, would come upon the heir, and extort something very handsome from him; but that Mr. Hogarth had said sternly that she could not do it, for she had not a scrap of evidence that she dared bring forward to prove that she had ever been his wife. That he had no objection to provide handsomely for me, for I had proved that I was worthy of it; but for her, she had been a thorn in his side all his life; that he had done all for her that

he meant to do, and all that she expected him to do. This made Mr. McFarlane think that he had given her a sum of money to get rid of her claims, and not a yearly allowance. She had certainly parted with me for money, and took no further care for my happiness. Mr. McFarlane never told me this before, but he wished to put me on my guard about this letter.'

'My uncle, certainly, must have been a good deal excited when he made his will,' said Jane.

'Mr. McFarlane says he certainly was so, and has no doubt he would have altered it had he lived a little longer—provided you had not married Mr. Dalzell, which was his great fear for you.'

'Do you feel disposed, then, to answer this letter, or to prosecute any inquiries?'

'The whole affair is full of such unmitigated bitterness,' said Francis, 'that I shrink from stirring it up; but yet I certainly ought to know if this woman is my mother or not. Should not I, Jane? I rely on your judgment.'

'It is your affair, Francis, not mine. I can scarcely dare to advise.'

'What would you do under such circumstances?'

'I cannot tell what, with your character, I would do under such circumstances,' said Jane.

'But with your character, which is a thousand times better than mine, my dear Jane? Only think for me. Things have been taken so much out of my hands by this detestable will, that I seem to lose the power of judging altogether on any matter that relates to it. I cannot aid when I most wish to do it. My father did not positively forbid me to assist my mother. I suppose, if he had done so, it would have raised as vehement a desire to that course of action as I now feel to oppose all his other prohibitions.'

The expression of Francis' face was earnest—almost impassioned—as it turned towards Jane. She felt now that there was a reason for his apparent coolness—a reason that made her heart beat fast and her eyes fill. She did not speak for a few moments till she felt that her voice would not betray her, and then said:

'Since you ask my advice, I will give it, such as it is. I think I

should in your circumstances make some inquiries; and you have come to the place where you are most likely to have them answered. I dare say Mr. Phillips knows Mr. Talbot, for I have heard his name in conversation; and if you have no objections to telling him about this letter, he could write—or, better still, Mr. Brandon, who talks of returning very soon, could make personal inquiries about this Mrs. Peck. It is quite possible she may be an impostor; for a good deal has been said in the newspapers about your inheriting Cross Hall, and she evidently has not got the right account of the story. She supposes you get it as heir-at-law, and not by will. It is an easy way of extorting money, to give out that one is a near relation of yours, and especially one of whom you have cause to be ashamed. Her story of a yearly allowance does not agree with Mr. McFarlane's impression either; but that may be policy—not positive unfounded fabrication. The orthography of this letter is not good; but the expressions are more like vulgar English than Scotch. Your mother's name was Scotch; and it was, at all events, a Scotch marriage. Will you speak to Mr. Phillips on this subject. He is kind, sensible, and discreet.'

'Yes, I will. You think I ought to do so?'

'He is at home just now. Suppose I ask him to come to see you?'

Francis agreed, and was pleased with the kind reception which Jane's employer gave to him, as her cousin. He praised Miss Melville very highly, and said that in every point of view she was a treasure in his house. He then gave slighter praise to Elsie; but still spoke very feelingly of the position of both girls.

After a few such remarks, Francis asked Mr. Phillips if he knew Mr. Talbot, a solicitor in Melbourne.

'Yes, by sight and by reputation very well; but he was not a personal acquaintance of mine. Mr. Brandon was a client of his, and so was Peggy Walker; they could give you any information about him you might require.'

'I suppose it is of no use asking you such a question—but do you know anything of a woman called Mrs. Peck—Elizabeth Peck, a client of —?'

The expression of Mr. Phillips's face stopped Francis' hesitating disclosure.

'Have nothing to do with her,' said he—'a bad one, if ever there was one on this earth. Good Heavens! what am I to hear next?'

'She says she is my mother,' said Francis.

'Perhaps it is not the same woman,' said Mr. Phillips. 'Your mother! that must be a very old story; you look to be forty, or thereabouts. It must be a different person.'

The trouble of Mr. Phillips's manner was undergoing some improvement. He walked across the room two or three times, and then said more steadily:

'Has she written to you? Would you let me see the handwriting?' The address was in a different hand from the letter itself, so Francis could not but show Mr. Phillips the body of the letter.

'May I read it? It is a delicate matter, I know; but I will be secret—secret as the grave.'

Mr. Hogarth assented, and Mr. Phillips read the letter through, and then returned it.

'She says she is your mother, and for this very reason I believe she is not, for if ever there was a woman possessed with the spirit of falsehood, she is that woman. Mr. Hogarth, take no notice of her—do not answer her letter—send her no money; she is not so poor as she represents herself to be. I am glad you asked me about her, and no one else.'

'Who is she? what is she?' was rising to Francis' lips, but the sight of Mr. Phillips's evident suffering checked his questions. After a short pause, he said that Miss Melville had advised him to consult Mr. Phillips.

'Good God! did you say anything about this to Miss Melville?' said Mr. Phillips.

'Yes, I did! I came to consult her on the letter, but it will go no further; let us call her back. Where is she?' said Francis.

'In the drawing-room,' said Mr. Phillips, ringing the bell violently, 'with Mrs. Phillips and Harriett, and Brandon, who has just come in. Alice is out on some errand, I believe; so that Miss

Melville cannot speak to her, and she surely will not speak on your private matters to my wife and sister.'

Jane was soon brought back to the breakfast-room, in which she had left her cousin with Mr. Phillips, and was surprised at the disturbed looks of both gentlemen.

'Mr. Hogarth has asked me about a person in Melbourne, whom I know to be an arrant cheat and liar. Her assertions in this letter are, no doubt, false; it is in keeping with her character that they should be so. He will take no further notice of the matter; and I hope and trust that her name will never pass your lips even to your sister, while under my roof, or even after you have left it. Mr. Hogarth, you will do us the honour to dine with us to-morrow, at half past six? Mrs. Phillips and I will be most happy to see you'—and so saying Mr. Phillips hurriedly left the room, leaving Jane and Francis in the greatest bewilderment.

'I am not so sure that this Mrs. Peck is not my mother, for Mr. Phillips's opinion of her is exactly the same as my father's; but I think I will inquire no further. If inquiry is to grieve and annoy the best friend you have ever had, I will ask no questions. She may write again when she finds she gets no answer, and bring forward something more tangible than these vague allegations. But is this Mr. Phillips a passionate or vindicitive man?'

'Quite the contrary. I never saw him agitated in this way before. He is of a remarkably easy temper—most indulgent to those around him.'

'He is kind both to you and to Elsie?'

'Very kind indeed, and very considerate. If Mrs. Phillips were as much so, we would both be very comfortable indeed,' said Jane.

'Does she show you any temper?' asked Francis.

'No, she dares not do it; for I am useful, and save her much trouble, and I have so much confidence in myself that I will not be interfered with; but poor Elsie is so diffident, so humble, so anxious to please, that she is constantly imposed on by an ignorant, thoughtless woman. Every one imposes on Elsie. Miss Phillips is inconsiderate, too, though she should know better. The servants

impose on her, and the children, too—though she is so fond of the children, that I think on the whole they do her good.'

'Do not you find that Elsie being here in such a capacity makes your superintendence of the servants more difficult?' asked Francis.

'Yes; I require to be more circumspect and more firm; but my life is quite easy, compared to hers. If I could only restore Elsie to that moderately good opinion which she used to have of herself in her more prosperous days, a great grief would be taken off my heart. I am the strongest, why should not I have the most to bear?'

'Have you tried her poems in London personally?'

'I have, but without success, and she has quite lost the wish to have them published. Your good opinion of her verses only gave her a little temporary encouragement.'

'She writes none now, I suppose?'

'She has no time even if she had the inclination. Mrs. and Miss Phillips keep her so busy that I have difficulty in getting her out in the middle of the day to join me and the children in our walk or drive; but that the doctor insisted on as absolutely necessary, and I will not allow her to be deprived of it. He took quite a fancy to Elsie, and showed her much kindness. You ought to go to see him for your father's sake. But as to Elsie's poetry, she does nothing in this way except improvising to the children in the evening, as she is sitting at work. When they found out that she could, as they said, 'make verses up out of her own head,' they think all their stories should be transferred into ballads, and either said or sung to them. They are honest in their admiration of the talent, but rather exacting in their demands for its exercise; on the whole, I think, however, that it does her good, and I know the children are fonder of her than of me. I am so glad to see her preferred.'

'Do you see much of Mr. Brandon? Could not he restore your sister to the self-appreciation so essential to happiness and contentment?'

Jane shook her head. 'He is devoting himself to Miss Phillips, and Elsie scarcely ever sees him.'

'One consequence of her taking this situation,' said Francis,

somewhat impatiently. 'I fancy he admired her when I saw him at Peggy Walker's, months ago, and that he only wanted to be more in her society to have the impression deepened. Did you not think so?'

'His admiration went a little way, but not far,' said Jane.

'Not so far as to lead to a proposal?' said Francis.

'People are generally far gone before they reach that point,' said Jane, hoping to escape thus from a rather searching question; but a look from Francis, very sad, yet very pleasing to herself, made her change the subject altogether. She liked to believe that she was very dear to him; they could never marry; there was far too much to forbid it—duty, interest, near relationship. Francis' life and career were too important to be tacked to any woman's apron-strings, even though that woman was herself, and the plans she had so much delighted in she could see worthily carried out. She would not be the hindrance and stumbling-block to any good life, and least of all to his. But, until he met with a woman to be his wife and helpmate, she rejoiced to feel that she was first in his heart. When that event took place, as it ought to do before long, she would of course retire to a second and inferior position; but it was something to rest in with pleasure, that if it had been right and expedient, she would never have been displaced.

Sometimes mere possibilities—thoughts of what might have been—give very precious memories to cheerful tempers; while to those who are of a sad nature, they only enhance the gloominess of the present. Jane was not so cowardly as to let Francis see that she regretted anything for herself, and she proceeded to tell of her handsome salary, and how small her expenses had been, so that she was saving money; that Alice's salary would be equal at least to what she had at Mrs. Dunn's; and that the twenty-four pounds a year which he was allowed to give them was added to their savings; so that they were really making up a little hoard to begin business with Peggy when she left Scotland for Melbourne. She spoke of her money matters with frankness and confidence, and her cousin could not but see that she had now reasonable hope of prosperity.

They had had a very long conversation before Elsie came in. She

had had a number of troublesome commissions to execute, and had been detained beyond expectation, but had acquitted herself to Mrs. Phillips's satisfaction, and now came in with a little glow of pleasure on her face to meet her cousin, to feel the warmth of his affectionate greeting, to have a little talk about books and poetry, to refresh her for her monotonous and uninteresting daily work. Nothing was said about the letter Francis had received, and Jane and he seemed desirous to banish it from their memory.

VII

HARRIETT PHILLIPS DOES A LITTLE BIT OF SHOPPING, WHICH IS SOMEWHAT FATAL TO HER PROJECTS

Among other purchases which Elsie had made on the day of Francis' arrival, were the materials for a bonnet for Mrs. Phillips, which she had chosen, and which, as she was busily engaged in making up, so much excited Harriett's admiration, that she was seized with a desire to have one like it immediately, only that hers must be of a different colour, and a little modified in shape, to suit her different complexion and contour of face. On the following morning, as she was going out shopping herself, she asked Elsie to accompany her, to give her the benefit of her taste on this as well as some other purchases. Mr. Brandon was asked if he was not going down Regent Street? He said he was, and he would be very happy to go with Miss Phillips—as he had nothing particular to do, and Phillips was out, and Jane had the children at their lessons, and he did not find it amusing to be left *tête-à-tête* with Mrs. Phillips.

Miss Harriett was quite unaware of her own weakness, or she never would have asked a lover to go with her in a draper's shop. Elsie had seen something of Mrs. Phillips's unreasonableness and unscrupulousness, but this was the first time she had been with her sister-in-law, and she did not expect from a young lady of such professed good principles, and good-nature, such an utter

abnegation of these excellent qualities in dealing with tradespeople. She blushed for her companion, who did not blush for herself. She herself chose quickly, with the certain judgment of a fine taste and a practised eye; but what she fixed on as most suitable for Miss Phillips's complexion and style, was not always of a suitable price. When driven from the expensive to something cheaper, then it was shabby and not fit to wear. Miss Phillips had come out determined to get as good things as possible, and to pay as small a price as possible for them; she would not be put off with an inferior article, and yet she was not willing to give the value of a superior. Elsie, who had herself waited on ladies of this character, and felt her body ache all over from the fatigue of being civil to them, was sorry for the shopmen, who fetched out box after box, and displayed article after article, without anything being exactly the thing which their customer wanted; while Walter Brandon stood beside the two ladies, finding it harder than ever to feel sentimental about Harriett Phillips.

Leigh Hunt recommends men to choose their wives in drapers' shops; for if a woman is conscientious, reasonable, and expeditious there, he thinks a man may be sure she will be fit for all the duties of life. But perhaps his test is too severe for general use, for many of the best of wives and mothers, the kindest of friends, and the most pious of Christians, are very far from appearing amiable under circumstances of such great temptation. The obsequious manners of British shopmen, who never show any spirit or any resentment, tend to lull conscience, while the strife between the desire for display and style, and the love of money, makes many women at once fastidious and unscrupulous. To Brandon, Harriett Phillips's conduct appeared ill-bred and mean; he could not help contrasting her with Elsie Melvlle, and acknowledging that the latter was the real gentlewoman. He began also to observe a certain imperiousness in Harriett's manner to Elsie herself, which struck him as being particularly ungraceful, and the old pity began to re-awake the old love. He had sometimes wished to speak to Alice just a few words to show that he had not been offended or piqued at her

refusal, but never had had any opportunity, and on this occasion Miss Harriett did not seem disposed to give him any.

At last, after being in several shops, and turning over innumerable boxes of ribbons, laces, blondes, flowers, &c., all was purchased that was required, and even Miss Phillips was perfectly satisfied with the selection she had made.

'Oh, dear!' said she, looking at her watch, 'how late it is! I quite intended to be in time for luncheon, for we started so early. Morning is always the best time for shopping—at least, I find I am better attended to then. But we are too late, and Mrs. Phillips will not wait for us. We had better have something to eat here, for I am very hungry—so, Mr. Brandon, I trust you to find some place where we can make a comfortable luncheon; I have no doubt you know the best restaurateur, and afterwards you will get us a cab to go home in. I like to make gentlemen useful when I take them shopping with me.'

'I am quite at your service,' said Brandon, 'for, as I said before, I have nothing particular to do.'

'That is taking all the grace out of your gallantry,' said Miss Phillips, 'but if you acquit yourself well, I will forgive you that impolite speech.'

Brandon did as he was desired—took the ladies to a fashionable restaurateur's, asked them what they would like, and ordered and paid for a very good and very expensive luncheon. Then he brought a cab, and accompanied them home.

'I really wish my brother could keep a carriage of his own,' said Miss Phillips. 'That is one of the few extravagances I quite sympathize with Mrs. Phillips in her desire for. It is so disagreeable to have to trust to these hired conveyances. One does not know who may have been in them before, and might catch fever or something of that kind.'

'Perhaps one might,' said Brandon, 'though it never entered my head to think of such disagreeable things. But then I have never been accustomed to ride in a carriage of my own. Riding on horseback was my only means of locomotion at Barragong; and

Melbourne, up to this time, has no such luxury for ordinary people as a hackney-coach stand, so that I cannot help being surprised at the cheapness and convenience of cabbing it in London. Whereas both of you ladies have been accustomed to private carriages, and must feel this very inferior.'

'Oh, Alice! by the by, so you were, I suppose,' said Miss Phillips.

'I preferred riding on horseback in those days,' said Elsie; 'but I think the drives with Dr. Phillips, lately, were the most delightful things I ever had in my life. After being quite debarred from anything but walking so long, I feel this hackney-coach really luxurious, I assure you.'

'The drives in Derbyshire did you good, Miss Alice; you are looking better than when you came down,' said Mr. Brandon.

'Oh! much better,' said Miss Phillips. 'Papa said it was all nonsense her being so alarmed about her health; but, both she and Miss Melville were a little frightened—London suits her better than Edinburgh. I have not heard you cough, Alice, for a week or more.'

'Yes, my cough is quite gone,' said Elsie; 'and I have much better spirits.'

'But, by the by,' said Miss Phillips, 'I really want my bonnet to go out with to-morrow. Your London smoke is dreadfully destructive. I had no idea that mine was so bad till I put it on this bright day, and really it looks too shabby to wear, though I had intended to make it last another month. At home it would have looked better after three months' wear than it does after three weeks here. You know, Mrs. Phillips promised you should have it ready for me to go to the exhibition of pictures to-morrow, by middle day,' continued she.

'I fear,' said Alice, 'that I cannot get it done in time, for we have been so much longer in Regent Street than I expected, and it will be nearly dinner-time before we get home; and Mr. Phillips insists, that as my cousin Francis is to dine with you to-day, I should be of the party.'

'Indeed!' said Harriett, 'and so you cannot finish my bonnet in time—it is a great disappointment to me.'

'Mr. Phillips would not allow me to refuse, I know; and Jane, too, is anxious for me to have a talk with Francis.'

'And you would like it yourself, too?' said Mr. Brandon.

'Yes, very much indeed,' said Elsie, honestly.

'I will be gald to have the chance of seeing you. By the by, Phillips forgot to ask me; but I will forgive him, and invite myself.'

'Oh! you need not stand on ceremony,' said Harriett; 'you are in the habit of coming in and going out of the house like one of ourselves; but really, Alice, are you sure you could not do my bonnet for me? There is so little work on the bonnets now-a-days, and you might have it done by two o'clock. Is not that the hour you appointed, Mr. Brandon?'

'Yes; or say half-past,' said Brandon.

'Well, by half-past two. I am sure you have made bonnets in a greater hurry at your Edinburgh house of business often enough. I have seen how very quick you are. I quite wondered at the rapidity with which you got on with Mrs. Phillips's.'

'But that is not finished,' said Elsie, 'and I promised it for the same hour to go to the Exhibition. I am very sorry, indeed, Miss Phillips; but, unless you can induce Mr. Phillips to excuse my appearance at dinner, I cannot possibly do it for you.'

'Oh! very well,' said Harriett, coldly; 'I have a bonnet to wear, though it really is rather shabby; and Mrs. Phillips takes such pains to have everything fresh and fashionable, that I am sadly thrown into the shade. What a sum of money she contrives to spend every year on herself! but my brother is so exceedingly easy and indulgent, he denies her nothing. Don't you think her dreadfully extravagant, Mr. Brandon? I should be ashamed to spend money as thoughtlessly as she does. She does not care what she pays for a thing if it takes her fancy. Now, my bonnet will not cost two-thirds of what hers has done, and it will look quite as pretty, will it not, Alice?'

'A little different in style, but quite as well,' said Elsie.

'You see, Mr. Brandon, that if I have seemed to take a great deal of trouble over my purchases, it has been for some purpose. One

cannot economize without some thought being bestowed upon such things as these.'

Mr. Brandon could not but assent, but the act of politeness cost him an effort.

'Then you come to dine with us to-day, to meet this Mr. Hogarth? Do you know, I have a great curiosity to see him. His father and papa being such old friends, long ago, gives me quite an interest in him; and the extraordinary story of his succession to his Scotch property is so romantic. What is he like—is he presentable?'

'He was quite the rage in Edinburgh when I was there, about the new year—a reading man, and a man of considerable taste—just your sort, in fact. He is a great friend of Miss Melville's, though I fancy, Miss Alice, that you do not care so much for him.'

'I like him very much indeed, though I was longer in doing him justice than Jane was. The circumstances of our first introduction were very painful,' said Elsie.

'If he is a friend of your sister's, that is quite enough for me,' said Harriett. 'I do not think I ever met with any one so congenial to my tastes as Miss Melville is. Ladies are so superficial now-a-days; their education is all for show, and nothing solid or thorough in it. My dear father was so careful to give *us* a thoroughly good education. It is very seldom that we meet with any one so well grounded as Miss Melville is. It is a good thing for my nieces that Stanley met with her. Your uncle *must* have meant that you should teach, Alice.'

'Did Dr. Phillips mean that you should teach?' said Brandon, bluntly.

'No, no, certainly; but Miss Melville has learned so much that is quite valueless except in teaching—oh! a great many things quite out of the way; but I meant that the ground-work was the same. Poor Alice! all this odd training was thrown away on you.'

'Not thrown away,' said Brandon, firmly. 'If it were not for Miss Alice's diffidence she would soon let you know how much she has profited by it. You should hear Peggy Walker on that subject.'

'I am quite charmed with the estimation in which both you and

my brother hold that wonderful woman,' said Miss Harriett, consdescendingly. 'Stanley is quite enthusiastic about Peggy.'

'And so am I, and with as good reason. Your brother owes her much, but I think I owe her more.'

'More!' said Harriett; 'oh! I see. Peggy nursed and saved the lives of Emily and little Harry, and perhaps of Mrs. Phillips, too, and my brother is greatly indebted to her; but I suppose she nursed your precious self through an illness all but mortal, so you are still more grateful. I know that you gentlemen think a great deal of number one. I understand the thing clearly.'

Walter Brandon paused a minute. 'No, it is not that, Miss Phillips; but Peggy raised my opinion of all women. Her courage, her devotion, her self-denial, and her truthfulness made me think more highly of all her sex; and if ever I am blessed with a wife she will have cause to cherish the memory of that homely Scotchwoman.'

'To think that a gentleman who had a mother and sisters, should need such a lesson from a woman like Peggy,' said Harriett, incredulously.

'One's mother and sisters are always looked on as exceptional people—placed like saints in a consecrated shrine,' said Brandon; 'but here was a woman with no particularly careful training or education, battling with the world alone and unprotected, and doing always the right thing at the right time, and in the right way—and truly she has her reward. Those orphan children will rise up and call her blessed, and if she has no husband to do it, her own works will praise her in the gates.'

'I did not think that you knew as much of your Bible as to be able to make so long a quotation,' said Miss Phillips, who could not understand or sympathize with Brandon's enthusiasm; but Elsie fully appreciated this generous and well-deserved tribute to Peggy's character. She saw now that she had been too rash in her rejection of her only lover. It was only now that she had lost him for ever that she had discovered the real goodness of his character; but she was pleased, very much pleased to find out that Peggy's conduct had

been understood and admired by Mr. Brandon, and had done him such excellent service. To think him worthy was delightful, even though she should never see anything more of him henceforward. The colour rose to her cheek and the lustre to her eye, and when Brandon's glance met her bright face, he could not help confessing that she was very pretty, let the Phillipses say what they pleased, and the idea of having a little conversation with her in the evening was much more agreeable to him than Harriett would have at all approved of.

VIII

FRANCIS MAKES A FAVOURABLE IMPRESSION ON HARRIETT PHILLIPS

With all Harriett Phillips's success in society she had never had much admiration from the other sex. This she did not attribute so much to anything as to her own superiority; it really wanted a great deal of courage for an average mortal to propose to her. Her unconscious egotism had something rather grand in it; it was rarely obtrusive, but it was always there. Her mind was naturally a vigorous one, but it had moved in a narrow channel, and whatever was out of her own groove, she ignored. She appreciated whatever Jane Melville knew that she was herself acquainted with, but whatever she—Harriett Phillips—was ignorant of, must be valueless. Now a comfortable opinion of oneself is not at all a disagreeable thing for the possessor, and kept within due bounds it is also a pleasant thing to one's friends and acquaintances. Brandon had been disposed to take Harriett Phillips at her own valuation, and to consider her very superior to himself in many things; while she liked him, for his attentions gave her importance; and though he wearied her sometimes, she could make up her mind to pass her life with him without any feeling of its being a great sacrifice. But he must stay in England; all his talk of returning to Victoria was only talk; her influence would be quite sufficient to induce him to

do that. Though her heart was, in this lukewarm way, given to Mr. Brandon, she had a great curiosity to see this Mr. Hogarth, whom Brandon had called, in his rather vulgar colonial phraseology, 'just her sort'. She laid herself out to please the new comer; and Brandon was disposed to take offence—and did so. The events of the morning had made an impression on him; but if she had possessed the tact which sympathy and imagination alone can give, she might have appeased him, and brought him back to his allegiance. She did not guess where the shoe pinched, and she still further estranged the lover she had been secure of. She was charmed at the idea of making him a little jealous; it was the first opportunity she had ever had of flirting with another person in his presence, and the flirtation was carried on in such a sensible way that there was not a word said he had a right to be offended with. She only talked of things about which Brandon knew very little, and Mr. Hogarth a great deal, and she thought she was convicing both gentlemen of her great conversational powers. It was really time Brandon should be brought to the point, and this was the way to do it. While Brandon felt the chains not of love, but of habit, dropping off him, and wished that Elsie Melville was beside him, and not sitting between her cousin and another Australian, who was talking to her vigorously on his favourite subject of spirit-rapping and table-turning, and she was listening so patiently, and making little smart speeches—he could tell quite well by the expression of her eyes, though he could not hear the low sweet voice distinctly enough to tell exactly what she said. He recollected the party at Mrs. Rennie's, and how pleasant her voice was; and felt Harriett Phillips's was not at all musical, at least, when she was talking about the fine arts and to-morrow's exhibition to Mr. Hogarth; while Francis wondered at any one presuming to have so much to say while his cousin Jane was in the room.

'Now, as to table-turning, Mr. Dempster,' said Harriett, who fancied she saw Brandon's eyes directed to that side of the table a little too often, 'you will never convince me there is an atom of

truth in it. I am quite satisfied with Faraday's explanation. You may think you have higher authority, but *I* bow to Faraday.'

'Faraday's explanation is most insufficient and most unsatisfactory; it cannot account for things I have seen with my own eyes,' said Mr. Dempster.

'But to what do all these manifestations tend?' asked Jane. 'Of what value are the revelations you receive from the so-called spiritual world?'

'Of infinite value to me,' said Mr. Dempster, 'I have had my faith strengthened, and my sorrows comforted. We do want to know more of our departed friends—to have more assurance of their continued existence, and of their continued identity than we have without spiritualism. I always believed that nothing was lost in the divine economy; that as matter only decayed to give way to new powers of life, so spirit must only leave the material form it inhabits to be active in a new sphere, or to be merged in the One Infinite Intelligence. But this is merely an analogy—a strong one, but only an analogy, which cannot prove a fact.'

'But, Mr. Dempster, I think we have quite sufficient grounds for believing in immortality from revelation. In scientific matters, I bow to Faraday, as I said before; in religious matters, I would not go any further than the Bible. But if that does not satisfy you, of course you must inquire of chairs and tables,' said Miss Phillips, with a condescending irony, which she thought very cutting.

'The Bible is indistinct and indefinite as to the future state—so much so that theologians differ on the possibilities of recognition in heaven,' said Mr. Dempster. 'Now, eternal existence without complete identity is not to me desirable. That our beloved ones no longer have the warm personal interest in us which they felt in life—that they are perhaps merged in the perfection of God, or undergoing transmigration out of one form of intelligence to another, without any recollection of what happened in a former state, is not consoling to the yearning human heart that never can forget, and with all the sufferings which memory may bring, would not lose the saddest memory of love for worlds. This assurance of

continued identity is what I find in spiritualism; and it meets the wants of my soul.'

'What extraordinary heathenish ideas!' said Miss Phillips, who in her Derbyshire retreat had never heard anything of pantheism, or of this doctrine of metempsychosis as being entertained by sane Englishmen. 'If you have such notions, I do not wonder at your flying to anything; for my part, I have never been troubled with doubts.'

'The Bible is, I think, purposely indistinct on the subject of the future life,' said Elsie. 'Each soul imagines a heaven for itself, different in some degree from that of any other soul; but to me memory and identity are so necessary to the idea of continued existence that I cannot conceive of a heaven without it.'

'I do not know,' said Mr. Dempster, shaking his head. 'Till I saw these wonderful manifestations, I had no clear or satsifactory feeling of it, and now I have. The evidence is first hand from the departed spirits themselves, and their revelations are consistent with our highest ideas of the goodness of God, and of the eternal nature of love.'

'That which is seen is not faith,' St. Paul says, and the very minuteness of your information would lead me to doubt its genuineness,' said Francis. 'I do not think it was intended that we should have such assurance; but that we should have a large faith in a God who will do well for us hereafter as he has done well for us here. But though I may not feel the need of such assurance, I do not deny that others may. There is much that is very remarkable about these spiritual manifestations;—whether it is mesmerism, or delusion, or positive fraud, I think it is a remarkable instance of the questioning spirit of the day, unsatisfied with old creeds and desirous of reconstructing some new belief.'

'I should like you to come to a *séance*,' said Mr. Dempster, glad to find some one who was disposed to inquire on the subject. He had only recently become a convert, and was very anxious to induce others to think with him. 'I am quite sure that you will see something that will impress you with the reality of the manifestations.'

'I should like to go too,' said Mrs. Phillips.

'I certainly should not,' said Harriett. 'I think these things are quite wicked,'

'These questions have never given me any trouble,' said Mr. Phillips, 'and to my mind, Mr. Dempster, the revelations, such as I have heard at least, are very puerile and contemptible; but that there must be a singular excitement attending even an imaginary conversation with the dead I can easily believe, and I do not care for exposing myself to it.'

'Nor I,' said Brandon; 'as Miss Alice says, I have got my own idea of heaven, and I am satisfied with it. I think we are not intended to know all the particulars.'

Why did Brandon, in giving no original opinion of his own (poor fellow, he was incapable of that), give Elsie's argument in preference to hers? Miss Phillips felt still more inclined to be agreeable to Mr. Hogarth from this slight to herself, and began to think that an inquiring spirit, in a man at least, was more admirable than Brandon's lazy satisfaction with things as they are at present.

Mr. Dempster's eagerness after a possible convert was only to be satisfied by Francis making an appointment with him to attend a *séance* on the following evening in his own house. And then the conversation changed to politics—English, foreign, and colonial—in which Francis and his cousins were much interested.

Mr. Dempster was rather an elderly man, who had lost his wife and all his family, with the exception of one daughter, who was married and settled in South Australia. Though so enthusiastic a believer in spiritualism, he was a very shrewd and well-informed man in mundane matters. He had been a very old colonist on the Adelaide side; and, having been a townsman, had taken a more active part in politics than the Victorian squatters, Phillips and Brandon. They were all in the full tide of talk about the advantages and disadvantages of giving to their infant States constitutional government, and allowing each colony to frame its constitution for itself. The good and evil effects of manhood suffrage and vote by

ballot Francis for the first time heard discussed by people who had lived under these systems, and English, French, and American blunders in the science of politics looked at from a new and independent point of view. At what Jane and Elsie considered the most interesting part of the conversation, Mrs. Phillips and Harriett, who cared for none of these subjects, gave the signal for the ladies to withdraw, so they had to leave with them.

Jane saw the children to bed, and Elsie got on with Mrs. Phillips's bonnet, while the gentlemen remained in the dining-room; but both reappeared in the drawing-room by the time they came up-stairs. Elsie did not like to disappoint any one, and the idea struck her that if she got up very early in the morning, and things went all well with her, she could finish Harriett's bonnet also in time, for really Mrs. Phillips's new one would make her sister-in-law's look very shabby. It was the first new bonnet she had been trusted to make since she came; she had had *carte blanche* for the materials, and had pleased herself with the style, and Elsie believed it would be her *chef-d'oeuvre.* The idea of giving Miss Phillips such an unexpected pleasure made her feel quite kindly disposed towards her, though the feeling was not reciprocated, for as Harriett did not know of Elsie's intentions, she could not be supposed to be grateful for them; but, on the contrary, she felt a grudge at her for enjoying herself in this way at the expense of her bonnet. Harriett Phillips played and sang very well; her father was fond of music, and that taste had been very well cultivated for her time and opportunities, and she had kept up with all the modern music very meritoriously. Perhaps it was this, more than anything else, that had made her Dr. Phillips's favourite daughter, for in all other things Georgiana was more self-forgetful and more sympathising. Stanley, too, admired his sister's accomplishment; he had missed the delightful little family concerts and the glee-singing that he had left for his bush life, and if it could have been possible for his wife to acquire music it would certainly have been a boon to him; but as she had no ear and no taste, even he saw that it was impracticable; but Emily was to be an accomplished musician. She did not go to bed with the

little ones, but sat up to play her two little airs to her papa's friends—to teach her confidence, Mrs. Phillips said, but, in reality, to give her a little spur to application.

'As for Emily needing confidence,' whispered Brandon to Alice Melville, 'that is a splendid absurdity. These colonial children do not know what bashfulness or timidity means—not but what I am very fond of all the Phillipses, and Emily is my favourite.'

'She is mine, too,' said Elsie; 'she is an affectionate and an original child, with quick perceptions and quick feelings. I believe she is very fond of me; I like little people to be fond of me.'

'Not big people, too?' said Brandon, with an expression half comic, half sad.

Elsie blushed. Emily came up to her dear friend, Mr. Brandon, and her favourite, Alice. 'Aunt Harriett is going to play and sing now, and after that, Alice, you must sing. I like your songs better than Aunt Harriett's twenty times, because I can hear all your words.'

'I cannot sing,' said Elsie, 'I never had a lesson in either music or singing in my life.'

'Oh! but you sing very nicely; indeed she does, Mr. Brandon: and there is not a thing that happens that she cannot turn into a song or a poem, just like what there is in books, and you would think it very pretty if you only heard them. We get her to bring her work into our nursery in the evenings, and there we have stories and songs from her.'

'You are in luck,' said Mr. Brandon; 'but now that you have told us of Miss Alice Melville's accomplishments, we must be made to share in your good fortune.'

'No, indeed,' said Elsie; 'as Burns says, "crooning to a body's sel' does weel eneugh;" but my crooning is not fit for company, except that of uncritical children.'

'You know I am as uncritical as the veriest child,' said Brandon. 'I must have given you a very erroneous impression of my character, if you can feel the least awe of me; but I recollect your twisting a very innocent speech of mine, the first evening I had the pleasure

of meeting you, into something very severe. That was rather ill-natured.'

'Alice is not ill-natured at all,' said Emily. 'Aunt Harriett sometimes is. She is looking cross at me now for talking while she is singing.'

'It is very rude in all of us,' said Elsie, composing herself to give attention to Miss Phillips's song.

'I tell you what, you dear old boy,' whispered Emily. 'I don't think Alice will sing here, or tell you any of her lovely stories; but I will smuggle you into the nursery some day, and you will just have a treat.'

'What have I done since I came to England,' said Brandon in the same undertone, 'that I should have been banished in this cruel way from the nursery? Did you ever refuse me admission at Wiriwilta—did not I kiss every one of you in your little nightclothes, and see you tucked into bed? If I was worthy of that honour then, why am I debarred from it now?'

'You saved our lives, papa says—you and Peggy—and so we always liked you; and, for my part, I like you as well as ever I did now; but we are in England now, and it is so different from Wiriwilta—dear old Wiriwilta, I wish I was back to it. I wish papa was not so rich, for then we would go back again; but it's no use as long as he has got enough of money to stay here. The letters that came the other day—you recollect.'

'I got none,' said Brandon; 'I suppose mine are sent by Southampton.'

'Well, I don't think they had good news, or papa's face looked rather long, and he has been so quiet and dull ever since; so I am in hopes that things are not going very well without him, and then we will have another beautiful long voyage with you, and get back to dear, darling Australia again. Harriett wants to go back too.'

'What a chatterbox you are, Emily,' said her aunt, who had finished her song. 'It is quite time you were in bed.'

'Not quite, auntie; papa said I might sit up till ten to-night; and

Mr. Brandon and I are so busy talking about old times, that I do not feel it a bit late.'

'Old times, indeed,' said Harriett; 'what old times can a little chit like you find to talk of?'

'Oh, the dear old times at Wiriwilta, when we were such friends; and the time that I cannot recollect of when there was the fire, and Peggy and this old fellow saved our lives. I wish I could remember about it—mamma does, though.'

'Indeed I do,' said Mrs. Phillips, with a tranquil expression of satisfaction at the thought of the danger she had escaped. 'We was all in terrible danger, and all through that horrid doctor. Stanley should have let me have my own way, and taken me to Melbourne; but he would not listen to reason.'

'Well, Lily, you are none of the worse now, and I hope you do not feel it burdensome to be so much obliged to our old friend Brandon.'

'Oh no, not at all.'

'You need not be,' said he, laughing; 'don't attempt to make a hero of me: a mere neighbourly good turn happened to have important consequences. Peggy's conduct was far beyond mine.'

'But you were badly scorched,' said Emily. 'Do let us see the scar on your arm once more—I have not seen it in England.' Brandon indulged the child; turned up his sleeve, and Emily gave the arm a hug and a kiss.

This was rather a strange exhibition for a drawing-room, Harriett Phillips thought, but Brandon never was much of a gentleman. Even Stanley had sadly fallen back in his manners in Australia, and what could be expected of Brandon? Mr. Hogarth had more taste; he had the dignified reserve of a man of birth and fortune; he had made remarks on her musical performance that showed he was really a judge. It was not often that she had met with any man so variously accomplished, or so perfectly well bred. He had promised to accompany them to the exhibition of paintings on the morrow, and she had great pleasure in anticipating his society, if it were not for the thought of her bonnet.

IX

A BONNET GAINED AND A LOVER LOST

'My letters have come at last,' said Brandon, next morning, as he joined his friends at breakfast. 'My overseer, I suppose, wanted to show his economy, and posted them by the Southampton mail, which does not suit me at all. I would rather do without my dinner on mail-day than have my letters delayed for nearly a week. And now there is bad news for me, I must leave by the first ship. Had I got my letters when you received yours, I should have gone by the mail steamer and saved a month, but I cannot possibly manage to get off so soon.'

'Oh! Mr. Brandon,' said Mrs. Phillips, calmly, 'there surely is no such need for hurry.'

'Everything is going to the dogs at my station. I will probably have to buy land at a high price; and there appears to have been great mismanagement, from the accounts I hear. Another six months like the last and I will be a ruined man. It is very hard that one cannot take a short holiday without suffering so grievously for it. What were your accounts, Phillips; I think you said they were rather unsatisfactory?'

'Not very good, certainly; but not so bad as that comes to. You will look to Wiriwilta a little when you return, and send me your

opinion. I had better entrust you with full powers to act for me, for I should prefer you as my attorney to Grant.'

'I hope he will not be offended at the transfer,' said Brandon.

'Oh! I think not; he took it very reluctantly, for he said his own affairs were enough for him.'

'And perhaps a little more than enough,' said Brandon, with a smile. 'In that case I will be very glad to do all in my power for you.'

'I have no wish to return to Australia,' said Mr. Phillips, 'if I can possibly afford to live here. With a family like mine, England offers so many advantages. In fact, there is only one place in the world worth living in, and that is London.'

'Very true, if you have enough to live on,' said Brandon, shrugging his shoulders. 'I must go now to work as hard as ever to get things set to rights again, and perhaps in another dozen of years, when I am feeble, old, and grey, I may return and spend the poor remnant of my days in this delightful centre of civilization. But with me, fortunately, there are only the two alternatives, either London or the bush of Australia—there is no middle course of life desirable. If I cannot attain the one, I must make the best of the other.'

Harriett Phillips listened to all this, and believed that matters were much worse with Brandon than they really were. She had no fancy for a twelve years' banishment from England, nor for a rough life in the bush. Mr. Brandon had been represented to her as a thriving settler who had made money. She saw the very comfortable style in which her brother lived, and she had no objection to such an establishment for herself; but she was not so particularly fond of Mr. Brandon as to accept for his sake a life so very different and so very much inferior. She felt that she had been deceived, and she did not like being deceived, or mistaken, and she still less liked to make mistakes; and instead of blaming herself, she was angry with everyone else—her brother, her sister-in-law, Brandon himself—for leading her to believe that his circumstances were so much better than they were. Of course, he would ask her—he could not help doing so; but as to accepting him—that was quite a different question.

She had put on her old bonnet with a grudge at Elsie; and when Mrs. Phillips appeared in the drawing-room ready for the party to the exhibition in all the splendour of her new one, which really looked lovely, and she lovely in it, and Harriett caught the reflection of both figures in the large mirror, she felt still more dissatisfied with everybody than she had done before. The gentlemen were ready, and they were just about to start, when a light quick step came to the door, and a little tap was heard.

Harriett opened it, and was delighted to see Elsie holding in her hand the second bonnet completed—equally beautiful, equally tasteful, and apparently quite as expensive.

'Oh, Alice, how good of you! What a love of a bonnet! Come in and see Mr. Hogarth. Look, Mrs. Phillips—look at Alice's clever handiwork.'

And Alice was introduced a little unwillingly into the drawing-room to be complimented on her taste and her despatch, and to shake hands with the two gentlemen. Miss Phillips was too much engrossed with her bonnet, and with the improvement it would make in her appearance, to observe the earnest, anxious looks of her two fancied admirers, as they greeted her sister's lady's-maid; or that they looked with interest and concern on her tired face, which, though now a little flushed with excitement, bore to those who knew the circumstances traces of having been up very late and very early over her work.

'I knew she could do it,' Harriett whispered to Mr. Brandon, when Alice left the room; 'she is so excessively quick. I never would have said so much about it yesterday, if I had not known she could easily do it; and does not mine look as well as Mrs. Phillips's? I said it would.' And so she accepted Mr. Hogarth's arm, and went to see the pictures with a better judge than Brandon, in all the triumph of her new bonnet—the lightest, the most becoming she had ever had in her life: but her influence with Walter Brandon was lost for ever. He wished he had had Jane Melville, with her good common sense, or Elsie, with her sweet voice and winning ways, hanging on his arm instead of Mrs. Phillips, who was very uninteresting to him,

though her great beauty and excellent style of dress made her an object of interest to other people, and who always enjoyed being well stared at in public places. But Jane was engaged with her pupils at this time, and Elsie was always kept very busy, so that neither of them could accompany the party, and Francis Hogarth felt disappointed, for he had anticipated the society of one or both of them.

How curiously the egotist, who fancies every one is engrossed with him or with her, would be disappointed if he or she could see the real thoughts of the people about them. How Harriett Phillips would have started if she could have read the hearts of Hogarth and Brandon, and seen what a very infinitesimal share she had in either.

Francis was only impelled to pay attention to Miss Phillips by his natural sense of politeness, and by the wish to make the situation of his cousins in the family pleasant, as far as it lay in his power to do so; while Brandon, who had at last struck the key-note of Harriett's character, was astonished to find new proofs of her selfishness and egotism peeping out in the most trifling circumstances. He observed how different her manner was towards him, now that a man of property in the old country had appeared in the circle of her acquaintances, and he could not fail to see that an additional coldness had come over her when his circumstances were supposed to be less flourishing, and this made him rather disposed to make the most and the worst of his bad news.

In Derbyshire, where she had her own established place in the household, and where her father and her sister Georgiana gave way to her so much, she had appeared more amiable than she did now. The armed neutrality which she maintained with her sister-in-law had amused Brandon at first, but now it appeared to him to be unladylike and ungraceful to accept of hospitality in her brother's house without any gratitude or any forbearance. He began to question the reality of her very great superiority over Mrs. Phillips; with all her advantages of education and society she ought to have shown more gentleness and affection both to her brother's wife and his children. He analysed, as he had never done before, her

expressions, and weighed her opinions, and found they generally had more sound than sense; and her habitual assumption that she knew everything much better than other people, became tiresome when he did not believe in her superiority.

He began, too, to contrast the charm of a face, when the colour went and came with every emotion, with that of one so unimpressible as Harriett Phillips's—whose self-possession was nearly as different from that of Jane Melville as it was from the timidity and diffidence of Elsie. Jane's calmness was the result of a strong will mastering the strong emotiuons which she really felt, and not in the absence of any powerful feeling or emotion whatever. Brandon had learned to like Jane better as he knew more of her, and rather enjoyed being preached to by one who could practise as well as preach. He felt that if she was superior to him she did not look down on him; and she certainly had the power of making him speak well, and of bringing out the very large amount of real useful practical knowledge that he had acquired in his Australian life. Her eagerness to hear everything about Australia and Australians certainly was in pleasing contrast to Miss Phillips's distaste for all things and people colonial; but above all, Miss Phillips's want of consideration for Alice Melville had weaned Mr. Brandon's heart from her. It was not merely unladylike; it was unwomanly. He could not love a wife who had so little sympathy and so little generosity.

X

A SEANCE

Francis Hogarth did not forget his promise to Mr. Dempster, and went to his house at the hour appointed, to be witness of the *séance*. A number of his friends and fellow-converts were there, and the proceedings of the evening were opened by a short and earnest prayer that none but good spirits should be permitted to be present, and that all the comunications they might be permitted to hear might be blessed to the souls of all of them.

The medium was a thin, nervous-looking youth of about nineteen; but, as Mr. Dempster assured Mr. Hogarth, was in every way to be trusted, as his character was irreproachable, and of great sincerity and simplicity. Francis was very incredulous as to the appearances being caused by spiritual agency, and though he could give no satisfactory explanation of the extraordinary movements of tables, easy chairs, sofas, &c., he felt that these things were very undignified and absurd, as every unbeliever always feels at first; but the eagerness of the large party who were gathered together had something infectious in it. Many of them had known severe bereavement—many of them had been tossed on the dark sea of doubt and despondency—and the brief messages communicated by raps, or by the voice of the medium, gave them consolation and hope.

To Francis, the details communicated appeared to be meagre and unsatisfactory. The spirits all said that they were happy, which to some present was a fact of inestimable value, but to him it was a matter of course. He never had believed, since he had thought out the subject in early manhood, that God would continue existence if He did not make it a blessing. But to others who, like many before him, had intelligently accepted of a sterner theology, and who had been struggling through years of chaotic doubts and fancies for footing on which to rest, he saw that these assurances gave real strength and support. An hour had passed amidst these manifestations—the interest of the believers continued to be unflagging, but Francis felt a little tired of it. He had lost no dear friend by death. The future world had not the intense personal interest to him that it had to others. The dearest beings in the world to him were his two cousins, and they were divided from him by circumstances almost as cruel as the grave. How few have done justice to the sad partings, the mournful alienations that have been caused by circumstances! Bereavement in all its varied bitterness has been sung by many poets in strains worthy of the subject; but circumstances are so insidious, and often so prosaic, that their tragical operation has been rarely treated of in verse.

His thoughts recurred, as they always did when he felt sad or serious, to Jane Meville—to the will that had brought them together, and at the same time so cruelly parted them—to the unknown father, whose own life had been blighted by the loss of domestic happiness, dealing so fatal a blow to the son whom he meant to bless and reward, by placing him in circumstances where he could not help loving Jane, and forbidding—so far as he could forbid—the marriage of two souls made for one another. Francis was wondering if his father now saw the mistake he had committed, or regretted it, when he was startled by the announcement that his father was in the room, and wished to communicate with him.

'How am I to know it is he?' said Francis, starting up incredulously, but at the same time somewhat awed by the mere

possibility that such a one was there, out of the body, owning him as his son, which he had not done while he was alive.

'Does the spirit mean to communicate by raps or through the medium?' asked Mr. Dempster.

'By raps,' was the answer given.

'Take the alphabet in your own hand,' said Mr. Dempster, 'and ask the spirit his name, and then pass your finger over the alphabet—the rap will arrest you at the right letter.'

Francis passed his finger along the alphabet, half disdainfully, half in curiosity. The rap stopped him at the letter H. He had never thought the curious little taps sounded so unearthly before. Next he was stopped at E, then at N, then at R, and next at Y; and so on, till the full name of Henry Hogarth was spelled out.

'You wish to communicate with me;—then you love me now?'

The three quick raps meaning 'Yes' was the immediate reply.

'Are you satisfied with what I have done at Cross Hall since your death?'

Again the alphabet was called for, and the raps spelled out, 'Very much pleased.'

'Are you sorry for the will you made?'

'All will be well in the end,' was spelled out.

'Did you see your nieces' sufferings unmoved—their poverty, their disappointments, their unfitness for the work that you had set them to do?'

'They are better for what they have suffered,' was spelled out; 'and you too.'

'Does the letter in my pocket come from my mother?'

The three raps replied in the affirmative.

'Did you give her an annuity, as she says you did?'

A single rap, meaning 'No,' was the reply.

'What did you give her, then, to make her forego her claims on you?'

'A sum of money,' was the reply.

Francis observed a great difference in the character of the raps proceeding from Mr. Hogarth from those of the spirit last

summoned, which had been supposed to be that of Mr. Dempster's eldest daughter, who had died at sixteen, and of a lingering disease. The latter were faint, and almost inaudible to an unpractised ear, while those of his father were firm and distinct. There was never any power of knowing from what part of the room the raps would come, and as answer after answer appeared to come so readily to his questions, it is not to be wondered at that Francis felt excited and awed at the mysterious intercourse.

'Advise me, my father; tell me what to do if you see more and know than more I can do. Should I assist my mother, as she asks me to do?'

The single impatient rap, meaning 'No,' was the immediate reply.

'Is she not in poverty and want?'

Again the answer was 'No.'

'Should not I write to her?'

'No; have nothing to do with her,' was the answer.

'Can I ever have what I most desire in the world? You promise improvement—I want happiness,' said Francis, passionately, startled out of himself by the extraordinary pertinence of the answers to his questions, and careless in the company of absolute strangers as to what they thought of him.

'Patience! I watch over you,' was the reply.

'What do you do in the spiritual world?'

'I am learning,' answered the spirit, 'from one who loves me.'

'What is her name?' asked Francis.

The alphabet was in his hands; he was anxious not to let any sign of his give any clue in case of its being all imposture and extraordinary quickness of sight. He purposely passed over the letters, but was rapped back by the recognised signal till the name 'Marguerite' was spelled out.

'Yes,' said he to himself, 'you think all is well in the end; you have met Marguerite in the spirit world, after being separated for a life-time in this, and this is very sweet to you; but I want Jane now to help me to live worthily. Can I win her in this life?'

'After a time,' said the spirit, rapping by the alphabet this answer to his inaudible question.

'You then can answer mental questions,' thought Francis. 'What connection can Mr. Phillips possibly have with Mrs. Peck, or rather Elizabeth Hogarth? But to this inaudible question the spirit made no reply, and told him, through the medium, that he was disinclined for any further communication. Certainly it was a question which he felt conscious he had no right to put, after what Mr. Phillips had said to him. The spirit was in the right not to answer it.

'Are you convinced?' said Mr. Dempster, who had seen the surprise with which Mr. Hogarth had spelled out the answers.

'I am staggered,' said Francis. 'The general answers might have been given at random, but the names, I am convinced, were unknown to every one here except myself.'

'It always is the names that convince people,' said a friend of the host's.

'I have asked some questions as to the future,' said Francis. 'I do not know if it is allowable to do so. Do your spirits claim to have a knowledge of what is to come?'

'Oh, yes; they do—those of the highest class in particular,' said Mr. Dempster.

'I do not see how they can,' said Francis musingly. 'To know the future is a prerogative of Omniscience, and even the highest created intelligence cannot tell what His purposes may be.'

'How do we guess at the future with sufficient accuracy to direct us in the present but by generalization from experience? Now, a departed spirit certainly has had a wider experience—sees more into other souls and their workings than we can possibly do while encumbered with these robes of clay—and consequently can make a juster generalization,' said Mr. Dempster.

'But not an infallible one?' said Francis.

'No; certainly not,' said Mr. Dempster.

'But, as to the present, their views are sure to be correct?' said Francis.

'If they are good spirits, and not lying spirits. We prayed against their appearance, and I do not believe that the spirit who has been communicating with you was of that kind,' said Mr. Dempster.

'How, then, do you judge between lying spirits and true ones?' asked Francis.

'By the nature of their communications. A false or an immoral message cannot be delivered by a good spirit.'

'Then you still continue to be the judges of the spirits? You do not bow your morality to theirs—you select and reject as you see good?'

'Morality is universal and eternal,' said Mr. Dempster. 'Even God himself cannot make evil good or good evil by any fiat of his own.'

'Then have these manifestations taught you anything that could not have been otherwise learned?' asked Francis.

'They have taught *me* much that I could not have otherwise learned. I cannot say what other people may attain to through pure reason or through a simple faith in the revealed will of God. There are diversities of administration, but the same spirit,' said Mr. Dempster, with a simple earnestness that weighed much with Francis. But here Mr. Dempster's attention was called to a message from an old friend who had just died one of the saddest of deaths, having been lost in the Australian scrub twelve years before.

These raps were still stronger than those of Mr. Hogarth, being violent, and following immediately on the question wherever a negative or affirmative was used.

Mr. Dempster said he had been a powerful young man, of the most unquestionable determination, and that the raps were always consonant to the character of the spirit when in life. He eagerly turned to identify him. The name was correctly given; the date of his death; the length of time he had existed without food and water, and the clothes he had on when he died. Then a message was sent to his aged mother, who had so long mourned for her youngest born, that he was expecting her soon to join him in the spirit land. The place where the old lady lived was mentioned, and her state of health was described as being bad.

'All perfectly true, perfectly true, Mr. Hogarth. Poor Tom! His was a distressing fate. I expected that we should have something good in manifestations this evening, but I scarcely looked for anything so perfectly satisfactory as this. Every name and every date exactly correct. Are you not convinced now?'

'I am certainly very much staggered,' said Francis. 'Have you been thinking much about your friend or his mother lately?'

'Not particularly that I know of; but I liked him very much, and I often think of his solitary death.'

'Have you heard that his mother is in bad health?'

'She has been an invalid for years, and you heard her age; but we must make a note of the date, and ascertain if she is particularly worse to-night. I feel sure that there are not many days of this earth for her, and how blessed a thing it is that we have such an assurance of a reunion and recognition as these communications give to us.'

When Francis got into the open air after the excitement of the evening, he was inclined to think that all had been a dream or a delusion, but the answer and the names recurred with startling significance; the difficulty and almost the impossibility of any cheat or collusion, and the apparent sincerity of all who had been sitting by him during the manifestations, increased the bewilderment of his mind.

'I must see Jane about this to-morrow,' said he; 'her clear head can perhaps solve this curious problem; but if I had not seen it, I would not have believed what I saw. Will she believe without seeing? Yes, she will receive my testimony, for I would receive hers. After a time I may hope to be happy. How long a time, I wonder?'

XI

SPIRITUALISM, LOVE, AND POLITICS

Great was the grief of Emily when she heard that Mr. Brandon was going away in a week or two, and that he might never come back to England for a dozen of years; and now, instead of spending the rest of his time in London with them, he had to go to Ashfield, to spend his last days in England with his mother and sisters and nephews and nieces. She felt quite wronged by this conduct, and bade him good-bye when he came to take his temporary leave of them, with an amount of sulkiness rather foreign to her character. Lessons were a far greater bore than usual on that day, and both Emily and Harriett tried Jane's patience sorely. After they were set free for two hours in the middle of the day, Jane found her cousin was waiting for her to go out with him, and she wished very particularly to see him, on account of some news she had got from Scotland. He had not been satisfied to have none of her society on the preceding day, and had appointed with Mrs. Phillips to come when she would be at leisure, which that lady had forgotten or neglected to tell Jane or Elsie. It was Jane alone whom he wished to see—it was to her alone that he could speak about the communication with reference to his letter. Jane was sorry that Elsie was not asked to accompany their walk; but when Francis said he had something on his mind,

and proceeded to tell all the singular circumstances of the previous evening, she listened with the greatest attention and with a suspended judgment. When he came to the mental question which related to herself, he simply called it something on which his heart was greatly set—it might have been his allotments or his cottages; but Jane asked no questions, and took no notice of his want of completeness in his narrative. Then he told of the inquiry as to Mrs. Peck's connection with Mr. Phillips, which he ought not to have asked, and which had received no answer. He paused for Jane's opinion before he came to narrate Mr. Dempster's message from his friend lost in the bush.

'Now, what do you think of all this, Jane?'

'I am a little staggered, as you were,' said she. 'I wish you had heard more or less—it bewilders me.'

'Should I then follow this advice so strangely given?'

'I think the advice exactly corresponds with what you had resolved to do at any rate. It need not influence you either one way or the other. You asked my advice the other day, but neither from me nor from a departed spirit should you accept of or follow any advice which appears to your own soul not to be good. You cannot shift off your personal responsibility. As I said, it is your affair, not mine; and I feel sorry that consideration for me, and for my generous employer, has weighed so much with you that you scarcely give the claims of your mother their just due.'

'And the spirit said she was my mother, but at the same time advised, or rather commanded me to have nothing to do with her. I do not wish to have anything to do with her. What is it to be grateful for—such a loveless, joyless life as mine has been—thwarted even now in my dearest hopes and wishes.'

'Francis,' said Jane, 'you have a great deal to be thankful for, and so have I. With all the sufferings of the past year, I would not have been without it for the world. We have both learned much, both from circumstances and from each other.'

'Jane, I am weary of all this talk about progress and perfection. I

am hungering for happiness, as I told this strange interlocutor last night,' said Francis, earnestly.

'And you will attain to it, Francis! but do not set your heart on what it is not right, or wise, or expedient for you to obtain. And you cannot look me in the face and say that, if one thing is denied, you have not many sources of happiness.'

Jane looked at him with her sisterly eyes, feeling the pain she was giving, but determined not to show that she had any personal regret. It was very kind, but it was very discouraging. She felt for him like a sister—and nothing more.

'If I have any eyes,' said Francis, trying violently to change the subject, 'Brandon is still an admirer of your sister's. What in the world keeps him from declaring himself? Why does he not offer her all he has, and all he may hope to gain? He cares no more for Miss Phillips than I do, and she would never consent to accompany him to Australia. And Elsie looks so pretty and so sad, she needs a protector; she would be grateful to him; she cannot stand alone, as you do; and she knows she makes your position here much more difficult.'

'The truth is, Elsie refused him, and it is difficult for a man to make a second offer when he has such slight opportunities of seeing her, even if he has not made a transfer of his affections.'

'I would make an opportunity—I would write—I would ask point-blank to see her—I would speak to you about it, if I were in his place. It is cowardly in Brandon.'

'Why, Francis, you are very unreasonable. Elsie refused him as positively and uncompromisingly as possible on her way down to Derbyshire. I do not think she would do so now; but how is he to know that?'

'I would hint as much to him, if I were you. Why, Jane, a word from you might secure your sister's happiness for life, and you shrink from saying it.'

'Indeed I do,' said Jane. 'I think no good can come from interfering in such matters, and I am particularly ill-adapted for such a delicate communication. Besides, if one may judge by the last

few weeks, it is Miss Phillips who ought to recieve the offer of marriage, and not Elsie. If her brother were to ask what Mr. Brandon's intentions are, as he might very well do, the result would be a marriage of two very ill-assorted people. She cannot comprehend the real goodness and simplicity of his character, and despises the man whom she is scarcely worthy to wait on. She even looks down on her generous brother; she has no love for her brother's children, and no sympathy with anyone. I am really very glad to observe, with you, that her influence with Mr. Brandon has decreased of late; but he certainly has paid her a great deal of attention, and she expects a proposal.'

'Her face has no charm to me,' said Francis. 'Taken feature by feature it is handsome enough; but it wants play and variety, and it has not the perfect harmony of Mrs. Phillips's. That is a singularly beautiful index to a soul that appears to be nothing particular. I have heard it said that we have all our ugly moments. Have you ever seen such a time with Mrs. Phillips?'

'There are times when she certainly does not look beautiful to me, nor to Elsie either. But I wanted to speak to you of your own affairs. I had letter from Tom Lowrie this morning, in which he says that he hears from one of his old schoolfellows that you have been asked to stand for the Swinton group of burghs, and that every one says you will easily be able to carry them over the duke's man.'

'Ah! has he heard about it? I should have told you of it, but the more pressing personal interest of the letter from Melbourne, Mr. Phillips's strange agitation, and this mysterious spiritual communication, put it out of my head for the time, and a word from you would put it aside for ever,' said Francis, with the old wistful look.

Jane, like all women who are interested in public matters at all, and they form a very small minority of her sex, rather overestimated the importance of a parliamentary career. She knew the turn of her cousin's mind, his education as a man of the people, his position as a man of property, his earnest desire to do right, his patient habits of business, and his thorough method of research and inquiry, were all certain guarantees that he could not fail; and she

had the belief that his abilities, and readiness, and confidence would make him an eloquent and skilful debater. It appeared to her to be an object of great importance that a perfectly honest and independent member should replace for the burghs in her native country the nominee of a great family, who only voted with his party, and never had done any credit either to the electors or to the nation. She said truly when she spoke of her ambition finding its vent in dreams about him and her pupil, Tom Lowrie. She certainly had influenced Francis Hogarth's character greatly during the turning-point of his life; the ideas she had nursed in her trials had been on his mind with force and earnestness, and through him she could hope to give a voice to a number of her crotchets and theories. Where a woman writes as well as thinks, she does not feel this dependence on the other sex so strongly; for, though at a disadvantage, she can for herself utter her thoughts—but Jane, as my readers will have observed, was not literary. She was an intelligent, well-informed, observing woman, but her field was action, and not books. In her present situation she had very little time for reading; but, from all that she saw, and from all the conversation she could hear, she found hints for action and subjects for thought. To see Francis in the British Parliament was a worthy ambition, and to give up such a probable career for an inglorious and obscure life with herself was not to be thought of. His wistful looks and earnest tones were to be treasured up in her heart for ever; but her own love for him was not of that imperious and unreasonable nature that she could not live without him.

XII

CHIEFLY POLITICAL

'Do you think that you can really get in?' said Jane, eagerly. 'I know that my uncle said the Liberal interest was much stronger in the burghs of late, and you are really the fittest man they could have. I was quite pleased to hear from Tom that you are so soon appreciated. Of course, he is enthusiastic on the subject.'

'I do not know if I am appreciated or not, but the burghs are a little tired of a struggle between the Conservative duke and the Whig earl, always resulting in some one being put up on both sides, to whom there were no strong objections, and no strong recommendations—a mere nobody, in fact.'

'You are popular in the county, are you not?' asked Jane.

'No, not exactly. I do not think I could possibly carry the county, even if I could afford the contest, for I am not considered a safe person for the landed interest. I gained some éclat on the road trusteeship, by opening a road which was a great public convenience, but I lost more than I gained there, by my allotments, which are looked on as a dangerous precedent. The cottages make me popular with those who have no votes, and with the more enlightened class of farmers, but the old school of tenants object to them, and almost all the landlords fear that they may be asked to lay out

money in the same way. On the whole, I am considered rather a dangerous man in the county, but in the burghs I am popular, I think. I have the character of being a man of the people, who has not lost sympathy with his class, and I can afford to give them my time and services, such as they are.'

'If you go in, you want to do so independently,' said Jane.

'Yes, I do; and here I risk my election. The Liberal party want a certain vote, which they think they could secure better by sending up a stranger from the Reform Club, who knows little and cares less about the burghs, than by supporting a man who will look into political and national questions for himself, and who will not be a mere partisan. If they mistrust me and send some one to divide the Liberal interest, I can only save the Swinton burghs from the duke's man, by retiring.'

'But how foolish to divide the Liberal interest,' said Jane.

'My dear Jane, you forget that his party is dearer to a party man than anything else. The question to be considered—and I want to see how your nice conscience will guide you through the bewildering mazes of political morality—is this: Whether it would be right to pledge myself to the party, in which case I am sure of my return, or to remain independent, and so make it very doubtful,' said Francis.

'You cannot vote always with the Liberals—at least with the Liberals who form governments and oppositions,' said Jane. 'They are often in the wrong, and particularly so in the bestowal of patronage, which, I suppose, is a very important matter among party politicians. The appointments which the Whigs have made of late years have often been most shamefully actuated by family or party reasons, and not with a single eye to the public service. Many times the Conservatives are really more liberal than the Whigs—sometimes the Whigs are more Conservative than the Tories. It is of the first importance that there should be many men such as you in Parliament, who will watch over both parties; and, if this determined dualism is at work everywhere, how are such men to get into the legislature? But, surely, you could carry the burghs—

you can speak, can you not?'

'I don't know, I never tried; but I dare say I could beat Mr. Fortescue, the duke's candidate. He has never opened his mouth in the House, but to give his vote, and on the hustings he made no figure.'

'Try the independent course, by all means; you may be beaten, but then if you succeed, you will be so much more useful.'

'It will probably cost me a thousand pounds.'

'It is shameful that the duty of serving one's country for nothing should be so dearly bought. If you get in, you must try to introduce some measure to reduce election expenses.'

'A difficult matter. The object of the Parliament, when once assembled, is to make it difficult and expensive to get in. To keep the candidature within the limits of a privileged body is considered a great safeguard.'

'Not by me, or by you,' said Jane. 'I want you to get in because you know the feelings and the wants of the people who have no votes better than ninety-nine out of a hundred, who are members of Parliament. Oh! Francis, I feel quite sure that if you exert yourself you can get in. And what is a thousand pounds?—you have it to spare.'

'I am doubtful, said Francis, shaking his head, 'if I can afford to go into Parliament.'

'Have you not two thousand a year? and do not lawyers who can scarcely make a living go into Parliament? I am sure there is some perjury on the subject of property qualification—but as, perhaps, the latter is unnecessary, it is the less matter.'

'They go to increase their means, or their practice, or their influence, and generally take the first opportunity of accepting something better than the Chiltern Hundreds under Government,' said Francis.

'There must be something very wrong somewhere, if a country gentleman of your standing cannot afford to give his services to the House of Commons. Have you brought the requisition that was sent to you?' said Jane.

'Yes; do you really want to see it? I have it in my pocket, and if I

really felt in earnest on the subject, I ought to communicate with Mr. Freeman, the earl's political agent in London, to know how he will favour a man who would support the general policy of Government, but who will hold himself free to vote against them whenever he sees them in the wrong. My only means of securing the earl's influence is by convincing him that he cannot carry the burghs against Fortescue by such a man as he has to put up; and as I am rather doubtful on that point, I can scarcely assert it confidently. If he chooses to withhold his family interest he can make me fail; but if it comes to the push, I would rather retire than let Fortescue get in.'

'Electioneering, then, is very nice and difficult work,' said Jane.

'Very difficult for the scrupulous, the sincere, and the far-seeing.'

'Who are just the sort of people whom we want to see in Parliament.'

'Whom *you* want to see, Jane, but not whom the two great parties wish to see. Then, should I go to Mr. Freeman, do you think, with this requisition and a frank declaration of my principles, and hear what he says on the matter? If the earl supports me I may count on a majority of twenty—a safe enough one; and if not, shall I spend the thousand pounds in a glorious defeat; writing the boldest and most independent of addresses; making the most uncompromising speeches from the hustings, if I can find voice?'

'No fear of your finding voice, Francis,' said Jane, warmly.

'Regardless of the savour of rotten eggs; undaunted by the sneers at my birth and breeding; the tales about my father, the jeers at my mother; and only retiring at the last moment, when I have said all that I have got to say, but which, I fear, my audience were not much in a mood to hear. My own idea is, that I should succeed better in the calm argumentative debates in Parliament, than as a hustings orator, or a popular declaimer.'

'Yes, you will, and you certainly should try the second, that you may attain to the first. My uncle was asked to stand for these burghs some ten years ago, but he was too crotchety, and could not write an address that was at all likely to be acceptable to the

electors, so he gave up the contest before it began. Yet, you know, it would be well to have a few crotchety people in the House of Commons. The game of life, whether social or political, is not played by only two sets of black and red men—like chess or backgammon.'

'I have met a gentleman at Miss Thomson's pretty frequently,' said Francis, 'who struck me as having the most remarkable qualifications for a member of Parliament. He has a habit of recurring to first principles which is rather startling, but which always forces you to give a reason for the faith that is in you, and which either confirms your opinion satisfactorily, or changes, or modifies it. He has retired from business on about £700 a year—which he has made in America, principally—has no family, no cares, and plenty of leisure—is the most upright of men, and knows more of the principles of jurisprudence, and the details of commercial matters than any one I ever knew; but no constituency would choose him, and he cannot afford to throw away a thousand pounds for the privilege of having his say out. He is one of the electors of Swinton, and particularly anxious that I should contest the burghs. His own vote he can answer for, but he boasts of no large following; though he is a man who ought to exert mental influence, he is too far ahead to be popular. If I were to stand, and were to succeed, I will find him a most useful prompter; and with you to inspire enthusiasm for the public service, and this Mr. Sinclair to suggest principles and details, I ought to distinguish myself.'

'I am quite sure that you will,' said Jane; 'so my advice is to lose no time in seeing Mr. Freeman. I cannot believe that people who call themselves liberal can act so illiberally as to endeavour to stifle independence. You will tell me a different tale to-morrow.'

Francis did as Jane advised him, and as he himself thought he should do, and waited on Mr. Freeman. It happened to be a time of a lull in party politics; there was no question strongly before the public mind on which Whigs and Tories were so equally pitted that one vote was of extreme importance; there was no near prospect of

a change of Ministry, and the great Whig houses had been much baited lately about their family selfishness and their party selfishness being quite as bad as that of the old Tory set. So it appeared to Mr. Freeman at the present crisis to be a very wise and expedient thing to offer support to an independent man like Mr. Hogarth, for it was very questionable if the duke, who had been more liberal in his expenditure in the towns, would not carry it against a mere club man, and they had no better man to spare. Mr. Hogarth, at least, was sure to ask nothing of the Government. His support, when they got it, would cost nothing; his adverse vote would be only on outside questions, as a rule. It would look very well for the county election, which was to be a very tough affair between a younger son of the duke and a younger brother of the earl, that Mr. Hogarth, of Cross Hall, should have the earl's cordial support in the burghs. His vote was secure for the Honourable James, and all those he could influence, he hoped. Francis said he could answer for his own, but his tenants must please themselves.

'Oh, yes, certainly; but tenants generally find it for their advantage to vote with their landlord,' said the agent.

'I will give my tenants distinctly to understand that they must vote from conviction, and that that will please me. That is my view of being a Liberal,' said Francis.

'And if all the other county proprietors had the same view the Honourable James would walk the course; but we must oppose all the stratagems of war of an enemy who takes every advantage, and strains to the utmost the influence of property and patronage.'

'I want to go in with perfectly clean hands,' said Francis.

'Bless you, so does everybody,' said the parliamentary agent; 'but somehow there is a lot of queer work must be done to get fairly seated on the benches.'

'I not only wish it, but I mean to do it,' said Mr. Hogarth.

'Well, well—I hope you will be able to manage it. I must introduce you to the earl. I think he will say, as I say, that he will give you cordial support; so that the sooner you get your address out the better—as soon in the field as possible, and don't fall asleep

over it. The other party are like weasels—they are not to be caught napping; and will undermine what you fancy secure ground, if you only give them a chance.'

The result of Francis' interview with the earl was as satisfactory as that with the agent. Party for once was inclined to waive its high prerogative, and to allow a person to slip into Parliament without any pledge as to future action. His manner prepossessed the earl; he received an invitation to dinner to meet a few political friends, and to talk over the canvass for the county, which was one on which all their strength was to be expended. Harriett Phillips was all the more interested in Mr. Hogarth when he had been invited to dinner with a peer of the realm, and stood a good chance of adding M.P. (though only for a Scotch group of burghs) to his name. Even Mrs. Phillips felt a little excited at the idea of a British member of Parliament, and seemed to view both Jane and Elsie with more favour than she had done before; while Mr. Phillips, anxious to do away with the impression of his first interview with Mr. Hogarth, was quietly and cordially hospitable, and hoped that the Swinton burghs would return him, that they might have the pleasure of his society in London for the coming sessions. Francis spent a week or more in London, and promised Miss Phillips to pay a visit to her father in Derbyshire by and by. Mr. Brandon was completely at a discount, and as fairly out of the circle of Harriett's probable future life at Ashfield as if he had sailed for Australia.

XIII

GOOD-BYE

While Jane and Francis were discussing the state of Brandon's affections, the object of their solicitude was going as fast as the railway could take him to Ashfield, where his widowed mother lived with his unmarried sister, a confirmed invalid, and a widowed sister, Mrs. Holmes, the mother of those wonderful nephews and nieces whose ignorance on the subject of dirt-pies had so much impressed Emily Phillips. Brandon had always been very glad to go to see them, and to stay a short time, but the intolerable dullness of the place had always driven him back to London. Australians generally prefer a large town as a residence, and London most of all; for though their relatives in small country towns or rural neighbourhoods fancy that it must be so much more lively with them than it is in the bush, there is a great difference between the dullness where there is plenty of work to be done, and the dullness where there is absolutely nothing.

Mrs. Brandon was a conscientious and, to a certain extent, rather a clever woman, but she had many prejudices and little knowledge of the world. Mary Brandon was the most amiable and the most pious and patient of sufferers, who only got out in a Bath chair, and received a great deal of care from her mother, while Mrs. Holmes

devoted herself to her children with a fidelity and an exclusiveness that made her influence elsewhere almost infinitesimal. All of them loved Walter dearly, and were very anxious that he should be married—most disinterestedly—for their circumstances were straitened, and but for Walter's assistance, which had been given whenever he could possibly afford to do so, they would have found it difficult to make ends meet. Mr. Holmes had been unfortunate in business, and the widow had sacrificed part of her jointure, and the invalid sister as much of her little fortune as was at her own disposal, to assist him in his difficulties. Their generosity had the usual result of only delaying the crash for him, and of finally impoverishing themselves.

One most promising brother had died at the close of a long, expensive professional education, which he had expected to turn to great account for the benefit of his sisters. Walter himself had been sent out to Australia in his father's lifetime with a better capital than could have been given afterwards, so that he always considered that he had got more than his share, and that his assistance was nothing at all generous.

The young Holmeses were taught and guarded by their mother night and day; she accompanied their walks, she overlooked their games, she read all their books before giving them to the children to read, and cut out or erased anything that she thought incorrect in fact or questionable in tendency. She allowed no intercourse with servants, and almost as little with playfellows of their own age. And when Uncle Walter from Australia came first to disturb the even tenor of their way by lavish presents of sweetmeats, cakes, and toys, and by offers to take the whole family to every attainable amusement, he was first reasoned with, and then, as he was not convinced, he was put down, his gifts returned, and the children instructed to say that they would rather not have the treats he offered. He certainly preferred the wild spirits and rebellious conduct of the little Phillipses, even in their worst days, to the prim good-child behaviour of his own nephews and nieces.

He had the pleasure of telling Mrs. Holmes on this occasion that

the wild young Australians had been reduced to something like order by an admirable governess whom he had been the means of procuring for them: that in spite of all the over-indulgence she had suffered from, Emily was proving a very tolerable scholar—that she had good abilities and an excellent heart, though she did climb on his knee for comfits, and beg to be taken to Astley's. Mrs. Holmes wondered at his procuring a governess for the children, and asked a good deal about her, with the view of ascertaining if her brother was fixed at last; but he talked about her with perfect *nonchalance*, saying that she was a particular favourite of an old servant of his called Peggy Walker, and that her account of Miss Melville's qualifications was perfectly satisfactory, as the result had proved. Mrs. Holmes was bewildered as to the curious social relations of Australian people, but her mind was set at rest about Jane Melville.

'But, Fanny,' said he to his sister, 'you know I have come to bid you good-bye in a week or ten days. I cannot help it; things look so badly just at present that unless I am on the spot I cannot see my way at all clearly. I have little doubt that I will work things all right again; the master's eye makes all go well. There need be no difference in the little allowance I sent to my mother and you—that will be sent home regularly as before. But I want to assist you otherwise if you will allow me to do it. You have enough to do to bring up those six children of yours, even with my little help. I will take your boy Edgar with me; as I am not going overland it will not be so expensive. I will train him to be useful to me, and make a man of him.'

'No, no, Walter, I could not let him be away from under my own eye; he is so young—his education is not finished,' said Mrs. Holmes.

'And never will be, if you keep him always at your apron-string. You cannot do it, Fanny; you must turn him into the world some day, and surely he will be better turned out under my guidance than under none at all. Why, the lad is sixteen, and though he is uncommonly ignorant of the world, he knows enough of books and that sort of thing to acquit himself very fairly in Australia. I

promise to do my very best for him, and he can be of great service to me very soon, if he has only a head on his shoulders. And though it is very hard to find out what your children are fit for, I dare say the boy has average intelligence.'

'Average intelligence!' exclaimed Mrs. Holmes; 'his memory is admirable. If you would only examine him in history, or geography, or Latin, or scientific dialogues, or chronology, you would find —'

'That I do not know the tenth part of what he does, no doubt,' said Brandon. 'But that is not what will make him get on in the world. You cannot afford to give him a profession.'

'I fear not. I wish I could. Perhaps I might by more economy. The education of my children has cost me very little hitherto, only the classics and mathematics from the curate. I should like to bring Edgar up for the Church.'

'But, my dear Fanny, if you were to give him a profession, you must send him away from you. If I take him I will do my utmost to get him on, and I will really look after him, and keep him out of mischief, better than you can do at a public school or a university.'

'Oh! Walter, you know what a state Victoria is in—full of runaway convicts, and all sorts of bad characters, attracted there by the gold-diggings. I should not like Edgar to meet with such people.'

'At my sheep stations he will see little or nothing of these people. I will keep him busy, and by and by, when he comes to man's estate, I will give him a start; and if you think I succeed with Edgar, I will take Robert, too, when he is old enough.'

'I know, Walter, that you mean very kindly by me and mine, but I do not care so much for my boys being rich, or getting on, as you call it; I want them to be good. I do not wish to throw them into the world till their principles are fixed, and strong enough to withstand temptation. Edgar is very young, and you are not firm enough to have the guidance of him.'

'I can be firm enough in important things,' said Brandon; 'but there are a number of little matters that a lad should learn to

determine for himself. Let us ask Edgar if he would like to go. Don't say anything for or against. For once let the boy exercise his choice, and have the freedom of his own will. You may reverse his decision afterwards if you see fit.'

Mrs. Holmes assented to this, but with some fear and trembling. Edgar was called in, and his uncle kindly and fairly made him the offer. The lad hesitated—looked at his mother, then at his uncle, then at the floor.

'What do you think I should do, mamma?' said he.

'Your mother wishes you to make your own choice,' said Brandon.

'No, no; I cannot part with you yet, my dear boy.'

'Nonsense, Fanny; do not stand in the boy's light,' said Brandon, a little ruffled at being taken at his word, and the lad's decision reversed by his mother.

'I don't want to go if you do not wish it, mamma,' said Edgar, looking rather ashamed at his choice.

'Consult our mother and Mary on the matter, Fanny; I believe they will be more reasonable.'

The advice of both grandmother and aunt was to the effect that Mrs. Holmes should take advantage of her brother's kindness, and entrust Edgar to his care. It was not without a great effort that she made up her mind to part with her son, and she had many serious compunctions of conscience afterwards; but as his letters home were regular and very prettily expressed, and as his uncle Walter generally added a few lines to say that the boy was doing remarkably well, and growing strong and large, she took comfort, and hoped that all was for the best.

Brandon was rather surprised at the cool reception he got from Harriett Phillips on his return; it was a relief to him to see that she could part from him without regret, for he felt none at leaving her. He had been putting on his Australian set of feelings, and preparing to like his bush life very much, as he had done in reality before. He had Edgar with him when he came to bid the Phillipses good-bye, and Emily was much amused at the idea of this model lad

going out to Melbourne in a large ship, and seeing dear Wiriwilta before she could do so. She gave him messages to some of the people, and desired him to inquire after the welfare of her pet opossum and her rose-crested cockatoo, and write her a full, true, and particular account of them all, and of how he liked the colony, which Edgar readily promised to do.

'And so this Mr. Hogarth has left London, Emily?' said Mr. Brandon.

'Oh, he has gone home to see about getting into Parliament—what stupid work it must be!'

'Don't talk so absurdly,' said Aunt Harriett.

'I see by the newspapers that he is likely to be put up; and you think it stupid work, Emily, do you? You are a young lady of taste. I think the same.'

'He is quite sure of success,' said Harriett Phillips, who thought the question and remarks might have been addressed to her, as the best informed person in the house.

'Miss Melville will be pleased at her cousin's going into the political line,' said he.

'Indeed, we are all pleased. I never saw any one so fitted to shine in Parliament,' said Harriett. 'He has promised, when the election is over, to visit papa; their politics will suit, I think.'

'And how is Miss Melville?' asked Brandon.

'Quite well, she is always well; but we have been very much troubled about servants of late. I believe really that all the good servants have gone to Australia, for we cannot hear of a housemaid or nurse to suit us, and it puts every one about. I know it annoys me, and Miss Melville (who holds rather a singular combination of employments, and I must say that she certainly discharges both of them extremely well) is particularly engaged just now, making up her housekeeping books.'

'And how is Miss Alice Melville? She is not so invariably well as her sister is.'

'No, she mopes more. She has not half the spirit of Miss Melville; but I believe she is quite well just now.'

'Well', said Brandon, with a half sigh, 'I have come to bid you all good-bye; no one can tell when we may meet again.'

'Oh! no fear,' said Mrs. Phillips, 'we will see you here again in a year or two. Mr. Phillips is often grumbling about his affairs, but I know it just ends in nothing.'

'By the by, Emily,' whispered Brandon, 'you promised if I was a good boy that you would give me a great treat. You will never have another opportunity.'

'Oh! yes,' said Emily, 'I recollect quite well—come along with me,' and Brandon followed the child to the nursery. Elsie was singing something to a tune that sounded like that of 'Chevy Chase,' a great favourite with Brandon in his childhood—but she caught the sound of footsteps at the door and stopped abruptly.

'This is our nursery,' said Emily; 'mamma says it is far better than the old one at Wiriwilta, but I do not like it half so well. I have brought Mr. Brandon here, Alice, to hear your songs and your stories, as I promised him the night you would not sing in the drawing-room when he asked you.'

'Go on, Miss Alice, I beg of you; do not let me interrupt you. Indulge me for once—that old air carries me back many years,' said Brandon.

'Oh, no,' said Alice; 'I could not venture on a stanza before you. You cannot imagine what doggerel I make to please the children.'

'It is not doggerel; it is beautiful,' said little Harriett; 'it is the best song of all, and the newest—the one that Alice has made about the fire, when we were such tiny babies; and how poor mamma was so weak and ill, and papa was away, and the flames were all around; and Peggy and Jim—you recollect Jim, black Jim, Mr. Brandon—and Mrs. Tuck—Martha, you know—were working so hard to save us; and then when Mr. Brandon came up on his horse, Cantab—we told Alice his name was Cantab—she knew all the rest of the story—and rode so fast and got off in such a hurry, and fetched water and quenched the fire. Oh! Mr. Brandon, it is a lovely song.'

'And all made up after our talk of old times the other night; for I thought it was just the thing for a ballad, and Alice will do anything

I ask her. You see that we *will* make a hero of you, and we will sing this song in your praise when you are far away,' said Emily.

'Then I am not be forgotten,' said Brandon, speaking to Emily, but looking very hard at Elsie. 'I do not wish to be forgotten by any one here; but I do not care for being remembered as a hero, which I do not deserve to be—but as a—a friend.'

'Our friends here have been so few that we are not likely to forget any of them, and with Emily beside us we stand a good chance of hearing your name frequently,' said Elsie.

'And you made a song about me—actually about *me*,' said Brandon, looking as if he wished the five young Phillipses out of the way.

'Oh! Alice can make a song about anything,' said Constance; 'she made one about my little kitten.'

'And such a nice one about my humming-top—how it goes whiz—whiz,' said Hubert.

'And Peggy told Alice and Miss Melville about the fire, and all about you long ago—long before she saw any of us,' said Emily. 'She made up a pretty story to amuse them just as Alice does for us when they were sad and dull—only Peggy's story was all true, and Alice's are mostly not.'

Brandon's quick eye could observe the faintest additional flush pass over Elsie's already crimson cheek, and guessed that Peggy's revelations had been a little too true and minute. What motive had she to conceal anything about him when she was relating her own experiences to divert the minds of the two poor girls in their troubles and perplexities? Was this the solution of his refusal in the railway carriage? If it was. he should try again. He had been a fool, an idiot, to give up so readily at the first nay-say. Now, it was too late; his passage was taken out for himself and Edgar, and he was to sail on the morrow; but if things looked decently well at Barragong on his return he must write, though he was no great scribe.

'Shall I not call Jane?' said Elsie, who felt embarrassed by his looks and manner, and dreaded his saying anything particular before a group of the sharpest children in the world. 'She is

extremely busy, but if you have come to bid her good-bye, she must see you for that.'

'You used to talk of going to Australia—to Melbourne, I mean—with your sister and Peggy, when she returns.'

'We hope to be able to do so,' said Elsie.

'Then I will see you again—I *must* see you again. Don't call your sister yet—don't.'

Here Brandon was interrupted by the entrance of Miss Harriett, whose curiosity as to where Emily had taken her friend had led her to the nursery, a place she seldom visited.

'Why, Emily, what a thing to bring Mr. Brandon into the nursery! You are a dreadful girl! I must tell Miss Melville of this.'

'I have only come to bid good-bye to some friends,' said Brandon.

'They should have come to you in the drawing-room, only those children are so fond of their liberty that they prefer the nursery, where they can torment Alice to their hearts' content, to anything like restraint in the drawing-room. What a litter the place is in! I do wish we could get a nurse.'

'I must see Miss Melville, too, and bid her good-bye,' said Brandon.

'She is in the housekeeper's room,' said Harriett. 'As you have been introduced by Emily into the nursery, perhaps you will let me take you there.'

'Good-bye, then, Miss Alice,' said Brandon.

'Good-bye,' said she.

Brandon could not drop a word of his intention to Jane, for Harriett Phillips was at his elbow when he made his adieu; but somehow Elsie treasured up his parting looks, and embarrassed expressions, with as much fidelity as if he had made an open declaration of love. Many a woman's heart lives long on such slight food as this. And the next day, Brandon was on board, and soon on the high seas, on his way back to his sheep-stations and his troubles.

XIV

FRANCIS HOGARTH'S CANVASS AND ELECTION

There can be little doubt that Jane Melville was a good deal influenced in her decision as to the position she ought to hold with Francis by the letter she had received from Tom Lowrie on the morning of the day in which her cousin had betrayed to her more unmistakably than ever the state of his own heart. It was something more for him to give up, and, as I have said before, she rather overestimated both the importance of the public duty and the amount of success in it which Francis was likely to attain to. It might seem to impartial observers rather Utopian to hope and expect some regeneration of the political world of Great Britain from the return of an intelligent country gentleman of independent and original principles, for a few obscure Scottish burghs, to be one of an assembly of six hundred and fifty-eight legislators, but it is from such Utopianism, felt, not in one instance, but in many, that the atmosphere of politics, both in Great Britain and in Australia, can be cleared and purified. When people, whether as electors or candidates (or, as in the case of Jane Melville, even those who are neither), take an exaggerated view of the trouble, expense, and annoyance attending the discharge of public duty, and form a low estimate of the good that each honest energetic individual can do

to his country by using every means in his power to secure good government, to promote public spirit, and to raise the standard of political morality, the country is on the decline. It may grow rich, it may increase in national prosperity, but, as a nation, it wants the soul of national life and national freedom. I prefer Jane Melville's rather unreasonable hopes to the pusillanimous fears—the *lassez-faire* policy of those who think they know the world far better, and who believe the game of public life is not worth the cost of the candle that lights it up.

If she had been the only woman in the world, or the only woman likely to suit Francis, and to make him happy, she would have felt very differently; but surely he could have no difficulty in finding, among the hundreds of thousands of marriageable women in Great Britain, some one as likely (she even thought, more likely), to satisfy his heart than herself. It was only because circumstances had made him know her so well, and because he had been so intimately connected with no one else, that he believed he loved her. He was a man whom any woman might easily learn to love; and if she steadily held out to him that she was only his dear sister—his faithful friend, and that she could never be anything else, he would ere long form a tenderer tie. But she hoped and wished that his lot might be cast with a good woman, who would not grudge her the secondary place that she felt she could not give up. She tried to convince herself that it could be only friendship really on his part; but he had been so unused to affectionate friendships, especially with one of the other sex, that he was very likely to mistake his feelings.

The state of her own heart she did not like to look into very closely; she knew that Francis was inexpressibly dear to her, but the absolute absence of all jealousy made her doubt if it were really what is called love. She could look forward without pain to another person becoming more to him than herself. My readers will think that if it had been really love, it would have forced itself upon her, and burst through all the barriers that were laid across its course. But love in a strong nature is a very different thing from the same

amount of love in a feeble nature. If it had been her own property and career that had to be given up for his sake, her love would have probably conquered all private ambition; but the very high estimation in which she held her cousin, fought against her instinctive wish to make him happy. And if the irrevocable step were taken, what security would she have that he might not regret it?

She dwelt in her own mind on the disparities between them, which, but for the peculiar circumstances in which they had been placed by her uncle's will, must have prevented the formation even of the friendship, now so close and so precious. She was perhaps scarcely aware that such contrasts are more favourable to the growth and the continuance of love than too near resemblance in character and temperament. She was so different in many ways from him—he was literary—she was practical; he was poetical and artistic, and by no means scientific—she was destitute of taste, and saw more romance in the wonders of science than in much of the poetry he admired so much; he was aristocratic by temperament, and only forced by her influence at the turning-point of his life into her democratic views—she could not rest from the over-activity of her nature, while he liked repose, meditative, literary, and *dilettanti.* The strong sense of duty, which certainly was the guiding principle of his nature, led him to exertion; while Jane worked because she could not help it. With Jane's temperament Francis never would have stayed for fifteen years clerk in the Bank of Scotland, while there were new countries to conquer, or new fields to work in. He found pleasure in beautiful things; all disorder or disorganization was positively painful to him. To begin again a life of comparative poverty, burdened with the care of Elsie, would be far more trying to him than to her; for though she had been brought up in greater affluence, she cared less for the elegances of life. She loved him far too well to allow him to sacrifice a great deal more than she thought she was worth for such a doubtful good, and she entered heart and soul into the prospects of this election, as the thing which would decide Francis' fate, and would give him still nobler work to

do, to keep him from regretting what it was better he should not obtain.

The spiritual communication on the subject of Francis' hopes, to the effect that after a time he should succeed in the object dearest to his heart, had made far less impression on her mind than on his. She had not heard the unearthly taps; she had not been startled by the appropriate answers; she had not herself had her hand arrested at the letters which spelled out the unknown names. Her curiosity led her to attend a *séance* with Francis at the same place, but everything on that occasion was a failure. The spirits had not got rightly *en rapport* with her; her dead relations were misnamed; their messages were uncharacteristic; and the spirit of Mr. Hogarth never could be summoned up again. She therefore determined to dismiss the whole subject from her thoughts, and advised Francis to do the same. Mr. Dempster, however, was not willing to relinquish his half-made proselyte; and certainly, the less Jane was inclined to believe in these manifestations the more she became attached to the simple-minded pious visionary who rested so completely in them.

Jane's own life was particularly full of work and of worry at this time; for, as Miss Phillips might have taken part of the blame to herself, if she had conceived it possible that she could do wrong; for it was on her account that the housemaid had given warning—she said that two missusses, that was, Mrs. Phillips and Miss Melville, was enough for her, and she could not submit to a third, and she couldn't abear Miss Phillips's interference. The nursemaid took umbrage at Elsie sitting so much in the nursery with the children, though it was what Mr. Phillips liked, and what the children delighted in; and besides there was no other convenient place for her except her own bedroom, which was too cold for comfort and too dark for fine work. Elsie's position in the house was rather anomalous, and certainly added to Jane's difficulties.

While Francis was busily engaged with his canvass, Mr. and Mrs. Phillips took a short tour on the Continent. Harriett would have liked to accompany them, and threw out hints to show that she expected an invitation; but her sister-in-law thought they had done

quite enough for her, having her all that time in London, and taking her about everywhere. Jane was to be left in charge of the children, and Elsie was to go with her mistress. Now that Mrs. Phillips had a lady's-maid, she could not possibly travel without one; and as neither her husband nor herself knew any modern language but their own, Elsie might be useful besides as an interpreter, as she understood French very tolerably, and had learned a good deal of Italian. There might be advantage by and by from being able to advertise French and Italian acquired off the Continent, for perhaps a school might suit the Melvilles better than going into business; so Jane was very glad indeed that her sister, who would profit most by it, should take the trip rather than herself. Miss Phillips returned to Derbyshire, as she had no desire to stay even with such a congenial companion as Miss Melville, with the drawback of a houseful of children.

In the meantime Francis' canvass went on briskly; Mr. Sinclair constituted himself his most active agent, and certainly took more trouble and fatigue about it than any paid agent; but he sometimes seemed to do his cause more harm than good by his constant recurrence to first principles, which alarmed the jog-trot old Whigs, and occasionally even the out-and-out Radicals.

The five burghs, whose representation Mr. Hogarth was about to contest, were grouped together because they lay in adjoining counties, and not because they had any identity of interests. In the good old times, before the passing of the Reform Bill, each burgh sent one delegate to vote for the member. The delegate was elected by the majority of the town council, and as that body invariably elected their successors, the representation of the citizens, either municipal or parliamentary, by such means, was the most glorious fiction that has ever been devised by the wisdom of our ancestors. The double election in this case had no good tendency. The Reform Bill was, on the whole, a very good thing, more because it was a great change in the representation, which was carried out without endangering the constitution, and was an earnest of still greater reforms being made in the future, than because there is any very

great improvement either in the character of the electors or their representatives; but to Scotland it was a greater boon than to England; for the semblance of representative institutions without the reality was a mockery to a free people, and a very mischievous mockery. In 185— the burghs had each their registered voters on the roll, who each voted for his favourite candidate, so that the votes of five hundred men in one burgh could not be neutralized by those of eighty men in another.

The stronghold of the Conservative party lay in Swinton, the genteel, and Freeburgh, the county town. The Liberals mustered very strong in Ladykirk, which had taken to the woollen manufactory within the last quarter of a century, and had increased very much in extent and population, so that it had far more voters paying 10*l.* rent than any of the other towns. In Auldbiggin and Plainstanes parties were so equal that no majority on either side could be reckoned on, but the Whig majority in Ladykirk was expected to overtop the Tory majority in the two first towns by as much as would secure Hogarth's return. The Honourable Mr. Fortescue was again to be put up for the Tory interest, for though he had not distinguished himself last parliament, he was a perfectly safe party man, and connected by marriage, not with the duke, but with a Tory marquis, next in consideration in the district, who had great influence in the county returns.

Mr. Fortescue found he had a different man to fight with in Francis Hogarth from his opponent last election, Mr. Turnbull; so he felt he needed more backing, and brought with him a Mr. Toutwell, a great gun with his party, who went his rounds both with and without him, and acted as his mouthpiece.

'One has confidence in an experienced man,' said this gentleman, in a confidential way, to the electors, when he met them singly or by twos and threes. 'If the earl had put up a man of greater parliamentary experience, he might have had a chance to oust Mr. Fortescue, but his picking up this quill-driver, who has spent his life behind a bank-counter, and offering him to the burghs, is really an insult to the constituency. Mr. Fortescue is no orator—there is

enough of us in the House to speak, Heaven knows—there is only too much talk about nothing; but Mr. Fortescue's vote was never given wrong—never once did he forsake his colours! Don't look to the speeches—look to the division list, and there you will see that you can trust your member. As for this Hogarth, there is not a single thing that he has done that inspires confidence, even with his own party. He is far too Radical even for the earl. I cannot imagine how that old fox has been so misled as to take him up—probably for a consideration. Look at those allotments he has made over or given away to his labourers—the most dangerous innovation that could possibly be made in such a country as this. When the non-propertied classes see such things, they fancy they should all share in the spoil. This is how Socialism is to come in upon us. These levelling and no doubt godless views prepare the way for such revolutions as we have seen with so much horror across the Channel. Old Cross Hall was a sceptic of the worst kind, and picked up his views of religion and politics in France, and this new man could not rest till he too went to France to improve his mind in the same way. These cottages he has built on his estate, no doubt to increase his popularity, and perhaps at Ladykirk they may go down, but in Swinton and Freeburgh people see things differently, and even Plainstanes and Auldbiggin like no such new fangled notions put into working people's heads. The idea of compelling proprietors to build such palaces for their tenants' labourers, when the labourers themselves do not ask for them, and do not care for them when they get them!—and I hear that Hogarth says they should all build houses just like his. Mere clap-trap to win political influence—for his own people break the windows, and take no care of their fine new houses. I am sure property is burdened heavily enough without this absurd crotchet for additional spoliation. Old Cross Hall was crazy enough to leave him a lot of money as well as the estate; he certainly might have left the money to the poor girls he had brought up like his daughters, and not have left them to starve, and to be a burden on the country; and young Cross Hall can see no better way of spending it than in throwing it away for the

chance of this seat—but he has no chance. The bank-clerk's hoards will be somewhat diminished before all his expenses are paid. We need take no trouble—indeed, Mr. Fortescue might walk the course.'

But, in spite of all this careless talk, Mr. Fortescue, and Mr. Toutwell too, did take a great deal of trouble, and employed every possible means to secure the certain majority of thirty which they spoke of. The greatest hope they had was in a split between the new man and the earl's party, and Mr. Fortescue's agents managed to make the most of every little point in dispute.

Reports reached the earl from different quarters, mostly reliable, that the return of Mr. Hogarth would not at all strengthen his party in the country. He had but a small following, and was comparatively little known. The county voters were mostly tenant-farmers, who generally voted with their landlords. The race of portioners, or small proprietors, was dying out in —shire, as it is in all the British island, and large proprietors were very much opposed to Cross Hall, on account of his loose views as to the rights of property. At Newton, however, which was a large manufacturing town of recent growth, and not a royal burgh, but which was of very great importance in the county representation, Francis Hogarth was extremely popular. He was the real friend of the people—the only man in the county who seemed to understand anything about the rights of labour. The electors of Newtown felt aggrieved that they, who were far more numerous than those of any of the five royal burghs, were thrown into the county representation, where their votes did not count for one-fourth of what they would do in the burghs. They felt personally interested in the return of Cross Hall (as he was generally called), and would not leave a stone unturned to secure it. The non-electors of Newtown—a still more numerous body—regretted that they could do nothing to further his views, except by going *en masse* to Ladykirk on the day of the election, and combining with the non-electors there, so as to make as great a physical demonstration as possible, for they considered that Cross Hall, if returned, would be their

representative—ready to fight their battles, and to redress their grievances.

'Be careful, Mr. Hogarth, be careful,' said Mr. Prentice, his Freeburgh agent. 'Say nothing that may awaken jealousy or mistrust among our own party. You are much too frank in your assertion of your opinions—correct enough, no doubt; but your people are not prepared for them, and your majority is not so large that you can afford to lose a single vote.'

'It certainly is not large in your burgh,' said Francis.

'A minority of twenty-three is the most favourable thing you can expect here—I think twenty-four. At Swinton there is a certain minority of fourteen, which the least imprudence on your part would double. Auldbiggin and Plainstanes are ties at present, so your majority at Ladykirk should be large, to cover up our deficit. We have the hardest work to do, with the least credit; we should have double pay at these losing burghs,' said Prentice, laughing. 'But, for Heaven's sake! Mr. Hogarth, keep your friend Sinclair quiet. If he would only take a fever or something of that kind, to keep him in bed till he is wanted to vote, it woud be a real service to the cause. You must address the electors to-night at a public meeting, and if possible, keep Mr. Sinclair away. We will get Mr. Hunter, and Mr. Thirlstane, and a few others, to speak in a quiet, taking way, and you need not say too much yourself, and do not make it too distinct. I have been agent here ever since the passing of the Reform Bill, and I should know what electioneering for these burghs is. Our people admire fine speaking—a few flowers of rhetoric. A little oratory and enthusiasm are very telling, but you need not pin yourself down to any definite course of action.'

'I am, perhaps, too much disposed to an indefinite course of action; my principles I wish the electors to confide in, and I will act up to them as the occasion may offer,' said Francis.

'But if you are too broad and direct in your assertion of principles, you may offend a third part of our sure votes. Nothing like a few good large words, with not much meaning, for these burghs. By the by, there is a deputation from Ladykirk come to wait

on you, before you speak at this meeting. It is nearer for them to come here than to Swinton, so it is more convenient.'

In fact there were two deputations awaiting the Liberal candidate—one from the electors of Ladykirk, headed by Sandy Pringle, a man who had risen by the fabrication of woollen yarn from a weaver into a millowner, though not in a very large way; and the other from the non-electors of Newtown, who, though they had no legitimate right to take up Cross Hall's time, wanted a few words with him before election. Their spokesman was Jamie Howison, of the class called in the south country, in common parlance, a *creeshey weaver*, who had not risen, and was not likely to rise.

Both deputations appeared at once, which to a man less honest and direct than Francis, would have been inconvenient. He might have requested one to retire while he gave audience to the other, but he had so little the fear of Mr. Prentice before his eyes, that he really wished every elector and every non-elector to hear his sentiments and opinions as fully and openly as possible, and he received both of the deputations together.

He first heard what his own would-be constituents had to say, and satisfied them as to his perfect independence of the great Whig families, and that he meant to keep his judgment unbiassed by party politics.

'Then what about the extension o' the suffrage?' asked Sandy Pringle; 'we want five-pound voters at Ladykirk.'

'That is a question likely to be kept in abeyance during the sitting of this parliament,' said Francis. 'If it is brought forward I must say that I cannot at present vote for extension of the suffrage.'

'Oh! we thocht ye were an oot-an'-oot Leeberal—nane o' your finality Whigs that took ae bit step in the richt direction, and then durstna venture further. Ye maun vote for the five-pound vote if ye are to be oor man,' said Sandy Pringle.

'We thocht ye would be for a baulder step than a five-pound vote,' said Jamie Howison; 'ye're said to be the puir man's friend. Is it fair that the like o' huz, that mak the country what it is, should

hae nae voice in the elections? We're for manhood suffrage, an' the ballot, and we look to you to be oor advocate, for we thocht ye was to be oor member. If so be as we had had our richts, and had votes to gie, ye should hae them a'.'

'It's fear—it's fear of the earl and the Freeburgh gentry that keeps him frae speakin' oot his mind,' said Sandy Pringle; 'but his heart is a' richt. He kens what's wanted, and if he's no thirled to the Elliotts and the Greys, he can vote as he thinks fit. I think we can depend on him.'

'My friends,' said Francis, 'I wish to show no fear and no favour. I would not say to you what I would not say to the earl, nor to the earl what I would be sorry or ashamed to let you hear. I wish you to know, as clearly as I can explain them, my political principles, so that I may raise no unfounded expectations and disappoint no one wilfully or designedly. I think with you that it is a great evil that the working man has no voice in the election of the members of the Legislature. I hope to live to see the day—and I will labour to advance it—when every man shall feel his influence in greater or less measure in that most important part of the duty of a free people; but have any of you ever seriously considered the effect which would follow the adoption in Great Britain, at present, of manhood suffrage, or even of reducing the franchise to a five-pound vote?'

'There would be far mair economy in the public service,' said Sandy Pringle.

'There would be far less jobbery an' corruption in government pawtronage,' said Jamie Howison, the Newtown weaver.

'They couldna swamp the consteetuencies by makin' fictitious votes,' said Sandy.

'They micht bribe, if the franchise was limited,' said Jamie Howison, 'but with manhood suffrage an' the ballot, a man micht vote just as he liked, and huz working men hae oor richts, an' oor feelins, an' oor interests, just as dear to huz as pedigrees an' acres to the aristocracy. We want nae ten-hours bills—what richt hae parliaments to dictate to huz, an' keep huz frae sellin' a' we hae to

sell, oor time an' oor labour? We want to be let alane to mind oor ain business, an no to be treated as if we was bairns that didna ken what was for their gude. Na, na, Maister Hogarth, when ye gied thae allotments to your hinds, ye showed that ye kent what they were fit for, an' ye *maun* see that the bigger a consteetuency is, the purer it is like to be.'

'My friends,' said Francis, 'the effect of any great extension of the suffrage, as things are at present, would be to put the *whole* political power into the hands of the least educated classes of the community.'

'Not the whole with a five-pound vote,' said Sandy.

'Surely, not the whole, even wi' manhood suffrage,' said Jamie. 'We dinna want it all, only oor fair share.'

'But it is in the nature of things,' said Francis, 'that it must be so. Your five-pound voters, Mr. Pringle, would outvote the ten-pound voters enormously. Your non-propertied electors, Mr. Howison, would out-vote even the five-pound voters, and would, in every constituency, carry their candidate by an overwhelming majority. This would not be good either for the country or for you.'

'But the rich have the House of Lords, where they are paramount,' said Sandy Pringle.

'A very feeble barrier that would be found against the abuses of democracy,' said Francis. 'You know well that in all emergencies the Lords must give way to the Commons.'

''Deed maun they,' said Jamie Howison, 'and the only chance of justice for huz that they maun. But, Maister Hogarth, ye see that property, an' education, an' rank, an' a' that, hae had it a' their ain way for hundreds o' years; it's time that we should hae oor turn. We arena like the French (in the days of the auld revolution); we would respect property. Even if we had owre muckle power, I think we wad mak nae bad use of it. It's hard to keep huz oot o' oor richts for ever because ye think we micht get a thocht mair than is good for us.'

'But,' said Sandy, sagaciously, 'ye acknowledge that things as they are are na fair. What wad ye do to mend them?'

'You recollect a proposal of Lord John Russell's, some years ago, to reconstruct the electoral districts, by making them each return three members, and allowing each elector to vote for only two, so as to secure somewhat of the rights of minorities,' said Francis.

'Oh! we misdooted that; for we thocht it was a treacherous thing on Lord John's part,' said Sandy. 'It is hard eneuch for the Leeberals to get their dues wi' this restricted franchise; an' this arrangement would mak the Tories stronger than they are noo.'

'But is it not just that a minority of a third should be secured their third share in the representation?' asked Francis.

'Oh! ye're gaun to first principles, like your freend, Maister Sinclair. Nae doot it's a' richt, but it wadna answer. The third in ae district maun do without their man, an' in some other they micht hae the best o' it. That wad mak a' odds even.'

'It does so in a great measure at present, though not so much so as I could wish, but every extension of the suffrage will tend to extinguish the minorities more and more. You cannot say that, in any electoral district you could name, with manhood suffrage the working classes would not enormously outnumber the educated classes.'

'An' we maun wait for the reconstruction of the districts afore there is any chance o' justice?' said Jamie Howison. 'I'm thinking we'll hae to tarry lang for our richts.'

'Not so long, if you steadily keep in view that this is the *first* step. Lord John Russell's proposal was an approximatation to a right principle, which, if it had been properly supported, might have given the fairest opening for greater reforms. If the Conservatives had voted for a really Conservative measure like this it would have been carried, but as it was brought forward by a political opponent they voted against it, though they now taunt him with introducing it. If the Whig party had seen the importance of it, and had vigorously supported it, it might have facilitated the extension of the suffrage, a measure which none of you can desire more earnestly than I do. I have conversed recently with some colonial gentlemen returned from Australia on the working of their

manhood suffrage and the ballot, and from one of them I got an idea which appears to be a still better one than Lord John Russell's. It was embodied in a Municipal Bill for an infant city—that of Adelaide—drawn up by no less a person than Rowland Hill, then Secretary for the Colonisation Commissioners. I believe it was a deplorably bad town council for Birmingham that led his acute mind to ponder how to secure the rights of minorities, as it was the enormous expense of a correspondence he entered into on the subject of the coal-tax grievance that led him to make the calculations and to devise the system by which letters could be carried all over the kingdom for a penny.'

'Well, and what does Rowland Hill say about the minorities that ye care muckle for?' asked Sandy Pringle. 'We hae a' great respect for Rowland Hill, and what he has to say on sic a subject should weel deserve a hearing at ony rate.'

'He had an arrangement by which a quorum of the citizens could plump for one member of council, giving additional force to their vote. As they voted for one instead of eighteen, their vote was worth eighteen. By concentrating their vote they proportionally increased the power of it.'

'Oh! we ken that plumping aye makes the vote mair valuable,' says Sandy.

'Simply because your one vote is an advantage to your member, which is not given to any other; but this system gives a much greater reward for concentrating your vote. In Lord John's case the thing was incomplete, for unless you have the power of giving your two votes to one man, a minority of a third cannot get in a member. It is the cumulative power given by Rowland Hill that secures that minorities will not be extinguished. This subject will receive my careful attention, if I am returned for the burghs, for I consider it by far the most important question of the day, and if I can get the working classes to sympathize with me, I hope for success in time. Also a revision of the partnership laws, so as to afford every facility for working people to co-operate with each other, for it is only by that means that much can be done to

improve their condition. Those Rochdale pioneers are going on most satisfactorily with their co-operative store, which they are now extending to other undertakings of a greater magnitude, and I hope soon to see hundreds of similar associations in Great Britain and Ireland. But we want more freedom for limited liability companies, instead of so many difficulties being thrown in their way by over-legislation. I do not want to treat working people as children, but to encourage them to help themselves. I have had to work hard myself, and I know what it is.'

'We will lippen to you,' said Sandy Pringle, 'and even though in some points we may not see things exactly as ye do, we want a man, an' no a mere thing to hae a name, an' be coonted like thae Fortescues and Turnbulls they are puttin' up.'

'Little good, little ill, like a spale amang parritch, was that chap Trummle,' said Jamie Howison.

'I am sorry I have been so short a time in the district, so that I am so imperfectly known to you, but I hope in time to show that I deserve your confidence,' said Francis.

'But what about the ballot?' asked Jamie Howison.

'I have not quite made up my mind about the ballot,' said Francis. 'It is humiliating to confess to such ignorance, but there is so much to be said on both sides that I am puzzled. I should like public opinion to be so much improved that there would be no necessity for the ballot, but perhaps without it we cannot regenerate public opinion. I am quite open to conviction on either side on this as on many other political questions. Now I think you understand my principles. I will vote for whatever I think right, no matter from what side of the House or from what party it emanates. If you can trust to my intelligence and my integrity, you will vote for me, but I make no pledge.'

'And we will ask nane,' said Pringle, 'we will lippen to you.'

'But Maister Hogarth,' said one of Jamie Howison's colleagues, 'we look to you to mind the interests of them that has nae votes, and that is a large body, as ye ken.'

'Yes, a very large body indeed, when you include the women and

children,' said Francis.

'Oh! the women and children,' said the weaver, with a disappointed air, 'I was na thinking of them; they are weel enuch—the men taks care o' them.'

'Not always the best care in the world,' said Francis. 'Children need protective legislation to guard them from being overworked by parents and masters. Women are supposed to be free agents, but they do not really get all the rights of free agents—they should be empowered to protect themselves; the law should support them in obtaining their just rights. A wife ought not to be treated as a chattel; her earnings should be protected if she wishes it. And women, too, should have a wider field of labour. The difficulties which are thrown in the way of the weaker sex, in their attempts to earn a livelihood, both by law and by society, are very unworthy of the age we live in.'

'Weel, Maister Hogarth, though I dinna just see the needcessity for bringing in women to compete wi' men at their trades, we could do ill without them at our mills, an' maybe ye're in the richt. Ye'll find us Whigs at Ladykirk united, and in that case ye're safe to carry the day,' said Sandy Pringle.

Francis' return, however, ran more risk than either he or Sandy Pringle counted upon, for the suggestion carefully circulated by Fortescue, Toutwell, and the Tory agents, and feebly denied even by Mr. Hogarth's own Swinton agent, that he was a most unpopular man in the county, and that it was a mistake on the earl's part to support him, very nearly brought down a member of the Reform Club to force him to retire after his canvass was made, and his majority counted as small but safe. This shabby proceeding was only averted by the firmness of the Newtown Whigs, who were indignant at such treatment of a man so independent and so able as Mr. Hogarth, and they declared to the earl, through their agent, that if he did not with his party support Cross Hall for the burghs, they would set up Mr. Sinclair for the county and vote as one man for him, so that Lord Frederic would have an overwhelming majority over the Honourable James.

This threat of a certain defeat for the county restored the earl to his original intention of giving a mild support to Hogarth, who certainly would be a better man than Fortescue. There was the usual amount of personal abuse levelled at the banker's clerk—neither his father nor his mother was spared—there were caricatures of him in mean lodgings and shabby raiment, doing things for himself, which he recollected doing, and which he was not ashamed of having done. If Francis had been made a duke, instead of merely trying to be a member of parliament, he would never have been ashamed of his past life, nor would he have been distressed or disturbed by the unexpected honour. He would have taken it as a matter of course. His speech from the hustings was clear, manly, and dignified, and far surpassed that of Fortescue, even with Toutwell's diligent prompting. Mr. Sinclair's speech was received with cheers and hisses, but in print it read exceedingly well.

Then followed Mr. Toutwell's very rhetorical, very sarcastic, and, as his own party said, very telling speech; but to Jane, who read this report with the greatest interest, it told nothing.

The result of the poll was a majority of three in favour of Francis Hogarth, Esq., of Cross Hall, who was accordingly declared duly elected, and took his seat along with Lord Frederic (who had got in for the county by a majority of twenty-seven, much to the earl's chagrin, who had supported Cross Hall for nothing, after all) and the other members of the new parliament.

XV

MRS. PHILLIPS'S FIRST GRIEF

Mrs. Phillips was somewhat annoyed at her husband's treating Elsie Melville on their continental tour more as a travelling companion than as a paid dependant. Where was to be the glory of this journey through France and Italy, of which she would have to boast all her life, if her maid and herself were to be on such terms of equality? In vain Mr. Phillips said he had disliked the difference that was made between the two sisters, and had only submitted to it in London on account of the servants, and that he was glad to take this opportunity of treating Elsie as her birth and education deserved. In vain he pointed out that French ladies conducted themselves to their dependants with less distance and hauteur than Englishwomen, and that in France it was proper to do as the French did. Mrs. Phillips felt offended, and, for the first time in her life, a little jealous—not very jealous, for she was so conscious of her own beauty, and so unconscious of her defects of mind and temper, that she had a strong substratum of confidence in her husband's affection—but at this time, Elsie was looking really very pretty; her movements were quick and graceful—a great contrast to Mrs. Phillips's slow, dignified, Juno-like deportment—and her conversation so sparkling and amusing, that she thought Mr. Phillips

looked at her too much, and talked to her too much. When they spoke French together—for Mr. Phillips was trying to revive his more than half-forgotten schoolboy French, and found he could do it more easily with Alice than with the foreigners—Mrs. Phillips had a vague sense that they were talking about something that they did not want her to hear. Elsie would have enjoyed this trip exceedingly, but for Mrs. Phillips's unreasonableness and caprices; but, even in spite of them, she brought away many delightful recollections of scenes and people. When on this tour, she felt as if she could write verses again, if she had only time and quiet.

When in Paris she called on Madame Lenoir with a letter of introduction from her cousin. She received Elsie very kindly, and asked her and the Phillipses to her 'at homes'; but as all the people there talked French, Mrs. Phillips did not find them at all entertaining, and she thought French hospitality a very shabby affair. They did not remain long in Paris, but went down to Italy, and visited Florence and Rome. Mr. Phillips wished he had had his two eldest girls with him in Italy, and promised to himself that next time he took the journey they should accompany him.

When they returned to London they found that all had gone well in their absence—Francis had won his election; Jane appeared to be in excellent spirits; and the children had made good progress with their lessons. Mr. Phillips appeared to miss his old friend and neighbour, Brandon, very much, and could not find any one of his colonial acquaintances who could fill up the blank which his departure from London had made. Besides, they were always losing somebody out of their pleasant circle. Every mail steamer, and every fine clipper ship that sailed for Australia seemed to take one or more from them; and though new people did come, they did not appear to be so agreeable as those who went away. Mr. Phillips could not remain contented in London, so he proposed a trip to America with his wife and Alice as before; but Mrs. Phillips disliked the sea, and did not feel very well, so she said she would rather stay in London with the family, though it was getting rather late in the season for London. She did not care to go to Derbyshire without

him, far less to go to Scotland; so, if he could be so cruel as to leave her, she would prefer London. If Emily had been a little older, Mr. Phillips would have taken her with him, for he disliked travelling alone, but she was too young, as he himself acknowledged.

Elsie could not understand the cause of Mrs. Phillips's peculiarly disagreeable conduct to herself lately, and she was almost on the point of leaving her, and taking another situation, when the children, one after the other, took scarlatina, and in such a house of sickness she—their favourite—could not be spared. All lessons, of course, were at an end. Mrs. Phillips looked into the nursery several times a day, and said how sorry she was to see the children so ill, and how she suffered from her anxiety about them; but it was Jane and Elsie who took the real charge of the little patients. The mother did not seem really alarmed, though the children were really very ill; the only thing she did that appeared like apprehension was making Jane write to Mr. Phillips to return to England without delay as soon as the children were seized with the fever. Jane also wrote to Dr. Phillips, and Vivian hurried to London, and stayed with his brother's family until his return, which was a great lightening of the load of responsibility which the sisters felt rested on them. In spite of every care and all that either doctor or nurses could do, little Eva fell a victim to the disease; and, after her death, Mrs. Phillips for the first time seemed to realize the danger of the others. Everything had gone so prosperously with her since her marriage; she had known no sorrow, and little annoyance; she had always had her husband at her side to smooth everything for her, so that she really scarcely knew what the contingencies and trials of life were; but this death, happening when the father who loved his children so dearly was absent, affected the indolent and generally unimpressible woman very strongly. She felt that she was somehow to blame about it. 'What will Stanley say when he comes home? Oh, what will he say to me for losing his darling child? Oh, why did he go to America, and leave me with such a charge? And the others will be sure to die, too!'—were her constant lamentations.

Her grief made her quite unfit to take any charge of the

survivors, and yet she was incredulous when she was told by her brother-in-law, or by the Misses Melville, that they were really recovering. It was not till her husband returned, which was as soon as he possibly could, and assured her that they were quite out of danger, that she gave any credit to it. Mr. Phillips felt the loss of one of his children more keenly than most men, but he was grateful to see that he was likely to save the others, and he did full justice to the care and attention which they had received from Vivian and Jane and Elsie.

Francis Hogarth was in London, attending a short parliamentary session, when the children were so ill, and was constant in his inquiries as to their health. Dr. Vivian Phillips forced Jane and Elsie out to hear their cousin make his first speech one evening, when the patients were decidedly convalescent. Jane was very much pleased with Francis' *début*, and though Elsie thought it rather tame, because it was not on an important subject, and was very calmly delivered, she was glad that he had not broken down, for it seemed a most imposing assembly for a stranger to address. Francis had visited the Derbyshire Phillipses, according to promise, after his election was over, and had been a good deal interested in Dr. Vivian, both on account of his own qualifications, and because Jane Melville had been interested in him. He now felt that Jane and the young physician were placed in very intimate relations with each other, and he naturally enough fancied that what he so much wished for himself would appear desirable to a man so acute and sensible as Vivian Phillips. Her calm temper, her promptitude, her method, were all shown to great advantage in a sick room. He forgot that Elsie's gentle tender ways and her overflowing sympathy might be equally attractive, but Dr. Vivian was quite used to all sorts of sick rooms, and to all sorts of nursing, and nothing was very striking to him, so that he fell in love with neither sister, though he liked them both very much.

Jane in particular, was one of those women who may count herself fortunate if she meets with one real lover in her lifetime. William Dalzell was not to be counted, except perhaps as a blank,

but by means of the most favouring circumstances, she had taken Francis Hogarth's heart into her possession, at least for time, and this was her one prize in the strange lottery of love. No other attachment she was likely to inspire, as she felt herself, but her lover was not so clear-sighted. Dr. Vivian Phillips had a great respect for her, and enjoyed her society now and then as a pleasant change from the more insipid company of his sisters or their female acquaintances, but to spend a life with her would be too fatiguing. She seemed always to require him to think his best, to say his best, and to do his best in her company. Now a wife just intelligent enough to appreciate his own abilities, but willing in all things to be guided by him, was a desirable thing; but one so thoroughly his equal as Jane Melville would allow him no repose.

The children did not gain strength rapidly, and Emily in particular made a most tardy recovery. Her illness threatened permanently to weaken her constitution, particularly as winter was fast approaching, and she had felt that season in England very trying during the preceding year. Her uncle Vivian strongly recommended that she should winter in a milder climate to re-establish her health, and Mr. Phillips thought going to the south of France, where the girls might acquire the language without much trouble, would be a good arrangement; but when he mentioned it to Emily herself as an excellent idea, the child languidly put it aside.

'Why not take up back to dear old Wiriwilta?' said she. 'We were never ill there. It is warmer and drier than France; and if Miss Melville and dear Alice go with us, we can learn lessons just as well there as here. I am tired of this great London, with its smoke and its noise.'

Mr. Phillips was not a man to disregard a sick child's longing at any time; and when his brother said that, though he would regret the departure of the family from England, her native air was probably the very best she could have, and the long voyage in a good ship would benefit all the children, he turned his thoughts towards Australia, as he could not have believed possible three months before. The accounts he received from Dr. Grant as to his

affairs were satisfactory enough, but the returns were not at all what he had expected; and he found that his London establishment was very costly. He might return to England in a few years, but the children were so young they might go on with Miss Melville very well at Wiriwilta for some time. A very fine ship was on the berth; Mr. Dempster was going in it, and several other acquaintances; so that, though he would have preferred waiting for Brandon's report of how things were going on, he decided on leaving England before the season was so far advanced, on Emily's account.

Mrs. Phillips was in consternation at hearing her husband say he was really going to return.

'I thought you was never going back to Australia again, Stanley. You promised me you would not. What will you do about the children's education?'

'We will take Miss Melville with us, and I have no fear but that they will all do very well. Their music, certainly, is not provided for; but something may turn up for that. Our first business is to get them into good health.'

'But Miss Melville will never go without Alice,' said Mrs. Phillips.

'Probably not; but we can take Alice, too.'

'I thought you said we was spending too much money, and that we must retrench,' said Mrs. Phillips.

'Our children's education is the last thing I should think of retrenching on,' answered her husband. 'I have heard you say that Alice saves her salary in your milliners' bills. I have scarcely seen that proved, however, Lily; but Miss Melville saves me two hundred a year—that is clear enough, in black and white. It would be false economy to grudge her salary. Besides, Emily would be broken-hearted to part with Alice, so that I will offer to take both sisters with us, if they will come.'

'We don't need such a housekeeper as Miss Melville at Wiriwilta. The house used to keep itself,' said Mrs. Phillips.

'I know I had more trouble with it than was pleasant or convenient,' said her husband. 'I think things will go on much more comfortably there if Miss Melville continues with us; and after all

their exceeding kindness and care of our poor dear children during their illness, I know that you too must be disinclined to leave them behind us.'

'Oh, yes! really they were very good to the children. I was not strong enough to do much for them myself; and I don't feel inclined for the voyage just at this time. Let us go overland, and it will be sooner over.'

'No; we cannot go overland; there is very little pleasure going overland with four young children, and as I suppose you will want one servant, as well as Miss Melville and Alice, you must think of the expense.'

'I hate the sea, and you know I must be on shore before the end of February. And you recollect Mr. Brandon, for all his difficulties—saying he was ruined and all that sort of thing—would have gone overland, if he had only had his letters soon enough.'

'Because he was only one, or, with Edgar, two, and time was of more importance to him than the difference in passage-money. A fine long voyage will restore our children to health, and it does not matter to me being a month or two longer on the voyage. I think we are sure to be in Melbourne time enough for you. If it were only you and myself, Lily, there is nothing I should like so much as the overland route. There is so much that I should like to see and to show to you, but under present circumstances it is impossible.'

No arrangement could have suited Jane and Elsie so well as Mr. Phillips's proposal, as a personal favour to himself, that they should accompany his family to Melbourne. It was the destination they had long aimed at; and as they were neither of the station nor qualifications to obtain free passages in any immigrant ship, they joyfully agreed to his liberal offer.

'But,' said Jane, 'we must be perfectly frank with you. We have had a great desire to begin business in Melbourne together. We must tell you that we have often planned to join our savings to those of Peggy Walker, when she returns to Melbourne, as she will probably do ere long. Plans, of course, may not be carried out, but if

ours are, we may leave you when you depend most on us. I am quite satisfied with my position in your family, but——'

'But neither you nor I are quite satisfied with your sister's,' interposed Mr. Phillips. 'It was the best arrangement that at the time could have been made; but you would never consent to go with us to Australia, and leave Alice to work here by herself; so, if she sees anything, either in Melbourne or in the bush that will suit her better, she is quite free to accept of it, and to leave Mrs. Phillips. Her services and your services to our children in this recent affliction can never be forgotten by us. I can assure you, Mrs. Phillips feels deeply indebted to both of you.

The party to Australia was increased from an unexpected quarter. Harriett Phillips had found that she had made no impression whatever on Mr. Hogarth. He had paid his visit to her father, but had taken almost no notice of her, who had been the person who invited him: in fact, he had markedly preferred her elder sister. His head had apparently been so full of politics, or something else, that he had not been half so agreeable as when she had met him in London, so that she was now very sorry that she had treated Mr. Brandon so cruelly during the last days of his stay in England. He certainly would have proposed if she had not dicouraged him so much; it was really almost wrong in her to try to make him jealous, and she had succeeded only too well. After having entertained the idea that she could be married to him if she pleased for several months, she missed the pleasing excitement of a lover when she returned to her flat country life.

Now that her brother had actually made up his mind to leave England, she would also miss the change and the gaiety of a London winter, which she reckoned on having every year; so she astonished him by saying that she should like of all things to accompany them to Melbourne, and to see a little of bush life at that dear Wiriwilta that Emily was always talking about. She did not think that she would care to stay long, but for a year or two she really thought the life would be very pleasant for a change, just to see how things were done in these outlandish uncivilized places. She said, too, to

her brother, that she thought she could be of service to Mrs. Phillips and the children. The society of Victoria was so indifferent, that it would be desirable to form a pleasant little coterie of one's own. The children's music should really be kept up; and she would be most happy to give them lessons. If her papa and Georgiana and Vivian could only spare her for a year or two, she should really like extremely to go. She would feel it so sad when Stanley left for an indefinite period again.

Mr. Phillips was pleased with the proposal; it showed a more friendly feeling towards his wife and family than she had ever evinced before, so he offered to pay all her outward-bound expenses, at any rate, for her. If she liked Australia, perhaps she might stay there with them altogether; or, indeed, she might find a home for herself there, and settle in the colony. Harriett said such a thing had never entered her head—that she went merely on a visit; but she set about getting her outfit in a very business-like way. It was an exceedingly busy fortnight for Jane and Elsie; but by dint of great applications to ready-made warehouses, everything was really got ready in time, and Mr. Phillips had again to admire the thoughtfulness, the foresight, and the method which Miss Melville showed in all her arragnements, while Elsie's busy fingers were employed from morning to night in doing an endless variety of little things that were needed to supplement the ready-made stock of clothes.

XVI

ANOTHER GOOD-BYE

Emily brightened up wonderfully at the prospect of a return to her old home. She seemed to gain strength every day, and no objection could be made to her going up to Edinburgh to pay her long-promised visit to Peggy Walker before she left England. Mr. and Mrs. Phillips and little Harriett accompanied her, and they took Jane Melville with them, for Elsie could not be spared from the needlework, and she did not wish so much to go to Scotland as Jane did.

Peggy was delighted to see her two nurslings, and also to see the young lady to whom she had given a home when she most needed one. Tom eagerly showed Jane what he had done in her absence, and received the commendation he deserved for his industry and his success. Grandfather was very weak, but in very tolerable spirits; this visit from Peggy's friends would be something for him to think on for the short remainder of his life. Mrs. Phillips's beauty and her fine clothes were something new to him; and the liveliness of the girls, and the politeness of their father, and Miss Jean's kind inquiries and kind looks all did him good.

Francis Hogarth met, by appointment, his cousin Jane at Peggy

Walker's, where she meant to bid him good-bye, but he was not disposed to do so.

'You *must* come to Cross Hall, just to give a look at it before you bid the country farewell for ever. Mr. Phillips, do come round by Cross Hall, and let Jane see her old home once more.'

'I want so much to see Cross Hall, that Alice tells us such pretty stories about,' said Emily.

'Cross Hall! is that the name of your place?' said Mrs. Phillips. 'I would like to see it too, very much. Mr. Phillips will go, of course, if we all wish it.'

Jane expected to suffer something in this farewell visit. It was not to be long, but it must be trying. Francis was cruel to ask it, and Mr. Phillips inconsiderate to accept of his invitation. There were some things to be done that were not painful. When they left the train and got into Francis' carriage—which was her uncle's old one, in which she had been used to ride—for a five-miles drive, they passed the gates of Moss Tower, and saw William Dalzell and his young wife riding out, and bowed to both. Then they went to Allendale, for Miss Thomson had expressed the strongest wish to see Miss Melville before her departure for Australia, and Jane, too, was very much pleased to see again one whom she held in such high esteem. There, for the first time, she saw Mr. Sinclair, whose appearance and conversation were quite equal to her expectations; but even he was not so great an object of curiosity to her as Mary Forrester—a niece of Miss Thomson's several years older than the girl who had got her new frock at Mrs. Dunn's, in Elsie's time. Mary was then on a visit to her aunt, and apparently had the charge of two lovely children, cousins of her own, and grand-nephew and niece of Miss Thomson's. Their parents had gone a voyage in search of health, and Aunt Margaret had invited them to spend the winter at Allendale, and cousin Mary to keep them company. Jane thought she had never seen a more charming girl than Mary, who was evidently a great favourite with her aunt and Mr. Sinclair. Frank, intelligent, and graceful, she looked like a sunbeam in the house. The little Phillipses knew at once that she liked children, and

wondered if she knew any of the delightful stories and ballads for which Elsie was famed. The little Munroes would take the Australians out of doors to see the poultry and the wonderful peacock, so Mary and Jane accompanied their charges. Mary had heard so much of Jane that she was disposed to be interested in her, while a new tide of ideas flowed into Jane's mind in relation to this stranger. In all probability this was the girl to whom Francis was likely to become attached when she left the country. And now that it was no unseen, and perhaps impossible, person whom she was to fancy as his wife, but a really pretty and amiable girl, did the thought now give her pain or awaken any sharp pang of jealousy? Her heart filled with many emotions at the thought, agitating and painful enough, but there was no jealousy. The more she fancied that Francis could love her, the more Jane felt that she must love her too.

'I really half envy you, Miss Melville,' said Mary. 'I wish I could do something for myself. You cannot think how anxiously I watched and wondered how you and your sister got on, and how delighted I was when you got the situation with Mrs. Phillips. Your cousin too—it must have been a sad weight off his mind. A generous man like him must have felt the terms on which he got the property very cruel.'

'Yes,' said Jane, 'I know he felt it very much. We have great cause to thank God that things have turned out so well as they have done.'

'Well, Miss Melville, do you know I feel quite ashamed to think of the amount of money which our family has cost Aunt Margaret; and after all she has spent on my education, and I really did try my best to learn too, I feel almost guilty in looking for a situation. There are so many wanting employment, that it seems like taking bread out of their mouths; and here am I, a full-grown woman, dependent on other people for mine. There are four girls of us, and only Grace at school now, but yet none of us are doing anything for ourselves. I spoke to Aunt Margaret about taking a situation, but she said she must have me at Allendale for the winter, on account

of Archie and Maggie. After that is over, I may speak of it again. You are going to Melbourne, where I have got a brother doing pretty well; but one does not like to be dependent even on a brother. If you think there is any opening there for us, will you let us know through your cousin? we see him very often.'

'Then you stay at Allendale for all this winter?' said Jane.

'Yes, and it will be very pleasant. I like living with Aunt Margaret so much, and John and I were always the two who drew together most of the family; and then Mr. Sinclair is the dearest old gentleman in the world.'

'My cousin seems to be a favourite of your aunt's,' said Jane.

'I never saw aunt take to any one at once as she did to him. What a pity your uncle did not take him home; it would have added very much to his happiness and to yours.'

It was not like the parting of strangers that took place between Jane Melville and Mary Forrester.

'Will you let me kiss you?' said Jane, timidly, as she said good-bye. This was rather a remarkable proceeding on Jane's part, for she was not addicted to the promiscuous osculation so common among young ladies, but she felt for Mary Forrester no common interest.

Mary frankly granted the little request, and they parted to meet again—when, and where, and how?

The party then went to Cross Hall, which was unaltered since Jane had left it; and while Mrs. Phillips and the children were resting after their journey, Francis took Mr. Phillips and Jane to look at the cottages he had built, and she mounted her old horse to ride out to see the allotments, which, even in this short time, showed signs of improvement. There were words of greeting to be said to everybody and to every animal about the place. The old servants were eager to tell her of all that had been done, and all that was to be done; they were glad to see her in good health, and apparently in good spirits. Many sad reports had reached Cross Hall about their straitened circumstances when in Edinburgh, and about poor Miss Elsie falling into a decline; and to see and hear that all was so well with the sisters was a pleasant thing for all who were

attached to them. After all this had been gone through, and she went into the room which had been hers and Elsie's for fifteen years, to dress for dinner, the past, the present, and the future all came upon her at once, and she felt as if she could have given the world for the opportunity to give way. Everything was exactly as she had left it; all the furniture which had been taken to Edinburgh had been brought back and placed as it used to be.

'Can I help you, any way, Miss Jane?' said Susan, the upper housemaid, tapping at the door.

'No, thank you,' said Jane: then recollecting herself, and hoping that the presence of the girl might help to steady her nerves—'but stop, do come in for a little, and brush my hair. I am too tired, I think, to do it; and my head aches a little.'

'Is everything right here? The master said I was to tell him exactly how things used to be, that ye should see nae change.'

'All is right,' said Jane. 'If Elsie were here I might forget that I ever had left Cross Hall; and I see that our people have no cause to miss us, so that we can go to Australia with lighter hearts.'

But for all this talk about a light heart, the tears would come into Jane's eyes slowly as she looked out to the familiar scene and heard the well-known voices, and thought that to-morrow she must leave Cross Hall and Scotland and Francis for ever.

Mr. Phillips helped her well to keep up conversation at dinner and during the evening, but after the children had gone to bed and Mrs. Phillips had retired, he thought the cousins might wish to have their quiet talk by themselves, and wished them good-night.

'You have not been in the library yet Jane,' said Francis; 'shall we adjourn there? I have a little, a very little business to talk over with you, and I am going to bid you our real farewell to-night, for I am not going to see you on board ship. I dare not.'

Jane followed him to the library. She had not been in it since they had searched through her uncle's papers, and had read the letters of Madame de Vericourt together. Francis took from the drawer, which still contained those yellow letters, a paper on which was some writing and figures, and a parcel of bank-notes.

'You recollect that you asked me to store the furniture that you left in your room till you saw fit to claim it. After Elsie decided on staying at Mrs. Phillips's, I sent to Peggy's for what you had there, as I think I wrote to you, and Susan saw that everything was placed just as it used to be. Was it so?'

'Yes; exactly so.'

'I do not want to part with any of it, but I got a valuation taken of it the other day, which you see here, and I give you the market price for all the things. There is no favour in such a commercial transaction as that surely, so here is a little addition to your slender capital. You will find the money all right, I think, odd shillings and all.'

'All right,' said Jane, compelling herself to count the notes according to her old methodical way.

'And you like my cottages, Jane, and you hope great things from the allotments, and you were pleased with my two speeches in parliament? Oh! Jane, if I am ever worth anything I will owe it to you, and now you are going to put half the globe between us, I feel as if I had lost more than half of myself.'

Jane could scarcely trust herself to speak.

'It is better so, Francis.'

'If you miss me as I know I will miss you, write and tell me so. You *know*, Jane, I love you,' said Francis.

'I feared it.'

'Why should you fear it? Is it not the most natural, the most reasonable thing I could do? If you loved me you would not fear it.'

'I thought that in all your many avocations, and especially in public life, that you would forget this fancy, but it is well that I must leave the country, for then I may hope that you will form another attachment. Write to me when you do so, that I may know I have not permanently deprived you of domestic happiness, and that I may pray for you both. You think you owe me much, but to you I owe still more. Till I knew you I had no religion, I never knew the privilege of prayer. Even though we may never meet again on earth, we can look forward to a happy meeting in heaven.'

'Now, Jane, when you women bid good-bye to a friend of your own sex, as dear to you as I am to you—for in a sense I am dear to you, am I not?'

'Yes, very dear to me,' was wrung out of Jane, by Francis' earnest looks and words.

'Well, when you bade farewell to Peggy this morning, she took you in her arms and kissed you—you kissed Mary Forrester, a stranger to you—and you are going to leave me—perhaps for ever—me, who would give my life to serve you, who would give up fortune, fame, almost duty for your sake, and you will shake hands coldly, and say—"Good-bye, Francis."'

'Not coldly, my friend—my brother. Do not think I can part from you so,' and by an irresistible impulse, she turned to her cousin, and felt herself folded for a few seconds in his arms, and kissed with passionate tenderness.

'This is what might have been ours for life, but for this accursed will, and your notions of what is best for me, and perhaps a natural disinclination towards my suit. Reflect—think—before it is too late; make your choice;—love in poverty and obscurity, perhaps—but still love.'

'Love is not all life, either for you or for me;—it is better for us to part.'

'Then you make your choice;—but Jane, if you change your mind, write to me, and let me know. I tried to leave off writing at one time; but it did no good, for I could do nothing that did not remind me of you. Then it *must* be good-bye. May God bless you, my beloved one, now and for ever!'

'May God bless you, my dear Francis, and now farewell!'

Another sort of farewell from her dismissal of William Dalzell! Centuries had seemed to have passed over her since that first eventful day of her life. She scarcely could identify herself with the woman who had so calmly and so kindly extinguished a fancied partiality, as she sat down in her own room and trembled from head to foot at the thought of the pain she had given, and the love she had rejected. In the one case she was perfectly certain that she

had done right, in this she was not by any means so clear. As she heard her cousin restlessly pacing up and down the library, she felt tempted to go to him and say she would share his fortunes, and even destroy them for him if he wished it. She looked at the mirror, and wondered at her being able to excite such an attachment; she looked into her own soul, and did not see anything in it to warrant a man in giving her such a power over him. Duty was clear as to the dismissal of William Dalzell, and the result had proved that she was in the right; and now, when duty was so terribly difficult, surely time, that tardy, but certain adjuster of life's inequalities, would justify her both to Francis and herself. William Dalzell's love had appeared to evaporate; but Francis' had grown more intense and passionate till she felt she could scarcely look at him.

But it was true that she had admired his speeches, and that she was ambitious for his success in all his plans. Every one who knew anything about the subject said that Francis Hogarth was the most promising young man who had entered the walls of parliament at this recent general election. He had given great attention to public business; he had mastered the details with ease; and the principles seemed to be intuitive with him.

He had become acquainted with a small band of outsiders like himself, men of independence and originality, who kept aloof from party, but whose votes were of importance to both parties, and whose approbation was of far more value than that of the strongest partizan. No one could tell to what height he might not rise from such a beginning; the ministry had noticed him favourably, and he was as likely as not to be offered office before the parliament had expired.

Mr. Sinclair had told her how his hopes rested on the new member for the burghs, and how many public matters and reforms they talked over together with constance reference to first principles.

Jane was proud of the conquest she had made, and proud of her influence over a man so able, and so upright; but now she felt it was dangerous to see too much of him, and his parliamentary life

had brought him into far more frequent contact with her now than ever before. She had led him so far in the right direction, but now she feared for her own resolution; she knew she could not withstand many such scenes as she had just gone through, and she saw that there was great wisdom and propriety in her leaving the country that he lived in. From her distant home across the ocean, she could hear of his labours and his triumphs, and, she hoped, after a time, of his happiness. But while she reasoned with herself as to the propriety of leaving him, she felt all the bitterness of the lifelong separation. She could no longer disguise the truth from herself—he was as truly half of her as she was of him—and she shivered at the thought of a life to be gone through in which she should never more see his face, or hear his voice. It was as sad a night, and as sleepless, as that she had spent in her cousin's house in Edinburgh, when all doors had seemed to be shut against her, except the faint chance of a sub-matronship in a lunatic asylum. Now, two doors were open to her—one to a life of toil and dependence for herself and probably a happy life for Elsie, at the antipodes; and the other, a life of love with the man who had all her heart, and who deserved it all, with a dependent life for Elsie. Even though her own hand had closed the door, she could not help lingering at the threshold, and grieving that she was shut out from the only paradise she cared for.

So the good ship sailed next week, bearing Jane from the man who loved her, and whom she loved, and Elsie and Miss Harriett Phillips towards the man whom they both thought loved them.

VOLUME THREE

MR. HOGARTH'S WILL

I

MR. BRANDON'S SECOND PROPOSAL TO ELSIE, AND ITS FATE

On Mr. Brandon's arrival at Melbourne after a longer voyage than he had expected in a ship with such a high character as the one he sailed in, he hurried up to Barragong, and was much gratifed to find things there did not look so badly as he had been led to expect. It was his overseer's want of confidence in himself that had made him exaggerate everything that was going wrong, or was likely to go wrong. In fact Mr. Phillips's affairs were suffering much more from the want of the master's eye than his; but Dr. Grant had a better opinion of his own management, and wrote more cheerful accounts. Brandon regretted that Powell had left his employment, for if he had been in charge of Barragong there might have been three more happy months in England for his master.

As his affairs were really in a sufficiently satisfactory state, he felt that he must write to Elsie Melville, renewing his offer of marriage, and endeavouring as far as he could to give her confidence in the stability of his character. How exceedingly awkward he felt it to be to have to write this instead of saying it. How incomparably better such things are done by word of mouth, particularly when one is not a ready and clever letter-writer. He would in the personal interview have felt the effect of one sentence before he ventured on

another—he would have assisted his halting phrases by all the advantages of tone, gesture, and expression of countenance. Though he had failed once in his attempt to win her affections, he had been far more stupid than he was now, and he was now more anxious for success. The more he had thought over the person, the manners, and the character of Elsie Melville, the more convinced he was that she was the one woman in the world for him; but he was by no means so sanguine of being accepted as he had been, particularly when he had only the pen to trust to. There was no saying what so clever and so literary a girl as Elsie Melville was would think of his blundering declaration. The paper looked cold and blank and uninviting—it really was hard to make it the only means of telling her how much he loved her. No kind wishes towards the overseer whose fears and scruples had hurried him away, or towards Miss Phillips, who had interrupted him when he was about to say something he had hoped Elsie could not mistake, accompanied the half-dozen different attempts at a love-letter, which were written before he could please himself. Emily was his friend; Jane, he thought, would be his friend too. Elsie was really a kind-hearted girl, and if he could only convince her that he would be miserable if she refused him, she might pity him a little. He had not the same objections to a little pity that she had on that day in the railway carriage, when he had been so confident of success. But when he reflected on what Peggy might have said with truth about him, and when he put to that the fact that immediately after his refusal by Elsie he had devoted himself to Miss Phillips, there was no doubt that Elsie had some cause to suspect the steadiness of his principles. It was difficult by writing to hint at these things without saying too much, but they must not be passed over in silence either.

At last the letter was written and committed to the country post-office nearest to Barragong—not that he was satisfied with it, but he must not lose the mail. If she was good enough to accept of him, she was to draw upon him for a specified sum for passage-money and outfit, and come out in the mail steamer following her answer.

It was not a brilliant letter, but it was honest and straightforward. However, as Elsie had sailed for Melbourne before it reached England, it was of the less consequence what it was.

Pending her answer, Brandon felt very unsettled. He could not set himself to work systematically, and all the neighbours said that his visit to England had spoiled him for a colonist, as it did with most people. He missed his pleasantest neighbour, Mr. Phillips, and he missed the children. Though Dr. Grant in one direction, and Mr. M'Intyre in another, thought they were ten times better than the Phillipses, Brandon did not feel that they could make up to him for their absence.

Dr. Grant was certainly mismanaging, to a considerable extent, Mr. Phillips's business, and muddling it as he did his own affairs. He had now been many years in the sheep-farming line, and in the best of times, for he had bought very cheap—much cheaper than either Phillips or Brandon, and he had quite as large a capital to start with; but he had a bad way of managing the men on his stations; he gave the same wages as other people, certainly, for he could not help that, but he always gave them with a grudge, and seemed to think his employés were picking his pocket. He had a harsh and dictatorial way of giving orders—very different from Brandon's and Phillips's pleasant manner—and he consequently had never been well served. His men had been the first to leave at the time of the diggings, and the consequences had been most disastrous. From sheer want of hands, he had sacrificed one of his runs with the sheep on it to Powell, and now he grudged to see how very handsomely Powell had been repaid for his money and time in this transaction. The fortune that Powell had made ought to have been his—Dr. Grant's own—instead of filling the pockets of a man who had only sprung from the ranks.

The same style of mismanagement was carried into Mr. Phillips's affairs; and yet when Brandon relieved Dr. Grant of the burden he had so unwillingly taken up, the latter felt rather hurt, for he had had a handsome salary for the charge of Wiriwilta and the other stations, and he would certainly miss the money; and, besides, he

thought it showed a want of confidence in himself on Phillips's part.

At Wiriwilta, however, there was a feeling of pleasure at the exchange, and Brandon had the satisfaction of really benefiting his friend without taking any very great deal of trouble.

In this restless state of his mind he had great pleasure in the society of Edgar, who attached himself to his uncle with quiet fidelity. He soon learned to ride, and to ride fearlessly and far; he learned too to use his limbs, his ears, and his eyes, so that Brandon found he really had a head on his shoulders, which he had been rather doubtful of when the lad had been kept so constantly at his books.

One day when the boy had been talking with enthusiasm of Australian life, and expressing his longing after more adventures, his uncle, who also was eager for change, proposed to Edgar an overland journey together to Adelaide. He had heard that some particularly fine sheep were to be had in South Australia, and he wished to add this variety to his own flocks as well as to those of Mr. Phillips. He had always had a great wish to see the Adelaide side, and this journey would amuse and employ him till he could get his answer from Elsie. If she accepted him, and came out, as he wished, without delay, he might never have another opportunity for making the visit, for he would not be inclined to leave her, for a while at any rate.

Edgar was delighted with the proposal, and helped his uncle with the few simple preparations for their long ride with a vigour and despatch that showed he had the stuff in him for a good bushman. How his tender mother would have trembled at the thought of the perils and hardships of such a journey but as she knew nothing about it till it was safely over, she was spared all anxiety. Brandon was not altogether insincere when he told Elsie and the Edinburgh ladies that the finest prospect he ever saw in Victoria was the prospect of getting out of it, but the present pleasure made him forget many past ones. He had a real enjoyment in the bush life he then talked so contemptuously about. Camping out was to him no

hardship, and to Edgar it was a delightful novelty. It was varied by nights spent at sheep stations, where a hospitable welcome generally awaited them, and an amount of comfort varying according to circumstances. When they crossed the Victorian border, and came to the South Australian side, the welcome appeared to be equally hearty. Edgar Holmes could not help admiring the want of suspicion and the liberality of these absolute strangers.

Brandon went about his purchase of sheep on his way to Adelaide, and made what he thought a very satisfactory bargain. It was to be a joint speculation between himself and Mr. Phillips, and he was sure it would turn out very well. When he had left directions as to delivery, he and his nephew went down to Adelaide, to see what they thought of that little colonial capital. Edgar was charmed with Adelaide, and preferred it out-and-out to Melbourne, but as he had only passed through the latter, and had got acquainted with none of the people there, his preference was perhaps not worth much. Brandon, however, could not help confessing that the Adelaide men had some cause for the patriotism so strongly, and, as he had thought, so tiresomely expressed at the time of the diggings. It had less bustle than Melbourne, and certainly was not so wealthy; but it was a quiet, cheap, and hospitable place, and its prosperity rested on a very solid basis. The amount of cultivation, both agricultural and horticultural, contrasted favourably with that of Melbourne, which had been almost exclusively pastoral till the gold diggings broke out, and had had many drawbacks, in the shape of land regulations, to its becoming a corn and wine bearing country.

Brandon took up his abode at the York Hotel, of course, and met with some pleasant people in and about Adelaide. Some of them he had known in London, and they introduced him to others. If his heart had not been fixed at this present time on Elsie Melville, he might have taken a fancy to one of the Adelaide girls whom he met. They were not so formidable in the array of their accomplishments and acquirements as the modern English young lady; they were frank, agreeable, and not ignorant of domestic matters, and they had no apparent horror of the bush. But Brandon's affections

were really engaged, and he put considerable restraint on his flirting powers during this visit, which all engaged men ought to do, but which, I must say, I have found very few engaged men do; they feel so perfectly safe themselves that they care very little for what construction other people may put on their attentions, or their polite speeches.

Brandon had sent directions for Mr. Talbot to get his letters and forward them to him in Adelaide, for he was now daily expecting Elsie's answer. In case of his being accepted, he would cross over to Melbourne in time to receive her from the next mail-steamer, would marry her there, and take her home to Barragong, and thus save himself two long land journeys.

But the mail-steamer had come with the Adelaide mails, and the next after that with his own letters, but not a word from Elsie or from any of the Phillipses. He had had a few lines from Emily the preceding month, to say that dear little Eva was dead, and that they were all getting better. The address was either in Jane's hand writing or in Elsie's, but he took if for granted that it was Elsie's, and had treasured it up in consequence of that supposition. But this month there was not a word from any of them. There had been plenty of time for an answer, for his letter had been sent *via* Marseilles, so that Elsie had had ten days clear to make up her mind and reply to what she ought to have thought an important communication.

It was using him extremely ill to treat his letter with so much contempt. He was never more near being very angry in his life. It was strange that Elsie Melville, whose manner was so remarkably gentle and winning, should on two important occasions have treated him with such marked discourtesy. No doubt, his letter was not worth very much in itself; but to him it was great consequence. If she wanted a month for consideration, why not write and tell him so? Or, if she feared to commit herself, she might have got Jane to write. Could she have taken the fever? That was a solution—but a very sad one—of her conduct. Jane would have certainly written in that case if she had not got the fever too. He

would alter his plans: he would go back overland; or, rather, he would sail up the Murray, and not pass through Melbourne at all. So he took his passage and Edgar's by one of the Murray steamers, and felt that if he was not a very ill-used man, he ought to feel a very unhappy one.

II

MRS. PECK

In a poor-looking room of a small wayside public-house, about twenty miles out of Adelaide, were seated one evening, shortly after Brandon's departure up the Murray, a man and a woman, neither of them young or handsome or respectable-looking. If they had been so once they had outgrown them all. The woman certainly had what is called the remains of a fine woman about her, but her face had so many marks of care, of evil passions, and of irregular living, that it was perhaps more repulsive than if it had been absolutely plain in features; her dress was slatternly and ill-fitting, her gray hair untidily gathered under a dingy black cap, with bright, though soiled yellow flowers stuck in it; her eyes, which had still some brightness, had a fierce, hungry expression; and the very hands, thin and long, and with overgrown nails, had less the appearance of honest work than of dishonest rapacity. The man was a rougher-looking person, more blackguardly, perhaps, in appearance, but not so dangerous. He had been at the nearest post-office, and brought a letter addressed to Mrs. Peck, which the woman tore open and read with impatient eagerness.

'This is from Mr. Talbot at last,' said the man. 'Long looked for—come at last. I hopes as how it is worth waiting for.'

'Worth waiting for!' said she, stamping on the letter with her foot, and standing up, with such a look of frenzy that her companion moved a little out of the way. 'Hang him, and his clients too!'

'Won't this man come down with the ready, Liz? Does he send to make inquiries? A cool hand—cooler than the old man. Won't out with the blunt till he knows what he's paying for.'

'It's not about him at all,' said Mrs. Peck. 'Not a word has he ever said, good or bad—taken no notice of my letters, no more nor if I had not been such a mother to him. I should have had an answer to my second letter by this time, and I know it was directed all right; he must have got them both. I'll have it out of him, though. I'll have my revenge, as sure as I am a living woman.'

'Don't go into such a scot, woman. Then, if it is not from young Cross Hall, what has that lawyer said to put you into such a tantrum?'

'Oh! just a request to keep on this side of the border, or he'll not warrant my getting a farthing out of Phillips. He offers three pound a quarter more if I don't show my face in Melbourne! Such a beggarly sum it is after all! To think that I should only have two children, and them turning out such ungrateful cubs to me!'

'Two children, Liz?' said the man with a sneer. 'Well, if I was Phillips I'd like to keep you at a civil distance just at present, for you look as like to brain him as not.'

'There's the both of them rolling in wealth. Frank got all Cross Hall's property, and all through me; and Betsy, with her London establishment and her carriage, no doubt, and her children dressed like duchesses, and herself, too—and look at me!'

'Well, just look at you, Liz. I fancy that the sight of you would do them no credit. You're well enough off with Phillips. I think this is a very handsome offer. Though we're both sick of Adelaide, we can stop here a bit longer—at least, till we can see our way clear to get out of it.'

'Do you think I don't care for my liberty? and I hate the Adelaide side. It was all your doings coming across here at all, and a precious

mull you've made of it. I fancy they must be thinking of coming back to Melbourne, from this notice to me to keep out of the way. And do you think I don't want to see my own daughter? Did not I put her in the way of all her good fortune? Did not I dress her the day she first saw Phillips, and did not she look like a angel?'

'And he was spoon enough to marry her, which was more than either you or me expected. As for the girl, she was glad enough to go away from you; you never cared so much for her.'

'Did I not, when I saw she was growing up so handsome and a credit to me?'

'Yes, yes; we both wanted to make our own of her, and I think we did not do amiss, considering,' said Peck. 'We've had bad luck in Adelaide, but things may change—money goes farther here.'

'Money never goes far with us,' said Mrs. Peck, 'and Melbourne is the place where we can get on best. If I had Frank's money, which I must and shall get out of him somehow, we could manage to rub along here, but without it we never could. The black-hearted scoundrel, not to send me a farthing—me who could—'

'You had better threaten him with what you can do in your next letter. I always thought that style of working the oracle would pay best; but perhaps the motherly affectionate dodge was the best to try first. Threaten him in your next.'

'I don't think I'll condescend to threaten him; I don't care to save him from what he deserves for his shameful ingratitude to me. I could make better terms with Cross Hall's nieces than I could do with Frank. Surely they would give me more for my secret than he would do to keep me quiet. They were left beggars, I know, and the estate is worth a great deal to them.'

'Hang it, Mrs. Peck, that is a glorious idea, but don't be too hurried in your movements. You don't care about your own share in the business being known?' said Peck.

'I care for nothing if I could only get my revenge on him, and if I could only get as much out of the Melville girls as would allow me to snap my fingers at Phillips. I would rather relish publishing my connection with him. I would like to bring down Betsy a peg.'

'There's where you always make a mull of it, Liz. Your infernal temper always gets the better of you. Revenge and spite are very good things in their way, but I don't see that they pay. I think you would be very mad to give up so much a year for the pleasure of vexing Phillips and Betsy; and as for the Melville girls, how are you to get at them? There is not shot in the locker to take you to England, and letters are very risky things to write. You're sure to let out more than is safe, and if you let out too little the girls will see no advantage in it.'

'I hate letters,' said Mrs. Peck, moodily; 'but I would like to get at the girls by word of mouth.'

As this interesting pair were engaged in conversation, a traveller of a very different description alighted at the door of the inn, and requested lodgings for the night. He was well-dressed and respectable-looking; he was probably as old as either of them, but his face and air gave tokens of a quieter life and a calmer temper. His horse was knocked up, so that he could not go on to a larger and better-appointed inn than this, which was five miles nearer town; but when he saw the name over the door and the host and hostess, he was reconciled to the inferior accommodation. But he rather objected to the company that he found in the inn parlour, and did not seem pleased with the proposal that he should take supper with them.

'Oh, Mr. Dempster,' said the host, 'I fancy you have got nice since you were in England. These people are decent enough, I reckon, though rather down in their luck, like some others of us. I wish I had such a house to receive you in as that I built on the — Road. I had plenty rooms there; but you see it was not licensed, and I was ruined—at least brought down to this.'

'Well, Frankland, I suppose I must submit,' said Mr. Dempster, 'as you say you have no other place for me; but I never would have thought these were particularly decent people.'

Whether from spiritual influences or not, Mr. Dempster felt a great repugnance to this man and woman. The influence might

have been partly spirituous, for there was a considerable fragrance of strong liquor about them both.

In spite of the unpromising appearance of the house, the hostess produced a very tempting-looking supper for hungry people. She sat down herself to make tea for the company, and was delighted to see Mr. Dempster, and to have a little talk with him about old colonists and old times. She was a very old colonist herself, and had known many ups and downs, generally in the same line of life.

Active, civil, and much-enduring, she was an admirable hostess, but her husband was rather idle and speculative, and had invested the savings of many years in the erection of a large hotel in a place where, in the opinion of the Bench of Magistrates, it was not wanted, and the licence was refused, so they had come down in the world in consequence, and had taken this small inn, where they could just make ends meet. Mrs. Frankland missed the old customers who used to call, and felt this visit from Mr. Dempster something like a revival of old days, and asked him as to the changes he saw in Adelaide; and as Mr. and Mrs. Peck were Melbourne people, who did not know anything about the old colonists, Mr. Dempster spoke to her with freedom.

'You have been visiting your married daughter, I suppose,' said Mrs. Frankland.

'Yes, that is the first thing I had to do on my return.'

'A fine family she is getting about her, I hear; but I have not seen her for awhile. This house is not good enough for her to stay a night in.'

'Yes, she has a very fine family—another little fellow since I left Adelaide.'

'You must feel it lonesome now,' said the hostess.

'Yes: it is the way of the world, and one should not murmur at it; but yet a man must feel it very much when his only daughter, and one so much his companion as my girl was, chooses a home for herself, and surrounds herself with new ties and new cares.'

'You should see and get some one to take care of you,' said Mrs. Frankland, cheerily;—'a pleasant, kindly body—not too young. You

must have met many such in England, who would have been glad of the chance.'

'Yes, and who would have grumbled at the colony whenever she came out, and given me no peace till I took her home again. Now my business and my interests are all in South Australia. Besides, I like the young women best, and they would never look at an old fogie like me; so I must content myself with my memories of the past and my hopes for a future life. My home is not so lonely as you fancy it, Mrs. Frankland. Even here I feel the departed ones are near me. The veil that separates this world from the next is a very thin one; and if our intercourse with each other is less complete than in the days when we were together in the flesh, it is none the less real. I have become a spiritualist since I went to England.'

'A what?' asked the hostess.

'You must have heard of table-turning, and all those strange manifestations?'

'La! Mr. Dempster, I never thought of *you* giving in to a pack of nonsense like that. I beg your pardon for my rudeness, but really you *do* surprise me.'

'What would you think of spirits who can read unseen letters—tell the names of persons whom none of the company knew—find out the secrets of every one in the room? You recollect Tom Bean, who was lost in the bush twelve years ago, and more; his spirit appeared to me in London, and gave me a message to his old mother, to say he was expecting her soon; and the old lady did not live three months after.'

'Well, that is strange, but I would be very hard to convince. But yet, Mr. Dempster, that is no reason why you should not get a nice tidy body to make you comfortable. The spirits would not surely begrudge you that. And so you had a pleasant voyage, and went round by Melbourne so as to see all that was to be seen. Did any of the old colonists come out with you?'

'We had a large party altogether— Mr. —— and his family, who had just been home to finish their education.'

'And you admired the young ladies, of course, but really they are too young for you. Have they grown up handsome?'

'Not particularly handsome, but very pleasant-looking; but if you talk of beauty, it was a Melbourne lady who bore off the palm on board ship. Unfortunately, she was married, and it would have been very improper to take a fancy to her, but Mrs. Phillips is superb.'

'Mrs. Phillips of Wiriwilta?' said Mrs. Peck, eagerly.

'Yes, I fancy that is the name of the place; at least the children used to talk about it by that name. Mr. Phillips is a sheep-farmer on the Victoria side,' said Mr. Dempster.

'And you say she is handsome?' said Mrs. Peck.

'Perfectly beautiful!—but uneducated, and somewhat capricious. I fancy her face must have captivated her husband, who is a very intelligent, agreeable man.'

'I suppose they are rich now?' said Mrs. Peck.

'Oh! very well to do, I fancy. I visited them a good deal when I was in London.'

'How many children have they?' asked Mrs. Peck. 'I knew them long ago.'

'They lost one with scarlet fever before they sailed. There were four on board ship; but there are five by this time, for Mrs. Phillips stayed in Melbourne for her confinement, and had a little boy within a week of landing.'

'Is her husband with her?' asked Mrs. Peck, eagerly.

'Oh, no! I think Phillips went up to his stations; he had a number of things to see to. What do you know about them?' asked Mr. Dempster, rather surprised at Mrs. Peck's curiosity.

'I was once in their employment at Wiriwilta, and Mrs. Phillips was uncommonly good-looking then. There was not so much style in those days as I suppose there is now.'

'Probably not; we have all had to work hard for what we have earned in these colonies and Phillips must have made his way like the rest of us. They had a very pretty little establishment in London.'

'Kep' their carriage, no doubt,' said Mrs. Peck, with a thinly-disguised sneer.

'No, they did not; but if it's any satisfaction to you to know it, Mrs. Phillips has had a tour on the Continent, and has had a lady's-maid.'

'A lady's-maid,' said Mrs. Peck; 'well! well! and the children, I suppose, are being educated up to the nines?'

'They took both the governess and the lady's-maid with them to Melbourne,' said Mr. Dempster. 'They were sisters, and very superior young ladies. In fact, to my taste, Mrs. Frankland, the lady's-maid was more charming than the mistress; not so regularly handsome—but very lovely—while as to intelligence and refinement there was no comparison. If she had been a dozen of years older I might have been a little presumptuous.'

'Was this Mrs. Phillips so very far behind as that her maid was so superior to her?' asked Mrs. Frankland.

'It happened that these sisters were the young ladies of whom, even in these distant parts, you may have heard something; who were brought up to inherit a large property in the south of Scotland, by a very eccentric uncle, who left everything he had to a son whom nobody had ever heard of before, and left the girls absolutely penniless.'

'Was not their name Melville?' asked Mrs. Peck, eagerly and fiercely.

'Yes,' replied Mr. Dempster, astonished to find his chatty communications to his old friend, Mrs. Frankland, taken up in this way by this unprepossessing-looking stranger. 'Yes, their name was Melville, and I never in my life met with more amiable, more intelligent, or better-principled girls.'

'I saw about it in the papers,' said Mrs. Peck, endeavouring to subdue her delight and exultation at the idea of the girls she wished so much to come in contact with being so near her as Melbourne. 'I took a great interest in it. I like these romances of real life. And so, Mrs. Phillips is up, and these girls are down, and glad to eat the bitter bread of service. It is very amusing.

Was Mrs. Phillips much taken up with them on account of their misfortunes?'

'I do not know,' said Mr. Dempster, drily. 'If you have served Mrs. Phillips you will know that she is not the same at all times.'

'Then there was a large party of them on board; a servant, no doubt, and these two Melville girls, and the children?' said Mrs. Peck.

'There was also a sister of Mr. Phillips's—rather a fine woman, too—come out on a visit.'

'And a fine lady, too, I dare say,' said Mrs. Peck. 'Mr. Phillips holds his head pretty high. I warrant his sister and Mrs. Phillips would have some sparring. And the chilren are good-looking, I suppose? I saw none of them since the first was a baby. What are they like?'

'They are very pretty children, and getting on well with their studies. The eldest Miss Melville is the most thoroughly cultivated woman I ever saw.'

'Oh, leave Cross Hall alone for that,' said Mrs. Peck. 'He was always crazy about education, and that sort of thing.'

'Cross Hall!' said Mr. Dempster. 'I suppose you will say next that you know Francis Hogarth, of Cross Hall, member of Parliament for the Swinton burghs?'

'Member of Parliament, too!' said Mrs. Peck, with the same subdued fierceness as when she first took Mr. Dempster up about the Melvilles. 'Member of Parliament! Ungrateful dog!' she said, under her breath; but her expression of vindictiveness was not altogether lost on Mr. Dempster. 'Oh yes! I know him; or at least I know all about him. Nobody did know anything of him till he came into the property, you know; but I really know more about him than most folks. There are some people that would give their ears to know what I do; but there is a saying in the north, where I was born, "Least said is soonest mended;" at any rate, least said to them as it don't concern.'

'If I had you at a *séance,*' said Mr. Dempster, 'I could get all your

secrets out of you, whether you liked it or not. Yes, Mrs. Frankland, I really could.'

'I don't think it can be right,' said the timid hostess, who, though she was very fond of hearing the news, preferred to get them from living persons and not disembodied spirits. 'Mrs. Peck, you are taking nothing.'

'I got bad news just before tea, and that took away my appetite; but I have got over that now, so I'll trouble you for a mutton chop, Mr. Dempster, and Peck, just pass me the pickles, and be good enough to give me a hot cup of tea, Mrs. Frankland, for this one is as cold as a stone;' so Mrs. Peck felt inclined to make up for lost time, and made a very hearty supper. She wound up with two glasses of brandy-and-water hot, and she got Peck out of the way, for she wished to have a quiet talk with Mr. Dempster.

Mr. Dempster was not disposed to encourage her confidence; her strange inquiries about people he had been greatly interested in, recalled the séance which had so much startled Francis Hogarth, and he suspected that this must be the person who had written the letter the spirit had been questioned about, and, consequently, that she was Hogarth's mother; no mother, certainly, to be proud of! The spirit said that her son ought to have nothing whatever to do with her, and Mr. Dempster was disposed to obey all spiritual communications. Besides this, all his instincts were strong against any intercourse with a woman so disreputable-looking, with an expression of countenance alternately fierce and fawning.

Now the fawning manner was put on. Mrs. Peck had an object in view—she wanted money to take her to Melbourne, and to take her immediately, and this easy-going, benevolent-looking Adelaide gentleman seemed to be the most likely victim she could meet with.

She had long wished to see her daughter apart from her husband, and there never had been such a chance since she was married; and to get hold of one or both of the Melville girls at the same time was a conjunction of circumstances absolutely and marvellously favourable. Her last remittance from Mr. Phillips had been received a month before, and was spent as soon as it was got. Peck, with

whose fortunes she had for many years connected herself, had not been lucky of late. He had come to Adelaide at race time, and had not got on well with his bets. He had done a little in gambling, but had got into a sort of row at a low public-house, and been taken up and fined for being drunk and disorderly, and dismissed with a caution; so he had gone up to the sheep-shearing, and then had worked a little at the hay-harvest, and again at the wheat-harvest. He could work pretty hard at such times, and make good wages; but he had no turn for steady, regular work, and neither had she. If she had been in Melbourne, she could have borrowed the ten or twelve pounds needed for her passage-money, and a decent-looking outfit from people who knew her there, and guessed that she had some hidden means, either from friends or foes; but in Adelaide she was unknown except from her connection with Peck, which did not inspire confidence.

This Adelaide gentleman had just come from London, and could know nothing about her, so she was determined to use her plausible tongue, and get the money out of him.

As Mr. Phillips said, she was possessed with the spirit of falsehood. She always had a disinclination to speak the truth, unless when it was very decidedly for her own interest to do so, or when she was enraged out of all prudence. So now, when she wanted to get an advance from Mr. Dempster, she forgot the agitation and the eagerness which she had shown about the Phillipses, the Melvilles, and the Hogarths, and opened up a quite new mine of anxieties and fears. Her secret, such as it was, should not be told to any one but the parties to whom it was valuable, and who would pay her handsomely for it, so she must now prevent this friend of the family from even guessing at what her schemes were.

III

RAISING THE WIND

As Mrs. Peck sipped her brandy-and-water, putting a constraint on herself in so doing—for her natural taste would have led her to swallow it in large gulps, but that would not have answered her purpose of impressing Mr. Dempster—she began to talk of the letter she had received from Melbourne, which had distressed her so much. Her daughter was ill and dying, and her son-in-law had written to her to beg that if she possibly could she would come across to see poor dear Mary before she was no more; but, poor fellow, he was always hard up—a decent well-meaning fellow he was—but he wanted push, and things had never gone rightly with him.

'They have never had the doctor out of the house since they have been married, and many births and many deaths keep a man always poor, Mr. Dempster, as well you must know; and it's many's the five-pound note as I've given to them out of my small means to help them through at a hard pinch, and he thinks, of course, as how I can just put my hand in my pocket and pay my passage in the first steamer as quick as he thinks for to ask me; and so I would, and would never have begrudged it, for my poor Mary's sake, but things has gone so contrary with me and Peck for this year back that I

ain't got a penny to lay out. And there's the poor soul laying so bad, and thinking as I'm on the road, I dare say, and me can no more get to her without wings nor she can to get me.'

'What is your son-in-law by trade?' asked Mr. Dempster.

'Why, he ain't got no trade to speak of, but he's warehouseman to Campbell and Co., in Melbourne, the merchants, you know,' said Mrs. Peck.

'Then he must have a good situation and regular payment—he ought not to be so badly off,' said Mr. Dempster.

'There's such expenses with a family in Melbourne, where there's much sickness especially. A very decent, good-tempered fellow he is, and don't spend his wages away from his home. Poor Mary! I well remember the day she was married, and how pretty she looked in her white gown, and how she says to me, "Oh, my mother! I can't abear to leave you, even for James," and now she is agoing to leave all of us. And when little Betsy was born, and I was a nursing of her, she looked up and says she, "Oh, mother! I don't think as I'm long for this world;" but I roused her, and said she wasn't a-dying then, and my words was true, for she was not going then; but now to think my being so far from her and her so bad.'

Then Mrs. Peck wiped her eyes energetically and sobbed a little. Mr. Dempster seemed to be soft-hearted and simple-minded. She thought she had made an impression, and she endeavoured to deepen it.

'I am a very old colonist. I have been in Australia this thrity year and more, travelling about from place to place. When you and Mrs. Frankland were talking about changes and ups and downs, I thought on a many as I have seen in the other colonies. There's them as I remember without a sixpence as is now rolling in gold. I don't know the Adelaide gentry so well, but I reckon they chop and change just like the others. It is very unlucky for me to be here just at this present time, for I know of a many in Sydney that I might have applied to for a little loan, and they'd have been glad to give me assistance; but, unfortunately, I am on the Adelaide side, where

nobody knows me. There's the Hunters, of Sydney, that I was nurse in the family.'

'And the Phillipses, of Wiriwilta, too, who I dare say, would be most happy to help you if you were straitened on the Melbourne side,' said Mr. Dempster, drily. 'Mr. Phillips is a more liberal man than Mr. Hunter.'

'It is not Mr. Hunter I'd look to, but his wife; she has the generous spirit,' said Mrs. Peck.

'The Hunters are at present in London—at least, Mr. Hunter and the family are. Mrs. Hunter died four years ago,' said Mr. Dempster.

'That's a pity. Oh, dear, dear! I am sorry to hear that news. Poor, dear lady; but in the midst of life we are in death,' said Mrs. Peck.

'No doubt we are,' said Mr. Dempster. 'No one knows that better than I do, for I am always living amongst the dead, and they occasionally help me to judge of people. I get a good deal of insight into character through their means; and my impression is, that there is not a word of truth in all you have just been telling me. You want to go to Melbourne, no doubt, but it is not to see a dying daughter. You have other plans in view which cannot be carried out here.'

Mrs. Peck was somewhat taken aback by this blunt expression of opinion coming from a man apparently so suave and gentle. 'Indeed, sir,' said she, 'I never heard nobody doubt my word afore; but this comes of leaving the place where you are known. It is to see my daughter that I am most wishful to go to Melbourne. No doubt I might have other reasons, for I don't like Adelaide; but it's this letter and this bad news that has made me so set on going. But I was asking no favour of you. If I did want a loan of a trifle, I'd have paid back every farthing of it with good interest. But I think I had better draw on a friend of mine in Melbourne. I suppose that if I did that, I could get the draft cashed at any of the banks?'

'You could get it cashed anywhere, provided you showed your authority to draw, and convinced the person to whom you applied that your friend was good for the money. Under these conditions I should not mind advancing it for you myself.'

'But you'd be rather hard to convince, I fancy,' said Mrs. Peck. 'After the unhandsome way you have doubted my true story, I would not like to apply to you. But any advance that any one would make to me would be as safe as the bank. I have an annuity, and have had it for many years.'

'No,' said Mr. Dempster, 'you have no annuity; you got a sum of money instead.'

Mrs. Peck started at this confident assertion, and coloured indignantly. 'How can you speak so positive about things you can know nothing about? I have an annuity from another quarter.'

'For valuable services, I suppose,' said Mr. Dempster. 'Well, if you can prove that you are still in receipt of an annuity, and if you can lodge an order to forestall it, I dare say you can get an advance from any Adelaide bill discounter; but I myself would rather not do business with a person who I feel is not to be relied on.'

To put an end to the revelations, true or false, of this unpleasant old woman, Mr. Dempster asked to be shown to bed, as he was tired; and he found his room, though small, was as clean and comfortable as Mrs. Frankland had been used to give to him in her more prosperous days.

Mrs. Peck's first attempt had failed, though it had appeared very promising. She thought she would next try Frankland, who, though he was poor, might be victimized to the extent of ten pounds. She did not think she could affect him by dwelling much on the desire she felt to see her dying daughter, though for the sake of consistency it was mentioned as her motive to get to Melbourne just at this time; but she had several sums of money due to her in Melbourne, and she was afraid, from the letter she had just received, that she would lose them if she kept out of the way; there was nothing like being on the spot—nothing like prompt measures when one wants to get in money. Mr. Talbot's letter was sufficient warrant for her to raise money on Mr. Phillips's annuity, but not for the purpose of going to Melbourne, which she had unluckily betrayed. It was also rather disagreeable in its tone, and not likely to inspire confidence in any one who read it. So she had only her own

representations to trust to, and she certainly gave a very minute, and at the same time glowing account of her debtors and her expectations from them; but what with one thing and another she had really never been so hard up in her life. Peck had not got all his wages for harvesting, and she had been so foolish as to lend a little money in Adelaide, which she feared she could not get back. Indeed, they had a score at the inn that had lain too long; but if she could only get her own she could pay all and be quite easy. She spoke of a rate of interest for a trifling advance that rather dazzled Frankland, and he was wondering if he could not manage to raise it, when his wife came into the room, and stopped their talk by saying it was bed-time. When she was told of Mrs. Peck's wishes and her offers, Mrs. Frankland peremptorily refused to listen to them, saying they had no money to advance to any one. Frankland had brought them down low enough in the world by being so free in lending and in spending. If she had not taken care of the business, and worked early and late, and looked after the money so far as she had it in her power, they would not have had a roof over their heads by this time. What with the licence that had just been paid, and the rent that must be paid before the end of the month, they would be cleared out, without advancing money to strangers that were in their debt already. As Mrs. Frankland was really the bread-winner, and at their present low water the purse-keeper also, Mrs. Peck saw it was of no use to press her offers on her husband in the face of such formidable opposition.

On the following day she started early in the mail conveyance for Adelaide, leaving Peck behind as a pledge for the settlement of the bill, and determined to raise ten or twelve pounds somehow.

With Mr. Talbot's letter in her hand she presented herself to a bill-discounter in Adelaide. He understood her position at once; that she was somehow connected with, but very obnoxious to a wealthy client of Mr. Talbot's, for Mr. Phillips's name was not mentioned in the letter; and also that, like most people of her class and habits, she had spent her money before she got it. Of course she said nothing of wanting to go to Melbourne, in which case, by the body

of the letter, it would be almost certain that her annuity would cease, but the discounter wanted some security against such a contingency, and asked her if she meant to stay in South Australia, according to agreement. Mrs. Peck was willing to say anything, to swear anything, and to sign anything, for his satisfaction on this point, but her very fluency made him suspicious.

'I cannot advance this money,' said he, 'even on the deposit of your order to arrest what is coming to you, unless I have some collateral security, or some other name, in case of your going to Victoria.'

Mrs. Peck could get no one to corroborate her statements but Peck, who could be of no service to her. She felt rather in a fix.

'What should take me to Melbourne?' said she, in accents of great surprise. 'It is so much against my interest to go there, that I would never be such a fool as to quarrel with my bread and butter; but it so happens I am much in need of money just at the present. I am expecting money from Scotland every mail. Indeed, it was trusting to that as put me so back this quarter. I never doubted that I'd get a handsome sum from Scotland; I've got the rights to it, and if it don't come by next mail, I will prosecute. You are sure to get your money well paid, with good interest, if you do run just a little risk.'

'That may be all very well,' said the bill discounter; 'but, in the meantime, can you not get any one to back you in this? I like good interest, but I cannot lend without better security.'

'There's the best of security. Mr. Talbot's next payment is due in two months, and I make it over to you; and if that does not satisfy you, I would give you something more next pay day, as much as would cover your risk and your trouble, and your interest, handsome enough.'

'Not at all handsome, if I chance to lose it all. One needs to keep one's weather eye open, in dealing with old hands like you, Mrs. Peck.'

'Then you won't do this for me—such a trifling accommodation as it is?'

'Not without some one to back you,' said the money-lender.

'I daresay I can easily find that, if you are so stiff,' said Mrs. Peck, as she flounced off in great indignation, and with very little hope of succeeding in what was required .

Here was she in possession of a secret worth so much to her, and unable to turn it to account for want of a beggarly ten or twelve pounds. The bill discounter was too sharp for her; she must try a good-natured man next, one who would be willing to do her a kindness—but here again, Mr. Talbot's letter, her only authority to give any security, would injure her more than with the keen man of the world. There was a steamer to sail on the morrow for Melbourne, and no other for a week or ten days; every day was of the greatest consequence, for now that she had made up her mind not to make terms with Francis, but to do so with his cousins, she was eager to carry her resolution into practice, and she must get on board the Havilah, if possible.

She had lived some weeks in Adelaide in rather a poor way, and in rather a poor neighbourhood, when she and Peck had come first across. She had made acquaintance with a very few people, and had left Adelaide slightly in debt, but in her eagerness she was inclined to overlook those circumstances, and to hope that some one or other of her late neighbours might be prevailed on to be a guarantee to the money-lender merely as a matter of form, and he might be induced to accept of it; so she turned her steps in the direction of her old residence.

She looked into the shop where she had been accustomed to make her purchases of groceries, with an intention of paying the eleven shillings which she owed if things looked promising, and if it would be a good speculation.

'Well Mrs. Smith, and how are you?' said she to the woman who kept the establishment with the favourite old Adelaide sign of 'General Store.'

'Much as usual, Mrs. Peck. You went away rather in a hurry,' said Mrs. Smith.

'Oh! Peck had to go off to the sheep-shearing, and I had the offer

of a good nursing in the country, so I had to move at a minute's warning, you see. But how are you getting on here?'

'Much as usual, Mrs. Peck; but the news is, that my man came home last night, after being at them diggings for four years, and not writing me a word, good or bad, for three and more; and now he expects me to be as sweet as sugar to him after serving me so; and me had all his children to keep and do for, and got no help from him no more nor if he was dead; and now he says as how I give him the cold shoulder.'

'Well, to be sure, and no wonder either! When a woman's been served so, she has the right to look a bit stiff,' said Mrs. Peck, who had heard during her stay in Adelaide that Mrs. Smith had passed judgment by default, and was going to take to herself another mate, which was nothing more than the absent Smith deserved.

'Well, to be sure, that beats cock-fighting; and what does Harris say to all this?'

'Why, in course, he's off, and I'm in such a quandary,' said Mrs. Smith.

'You wasn't married to Harris, out and out, was you?' said Mrs. Peck, who had a keen relish for such interesting news as this.

'No; there was two or three things as put it off; but the banns was gave in last Sunday, and I had got my gown for the wedding, and lovely it looks—and here's Smith as savage as if he had been writing to me every month and sending me money.'

'I suppose he's come home as poor as a rat, like the rest of them?' said Mrs. Peck.

'No, no, I cannot just say that,' said Mrs. Smith, relenting a little, 'He says he never had no luck till the last six months, and now he has come back with three hundred pounds; and he's been behaving very genteel with it, I must say, and brought presents for me and for the children—there's a shawl for me as is quite a picter—so rich in the colours; but I can't say I feel quite pleased at the way he neglected me so long. And poor Harris, too; I can't just get him out of my head all at once.'

'That's natural enough,' said Mrs. Peck with a sympathizing sigh.

Here Mr. Smith came into the shop, and started at the sight of Mrs. Peck.

'Well! who'd have thought of seeing you here, Mrs.——? I don't rightly recollect your name, but I know you as well as possible,' said he.

'Mrs. Peck is my name,' said she impressively. 'I recollect you well on Bendigo.'

'Many's the time I've seen you there,' said Smith, in an embarrassed tone of voice. 'I hope as how you have your health, Mrs. Peck. Susan, my dear, you'd better give Mrs. Peck some refreshments. Step in, Mrs. Peck, I'm just a day home, and I ain't come back too soon, neither, as it appears. Susan, my dear, get out the spirit bottle. Will you have brandy with hot water or cold, Mrs. Peck?'

'With cold this hot day. I've been half baked travelling in that mail omnibus twenty miles, and the wind blowing through it like a flaming furnace; and now your Adelaide dust is making me as grimy as I'm not fit to be seen,' said Mrs. Peck, wiping her face with her handkerchief, and watching how Smith mixed her brandy and water. 'There's nothing pleases me like meeting with an old friend.'

'Nor me,' said Smith, 'if so be as she is friendly. Now, Susan, sit down and have a glass with us. Why, the woman looks handsomer nor the day I married her. I don't wonder at the risk I ran of being choused out of you; but it was rather too bad, too, was it not, Mrs. Peck? If my letters hadn't a miscarried you would never have thought of such a thing, Susan,' said he, with an insinuating smile, handing his wife a mixture similar to that he presented to his old friend.

'If they had been written there would have been no fear of their miscarrying,' said she rather sulkily.

'Here's Mrs. Peck—my good friend, Mrs. Peck—who will be a warrant how often I used to be a speaking of you, and a wondering what made me give up writing.'

'That I will,' said Mrs. Peck, who felt this little bit of romance

was quite in her line. 'Many's the time I've heard him speaking about you and the children.'

'Take another drop of brandy, Mrs. Peck,' said her newly-found friend.

'Thank you,' said she; 'it's better brandy than we used to get at Bendigo, but really I am in too much trouble just now to enjoy it, and I won't take no more nor the single glass. It's a bad world and a sad one, and I seem to have more than my share of trouble.'

'Dear me! Mrs. Peck, I am sorry to hear that; and I am sure I wish I could do anything to help you,' said Smith.

'I don't like imposing on people that I haven't no claims on, but I am in great need of twelve pounds just for a little while. I have an annuity, as I dare say you heard at Bendigo.'

'Yes, I heerd on it,' said Smith, who appeared indisposed to contradict or doubt anything that Mrs. Peck said.

'But we have been tried with the sickness and doctors' bills—Peck and me—and I am very backward with the world just at present. If anybody could lend me twelve pounds for two months, they'd get principal and interest handsome. You being an old friend turned up, and me knowing you so well at Bendigo, makes me bold enough to ask you for this little temporary assistance. I would deposit an order for the money with you if you will be so good as to advance it.'

'Certainly, Mrs. Peck, I am not the one to be backward when a friend is in need, and I know it will be safe enough to be paid. Susan, it is perfectly safe. Mrs. Peck had money regular every quarter, to my knowledge; and if she wants the money now, it shall be paid down on the nail.' And Smith told out the twelve pounds into Mrs. Peck's hands, and received an order for repayment on Mr. Talbot, which was not to be presented for two months.

Mrs. Peck was overjoyed at her unexpected good luck in meeting with this returned digger, whom she had known very well at Bendigo under another name, and where he passed himself off as the husband of another woman. She perceived that now he had found his wife in Adelaide, doing very well in business, he would

rather that she heard nothing of his own little infidelities, particularly in the first days of meeting, and his probable loss of the money he advanced was not too high a price to pay to purchase silence.

Everything had turned out most propitiously for Mrs. Peck, so far. The information from Mr. Dempster showed that all her objects of interest were collected in one spot, and this recognition of Smith put into her hands the means to get to them while Mr. Phillips was absent. She was flushed with hope and confident expectation when she made her purchases of some articles of ready-made clothing, and took out her passage in Melbourne in the 'Havilah,' to prosecute her plans for revenge on Francis and advantages to herself.

IV

MISS PHILLIPS MEETS WITH A CONGENIAL SPIRIT IN VICTORIA

As Mr. Dempster had reported there had been a division in the family of the Phillipses shortly after they landed. Mrs. Phillips wished to remain in Melbourne for a month or two, as she did not feel able to stand the long land journey at this particular time. Neither her husband nor herself had much confidence in Dr. Grant's skill, and she could have better attendance in town. Mr. Phillips having ascertained that Mrs. Peck was in Adelaide, and having, through Mr. Talbot, sent a request that she should remain there, which her own interest was likely to make her attend to, had less objection to her staying in Melbourne than he ever had before; so he took a suite of furnished apartments for her and those of the family who remained in town.

Jane Melville went at once to Wiriwilta with the children, who all longed to be there, and who disliked Melbourne more than London. Miss Phillips had her choice to remain in town or to go up to the station, and she decided on the former alternative, for she began to fear the station would be very dull, and would contrast unfavourably with the voyage, which had been lively and pleasant. There were some of her fellow-passengers whom she was unwilling to lose sight of; and Mr. Brandon was not at Barragong, but in

Adelaide, so, on the whole, she thought it would be preferable to stay. She gave as her ostensible reason for the choice, her wish to be with Mrs. Phillips during her brother's necessary absence. Mr. Phillips stayed with his wife till she presented him with a second son, and then, as she was doing very well, he left her in the care of his sister and Elsie.

He had been rather annoyed to find that Brandon had been amusing himself by taking a journey to Adelaide so soon after coming out to the colony again. Dr. Grant came down to meet Phillips, and represented that a great deal had gone amiss at Wiriwilta since he (Dr. Grant) had been supplanted in the charge of the stations; so that he thought it indispensable to go up with the least possible delay to look to all the flocks and the out-stations.

'It was the wildest thing in Brandon to start off in that way,' said Grant, 'with a poor lad of a nephew who did not know a wattle from a gum-tree when he came, and scarcely a sheep from a cow. *I* never would have done such a thing.'

'But he has gone to buy some new sheep, I hear,' said Phillips. 'Have they been delivered at Wiriwilta?'

'No, not yet,' said Grant; 'and I think that was the most insane part of the business. I am sure our Victorian flock-masters have always kept ahead of the Adelaide lot; and to go to the Adelaide side for sheep would be the last speculation I should care to enter into for myself, not to speak of implicating you in such a thing. The long overland journey will pull them down so much that you are likely to lose a third of them on the road, and what you do save will be in wretched order. Brandon was fairly ruined by going home to England.'

'Ruined!' said Harriett Phillips. 'He said he was ruined, or something like it, before he left. Are his affairs really in such a bad state?'

'Oh, it's not exactly his affairs, but he got unsettled and would not work as he used to do. He overturned most of my arrangements at Wiriwilta; and I am sure Mr. Phillips will not find himself any the better for his alterations. He is so foolishly confiding. Now, I

like to look sharply after my people, and then I see what work I get out of them.'

'I think you are quite right, Dr. Grant. I have remarked the want of that prudence in both Mr. Brandon and my brother. They think it proceeds from benevolence, but I attribute it more to indolence and the dislike to give themselves any trouble they can avoid,' said Harriett.

Dr. Grant was piqued at being deprived of Mr. Phillips's agency, for though he had protested against taking it, he had found it very lucrative; he was also piqued at Mrs. Phillips staying in town for her confinement, though he always declared that he detested practising, and only did it as an accommodation to his neighbours; but both things had added alike to his emolument and his importance, and he was extremely jealous of any slight being cast either on his business knowledge or his professional skill. On this occasion he offered to stay in Melbourne for a week or so after Phillips left, merely as a friend, to see how Mrs. Phillips was going on, and to take up a full and satisfactory account to the station. Though he was not her medical attendant, he was as much in the house, and far more than he had ever been before. When the week was over, he appeared to be in no hurry to go away, but wrote to Phillips instead; and hung about the house, went errands for her or her sister-in-law, took Harriett out for walks and drives, brought all his Melbourne acquaintances to call on her, and to inquire for Mrs. Phillips and the baby, and was himself engaged for several hours of every day in conversation with Harriett.

He had come to Melbourne determined to fall in love with Miss Phillips, whose likeness he had seen and admired at Wiriwilta years ago, and whose face and figure, when seen in reality quite came up to his expectations, while her air and manners were exactly suited to his taste. He knew that she had a fortune—not large, certainly, but tempting to a man who was not exactly poor, but always more or less embarrassed. Her perfect self-possession, her good education, her musical talents, her excellent connections, her stylish

way of dressing, her very egotism, were all charming to a man who wanted a wife who would do him credit.

His Scotch family was a good one; he was connected with many noble houses; he could tell long traditional stories of the feats of the Grants and the Gillespies, his father's and mother's ancestors; and it was wonderful how much the history of Scotland, and indeed that of the world generally, seemed to hang on the exploits of those ancient clans. Though Harriett was not a Scotchwoman (it was the only drawback to their perfect suitability), she appreciated these anecdotes wonderfully well. Dr. Grant laid himself out to please her in a much more marked manner than Brandon had ever done, and his success was much greater. He had a subdued feeling that his neighbour at Barragong was his rival, as he had seen so much of Harriett in England, so he lost no opportunity of mentioning anything that would tell against him.

Then he was of the same profession as her father and brother Vivian, and liked to hear her talk of them. Indeed, provided he got time and opportunity to speak about his own relations, connections, and friends—to give anecdotes of his schoolboy and college days, more interesting to his mother than to any one else heretofore—to describe how he had felt the colonial hardships at first, and how he had gradually made himself very comfortable at Ben More (which was the name he had given to his station, so much more suitable for a Scottish squatter than such native names as Brandon and Phillips had retained for theirs);—he would allow Harriett to give her school and society reminiscences too, to describe her home in Derbyshire—the furniture, the ornaments, the lawn, and the greenhouse—the county Stanleys, and the county balls. As they were generally *tête-à-tête* four or five hours a day, they had ample time for descanting on all these interesting topics. Any visitors who might drop in, or any visit that they might pay together only gave fresh food for further comparison of their own personal tastes and predilections. Miss Phillips's avowed contemptuous compassion for everything colonial did not at all offend Dr. Grant. He had never been thoroughly acclimatized himself, and he had vowed never to

marry any of the second-rate colonial girls, who, as he thought, had no manner and no style. It was surprising how well these two new friends agreed about everything and everybody.

Dr. Grant, from his education and his habits, considered himself a reading man, and a very well informed one. Miss Phillips, too, had thought Brandon greatly her inferior in literary acquirements, as in all other things; but it was singular to observe how little these two people, who were so congenial to each other, and who enjoyed each other's company so much, and had so much of it, talked about the many books they must have read. As for religion, politics, or any other of the great concerns of life, they never seemed to rise even on the surface of conversation; and when a book happened to be mentioned, it was dismissed with a casual remark, such as 'I read it,' or 'I did not read it,' or 'I liked it,' or 'I thought it stupid,' and then they turned to things which more nearly interested them, and these were things in which they themselves or some one related to them made some figure. If any of Miss Phillips's, or any of Dr. Grant's relations had published a book, that would have been mentioned and extolled, but they had not. Vivian's scientific attainments, which Harriett had thought rather a bore at home, were however something to boast of here; and Dr. Grant had an uncle who had made some improvements in agriculture in the north of Scotland, of whom he was never tired of talking.

Miss Phillips had remained in Melbourne to be with her sister-in-law, but she was very little beside her. Besides Dr. Grant, there were fellow-passengers who visited at the house, and whose visits Miss Phillips was bound to return, and there were also public places to go to with them; for she wished to see all that was to be seen in Melbourne while she was there; and though she generally criticised all the Melbourne concerts, and theatres, and balls, and private parties very severely, she accepted every invitation and joined every party that was made up for the theatre.

Elsie and the nurse had the care of Mrs. Phillips and the baby, though Elsie would have preferred being at Wiriwilta, with Jane and the elder children, for she missed their cheerful society, but she

could not be spared. Miss Phillips was in exceedingly good-humour at this time, and did not exact so much from Elsie as she had expected; but Mrs. Phillips missed her husband, and was rather petulant and capricious. She had been considerably kinder to Elsie since the death of her little girl. This first sorrow had done her good; but now, in her husband's absence, a good deal of the old spirit returned, particularly as she was much offended at the little attention which Harriett paid to her. Elsie was the real housekeeper, though Miss Phillips had the credit of it, and she was delighted to find how well she could manage. Her old experiences at Cross Hall had not been altogether thrown away; she had grown more thoughtful, and she felt she must depend on herself, for there was no Jane now to fall back upon.

Elsie was apprehensive that the coolness between the sisters-in-law would lead to an open rupture, for Mrs. Phillips had not been accustomed to be considered as nobody in her own house; but there appeared hope for peace in the fact that Dr. Grant must leave Melbourne; and then those long conversations must have an end, and at least three-fourths of the rides and gaieties which served as an excuse for her neglect. During the short absences from day to day which necessarily took place, and during the few angel's visits, 'short, and far between,' which were paid to her sister-in-law's sick room, Dr. Grant's sayings and doings, his compliments to herself, and his criticisms of other people, were the staple of Harriett's conversation to the invalid. If the absence of the one and the visits to the other were prolonged, it was just possible that Mrs. Phillips might be more fatigued; but she could not be so much ignored as she was at present.

V

DR. GRANT PROSECUTES HIS SUIT WITH CAUTION AND SUCCESS, AND BRANDON FINDS HIS LOVE-MAKING ALL TO DO OVER AGAIN

Harriett Phillips could not come out quite so strong in her contempt for colonial ways and colonial people, arriving when she did, as if she had landed ten or a dozen years before, but still there was a great deal that was open to criticism. Mr. Phillips and Mr. Brandon thought the colony had made rapid strides towards civilization and comfort since the great influx of wealth consequent on the gold discoveries had attracted to Victoria much that was unattainable before. Even during their absence in England there had been a great deal of building going on in Melbourne, and many other improvements had been introduced. The houses were better, and better furnished; the shops seemed to contain everything that enterprise could import or money procure; the ladies were handsomely and expensively dressed, and there were public amusements such as were never heard of in the early colonial days.

But still there was much even in Melbourne that was un-English and strange to a new comer.

Melbourne did not at all come up to Harriett's expectations, though what she had expected it would have been difficult to tell. She had wished to go to Victoria because it would be a novelty to her—it would be so different from England that it would be

amusing—but every difference that she observed, and she was very quick in observing such things, was always for the worse. There was, of course, the difference of climate, which led to many alterations in dress and manner of living, and which would reasonably lead to more if the English colonist was not so much wedded to old customs and costumes. The heat and dust Harriett found to be insupportable, and the dress which was most suited to it was so unbecoming, particularly the gentlemen's dress, with the endless variety of hats for head-covering. Dr. Grant, who stood a good deal on the dignity of his profession, when in Melbourne wore dark clothes and a black hat even in the heat of summer, and that weighed in his favour with Harriett. The noise and bustle of Melbourne was so different from what she had been accustomed to in Derbyshire—indeed it was more like Liverpool than any part of London she had seen—a poor edition of Liverpool; and that was the city of which the Victorians were so proud. She could not enter into the natural liking of a people for a town that they have seen with their own eyes grow from a mere hamlet of rude huts to a handsome, paved, lighted, commercial city like Melbourne—who identify themselves with its progress, having watched the growth of every improvement. They wonder that it does not strike strangers as being as astonishing as it appears to be to themselves.

Mrs. Phillips had no acquaintances in Melbourne; but Mr. Phillips and Dr. Grant knew a good many people, who were disposed to be very friendly to Harriett, but she did not feel very grateful for such kindness. She fancied that her position and education, and her being recently out from England ought to give her an overpowering prestige in these half-savage lands, and though she lost no chance of laughing or censuring anything which she thought colonial, she could not bear being talked of as a new chum, whose opinions should be kept for two years at least before they were worth anything, and whose advice was probably worth nothing at any time.

Amongst other subjects for censure, the great freedom of manners, particularly amongst young people of different sexes

towards each other, struck Miss Phillips forcibly. She had observed at evening parties, at picnics, and at places of public amusement, the very unrestrained way in which they talked and behaved, and she thought the colonial girls were badly trained, and that they ought to be more carefully watched by mothers and chaperones. At the same time she took full latitude herself, and did many things on the strength of her being in Australia, where people might do as they liked, that surprised even the colonial girls themselves.

If she remarked on their flirtations with their old friends, they could not help observing Miss Phillips's prepossession towards her new acquaintance, and laughing at the manner in which the two seemed wrapped up in each other. How could she endure his returning to Ben More, and leaving her, perhaps, for another month in Melbourne without his society, was a question which they frequently put to each other; but she solved that difficulty to her own satisfaction and as much to their amusement.

'I am very sorry to leave you,' said Dr. Grant one day to the object of his attentions, 'but I must go. Business must not be neglected. I cannot be flying about like Brandon, letting my affairs go to ruin. I hope you will not be long in coming to Wiriwilta, Miss Phillips.'

'Not very long I suppose,' said Harriett. 'Indeed, I think there is nothing to prevent Mrs. Phillips from going home now, if she would only believe so.'

'Nothing whatever,' said Grant.

'I am quite wearying to see Wiriwilta,' said Harriett: 'the children's letters are quite rapturous about its beauties, and Miss Melville, too, seems very much pleased. You will like Miss Melville, I am sure. You like Scotch people, I know.'

'If I do not like Miss Melvile better than her sister, my liking will not go very far,' said Grant.

'Do you know Stanley thought Alice quite pretty at first—I don't see it. Miss Melville is what people call plain, but I prefer her appearance to Alice's, and she is very clever and strong-minded. I quite expect you to fall in love with Miss Melville,' said Harriett,

with a little laugh.

'No fear of that. I have no fancy for strong-minded women. Not but what I like a good understanding and good sense in a lady, but let each sex keep to its own department. But, Miss Phillips, if you really want to go to Wiriwilta, I can drive you up—or, better still, you could ride. You are an admirable horsewoman, as I know, and I have an excellent horse in town that would carry you easily that distance without fatiguing you. It would be a beautiful ride. You would see the country so well as you go along.'

'I should like to go, of all things,' said Harriett; 'but what would Stanley say?'

'Oh, I will tell him it was quite unnecessary for you to stay with Mrs. Phillips, and it will be the easier for his horses to bring up the rest of them, if you have gone before,' said Grant.

'Well, I am really tired of Melbourne; I think I have seen all that is to be seen, and I dare say there are some preparations and arrangements I could make before Mrs. Phillips comes up, so as to make her more comfortable, though I dare say Miss Melville has done her best. Still, there are things that one of the family can do which strangers cannot be expected to attend to.'

'Certainly,' said Dr. Grant; 'I can imagine your presence at Wiriwilta will make things more comfortable for all parties.'

'And, by-the-by, Emily and Harriett will be neglecting their music, and I engaged to see to that so long as I remained in Victoria, as Miss Melville knows no music.'

'No music!' said Dr. Grant; 'that is a singular sort of governess to engage for young ladies up the country.'

'She is wonderfully clever about other things, and brings on the children very nicely. When I compare them with the girls of their own age whom I have seen in Melbourne, I cannot help congratulating my brother on having brought out a governess with him. It would have been better, of course, if she had been English, but Miss Melville is not painfully Scotch.'

'I hope you have no dislike to Scotch people,' said Grant. 'I myself

glory in my country.'

'Oh, I quite understand your feelings. If I had been born in Scotland, I should have felt the same, I dare say,' said Harriett.

'But, with regard to this drive or ride to Wiriwilta?' said Grant.

'How long should we be on the road?' asked Harriett.

'Two days, I think. We would stay all night at Mrs. Ballantyne's, a very old friend of mine, and an aquaintance of your brother. Ballantyne and I were fellow-passengers when we first came out. They will receive you with bush hospitality. I should like to introduce you to Scotch bush hospitality, and it is a pretty place, too; rather romantically situated.'

'I should really like to see it, for I want to study Australian scenery and Australian manners during my short stay in the colony, to see as much as I can while I am among you savages.'

'Then, shall it be a ride or a drive?' asked Dr. Grant.

'I think I should prefer driving,' said Harriett; 'but I must first consult Mrs. Phillips. I do not suppose that she can enlighten me much, but as Stanley's wife I owe her that courtesy.' So Harriett, with a condescending smile, took leave of her admirer.

Mrs. Phillips was in an exceedingly bad humour, but she made no objection to Harriett's going away. She did not quite believe in the zeal for the children's music or for her comfort, which Miss Phillips professed, but she was tired of having the name of her society without the reality of it. As for the impropriety of her sister-in-law's travelling all that distance with a single gentleman, either riding or driving, Mrs. Phillips had never decided any question of the kind for herself or others since she had been married. She had always acted as her husband thought proper, that is to say, she might often have made mistakes or done wrong if he had not prevented her, and the proposition did not strike her as at all objectionable. Elsie wondered if there was an engagement between her and Dr. Grant, when a young lady of such strict principles proposed so singular an expedition. Harriett was not at all quick at reading countenances, and was particularly dull in the interpretation of Elsie's; but as

some idea of the kind had dimly occurred to herself, she gave it voice and explained her views on the subject, in Elsie's hearing, to Mrs. Phillips.

'Of course I should never think of such an adventurous journey in England, but here it seems the fashion to do just as is most convenient to ourselves; and for your sake and that of the children, I think it is better that I should go first. Dr. Grant being a professional man, and such an old friend of my brother's, will be an excellent escort, and I am really desirous of seeing a little of the roughness of colonial life. We will stay all night at Mr. Ballantyne's, and reach Wiriwilta in good time the second day. I will see to have everything comfortable for you, Lily, my dear, before you come up. I wish you could accompany me. Dr. Grant says you could go up now, if you were disposed.'

'I am not going to Wiriwilta till Stanley comes himself to fetch me, for I am so timid with any one else driving on these dreadful roads; and as for what Dr. Grant says about my being fit for the journey, he is not my medical man this time, so I won't go by his advice. Besides, he don't understand my constitution as Dr. M— does,' said Mrs. Phillips.

'I feel very sorry to leave you, Lily,' said Harriett.

'Oh, I dare say I'll get on very well, even without you. Alice and nurse will do for me until Stanley comes. Tell him how I weary to see him the very first thing you say when you see him. Whenever he's done with going over the stations, beg him to come down. Alice has written for me to tell him to make haste. I am not strong enough yet to sit up to write.'

The idea that Harriett might hasten her husband's return to her, helped to reconcile Mrs. Phillips to the very cavalier treatment she received from that young lady.

Harriett enjoyed her drive exceedingly. Dr. Grant knew who lived in a great many houses that they passed, and they carried with them the great subject of agreeable conversation in themselves. The Derbyshire country and the Highland scenery was compared and contrasted with the Victorian, very much to the disadvantage of the

latter, which, indeed, did not look its best, but its very worst at this time. Mr. Ballantyne's station Harriett confessed to be rather prettily situated; but things in the house were much rougher than she had expected, and the house itself was of a very irregular and primitive style of architecture—the slab hut enlarged so as to be tolerably commodious; yet, still, the very house that the squatter had built, partly with his own hands, in the early days of the colony. He had not been a fortunate man, but he had got his head above water since the gold discoveries; and he was not so imprudent as to involve himself again by building a handsome house so long as the old one would do. Mrs. Ballantyne had an overweening opinion of the advantages of English society and English education, and received Miss Phillips with an amount of adulation quite beyond anything she had ever met with in her life; which was all the more effective from its being perfectly sincere. Her own children were but half educated, and very deficient in acquired manner; and they too looked with awe on Mr. Phillips's English sister, who was so self-possessed and so fashionably dressed. To a person less conscious of her own superiority, Mrs. Ballantyne's profuse apologies for everything and everybody would have been rather painful; but Harriett received them graciously, and told Dr. Grant that she felt quite delighted with this first specimen of bush hospitality, and with his Scotch friends.

Dr. Grant on his side was exceedingly proud of his companion, and felt quite sure of his success with her; he never had been so agreeable as during this long drive, and when they appeared at Wiriwilta, on the second day, in time for an early tea, both travellers were full of spirits, and not at all tired. Mr. Phillips was not at home, and not expected for some days. Jane was somewhat surprised by the appearance of Miss Phillips under such care, but received her politely and kindly.

Dr. Grant had to go home to attend to business, but promised to ride across to Wiriwilta, as soon as possible, to see if Miss Phillips had not suffered any fatigue from the long journey over such rough roads.

It was rather flat at the station for Harriett on the following day. She was disappointed with the house, for though it was a great deal better than Mrs. Ballantyne's, it was not so large or so convenient as she had expected. She could not take any interest in the many things which the children showed her, which they thought so beautiful—their pet animals, the few wild flowers they could find at this season of the year, their dear old trees, their pretty walks, the native boy Jim, Mrs. Bennett's baby, and the curious windmill that Mr. Tuck had made for them with his clasp knife and some twigs. She could not be troubled with such childish talk; she wanted rational conversation; but when Jane Melville sat beside her, and conversed in her own quiet sensible way, she felt even that to be unsatisfactory.

A new element had entered into Miss Phillips's life. She was, after her fashion, in love; and she was restless and dissatisfied without the presence of the beloved object. Dr. Grant was just long enough away to be very welcome when he came; and Jane was a little amused at the manner in which Harriett threw off her languid air of indifference, and talked to this (to Jane) most uninteresting Scotchman, who was so full of national pride and personal vanity. Jane was very cosmopolitan in her ideas, both by nature and by education. Her uncle had always had more pride in being a Briton than a North Briton, and never had fired up with indignation at Scotland being included or merged in England. She did not think Scotchmen intrinsically more capable than English; there was a greater diffusion of elementary knowledge in the northern part of the island, but she thought that in society Englishmen were more agreeable than Scotch, as a general rule, because they were more certain of their own position. Scotch and Irish people are apt to be afraid that they are looked down upon, and are too often on the look-out for slights to be resented, whereas Englishmen, who do not know much of continental feelings and habits of thought, have a comfortable conviction that the greatest country in the world belongs to them, and that nobody can dispute it. Dr. Grant was surprised at Jane's want of nationality, and confided to Harriett that

he was greatly disappointed in her; and in spite of Harriett's professed regard for Jane, she could not help seeing the faults which this keen-sighted observer pointed our.

One day when Dr. Grant and Harriett were in the enjoyment of each other's company, and flirting in their own interesting manner, and Jane was sitting beside them with the children, Mr. Brandon and Edgar made their appearance. Emily and little Harriet met Brandon with acclamations, and the little ones rejoiced over him in a very noisy manner, too. Jane gave him a hearty welcome, for she was really delighted to see his face again, but Miss Phillips and Dr. Grant were scarcely so affectionate.

'Well, here comes the recreant knight,' said Miss Phillips. 'What have you got to say for yourself, Mr. Brandon?'

'To say for myself! Oh! I have a great deal to say for myself. I have seen a great deal since we parted in London.'

'But why have you left your own business and my brother's, and gone wool-gathering in South Australia?'

'I have just gone wool-gathering, and that must be my excuse. Phillips will admire the sheep, I am sure. They have just got home in first-rate condition; easy travelling and plenty of time. But where is Mr. Phillips and Mrs. Phillips?'

'Oh, mamma is in Melbourne, and we have got a new little brother, and his name is to be Vivian, after uncle Vivian, you know; and papa is out over the runs, and will be back on Saturday; and I am sure he will be very glad to see you, and Edgar too, I dare say,' said Emily.

'And where is your sister, Miss Melville? Has she come out to Australia with you? Is she quite well?' asked Brandon.

'Quite well,' said Harriett; 'she is in Melbourne with Mrs. Phillips. We expect them out in a week or two, or perhaps as much as three weeks, for Mrs. Phillips fancies she cannot stand the journey for some time.'

'Alice has not seen Wiriwilta yet,' said Emily. 'I know she will think it very pretty; Miss Melville likes it very much.'

'And you have got quite strong, Emily?' said Brandon.

'Quite strong again. I can walk to the water-holes near the grove of young gum-trees and back again without being a bit tired. We have such lovely walks every day with Miss Melville. And do you know Mr. Brandon, my dear old Cockey died just after you and Edgar went away to Adelaide; but I have got another—such a beauty—and two such lovely parrots. Jim got them for me. You can't think how glad Harriett and I were to see Jim. And Mrs. Bennett has got another baby, and I'm to be godmother, and it's to be called Emily; and Mrs. Tuck has got another too, ever so fat. We have not seen our own baby brother yet.'

'But how does it happen that you did not write to me? I got one letter telling me little Eva was dead, and that you were getting better; but next month I did not hear a syllable, good or bad, from any of you.'

'Because we were on board ship by that time, before the mail from Australia came in. Papa thought we would be all here sooner than we were—but it was a delightful voyage. We had Mr. Dempster—you know Mr. Dempster—and such a lot of nice Adelaide children. I was so sorry to bid good-bye to Rose; she was my friend all the voyage; and there were some very nice gentlemen, too. It was quite as nice a voyage as the last, only that Miss Melville made us do lessons all the time; and perhaps after all it was as well that she did.'

'I never heard such a chatterbox as you are, Emily,' said her aunt.

'Did you find the voyage pleasant, Miss Phillips?' asked Brandon.

'Oh, yes, very pleasant indeed.'

'I did not think you would condescend to visit our rude latitudes,' said Brandon.

'Oh, I am really quite enjoying my visit. Stanley was greatly pleased at my proposal to come out, for he thought it such an excellent thing for the family. I am only on a visit, you know. I cannot say how I should like Victoria for a permanence, but I like the novelty for the present.'

'And your cousin is in Parliament, I hear, and likely to distinguish himself, Miss Melville,' said Brandon. 'I hope that you and your

sister do not despise us poor colonial people.'

'Certainly not,' said Jane; 'indeed, Francis says that he got most of his best ideas from Mr. Sinclair, who had been in Canada and the United States, and from a conversation between you and Mr. Phillips and Mr. Dempster the first day he dined with us in London. He says nothing sharpens an Englishman up like intercourse with such pushing, energetic, straightforward people as colonists.'

'That is high praise from a British member of Parliament. I owe him something for that. But did you see Peggy before you left?'

'Yes; we went up to bid her good-bye. I think she will not be long in joining us,' said Jane.

'Well,' said Grant, who, as well as Harriett, felt that Miss Melville was receiving more than her fair share of Brandon's conversation, 'you have not given at all a satisfactory account of yourself. You have been figuring away in Adelaide, I suppose, and enjoying yourself, and leaving your own affairs and Mr. Phillips's affairs to mind themselves.'

'And you have been figuring away in Melbourne, Dr. Grant,' said Emily—she could not bear any aspersion to be cast on her friend, Brandon—'and then you brought Aunt Harriett away; so you leave no one with poor mamma but Alice. I am wearying so to see mamma and the baby boy.'

'Suppose you go with me,' said Brandon; 'for I am going to Melbourne to-morrow to see them, and I have some business there besides.'

'Oh! that would be delightful. Miss Melville, may I go?'

'I think not, Emily,' said Jane. 'Your mamma will be soon here, and your papa will be disappointed to find you gone when he comes here. I should not wonder that he will take you with him when he goes himself, and that would be better, I think.'

'Much better,' said Miss Phillips. 'I wonder that you could think of such a thing as troubling Mr. Brandon to take care of you all that long way.'

Emily made rather a pertinent remark as to her aunt showing

her the example, at which Miss Phillips blushed, and Grant looked conscious but delighted. He could not conceive what was taking Brandon to Melbourne immediately on his return from Adelaide; he did not believe his assertion that he had business to attend to there. It was another sign of his being spoiled by his visit to England—it had completely unsettled him.

Now that Brandon had heard that his letter had never reached Elsie, and consequently that he had not been treated by her with discourtesy or unkindneess, he felt relieved; but, at the same time, a little sorry that all his trouble had been wasted, and that it was all to do over again. A few months ago he had lamented that he could not have it out by word of mouth; but now he regretted this letter had not, at least, broken the ice, and inclined her to listen to his suit. However, things had come to such a pass that he could not wait an indefinite time; he must go to Melbourne and learn his fate without delay. He left Edgar at Wiriwilta, where Emily thought him very much improved, and where the boy was exceedingly happy. He took a great fancy to Miss Melville, who was very different from the fond anxious women who had brought him up, but whose experiences with the Lowries had given her great interest in boys of that age, and who knew so much on all subjects that she never failed to win upon them, if they were tolerably intelligent and well disposed.

VI

MRS. PECK'S PROGRESS

All things continued favourable to Mrs. Peck's plans—she met with no disaster by sea in her voyage from Adelaide to Melbourne; the 'Havilah' brought her to her destination in three days, and she landed on the familiar shores with a light and hopeful heart. She was not long in discovering where Mrs. Phillips lived, which was in East Melbourne; and as no time was to be lost, she repaired to the house on the very day on which she landed, dressed decently and respectably, like the wife of an artisan, or perhaps with more of the appearance of a monthly nurse.

The girl who opened the door asked her name when she requested to see Mrs. Phillips, and she announced herself, not as Mrs. Peck, but as Mrs. Mahoney, under which name she had taken out her passage, and begged to see the missis by herself for a few minutes. Mrs. Phillips was then sitting in an easy-chair in the drawing-room, the nurse was engaged with the baby, and Elsie busy in Mrs. Phillips's room; so the stranger was introduced to have a quiet interview with her daughter.

'Well, Betsy, do you not recollect me?' said Mrs. Peck, in a subdued but intensely earnest voice, whenever the girl was out of hearing. 'Have you forgotten your own mother?'

Mrs. Phillips grew deadly pale, and was about to scream.

'Hush! Betsy, be quiet,' said her mother. 'I've only come to pay you a friendly visit. I've longed so to see you again all these years, and now I heard you was by yourself, I thought I must run all risks to get a look at you. Why, how handsome you've grown, and everything handsome about you, too;' and Mrs. Peck gazed with wondering admiration at the beautiful, well-dressed, queen-like woman whom she had parted with when a mere girl, and had never seen since her marriage. 'Rings on your fingers, and a gold chain round your neck, and everything you can wish for. Oh, Betsy, I made your fortune, and you never take a thought for me. I might be dead and buried, and you'd never care a straw. I have had a hard life, a very hard life—tossed about from place to place, and often in want of many things that at my time of life I need to get—and you in such luxury. My pretty girl, my beautiful daughter!'

Whatever might have been the resemblance between mother and daughter, there were but slight traces of it now. Mrs. Peck might have been beautiful at sixteen, but her life had not been so conservative of her charms as Mrs. Phillips's was; besides, Mrs. Phillips resembled her father much more than her mother, and he had been of a much more lymphatic temperament, and was at the same time a remarkably handsome man. Mrs. Peck was not yet sixty, but she looked old for her years, and more like the grandmother than the mother of Mrs. Phillips, whose easy circumstances, indulgent husband, and indolent, self-regarding life, with no emotion and little excitement, had kept her face free from a single line of care or anxiety. Her mother's face was ploughed up with innumerable lines, and her features seemed to work with every varying passion, while her expression was hungry, eager, and wolf-like, without showing anything more intellectual than cunning, even in its calmest moments.

'Oh!' said Mrs. Phillips, 'if Stanley was to find you here, he would never forgive me.'

'Is it your fault that I could not rest till I saw you again? I never

thought he'd be so cruel and unreasonable as to blame you for what I'd do.'

'But I heard you was in Adelaide, and Mr. Phillips says that, as long as you stay in Adelaide, he will see that you know no want. Oh, mother, you had better go back to Adelaide!' said Mrs. Phillips.

'Is that my girl as is talking?' said Mrs. Peck, disdainfully,—'my girl as I loved so dear, and was so proud of—that now, when I've come all the way from Adelaide, and risked all I've got to depend upon, just to please my old eyes with the sight of her handsome face, and my poor old ears with the sound of her voice, would banish me the minute I come! That's a pretty husband you've got—that you're so afeard of him. You deserve that your children should turn against you when they grow up. Oh, Betsy, how can you talk so cruel?' and the old woman caught her daughter's hand, and kissed it with much apparent, and no doubt some real feeling. 'You're not expecting of him home for a while; let me come and let me go while he is away—my name is Mrs. Mahoney. Say as how I am an old servant of your mother's, or an old servant you had at Wiriwilta, or the mother of some one you know—call me what you like, but let me just have the liberty to come and see you and the baby, and then I will go back to Adelaide, and Mr. Phillips need never know nothing about it?'

Invention was not one of Mrs. Phillips's talents, but her mother revelled in it, as I have said before. She delighted to go amongst people who did not know her, where she could give out an entirely fictitious history of herself quite new. Even to her intimate acquaintances her narrations were singularly inconsistent. When her interest demanded that she should speak the truth she did so, but it was with an effort; when the balance lay the other way she had no hesitation and no scruple.

'I ain't good at these stories, mother,' said Mrs. Phillips, 'and I don't just see what good it will do me to get into trouble with Stanley on your account. It is just the one thing he is unreasonable about. When he married me he said he made only one stipulation,

and that was, that I should have nothing to do with you or with Peck, and I said I wouldn't.'

Mrs. Peck here began to sob, and Elsie who was sewing in the next room, hearing a little noise, and afraid that Mrs. Phillips was not well, came in at this moment. Mrs. Phillips was quite at a loss to account for the emotion of her visitor, but her mother was equal to the emergency.

'I am sure, Mrs. Phillips, I cannot say what I feel,' said she, 'but your goodness really overpowers me. To think as the little girl as I knowed when she played with my poor Susan as is now no more should recollect me now she's growed up so beautiful, and had such a fine house of her own, and should help me in my troubles! It is quite too much for me. But all I want is just a little to start me in a way of business, and I'll be sure to pay it back again if I get on—and I have got a good connection, a capital connection—your liberality I can never forget;' and Mrs. Peck fumbled with her purse, and looked very hard at Elsie. This was the person whom she wished to see, even more than her ungrateful daughter, from whom she had expected a kinder reception. Elsie looked simple-minded enough—there was no doubt she would be easily dealt with, and much better by speech than by letter.

'This is your maid, I suppose?'

Mrs. Phillips assented.

Mrs. Peck turned to Elsie and said, 'I think as how the missis wants some sal volatile; she looks a bit faint—she don't seem to be strong yet.'

Elsie fetched the sal volatile, and gave Mrs. Phillips a little of it, and then returned to her work. She was puzzled at the stranger's speaking of Mrs. Phillips's liberality—for she was not generally liberal—and at her fumbling at her purse as if she had received money, for she knew that Mrs. Phillips had left her purse in her bedroom.

'You *must* let me come and go for the few days I am to stay in Melbourne, Betsy,' said her mother.

'Oh, I'd rather give you money, if you need it—at least, all I've got.'

'I fear I will need money to take me back, for I made such an effort to get across, but I could not help it. But I won't hurt you, Betsy, and I may do you good. What sort of girl is it that you've got?'

'Oh, a very clever milliner, and a handy girl enough. Stanley says he thinks her pretty, but I don't see it. He makes a great fuss over both her and her sister, but Jane is plain.'

'If he says he thinks her pretty, I'd not keep her in the house if I was you. I know what men are,' said Mrs. Peck.

'I don't think you know what Stanley is,' said Mrs. Phillips, with some dignity. 'I did not like it at first, but I ain't frightened now; and besides, they are both so badly off it's quite a charity to keep them.'

'If she is a milliner, I know of a capital situation,' said Mrs. Peck.

'Stanley would be in a pretty state if I let her go to a situation of your recommending,' said Mrs. Phillips.

'Oh, I don't mean to meddle with your affairs; but young people are very unwary. You think as how you're too handsome for your husband to think of looking at another woman; but I know the world better nor that. Howsomever, that is neither here nor there. But you know I am risking my annuity from Mr. Phillips by coming here to see you; but I heard in Adelaide that for the first time since you was married I might have the chance of seeing you, without making dispeace, which is the last thing I would wish to do. So, Betsy, if you will be reasonable, and let me come again, as Mrs. Mahoney (an old neighbour in New South Wales), and help me, as you say, with money to take me away, I will be as quiet as a mouse. It is a pleasure to see you, and to speak to you. Give me a little needlework, and let me sit with your maid, and just have a look at you now and then, and at the baby. I ain't seen none of your children, Betsy. Because you've been so well off, and had no cares, you shouldn't turn off your mother in that unfeeling way.'

'Oh, I wish I dare do it. But if Stanley was to come—he may come suddenly. I've sent him a message to hurry home. You can't think what a good, kind husband he is to me, mother. But he'd be furious if he found you here.'

'Oh, if he comes home you do not need me to work any longer;

and you can give the girl that message; and you can drop me a hint if I happen to be in the house. Even if he was to see me here, I know I could find some reason. I am never without an excuse.'

Mrs. Phillips was not particularly fond of her mother, who had been very harsh and violent-tempered to her in her childish days, while she was as fond of her husband as she could be of any one but herself, and she knew with what abhorrence he regarded this fierce, cunning old woman. She wished Mrs. Peck to be satisfied with this one visit and to come back no more, for she feared that Alice and the other servants might suspect something, and she had no confidence in her own powers of concealment. But Mrs. Peck had more ammunition in her chest; she again began to sob, and showed symptoms of going into violent hysterics, and bewailed her own hard lot and the cruelty of her ungrateful daughter so loudly, that she was glad to agree to her demands to make her keep quiet for the present.

Mrs. Peck then saw the baby, which she admired exceedingly, and accepted of some refreshments. Mrs. Phillips got her purse, and really gave her some money; and shortly after, her mother took leave, engaging to come back on the following morning to do some needlework, and uttering many blessings on Mrs. Phillips for her kindness and generosity in Alice's hearing. Mrs. Phillips looked greatly relieved when she was out of the house, but the apprehension of her return weighed considerably on her mind.

VII

BUSINESS INTERRUPTED BY LOVE

Mrs. Peck appeared on the following day, according to promise, carrying a little black bag, containing scissors, yard-measure, and a few other implements of needlework, all perfectly new; and after a short conversation with Mrs. Phillips and a little refreshment, she sat down beside Elsie to ingratiate herself with that young lady. Elsie thought she had never seen any one so ignorant of the work she had set about as Mrs. Mahoney appeared to be. She confessed that she was not skilful, and it showed all the more kindness in Mrs. Phillips to give her work when she had had so little practice, and did it so badly. She had been accustomed to go out as a nurse, she said; but she had got too old for that, and could not stand the sitting up of nights; and then she branched off into accounts of dreadful experiences in nursing, and deathbeds, and awful operations, that were enough to make Elsie's hair stand on end. She found fault with Mrs. Phillips's nurse as being too much of the fine lady, and told Elsie what she considered to be a nurse's duties, which she would like to do if she was only fit for it. Then she threw herself on Elsie's good nature for a little lesson in needlework, admired her quickness and taste and skill, wished she could do anything half as well, and asked her to be good enough to cut out

and place her work for her, and to lend her patterns, and altogether behaved with the most insinuating affability.

Although Elsie Melville looked simple-minded, she was by no means wanting in observation, and her situation with Mrs. Phillips and her sister-in-law had taught her a wonderful amount of prudence. She thought there was some inconsistency in Mrs. Mahoney's fluent narratives, and something very peculiar in her relations with Mrs. Phillips, who appeared to be restless and uncomfortable whenever she was in the house. Elsie was, however, good-natured enough to give her some instruction, for which great gratitude was expressed. On the third day of her visits, when apparently occupied in learning how to do featherstitch for trimming baby's pinafores, Mrs. Peck looked up from her work, and asked Elsie if she did not come from ——shire.

'That was my native county,' said Elsie.

'Do you know Cross Hall at all?' asked Mrs. Peck.

'I was brought up there,' said Elsie.

'I come from that county, too,' said Mrs. Peck.

'I did not think you had been Scotch,' said Elsie.

'I have been in these colonies for thirty-four years, and seen but few of my own country folks; but the English say they'd know me to be Scotch by my accent.'

'Well, perhaps your accent is a little like that of ——shire, when I come to think of it; but the turn of your expressions is not Scotch at all,' said Elsie. 'Thirty-four years is a long time, however; I may, perhaps, get rid of some of my own Scotticisms by that time.'

'I knew Hogarth of Cross Hall, very well, when I was young,' said Mrs. Peck. 'Do you mean to say you was brought up there?'

'Mr. Hogarth was my uncle,' said Elsie.

'Oh, you must be a daughter of his sister Mary's; I fancy there was only the one daughter that lived to grow up. But if Cross Hall was your uncle, how came you to be in this situation?' said Mrs. Peck, with feigned astonishment.

'My sister and I were educated by him; he was exceedingly kind to us as long as he lived.'

'But his property did not come to you;—the heir-at-law swallowed up all,' said Mrs. Peck, with a fierce glare in her eyes that she could not quite subdue. 'It is very hard on you.'

'We have felt it rather hard,' said Elsie; 'but still things have been worse for us at one time than they are now. Jane and I can earn our own living, and that is the position of most people in the world.'

'What would you give now,' said Mrs. Peck, 'if you could get back to Cross Hall, and be just as you used to be?'

'I cannot say what I would give,' said Elsie. 'But it is impossible. Unless we could restore my poor uncle to life, things could never be again as they used to be.'

'And the new man might have helped you, and not have driven you to seek service at the ends of the earth. Would you not like to serve him out?' said Mrs. Peck with the same subdued fierceness as before.

Elsie's instinctive sincerity would have led her to justify Francis, by explaining about the will, but she felt reluctant to say anything to this strange woman that she could help. Besides, though she knew nothing of the letter that had been sent by Mrs. Peck to her cousin, and left unanswered, at Mr. Phillips's earnest request, she was beginning to suspect something of the truth. Mrs. Peck's courting her so assiduously had puzzled her; and now the interest she felt in this story, which was all the more apparent to a keen observer from the efforts she made to conceal it, showed that she knew more about the matter than she liked at once to disclose.

Elsie had a good eye for likenesses, and could see family resemblances where no one else could; and it had always struck her as very remarkable that there was not the slightest resemblance between Francis and her uncle, nor between him and any other member of the family whom she had seen or whose portraits had been preserved. Not merely were the features and complexion unlike, but there was not a trick of the countenance or of the gait reproduced, as is generally the case with the sons of fathers who had such marked characteristics as Henry Hogarth. Though she had not heard of Mrs. Peck's letter, Jane had told her about Madame de

Véricourt's to her uncle, and in her own heart she had fancied that the reason why he had been so cold to Francis was, that he had been doubtful of the paternity; the very indifferent character of the woman he had married was not calculated to inspire him with confidence, and the absolute absence of all family likeness was an additional cause of distrust. He must have been satisfied on that point, however, in later years, or he would not have been so strong in his prohibition of his marriage with Jane or Elsie on account of his cousinship; but, in early life, he must, in Elsie's opinion, have had grave doubts on the subject.

She looked again more careful than before at Mrs. Peck. She was of the age to be Francis's mother, but otherwise she was quite at fault; there was not any likeness there either. A conformation of the little finger was rather peculiar, but it was an exaggeration of a little defect on Mrs. Phillips's otherwise very handsome hand, but not of Francis Hogarth's.

'If Francis has no right to the property, and we have, of course we should like to have our rights,' said Elsie.

'It was a Scotch marriage, you know,' said Mrs. Peck.

'Yes, but a binding one; he is received everywhere as my uncle's lawful son.'

'Yes, as his lawful son, no doubt. Do you know if he has brought forward his mother at all?' said Mrs. Peck.

'No; I suppose she is dead, or we should certainly have heard of her.'

'Dead, you suppose!' said Mrs. Peck, indignantly; 'that is the easy way of getting quit of relations that has got claims on you—just suppose them dead?'

'I do not know anything of the matter, except that she has not been heard of. If she were alive and heard of his inheriting this property, she would be sure to write claiming him, and probably asking for assistance, which I have no doubt she would at once receive, for he has ample means, and has the character of being both just and liberal.'

'And you think she would apply; and you have no doubt that she

ought to have got it? Any one would have thought that,' said Mrs. Peck, between her set teeth.

'Yes, certainly,' said Elsie; 'but perhaps she did not go the right way to work?'

'She did,' said Mrs. Peck, indignantly. 'I knowed her well, and heard all about it.'

This was to throw Elsie off her guard, for she did not wish to be identified at once; but it had not the effect desired, for Elsie felt convinced that this was the person who claimed to be Francis's mother.

Mrs. Phillips came in at this interesting poise in the conversation, and began to give Elsie directions as to some alterations in a dress.

'There's some buttons and trimmings to get to make it up with. Alice, you had better go to town and get them for me. You need a walk, at any rate; I do not think you've had your walk at all regularly of late,' said Mrs. Phillips.

'Indeed,' said Mrs. Peck, 'she has had no walk since here I've been, whatever she might have had before. It's trying work sitting still all day; I feel it myself, and all the more that I'm not used to it. If you'd be so good as excuse me for a hour or two; I'd take it as a great kindness if you'd let me go with Alice for a walk to do her bit of shopping, and to show her round Melbourne a bit. If I don't know Mebourne well, I ought to. I don't think I ever saw so good a hand as Alice has. I think I could make her fortune, if she'd only give me a little commission.'

'Oh, I don't think Alice is inclined to leave me,' said Mrs. Phillips; 'and, indeed, I am very well satisfied with her.'

'But this ain't exactly her sphere. She was a telling me as she was brought up with great expectations,' said Mrs. Peck.

'She has got over her disappointment about that, I think,' said Mrs. Phillips.

'I dare say you think it shabby in me to try to entice your maid from you; and really, after all, a comfortable home with a lady, as it must be a pleasure to serve and to wait upon, is perhaps the best

thing after all. But as I was saying, Mrs. Phillips, I would be glad to get out for an hour or two with Alice. I'll not do much work without her, for I'm sure to go wrong if she is not at my elbow. There's not many ladies so generous as you, to pay me for my blundering work; and Alice is wonderful patient too. I don't know how to thank her for the pains she takes with me, and I can't help being very stupid. After being used to active life, one don't take well to this sitting still. So I'll just put on my bonnet and shawl and go out a bit with Alice.'

Mrs. Phillips did not at all like this proposal, for she had an idea that her husband would very much disapprove of it, and would be still more angry at that than at her having her mother in her house; but then Mr. Phillips was away, and her mother was there, and the present terror conquered the distant one. She never knew what her mother might or might not say, if she thwarted her in anything: she had distant recollections of terrible punishments that always followed the slightest act of disobedience, or even carelessness, in her childish days; and though now she knew her mother would not strike her with her hands, she was in constant dread of her tongue. So that now Mrs. Peck took it for granted that she would be allowed to accompany her daughter's maid—she dared not refuse it. Alice scarcely liked the idea of going to walk to town with this strange woman; but at the same time her curiosity as to what she might have to say was very great. She felt that this Mrs. Mahoney had intelligence to give that was of great importance, and that she wished to be secure from interruption. Mrs. Phillips was constantly going in and out, for she was afraid to leave her mother long with any one, and always looked suspicious of what they might be talking about. Mary, the housemaid, and the nurse, too, seemed to be curious about this old needlewoman, and were often coming in unexpectedly.

When Mrs. Peck had put on her bonnet and shawl, and dropped her veil over her face, she looked sufficiently respectable for a companion to one so little known in Melbourne as Alice Melville, so she thought there could be no harm in going out for an hour or

two with her for the sake of ascertaining if she had any light to throw on the dark subject of Francis's birth.

When they got out of doors, Mrs. Peck appeared at first to be rather anxious to resume the conversation which her daughter had interrupted; but as they were pretty closely followed by two other pedestrians all the way into town, she made up her mind to attend to Mrs. Phillips's business first, so they went to Collins Street and bought the trimmings. Then Mrs. Peck went to a bookseller's shop and purchased a shilling novel that she said she had been told was very interesting, but she appeared scarcely to know the name of it, and took the first one the shopman gave to her.

Elsie thought she was a good deal more stared at than was agreeable, and also that the shopmen in both establishments addressed her with a good deal of familiarity. She had heard Miss Phillips complain of the great freedom and the want of politeness of Melbourne tradespeople and the inhabitants generally; but this was her first personal experience of anything of the kind, and she rightly attributed it to the company she was in. She felt, now, that she had made a great mistake in going out with this Mrs. Mahoney, whose rather loud remarks and vulgar appearance seemed to attract general attention, and she could only wish fervently that, with or without her secret, she could get back safely to East Melbourne. As they returned, Mrs. Peck proposed a detour by the Botanic Gardens, which Elsie had never seen. Mrs. Phillips would not expect them home soon, for she had proposed to show Miss Melville all about Melbourne; and the gardens were well worth seeing. On a week day they were quiet, and one could get a seat to have a little comfortable talk. Much as Elsie wished for the talk, she would not on any account lengthen her walk for it, so she declined the proposal.

'Then,' said Mrs. Peck, 'let us go out of the regular road we came by, and go round Fitzroy Square, and have a look round at all the churches and chapels that are built on the Eastern Hill.'

Fitzroy Square was not at that time enclosed or planted. It was merely a vacant space, intersected by numerous footpaths in various directions, and covered where there was no beaten path with very

dusty withered-looking grass. Elsie had no objection to go out of the thoroughfare; but, instead of pointing out the churches or anything else, as soon as Mrs. Peck had got safe out of any third party's hearing, she slackened her pace, and eagerly opened the subject which was nearest to her heart.

'I said, Miss Melville, that I could make your fortune if you'd only give me a handsome commission. Are you willing to drive a bargain?' said Mrs. Peck.

'If I can see my way clear to the fortune, I should, of course, be glad to pay you for the information; but I must know what you have got to say before I can guess what it is worth,' said Elsie.

'And I must know what you are willing to give, before I can tell what I know,' said Mrs. Peck.

'But I have really got nothing to offer,' said Elsie; 'you know how poor I am.'

'But suppose you and your sister was to get Cross Hall through means of me, what would you give me for that?' asked Mrs. Peck.

Elsie felt sure that this woman could not give the property to Jane and herself, for it had been left to Francis distinctly by will, by name and description; but yet she wanted very much to find out if he was really their cousin or not, so she said—

'I must consult with my sister on this matter, for it concerns her as much as myself, and also with Mr. Phillips, who has been to both of us the kindest and best of friends, before I could make you any definite offer.'

'No, no,' said Mrs. Peck; 'I want no interference of strangers, and I ain't got no time to waste here while you write up the country to anybody. I must go back to Adelaide in a few days, and surely your sister will see the advantages of your acting for her. What do you say to £2,000.'

To be asked £2,000 for what Elsie knew to be worth nothing, in a money point of view, appeared to her rather absurd. 'That is a very large sum,' said she.

'A year's income is not too much for such a secret as I've got.

Cross Hall must be worth £2,000 a year now, and more than that, and I must have something handsome to cover my risk.'

'Then you put yourself under the grasp of the law by what you have to reveal?' said Elsie.

'You must let me get clear off before you publish it,' said Mrs. Peck. 'I have been treated with the greatest ingratitude by Frank, and I'd like a little revenge. I'd like to pull him down from his high horse, and set him working for his bread as you have had to do; but at the same time I am a poor woman, and I must live.'

'I cannot tell what we would give you,' said Elsie, 'until I have something more distinct than these vague threats; but you may be sure that we will give you as much as it is worth. Trust to our honour for that.'

'Trust to a fiddlestick's end! I am too old a bird to be caught with such chaff as that. No, I must have it down in black and white. See, here is a paper that I want you to fill up and sign before I'll open my mouth on the subject.' So Mrs. Peck drew out of her black bag a paper containing an agreement to pay her £2,000 on condition that the estate of Cross Hall should be recovered for her and her sister through Mrs. Peck's information. She laid the paper open on the book she had bought, then she took a pen and a portable ink-bottle from the same repository, dipped the pen in the ink, and demanded Elsie's signature then and there.

Her eager eyes watched the girl's countenance as she read the agreement and weighed the pros and cons of the bargain she was making, and neither of them were aware, in their preoccupation, that they were observed. When Elsie looked up, puzzled as to what she was to do, and Mrs. Peck was putting her pen into her hand, she saw the figure of Walter Brandon approaching her with the appearance of haste and agitation. Mrs. Peck snatched the paper from Elsie's hand, and replaced it in the black bag, along with the other writing materials and the extempore desk.

'Alice Melville!' said Brandon, 'what in Heaven's name are you doing here in such company as this?'

Elsie turned as pale as death; she could not utter a syllable.

'Come with me—let me take you home. I heard from Mrs. Phillips that you had gone out; but I could not have imagined you to have such a companion.'

'Such a companion, indeed!' said Mrs. Peck, indignantly. 'I have been in these colonies more nor thirty years, and I'm good enough company for any fine lady's-maid as ever walked on shoe leather.'

'Oh, Mr. Brandon!' said Elsie, who had recovered her powers of speech; 'she was doing needlework at Mrs. Phillips's, and I was sent out on an errand, and she would come with me.'

'And we was just a looking over the bill, and seeing as our money was all right,' said Mrs. Peck, in the most plausible manner.

'No; it was not a bill,' said Elsie, who hated the idea of this woman telling lies for her.

'Did Mrs. Phillips actually send you out walking with this person?' said Brandon, with a look of the most intense contempt and disgust at Mrs. Peck.

'She said nothing against it; but she did not send me; it was all my own fault,' said Elsie, weeping bitterly. 'I rather wished to go with her.'

'My dear Miss Alice, you must have seen that this was no fit person for you to associate with. You are an innocent girl, ignorant of the world, as all girls ought to be; but you are not so easily deceived in character as not to see in this woman's face, language, and manners, that she is to be avoided as you would avoid death and destruction,' said Brandon.

Elsie only wept more bitterly than before. Brandon must despise her for ever now. She had been glad to come out to Victoria, because she thought if he still loved or cared for her she should hear of it. She had treasured his parting words and his parting looks in her heart; and now to meet him again in this way—to feel that he must look down on her as in the old days of his pity he never could have done—was dreadful. How was he to guess at the almost irresistible temptation that had led her to compromise herself so far?

'You had better go home now to your own dwelling, Mrs. Peck,' said Brandon; 'for if Mr. Phillips were to know that you had been

visiting his wife in his absence you would come by the worst of it. Needlework, indeed! Mrs. Phillips is a fool, certainly; but the idea of your doing needlework for her is very absurd. So you had better never show face there again.'

'Perhaps you'd like to know where I live, Miss Melville,' said Mrs. Peck, glaring angrily at Brandon. 'I lodge at No. —, Little Bourke Street, and can be heard of there, either as Mrs. Mahoney or Mrs. Peck. You can come there to see me.'

'Like to know where *you* live—go to see *you*!' said Brandon, in towering indignation. 'Now Miss Melville knows your real character she will keep away from you for ever. So now go off with you, as quickly as you can.'

'Good-bye, Miss Melville,' said Mrs. Peck, as she slowly went on her way to her own lodgings. She found she must go, but she would not be hurried by Brandon's wrath.

He waited till she was out of hearing before he tried to soothe the feelings of the agitated girl she had left under his care.

'Now where can I take you to? If Mrs. Phillips allowed you to do such a thing as walk through Melbourne with Mrs. Peck, she is not to be trusted with you. Oh, if Peggy were only here—but she is not: your sister told me she had not left Edinburgh.'

'Take me back to Mrs. Phillips; she will be as glad to get rid of this woman as you can possibly be,' said Elsie.

'But she must have known there was something wrong, for she looked confused and ashamed when I asked for you, and when I settled down to wait till your return, she seemed quite restless till I went away. Indeed, she sent me on an errand in quite a different direction; but I wished to come this way, and thought there was no hurry about her commission. I always knew her to be a fool, but not so wicked and false as this proves her to be.'

'I think this woman frightens her,' said Elsie.

'She has some hold on her, no doubt. Poor Phillips! we had better say nothing to him about it. So you would really prefer going home to her,' said Brandon.

'Yes, certainly,' said Elsie; and she paused for a little. 'But, Mr.

Brandon, I am in want of advice and assistance more than I ever was in my life. I must have it, and have it immediately. Can I rely on you as a friend?'

'Yes, as a friend;—certainly, as a friend,' said Brandon, who wondered what revelation was about to be made. Surely no love affair with some one else!

'I believe this woman is the person who calls herself my cousin Francis's mother,' said Elsie. 'I think she came to Mrs. Phillips's for the express purpose of ingratiating herself with me, in hopes of selling me a secret which she knows, and which she declares will give to Jane and myself the possession of Cross Hall.'

'Ah!' said Brandon, slowly; 'and is this her little game at present?'

'Now, I have often thought that Francis was not my uncle's son—there is not the slightest family likeness; and she is capable of any fraud or deception. I really knew she was not good when I went out with her, but we had no chance to speak without interruption in the house, and I did not think she was so well known in Melbourne as she appears to be. I know I have done very wrong, but I really had some excuse. If she can prove this—' and Elsie paused, in hopes that Brandon would say something to show that he felt for the greatness of her temptation.

'But, my dear Miss Alice,' said Brandon, 'she cannot take the property from your cousin. Was it not left to him by will, and left to him because he had proved himself worthy of it?—at least, I believe that is what your sister and Peggy have told me. She tries this game of hers with a girl who knows nothing about business. It is of no use whatever.'

'She has no idea about the will, and thinks that Francis got the estate as heir-at-law. But my view of the matter is this, that if Francis is proved not to be our cousin, he might marry Jane, and not lose the propery. That is what I aim at, for they love each other, I am quite sure.'

'If they do, I wonder he did not throw up the fortune, and set about earning one for himself. It was a good deal to give up, too—a seat in parliament, and such a career as appears before him. But

what are wealth and fame compared to love?' said Brandon, who had got rather into heroics.

'I do not like to say much to Jane about it, for it only distresses her; but I think—I am almost sure—that he offered to make the sacrifice, but that Jane would not accept of it. She rejoiced in his useful and honourable life. She would not consent to be his drag and stumbling-block. She must have felt it very hard, too; for I feel she loves him dearly. It was for their sakes that I was so anxious to discover this woman's secret. She wants to be revenged on Francis, who has not answered her letters, and has sent her no money. I am a little surprised at that; but yet I believe that he must have had good reasons for his conduct, for there never was any one more thoroughly conscientious and liberal than the cousin I want to lose—the brother I wish to gain. Would it not be a glorious revenge if this Mrs. Peck, in her spite, were to give him all he wants—the only thing missing in his cup of happiness?'

'Perhaps, then, it is a pity I interrupted you so soon,' said Brandon, admiring the generous enthusiasm of the girl; 'but you were too dear to me, too precious, to be left in such suspicious company a moment longer than I could help. I came to Melbourne with one purpose—and that was, to entreat you to reconsider the answer you gave to me in the railway carriage.'

'I did not know you so well then,' said Elsie. 'I thought you only pitied me; and now I fear I have given you cause to despise me.'

'Nothing of the kind,' said Brandon; 'nothing of the kind. I love you far more now than I did then; and though I was so stupid and idiotic as to fancy that Miss Phillips would suit me as well, whenever I saw you together her faults came out, and your virtues. I do not wish to take you at a disadvantage. Do not think it ungenerous in me to ask so much just when you are in trouble and perplexity, and need advice and assistance.'

'And just when I have appeared in such an unfavourable light,' said Elsie, in her low, sweet voice, a little tremulous with the excitement of the scene.

'But I will give you the best help I can, and the best advice my

poor head can supply, whether you return my love or not. Do not let that weigh with you for a moment. Nothing I can do can make me deserve you. If I am not bodily on my knees before you—for in a public place like this it would be absurd, and you would not like it—I am mentally on my knees, willing to accept whatever you may choose to give me—love, if possible; but if your heart is otherwise engaged, or if you cannot love such a commonplace fellow as myself, then I will *try* to be contented with friendship. Which shall it be, my dearest Alice?'

'Will you have any objection to accepting of both?' said Alice, in the same tremulous tone.

'None,' said Brandon, delighted, 'none whatever; indeed, one implies the other, though the other does not imply the one. I cannot express myself distinctly, you see, but you know what I mean. I am not at all a genius, and even this happiness cannot inspire me with fine language. But what can I *do* for you?—there is where I hope to show my sense of what I owe to you.'

'First, then, we must leave this place and walk home, for I think people are looking at us,' said Elsie, trying to collect her thoughts; 'and then you must tell me what I am to do with Mrs. Peck, if that is her name. Mrs. Phillips calls her Mrs. Mahoney. The paper you saw in my hand, which she snatched away, was an agreement to pay a sum of money if we were put in possession of Cross Hall. If I had signed it, it would have been of no value to her; but I hesitated about it, for I did not like cheating even her, and making her risk bringing herself to justice for nothing.'

'I will go to see her myself, and negotiate for you. I do not think I should have much scruple in outwitting her, for she really deserves it, and it is only letting her over reach herself. Will you give me full powers to act for you?'

'Oh, yes,' said Elsie; 'if she will only deal with you it will be so much better.'

'Upon the footing on which we stand together at present it is quite right and proper that I should do so,' said Brandon, accepting the responsibilities of his position with great satisfaction. 'You did

not get my letter. Emily and your sister told me you sailed before the mail come in, which contained that painful work of composition. I wrote to you whenever I got out to Barragong, and saw that I really had not been so nearly ruined as I thought. I determined to do it on the occasion when I parted with you in the nursery.'

'Shall I say, like Miss Harriett Phillips, that I conquered you by making a ballad in your praise? for these men can be led by nothing so well as by vanity and selfishness. No, I will not say it, for I do not think you are either vain or selfish. I should not like you if you were,' said Elsie.

'Say *love*, Alice, it sounds much sweeter, and goes more to my heart. You like your cousin, or no-cousin Francis, but you must *love* me.'

'Well, love be it,' said Alice; 'but I really love Francis a good deal, too—not as I love you, or as I intend to love you, for I really don't know how I feel just yet, but still not mere liking.'

'I am not at all jealous,' said Brandon, 'though all his literary talents and tastes should make me feel my own inferiority.'

'Even Jane never would allow me to say that you were inferior to Francis; she said your talents lay in a different direction. She was sorry that I refused you, and when I came to know you better I was very sorry myself.'

'When did you begin to soften to me?' asked Brandon.

'When you said Peggy had taught you so much—when you expressed yourself so warmly and so truly about her.'

'Had she not prejudiced you against me in the first place?' said Brandon, hesitatingly.

'Yes, she had,' said Elsie, with still greater hesitation.

'By something that she said of me? It was too true I deserved it; but the lesson she taught me has never been forgotten. I do not say that I deserve you, but I mean to try my best to deserve you. But was that your only reason for refusing me?'

'No; I had several. I thought myself a very unfit wife for you, and that you would be cruelly disappointed to get a low-spirited, sickly, useless girl who did not love or esteem you. I really thought I was

dying, and it would have been wrong to have thought of marrying under such circumstances; and besides, you could not have cared much about me, or you would not have transferred your affection so easily to a woman so very different in every way.'

'Well, it does appear very inconsistent,' said Brandon. 'When my letter is returned from England, you will see two pages of apologies, and reasons why I was so foolish; but I really thought there was somebody whom you liked better, until that very moment when I caught your eye and your expression when I praised our excellent old friend. Your glance at that time restored me to my allegiance; but the bad news of my affairs next day put love and marriage out of my head, till I came to part from you, and I felt how hard it was. But I am glad to see that I have not seriously injured Miss Phillips by trifling with her affections. She has met with her match at last. I never thought she could have been so well suited.'

'I really think they will get on very comfortably.'

'How could I ever fancy that woman amiable?' said Brandon. 'I thought her really an exceedingly agreeable and clever woman in Derbyshire: when I went out shopping with her on that memorable day, I saw spots on the sun; and the day before yesterday, at Wiriwilta, she appeared to be quite insufferable. I cannot think enough of my own good luck; I might have been her husband by this time instead of being your lover, which is much pleasanter. What an insipid slow life it would have been, though Grant, I dare say, looks forward to it with complacency. He always used to look down on the colonial girls that our neighbours married, and threatened to go home for a thoroughly accomplished wife; and now one of that stamp has come out to him, and saved him time and money. And Miss Phillips looks far more kindly on him than she ever did on me.'

'I do not call it merely good luck,' said Elsie; 'I think our affairs are in wiser hands than our own.'

'And that I should be grateful for that wise guidance, instead of idly congratualting myself that things have turned out so well,' said Brandon. 'I only know that I feel grateful, though I am in want of

words to express it. A man living alone, as I have done for so many years, feels at a loss to speak about these matters. I need a dear good woman like you by my side to teach me to open my heart, for I know I never will be ashamed to speak to you as I feel—though I might stand in some awe of a poetess, too.'

'Don't speak about my poetry,' said Elsie.

'Am I never to hear that song of Wiriwilta, in which I play such a conspicuous part?' said Brandon.

'Oh, I have forgotten it, for the children got tired of it, and asked for new songs and stories; it was never written down, and I never can recollect my own verses. It shows that they are not genuine poetry, for I have a tenacious memory for anything good of other people's. So, as it is lost for ever, you may imagine it to have been as beautiful as you please.'

VIII

MRS. PHILLIPS IS RELIEVED

Mrs. Phillips had been much alarmed at the sight of Mr. Brandon almost immediately after Elsie and Mrs. Peck had gone out. He asked for Miss Alice Melville as soon as he entered, saying he had a letter from her sister and messages from the children for her, so that he would stay with Mrs. Phillips till she returned, and sat down before the window looking steadily out to catch the first sight of her. Not having her mother's inventive turn, she was at a loss how to get rid of him. Brandon must not see Mrs. Peck, and Elsie must be warned to say nothing about her to him. She sat in torture for some time, and at last in despair she asked him in an awkward embarrassed way to be good enough to go for a nosegay for her, that she had been promised by a mutual friend at Richmond, that she wished very much to have. He could not help thinking something was wrong. Mrs. Phillips had always been very inconsiderate to Alice, and no doubt she had been sent to town on some errand that she was ashamed he should know about—probably to fetch a heavy parcel. So, instead of going to Richmond, he took the road on which he would be most likely to meet her, so as to assist her if possible, and as he came up to the square where Mrs. Peck and Elsie were talking, he met with a bush acquaintance, who, after

the usual greetings to the returned Brandon, pointed to the two female figures, and remarked—'There's Mrs. Peck back again to Melbourne, and a very pretty girl with her. I wonder if she brought her from Adelaide. I thought Melbourne had lost that ornament for ever, but here she is as large as life again.'

Something in the attitude and form of the girl in the distance reminded him of a person he had seen. He was sorry for the poor thing, and walked quickly towards the place where they were standing engrossed with their important business. To his surprise and horror he found she was really the person he thought she slightly resembled, and he lost no time in coming forward to stop the conversation.

Mrs. Phillips was astonished and distressed to see Elsie return with Brandon without Mrs. Peck. Where they had met, and how they had got rid of her, she could not imagine. Elsie went to take off her bonnet and return to her work, and Mrs. Phillips was left alone with Brandon. At his first word, his first question, how could she let Alice Melville go out of her house with a woman so well known in Melbourne as Mrs. Peck, Mrs. Phillips burst into tears.

'I could not help it; indeed, I could not help it. Stanley will be so angry if you tell him, and I am sure I did all I could to keep her away, but she would come, and she would take a fancy to Alice, and sit with her, and then when I sent Alice out for the buttons, she would go with her.'

'But why have you her here at all, Mrs. Phillips?' said Brandon, gravely. 'You must know that she is no fit person to be in your house, particularly in Mr. Phillips's absence. Confide in your good husband. If there is any part of your past life that you are afraid of her telling, believe me you will not better yourself by keeping in her power—tell your husband everything, and shake yourself free of this dangerous woman.'

'Stanley knows everything—everything about me—but he said I never was to speak to her again; and I am sure I never wished to; but how can I help it when she will come—and she is my own mother? But don't tell anybody, for Stanley would be so vexed. I

don't keep anything from him; don't blame me with that, Mr. Brandon.'

'Your mother?' said Brandon. 'Oh, that alters the case.'

'I know that she is not good, and not respectable, and all that; but she went on so that I was terrified to refuse her leave to come here to do some sewing. If Stanley had not thought she was in Adelaide, he would never have left me here. Everything goes wrong when he leaves me. There, when he went to America, we had the scarlet fever, and I lost my dear little Eva, and now there is all this trouble. Oh! I wish I had gone up to Wiriwilta—I would have done just as well there. But don't tell Mr. Phillips about this; I would rather tell him myself. He has been good to me—so very good to me;—you cannot think how good he has always been to me;—I do not keep things from him—indeed I don't, Mr. Brandon.'

Brandon felt more liking to poor Mrs. Phillips in her distress and in her tears than he had ever felt before. With such a mother, and such training as she had had in her early years, much could not be expected from her, and now her expressions of gratitude to her good husband touched him greatly. He had always thought her too insensible of her extraordinary good fortune—and in a general way, so she was; but during these last few days, seeing her mother, and shrinking from her, had made Mrs. Phillips have some idea of what her life might have been if Stanley had not been so fond of her, and so generous as to marry her, and take her away from what was likely to be her fate in such hands as those of her mother and Peck, and keep her so quiet and comfortable, and give her every luxury he could afford, and bear with her temper, her ignorance, and her stupidity; for in a vague way she knew that she had these faults. Was there ever a wish of hers that he could grant that he had refused? Even this unlucky stay in Melbourne had been at her own earnest request, and it had turned out so miserably, just because he was away. Never had she loved her husband so much as at this time when she had been displeasing him so grievously; how she had longed for courage to drive away the invader!—and now, though humbled before Mr. Brandon, she was

grateful to him when she thought that he could stay with her till her husband came, and that, so protected, her mother could not again visit her.

'No doubt Phillips will forgive you readily when you tell him the truth; and I forgive you too, under the very distressing circumstances in which Mrs. Peck placed you, though I did feel very indignant at your allowing the girl whom I love, and whom I mean to marry, to go to Melbourne with such a person,' said Brandon.

'You mean to marry Alice?' said Mrs. Phillips.

'Yes, and she has consented to have me.'

'Well, she is a good girl,' said Mrs. Phillips, 'and I am sure I wish you happy with her. I know you will get on better with her than with Harriett, for she is always so much taken up with herself, and never thinks about other people. The way she treated me when I was left here with her was shameful; but I'll not tell Stanley about it if I can help it, for I have got enough to vex him about without grumbling at his sister that he thinks so much of. But I like both of the Melvilles, and they were both very good to my poor little baby as died in scarlet fever, you know. We'll never get a husband for Miss Melville, for the gentlemen are all frightened of her; but it is just as well, for she is a capital governess, Stanley says, and the children like her—but they like Alice best.'

'And Miss Phillips and Dr. Grant appear to be making it up as fast as possible,' said Brandon, 'if I may judge from what I saw and heard at Wiriwilta.'

'I am sure, Mr. Brandon, you never saw such goings on all the time he was in town. They were together continually, and when he left Melbourne, she said she would like to go up the country too. I really don't think Stanley would have liked it.'

'Perhaps they are engaged,' suggested Brandon.

'Perhaps they were; but I think Harriett would have told me that, for she'd have been so proud of it, and I really think it was my dues to hear the first thing besides.'

'I have told you the first thing,' said Brandon. 'I have not been more than half an hour accepted.'

'Well, I am glad you have told me. I will miss Alice dreadfully, though. I suppose it will be soon?' said Mrs. Phillips.

'As soon as I can persuade her to take me for better for worse,' said Brandon.

'Oh, she won't need much persuading, such a good marriage for her as it is,' said Mrs. Phillips, who fancied she knew something of human nature. 'Emily will want to be bridesmaid, she is so fond of both Alice and you.'

'Of course she will wish it, and of course she will have her own way, as usual; but with regard to Mrs. Peck, will you or shall I tell Alice the relation between you and her? I should like you to be justified to her.'

'Oh, I'll tell her: I must wish her joy, and then I will tell her. And, Mr. Brandon, will you be good enough to stay in the house as much as you can till Stanley comes down from Wiriwilta, and then you will be able to send Mrs. Peck away, for I am too frightened of her to do it myself. I'll go and speak to Alice now.'

'Do; and send her in to speak to me, for I have got some business of hers that I must attend to, and I must have some directions from her.'

'Business!' said Mrs. Phillips, incredulously; 'I dare say you have got plenty to say to her, but I don't think as it's business.'

At the sight of Alice, Mrs. Phillips's tears burst forth afresh, and for the second time in her life (the first was on the occasion of Eva's death, when she had felt Alice so very kind), she threw her arms round one of her own sex for sympathy and consolation.

'My dear Alice, forgive me—I could not help it, I was so frightened. You must not tell anybody, not even your sister, about it; but that woman is my own mother, and I could not get her to go away. I did not like your being so much with her, but I could not help it, for she would do it. Do forgive me.'

'Certainly, I forgive you from my heart,' said Elsie.

'And Mr. Brandon has told me all about you and him, and I really wish you joy. You are going to have a good husband—not so good a one as mine, but still a very good one.'

'Thank you, Mrs. Phillips. I hope to be able to make him happy—at least I will try my very best to do so.' said Elsie.

'And you must make allowances for me, for you can see how I was brought up. I know I have been very often cross with you, but you must forgive all these old things; and I suppose it had better be before we leave Melbourne. We must write for Emily to come down, for she will want to be bridesmaid, and Mr. Brandon says she shall, and we must set to get your things all in a hurry.'

'There's time enough to talk of all these matters,' said Elsie. 'I have scarcely begun to believe that I am engaged yet.'

'Oh, but Mr. Brandon wants to speak to you on business, and what other business can there be? So go into the drawing-room, and he will perhaps show you that there is some need to think of these things.'

But Mr. Brandon did not bewilder Elsie with asking her to fix any time, though he was determined to be married before going out of town, if possible; but he had to get from her extracts from her uncle's will, which she recollected nearly word for word, and instructions as to how to proceed with Mrs. Peck; also, as much as she knew of Mr. Hogarth's letters to Madame de Véricourt, to show the relations between him and Elizabeth Ormistown, so far as she knew of them. There was also a good deal of other talk to go through on subjects personal to themselves, which they both thought exceedingly interesting, and Brandon would not believe till he looked at his watch that he had kept Mrs. Phillips out of her own drawing-room for two hours.

IX

MRS. PECK'S COMMUNICATION

Mrs. Peck was surprised and a little disconcerted when, on the evening of the day on which she had so nearly confided her secret to Elsie, Mr. Brandon walked into her lodgings unannounced; but she concealed her chagrin with her usual duplicity. Though she was desirous of further communication with Elsie, she preferred it to be with herself, and not through a person who had spoken so uncivilly to her.

'You did not think it worth while for me to give Miss Melville and you my address, but I see that you are making use of it without delay,' said she.

'Yes, I am, for I want to know if I cannot transact the business which I interrupted,' said Brandon.

'You! No; certainly not. I only deal with principals.'

'Miss Alice Melville empowers me to act for her in this matter, and this letter from her to me should satisfy you of that. It will not do for a girl to treat personally with a woman who compromises her by her company.'

'Oh, is that it?' said Mrs. Peck, who disliked the exchange of a simple young girl for a man of the world in the bargain she wished to make. 'Well, if I must deal with you, what do you offer?'

'If you can give the inheritance of Cross Hall to Jane and Alice Melville, a thousand pounds,' said Brandon.

'Say two thousand,' said Mrs. Peck; 'I will not take less than that. Are you a sweetheart of that girl's—or of her sister's? If you are, you can easily see that Cross Hall is worth far more than that.'

'I do not think you can give information that will be worth the money I offer,' said Brandon. 'Even supposing you were married before your irregular marriage with Mr. Hogarth, you will have difficulty in proving that marriage; and after so many years spent in New South Wales and Victoria under another name, it will be almost impossible to prove your identity.'

'I can prove that,' said Mrs. Peck, taking out of her black bag several letters of old date, generally with remittances, signed 'H. Hogarth.' There had been an annuity paid regularly after she had gone to Australia; but the last payment had been of a large sum £1,500 which she had accepted in lieu of all future annual remittances, and that had been sent more than thirteen years before.

'I was a fool and a idiot to take the money, for it went as fast as my money always did; but Peck wanted to start in the public line, and persuaded me to ask for that sum, and then in a year and a half it was all gone, and I had no annuity to fall back on,' said Mrs. Peck.

'Were you married to Peck or to Mrs. Phillips's father?' asked Brandon.

'No, not exactly married. I kept out of bigamy. I always kept that hold on Cross Hall; I would not marry any one right out, you know.'

'He might have had a divorce from you,' said Brandon.

'If he had known, perhaps he might; but nobody made it none of their business to tell him, and I said nothing about it.'

'It is rather difficult to tell when you are speaking the truth, and when you are not,' said Brandon; 'but I believe that you really are Elizabeth Ormistown, and I believe also that Francis Hogarth is not the son of old Cross Hall, as you call him; but I fear you cannot prove it, and without that the information is of no use to us, and worth no money.'

'If I can prove it, how much is it worth?'

'How much have you had already on the strength of it? You are first handsomely paid for the lie, and now you want to be bribed into telling the truth. I myself think £1,000 far too much, for if the case were taken to court, there would be very heavy law expenses before possession could be obtained. I offer, on Miss Melville's behalf, a thousand whenever they get the property.'

'Far too little. I'll not speak a word for the chance of a sum like that; I must have £2,000. What is £1,000?'

'Why, at your years, it would buy you a very handsome annuity, or you could lend it out at interest, and get ten per cent. for it, and have the principal to leave to any one you liked; or you might start in business with such a capital. Many handsome fortunes have been made in Melbourne on a smaller beginning; but if you think it insufficient, I can go away. My clients are not so very anxious about the property as to accede to such a demand as yours, and Francis Hogarth may be left in peaceable possession of the estate,' said Brandon, coolly.

'He must not be left with it. I must not let him sit there in the place he ain't got no rights to, after the way he has served me,' said Mrs. Peck.

'I believe it is more a piece of spite than anything else,' said Brandon. 'Well, here is the agreement for the payment of a thousand pounds. Will you accept of that, or shall I go?'

'You are too sharp for with me, a great deal too sharp on a poor old woman like me, but I'll take your offer in the meantime. Miss Melville said I was to trust to her honour to pay me as much as it is worth, and if she finds out as it's worth more, I expect she'll keep that saying of hers in mind, and act accordingly.'

Mrs. Peck signed the paper, and Brandon signed it also, as agent for Jane and Alice Melville.

'Now for your part of the bargain, Mrs. Peck, and stick to the truth if you can. I know that your imagination is apt to run away with you; but here it will be a disadvantage to have any flights of fancy,' said Brandon.

Mrs. Peck had for more than a week thought of nothing but this disclosure of her past life, and now that the opportunity had arrived, she really enjoyed telling it as much as if it had been wholly fictitious. It was quite as romantic as any of her fabrications, and it was a subject on which her lips had been sealed for thirty-four years, except to give vent to some occasional allusions, to Peck. It was interesting in itself, it was damaging to Francis, and it was likely to be lucrative to herself, for she hoped for a further reward from the grateful nieces, in addition to the thousand pounds which their agent offered on their behalf. She had thought a good deal over the story she had to tell, and gave a more consecutive and consistent narrative than was usual with her, for she felt the importance of making it appear to be a perfectly true story.

'Well,' said she, 'it's an old story and a queer one, but I do keep it in mind, and I will tell you the truth; for as you say, it is what will answer us both best. My name, as you know, was Elizabeth Ormistown, and I was born in the next county to —shire, where Cross Hall is. I have never seen Cross Hall myself, but I have heard of it. We had seen better days, for my father was a small shop-keeper, and my mother was a schoolmaster's daughter; but my father was the simple man, who is the beggar's brother, and he was caution or security (as they call it here) for a brother of his own, for two hundred pounds, and lost it, and then we went all down hill together. Mother was always very furious at him for his being such a fool, and even on his death-bed she never forgave him for bringing her down so low. She was very greedy of money, was mother, and never forgot any ill she had had done her. We was living in the country very poor, for I could not bear to go to service among folk that knew about us, when I fell in with a young man as I liked better than most; but as he was as poor as a rat, and only a working joiner, mother would have nothing to say to him, and she made up her mind to take me to Edinburgh, where she lived with a cousin, and I was to go to service. I had wanted to go before, but it was all mother's pride as kept me at home; I wanted to be well dressed, as all girls do, and I liked to be seen and to be talked to. I

had grown up handsome enough. You have seen Mrs. Phillips—she is the very moral of what I was, and I didn't like to be always wearing old things. And mother, she wanted Jamie Stevenson driven out of my head, so she made no objections to my going to a house where they took lodgers, mostly young men, in for the college. The work was hard, and the wages no great matter; but the chance was worth twice as much as the wages, for the lads was free-handed, particular if you would stand any daffing, as we called it then. Harry Hogarth was there the second winter I was in Edinburgh, and, though he was not like to have Cross Hall then, for he had two brothers older than him, he was just as free of his money as if he was a young laird. He had been in Paris before that, but his father had grumbled at his spending so much there, and said he must hold with Edinburgh for the future; and Harry was maybe trying to show the old man that as much might go in Auld Reekie as in France. He was said to be the cleverest of the family, and the old man was fond of him, and proud of him too, but he was very hard to part with the gear. Harry was my favourite of all the lads in the house, for he had most fun about him, and was the softest-hearted too. The old laird changed his mind in the middle of the winter. I mind well his coming to our place one day, and he gave me a very sour look when I opened the door, as if my cap and my clothes was too good for my station, and my looks, too, maybe; but he said that Harry had better go to Paris, as his heart was set on it; and he gave Harry a sum of money that made him think his father was not long for this world, though he looked all right. So he behoved to have a splore, as they called it: he entertained all his friends at a hotel to a supper, where they had a night of it, drinking, and singing, and laughing, to bid him farewell. When he came back it was grey daylight, and I was up to my work; and when he went past me, he saw me crying, as he thought, for grief at the thought of his going away. And really I was sorry, for I liked him the best of the lot, but my greeting was more with the thought of his giving me something handsome at parting than that he should take it up so serious. But he, in his conceit, thought I was breaking

my heart for the love of him, and he tried to dry my tears. So, instead of going away that day, he stopped another week; and then when he went to Paris, I said I would go with him; and he would refuse me nothing. So we went in separate ships, and met together in Paris; and I stopped with him at his lodgings, as is common enough in that queer town; and well I liked the place, and the sights, and the presents he gave me, and the clothes I had to put on; and he was good enough to me, though he laughed at me whiles; and many a day he called me greedy, but I aye got what I wanted out of him.

'Well, we had been three months in Paris, when he got word that his eldest brother had broke his neck when he was hunting, and that his father had taken the news so sore to heart that he was ill and not like to recover, so Harry had to go home with all speed. I would not stop in France without him, so we both came back again, and Harry went to Cross Hall and me to my mother's. I was not over willing to go to her, for I knew how angry she would be at me; but Harry said it was the best place for me for the meantime, and he promised to send me money, so that I would be no burden.

'As I dreaded, my mother was terrible angry at me; but when I told her how soft Harry was, she thought he might be brought to marry me, and she set her heart on managing that by hook or by cook. Her contrivance was, that I should pretend to be very ill, and send for him to bid me good-bye, and then she would manage the rest. So by her advice I took to my bed and coughed very bad, and she made my cheeks look deadly white, and my lips too; and when Harry came he was shocked to see me. His father was dead by this time, as well as his eldest brother, so his heart was especial soft, and he looked sore distressed at my being in such a bad way.

'"Oh! Bessie," says he, "what can I do for you? What can I get for you?"

'"'Deed it's no much that she wants now in this world; I'm thinking we'll lose her soon," said mother.

'"No, no," says Harry eagerly. "Let me feel your pulse, Bessie,"

says he. Mother forgot about his being a doctor, and did not like his going about in such a skilful way; but I was so roused and excited myself that my pulse was at the gallop. "Quick, but strong," says he; "not the least like death. Cheer up, Bessie," said he, "it's just a bad turn you've got—a chill, perhaps, but you'll very soon get over it. You ought to know that you're safe against fever at the present time."

'"It's on her mind," said mother. "It's her mind as is so disturbed. She eats nothing, and she sleeps none for coughing, and takes such spasms at the heart. I know she'll never get better, and she thinks just the same; and for my part I'd rather have laid her head in the grave than let her live to be such a disgrace to us all. To think of such a thing happening to a daughter of mine, and all through you."

'"Well, Mrs. Ormistown, it is a pity, but it was quite as much her doing as mine, and maybe a little more," says he, looking at me with a half-laugh; but I only sighed and groaned, and would not speak to him.

'"I'm sure, Bessie, when we were in Paris," says he, "you did not take it much to heart; and I'll do what I can to make you comfortable."

'"Don't mock us with talking about comfort," said mother, sternly. "If Bessie did not feel her sin and her shame when she was in that sink of iniquity with you, I trust I have been able to convince her of her position since she returned to me."

'"Indeed, Harry," says I, "morning, noon, and night, mother is preaching to me, and I really wish I was dead, to have a little quiet."

'"Tut, tut," says he, "if you were really ill, you would not speak so briskly about dying;" and he tried to soothe me down, but I kept very sulky—but yet when he went away he did not believe there was much the matter with me.

'"We must make you really ill," says my mother, when he was gone; so she got some stuff for me to take, and I swallowed it, and I really did think as I was dying. I never felt as bad before or since, and even mother was frightened that she had made it too strong, but she sent for Harry, and he was frightened too. She said that I

had poisoned myself, and was going to die with the scorn of every one.

'"Oh, if you would but acknowledge yourself her husband, it would be enough, quite enough, to let her die with her mind easy and her name cleared," says mother to him.

'Harry had no notion I took things so serious, but he supposed that my mother had driven me to desperation by her reproaches, so he said he would do as she wished, and mother fetched Violet Strachan, our cousin, and a woman called Wilson, from next door to be witnesses, and he said he was my husband, and I said I was his wife, in their presence. Harry thought that was enough, but mother wanted to make it surer still, for she wrote it out, and we all signed it, and here it is.' Then Mrs. Peck drew out this document from her bundle of papers.

'This is a marriage in Scotland. Without the paper it was a marriage, but mother liked to see things in black and white. Harry never could get out of it—though he said afterwards that he did not know what he was about when he signed it.

'Of course after mother had carried her point I was allowed to get well, but slowly, for the stuff had really half poisoned me. Harry was in London with his brother when my boy Frank was born; but he came to me as soon as he could, and by ill-luck it happened that the very day he came my old sweetheart Jamie Stevenson was paying me a visit, and Harry heard something that was not meant for him, and off he set without seeing me or the child either. He sent me a letter, saying I had cheated him first and last, and he would never look at me again.'

'Then your boy was not Henry Hogarth's son,' said Brandon, eagerly, who thought he had got hold of the important part of the story, 'but this man Stevenson's?'

'You're quite out in your guesses, Mr. Brandon, for as clever as you think yourself; it does not concern my story a bit, but I will say this, that my Frank was Harry's own son.'

'Then, were you married in this irregular way to Jamie Stevenson in the first place?' said Brandon, who saw no prospect of proving

the desired non-cousinship.

'No, I wasn't. But Jamie was doing better in the world then, and he was saying, thinking that I wasn't married, that for all that had come and gone, if the father would provide for the bairn any way handsome, he'd marry me yet, and I did not see much good in being the wife of a gentleman that would always be ashamed of me, and never bring me forward. Mother thought he would do that, but I knew the man better by this time. So I was telling Jamie that if I had only thought he'd have made me so good an offer I'd never have followed mother's counsel, but have taken him that I liked twice as well as Harry; and, may be, it would have been better for me if Harry had not been so soft and mother so positive. This was what Harry Hogarth heard that angered him so terribly, and he said I had cheated him. He sent me money, but he vowed he would never look me in the face again. Well, when Frank was about fourteen months old, Harry's other brother died. There was an awful mortality in the family at that time—three within two years; and then he came in for the property. Mother was in an awful passion at my having had anything to say to Jamie, and losing hold on my rich husband through my stupidity. But I was his wife, and must be provided for at any rate. So he wanted to make terms with me, and proposed that I should go out of the country altogether—to Sydney—where he would give me a decent maintenance for myself and the child. Mother, at first, would not listen to this, and neither would I; but wanted to go to law for my rights. But when he said he would expose everything about the marriage if we did, we gave in, and agreed to go to the ends of the earth to please him. And, after we had made up our minds to it, we rather liked the notion of getting out of Scotland. He would not trust to us going unless he saw us off; so he appointed to meet in London, where the ship was to sail from, and he would arrange all things for our going off quiet and comfortable; and then we was to part for ever. Mother, and me, and Frank, went to London, and took lodgings in a very crowded lodging-house, full of people just ready to sail for America or some other place—here to-day and away to-morrow—and there Frank

fell ill. He had looked a strong enough child; but I think the stuff mother gave me had hurt him, for he had every now and then bad convulsion fits. Being used to them, we did not take much notice of them; but now, when it was of such moment to us that the child should be alive, and that his father should see him, then by ill-luck, just an hour before the time appointed for our meeting, Frank took a worse fit than ever, and died in my arms. I was very vexed indeed, and sorry, for I liked the child, and he was a very pretty little fellow, but mother was furious.

'"It's a good hundred a year out of our pocket," said she. "If he had only lived to get on board, we need never have told Cross Hall about his dying afterwards—and he looked the picture of health only yesterday. I wish some one would lend us a child! Maybe the woman in the next room will. He never saw it, and he'd not know the difference between one child and another."

'So mother went into the next room. It was let to a woman with one child, and she was to sail for America the next day to join her husband, who had written for her. She seemed to be poor, and mother had no doubt that for a pound or so she would lend us the child; but when she went into the room the mother was out, and the child was lying on the bed asleep. Mother was very quick and clever. Our boy was so changed with the convulsions that I would never have known him again; and this boy was much the same size and age, and not very unlike him, so she slipped off the child's nightgown and put poor Frank's clothes on it, and dressed my dead child in the nightgown she took off, and put it in the bed. She would not give me time to cry, but got into a hackney coach and rode off to where we were to meet Harry. She told me afterwards that she meant to take back the woman her child, if possible; but, in case of not being able to do it, she got all our luggage which was ready packed, into the hackney coach, and paid the woman of the house all we owed her.

'When I saw Harry again he looked changed—far graver and duller. I was full of sorrow about Frank; and I cried sore when I saw his father. But then he thought I only cried, out of cunning, to get

something more out of him. Harry took the child in his arms and looked at it all over. "Poor thing," says he—"poor thing!" and I saw a tear drop on that stranger's face. My own boy—his own boy—he had never touched, and never looked at. I was jealous and fierce at both of them, in my grief and my rage; but mother was pleased to see him so taken up with the child, for she thought it would be all the better for us.

'"Well," says he, "are you ready to go on board this afternoon? for the ship will get off to night with the tide, and I will see you all right."

'"Yes," says mother, "we are all ready; but we want to know what allowance you are willing to make. You must take into consideration that we are banished, and have to leave everybody we know. What will you allow for Elizabeth, and what for little Frank?"

'"I think," said Harry, speaking slow, "that I will arrange differently about the child. As he is my son, I think he would be better in other hands than yours. Will you leave the boy with me?"

'I was just on the point of saying it was none of mine, nor of his neither; but mother saw her own interest in this, as she did in most things, and so says she—

'"It's cruel to part Elizabeth from her child, very cruel. Will you, that has treated her so bad, be good to the boy? Do you mean to acknowledge him?"

'Harry spoke slow again: "I don't know if I will be good to him, but I will try. I will put him in as good hands as I can, educate him, and acknowledge him, if he deserves it; and I fear if you bring him up he is not likely to do so."

'"It is for the child's own good, Bessie," said mother, eagerly. "You must sacrifice your own feeling, and leave him with his father, if he promises so fair. How are we like to get him educated where we are going? It is very hard on you, Bessie," said mother, coaxingly.

'I stood sulky, not knowing what to do or what to say.

'"And Mr. Hogarth will no doubt consider the hardship of your

case, and make it up in some other way to you," mother went on to say.

'Henry looked up at mother very sharp, and then he looked at me. Though he did not believe in my tears, he did not like to see them, for they reminded him of how I had served him before.

'"He is quite innocent now, poor boy, quite innocent," said Henry; "we must keep him so if we can," and he offered as much to me for my life as we had expected him to give for me and the child too; and it was so tempting that we closed with it at once, for it cost me nothing to part with a baby as was not my own. I had had a mind to tell him, but then I knew how enraged he would have been at my trying it on with him. Another cheat would have driven him wild, so I bade him good-bye and the child too.

'He took us on board and we sailed that night, and I never saw him or the child again. He sent me money regular till I asked for the fifteen hundred pounds and signed a quittance for the annuity like a fool, as I told you.'

X

MRS. PECK'S DISAPPOINTMENT

Brandon had listened to this strange story of Mrs. Peck's without interrupting her. After she had concluded, he thought for a minute and then said—

'Did you ever hear if the mother of the child you stole missed it?'

'How should I hear? We sailed that day for Sydney, and we never heard nothing about it.'

'What was her name?' asked Brandon.

'I don't know at all for certain; there was so many people in the house, that though she had been there three days, I had not asked nor had mother, but yet we must have heard it. I fancy it was Jackson, or Johnson, or Jones, or it might be Brown, but it was a common name as there's no recollecting. When mother took the child first, she thought she'd never know the one from the other; but afterwards she used to say that the mother might find out the difference. Both was much of a size, and my boy was much changed.'

'But,' said Brandon, 'there might be more or fewer teeth, or a difference in the colour and length of the hair, or in the shape of the limbs, though the features and complexion might be changed by the convulsions. Your child was probably more emaciated than the

other. A mother's eye might have seen differences that you in your hurried examination did not.'

'Oh, the other appeared to be teething too; but, as you say, I think it is most like she did see the difference, but being out of the country I heard nothing about it.'

'When did this happen?' asked Brandon.

'Thirty-four years ago and more we sailed from London Docks for Sydney,' said Mrs. Peck.

'Where did you lodge in London when this affair took place?'

'At a lodging-house in —— Street, near the Docks; I think the number was 39, but I am not quite sure.'

'Can you tell me the name of the ship the mother of the present proprietor of Cross Hall went to America in?' asked Brandon.

'No, but we sailed, as I told you, on the 14th May, 18—, in the 'Lysander,' and the other ship was to sail for New York on the next day.'

'Are you sure this woman was going to America?'

'Yes, for the landlady told us so, and I could see when we was in her room that she was making preparations for a voyage. I think there's no doubt of that.'

'Was there no mark on the child's clothes? no name on the boxes you must have seen when you were exchanging the two children?' asked Brandon.

'Not as I recollect of, nor mother either, for we have sometimes talked over it and wondered about it. Our time was so short that we took no notice of such things.'

'And how did you two precious colonists like Sydney?' asked Brandon.

'Oh, well enough. We held our heads high there, for we was free people, you know.'

'Though you had both done what you deserved hanging for,' said Brandon, under his breath. 'Where did Phillips meet with you and your daughter?—for I suppose Mrs. Phillips is your daughter: though your first experiment in child-stealing had been so successful, it might have tempted you to another of the same kind.'

'Oh, Betsy is my daughter, and an ungrateful one she is. We met with Phillips in Melbourne, just when we came first to Port Philip. Peck had run through the £1,500 that we got from Cross Hall, and we was hard up and obliged to leave Sydney under a cloud; but Peck, he said, such a handsome face as she had should be a fortune to us. It's been a fortune to herself; but as for me, she never thinks of me. And there's Frank, when I wrote to him after I had read in an old newspaper at the diggings that he had come into the estate, and asked him for a little help, he never condescended to send me an answer or to take the least notice of me that has done so much for him. If it had not been for me, where would he have been now? His mother was a poor woman. If you'd seen the poor old night-gown I took off of him—and there has he been educated like a gentleman, and getting Cross Hall, and being a member of Parliament too, and never to take trouble to write me a line or to send me a penny. I said I'd be revenged on him, and so I shall.'

'Well, Mrs. Peck,' said Brandon, 'I will just write down the particulars of this curious story, and you will sign it if you think I have put them down correctly.' So with clearness and brevity Brandon sketched the facts, if facts they were, which Mrs. Peck had narrated, and then he read what he had written.

'I don't see as there's any call to put in all about how I got Harry Hogarth to marry me; that has nothing to do with the case in hand,' said Mrs. Peck.

'I think,' said Brandon, 'that if the young man is to lose the property through this confession, he has a right to know what sort of mother he loses with it. I think you had better sign this as it stands. I have signed something for you, and you must do the same for me.'

Mrs. Peck signed her name rather reluctantly as Elizabeth Hogarth, known as Elizabeth Peck, and was proceeding to give some account of her relations with Peck, of rather a romantic character. Perhaps, after so long a stretch of trying to tell the truth, she needed some relief to her imagination; but Brandon soon stopped these revelations, and sent her thoughts in quite another channel.

'Now,' said he, 'I believe this to be a true statement—a perfectly true statement—but it is of no use whatever to be used against Mr. Hogarth. The property was left to him by will, as distinctly as possible.'

'By will!' said Mrs. Peck, looking aghast; 'my newspaper said he was the heir-at-law; but it would never have been left to him if Harry had not thought Frank was his son.'

'It was left to Francis Ormistown, otherwise Hogarth, for fifteen years clerk in the Bank of Scotland,' said Brandon, reading from Elsie's memorandum.

'But he is neither Ormistown nor Hogarth, nor Francis, neither,' said Mrs. Peck, triumphantly. 'He can claim nothing. Francis Ormsitown, or Hogarth, is dead—dead thirty-four years ago: this man has no name that any one knows. I will swear that the child Harry Hogarth took out of my arms was neither his child nor mine, and that he had no right to inherit Cross Hall. The nieces must have it; they were his nearest relations. None of his brothers left no children, and the Melvilles should get the estate, and I should get my thousand pounds.'

'I wish your oath was worth more,' said Brandon, regretfully. 'I wish you could prove what you state as a fact; but all you have told me is absolutely worthless in a court of law. You say you told a parcel of lies to one whom you should have kept faith with, for pecuniary advantage, and now you want to contradict them in hopes of getting a thousand pounds from the Misses Melville, and in order to revenge yourself on the boy whom you so cruelly injured. I am sorry to say nobody would believe a word of this story except myself; and I do.'

'But could you not look up in old newspapers to see if there was any stir made at the time about a changed child?' said Mrs. Peck, trembling with excitement and disappointment. She had been so long accustomed to look on this secret as capital to herself: her mother, and Peck, and herself had always thought that in case of Mr. Hogarth's death a good deal might be got out of the heir; and she had not parted with the certificate of her marriage, or of her

child's baptismal register, in case he had left no will, and the heir-at-law had to be found. She had sent copies of these documents, very admirably executed by a Sydney friend, who had been sent across the ocean for similar instances of skill, to Mr. Hogarth, so that he did not think she had any proof to bring forward to support her claims to be Francis' mother; but it was only recently that she had thought of making more favourable terms with regard to her other secret with the disinherited nieces than with the ungrateful heir, and their coming so near just when she was exasperated at Francis' neglect, had made her overlook the want of proof. She had now fatally injured herself with Francis, with a very faint chance of success with the Melvilles. She therefore repeated nervously, 'Look over the old newspapers—the mother must have known the difference—there must have been some inquiry about it that would prove my statement, which is all true, every word of it, as I hope for salvation.'

'Yes, that might be of some use; that might be seen to,' said Brandon, doubtfully. 'Our data are meagre enough. Your mother is dead, I suppose, and she is the only person besides yourself who knew of the crime you both committed.'

'She is dead and gone a dozen years ago, and it was her as committed the crime, as you call it, and not me. I won't answer for it to nobody.'

'Well, we must make inquiry in the house, though I fear that is hopeless, and in the newspapers. If you had had the sense to have got the mother's name, we might advertise in America; but I suppose you thought then that the less you knew about it the better. Though you cannot expect the thousand pounds—'

'But you promised it,' said Mrs. Peck. 'I'll say nothing more, unless I can get something first. You have basely deceived me. I never heard of a more scoundrelly action than getting me to tell you all that old story, and put myself into such a wrong box, on the pretence that I was to get a thousand pounds, and now you say that what you signed is waste paper. I'll get my own statement from you back again, before you leave this,' and

Mrs. Peck, with eyes of fury, planted herself at the back of the door. 'The next thing you'll do will be go and give information, I fancy.'

'Be cool, Mrs. Peck; I do not mean to injure you. As I said, though there is no chance of our depriving Mr. Hogarth of property left to him so clearly as this, I think I may take it upon me to say, as his friend— '

'His friend!' interrupted Mrs Peck. 'Oh, how you have deceived me! And you call yourself a gentleman, I suppose; and serve an old woman like that.'

'Yes; as his friend,' said Brandon, firmly, 'I think I may say that he would be disposed to reward you, if you can prove that you are not his mother. I do not hesitate to say that he would give you five hundred pounds for such information as would hold in a court of law that he is not your son.'

Mrs. Peck brightened up a little at this offer, though she could scarcely imagine any valid reason for it. 'I think I could prove that; I really think I could prove that. There was my cousin that we lived with in Edinburgh, Violet Strachan, one of the witnesses to my marriage. She saw a great deal of my child, for, till we went to London, we lived in her house, and Frank was born there. She knew that he took convulsion fits very badly, and that he had a brown mole on his shoulder that this boy cannot have. I don't know of any other birth-mark,' said Mrs. Peck.

'And this woman lived in Edinburgh. Do you think she is alive? Was she older or younger than you?'

'Oh, older by ten years,' said Mrs. Peck, feeling the ground give way under her. 'I hope she is not dead—she lived in 57, New Street, leading down to the Canongate, up three pair of stairs; her husband was a saddler, and she kept lodgers. His name was George. He would recollect something about Frank. Peck could swear that I have told him over and over again that my boy was dead, and that the boy Cross Hall brought up was none of mine.'

'But Peck's word is worth nothing,' said Brandon.

'Betsy could say something of the kind. I am sure she must have

heard us hint at it often, but she is not sharp. Perhaps she did not notice.'

'Does no one else know anything about it?' said Brandon, in despair.

'No one;—but surely I ain't got no cause to take such blame on myself, if it was not true,' said Mrs. Peck, sulkily.

'You unfortunately had a motive—two strong motives. A death-bed confession, for no hope of gain or revenge, might have carried weight—but this carries none. The only accomplice of your crime is dead. The mother from whom you stole the child is probably dead also, and at any rate gone out of England—you do not even know her name, or that of the ship she sailed in. The witness who you think could prove the non-identity of the present possessor of Cross Hall is most likely dead also, and if alive must be an old woman who has probably forgotten the trifling circumstance of the existence of a mole on a child after thrity-five years and more—and people outgrow these peculiarities. You have not the ghost of a case for the Melvilles. Hogarth might give you something for the chance that you are speaking truth, to get rid of your claims for ever, and the satisfaction of feeling that you are nothing to him.'

'That's what I ought to have done. Peck always said I was too hasty; and his words has come true,' said Mrs. Peck. 'I might have got something handsome out of the heir—and but for your interference I might have got something out of the Melvilles.'

'Nonsense!' said Brandon; 'they have nothing to give, unless you gave the property to them; and you cannot do that.'

'I'm glad you're to get nothing with your sweetheart,' said Mrs. Peck, maliciously. 'My daughter's maid, I suppose, is the person. Half of Cross Hall would have been a good fortune, but you're not to get it.'

'You must not come to Mrs. Phillips's again. I am going to stay in the house till her husband returns, and will protect her from you,' said Brandon.

'Protect her from her own mother!' said Mrs. Peck. 'Let them hold their heads as high as they like, they can't get out of that. I am

her mother, and if I like I will publish it. Her father was a gentleman. I was in clover when I lived with him; but he married, and then he died and left no provision for us; and then I fell in with Peck, and have stuck by him ever since. He is in Adelaide now, where I wish I had stopped with him with all my heart. Do you think as Phillips would overlook this if I went back quiet, and keep sending me the poor little allowance as I need to keep soul and body together, for I'm an old woman now, and past working?'

'I do not know. I will speak to him on the subject, and will probably see you again in a few days. If you can think of any collateral evidence in the meantime, it will be as well that you tell me. In the meantime, I must go to communicate to Miss Melville what you have told me.'

Elsie was sadly disappointed at the doubtful nature of the evidence which Mrs. Peck had to give. She had had such brilliant visions of the happiness which Jane and Francis might have together if it could only be proved that they were not cousins; and she could not help seeing with Brandon that the chance of establishing it was very small. Brandon told Mrs. Phillips the reason why Mrs. Peck had so assiduously courted Elsie, and then asked if she could recollect anything which she had heard from her mother, her grandmother, or Peck, which would corroborate these unsupported statements.

'I cannot say anything—I will not say a word till Stanley comes home, and then I will tell him. He would not like my mixing myself up with her in any way when he was gone, and I never will keep anything from him,' said Mrs. Phillips.

'You are quite right,' said Brandon, who, nevertheless, was rather impatient for any information she might give, and thought it might be valuable, from her hesitation about the matter. He had not long to wait, however, for Mr. Phillips came down on the following day, and heard all his wife had to say and all Brandon had to say.

'You know, Brandon, that it would be horrible to me to have my wife's name brought into a court of justice as the daughter of that woman—cognizant, even in a very vague way, of such a serious

crime,' said Mr. Phillips. 'And what purpose can it serve? You can neither enrich Jane or Alice Melville by proving that the crime was committed. Mr. Hogarth is as worthy a successor as the old man could have found, and neither of the Melvilles grudges him his good fortune. Alice will be as comfortable as you can make her, and I wish you both joy from all my heart, and I believe you will be happy. Miss Melville will be as comfortable and happy as we can make her till she chooses a home for herself. Why wish to rake up old stories for no good end whatever? I dare say the story is true. I said to Hogarth when he and Miss Melville consulted me about the first letter she wrote, that for the very reason she claimed to be his mother I believed she was not. I advised him not to write to her or send her money, and requested Miss Melville never to mention her name.'

'Out of consideration for you, then, he did not answer her letter, and this has been the result of it. But we have no wish to deprive him of his property; and the only end we aim at is to prove that he is not Miss Melville's cousin. Alice tells me they love each other; but their marriage is forbidden by the will, unless at the sacrifice of the property, which in that case goes to some benevolent societies.'

'Ah,' said Phillips, thoughtfully, 'in that case, if I thought Mrs. Phillips's evidence could establish it, it would perhaps be right to give it; but it cannot—I see it cannot. Mere vague hints, half recollected now that the subject has been brought prominently forward, though they may convince you and me, could not stand before a court of law. I think when you hear what Mrs. Phillips has to say you will confess that it would be wrong to put her and me to such distress, for so little good purpose. I am sure Miss Melville would be the first to dissuade you from such a course. It is for the sake of our children that I am so anxious to conceal the connection. I can trust to you and to Alice, I hope, never to mention it.'

Brandon felt the justice of Mr. Phillips's reasoning, and yet was very sorry that he could not gratify his promised wife by anything satisfactory in the way of collateral evidence.

'Now, Elsie,' said Brandon, who now took the privilege of love,

and called her by her pet name, 'what do you mean to do with this information? I think it quite useless for the end you wish to gain. Is it worth while to disturb Hogarth's mind, to lead him to make fruitless inquiries, to wear himself out in attempting to prove what I fear cannot be proved, to make him feel that he has robbed you with even less semblance of justice than before? Can you not leave him to his own life, which will be a useful and a distinguished one? Let us keep this vexatious confession, at least till you consult Jane.'

'No, no; I think as we have done everything without consulting Jane, we will make up our minds on this matter too for ourselves. I know Jane will say with you that we should not communicate the news to Francis; for anything that appears to sacrifice herself and to save other people is what she thinks she ought to do.'

'I don't think she can be very fond of Hogarth, after all.'

'But she is,' said Elsie, 'in her own quiet, deep way. She could give her own life for his; but she could not feel that she was worth the sacrifice he offered to make.'

'I feel I could throw up everything for you, Elsie,' said Brandon.

'But I should not like to see you do it, so I am very glad you have not got it to do. Poor Francis!'

'Well, I suppose he will marry some one else, and she will do the same, and they will always be very excellent friends,' said Brandon.

'But then the wrong is to the somebody else,' said Elsie. 'It seems quite wicked to think of such a thing. Can they not keep single for a purpose, as Peggy Walker did? Francis may immerse himself in politics to his heart's content; and Jane, she will be very happy in my happiness. You must love her; you must not be jealous of her. She has been everything in the world to me—my sister, my mother, my friend; and if she cannot have a home of her own, let her always be welcome to ours.'

'Always,' said Brandon. 'We must try to do our best to make up for what we cannot give to her. But you say that Jane would be disposed to keep back this?'

'Yes; but I will send it, and write to him besides. If I were in his circumstances I should think I had a right to know. I would rather

hear the truth so far as it can be ascertained about my parentage, than have it concealed for fear of hurting my feelings. He may act upon the information as he sees fit; so I will send him a certified copy of this confession, and write him a few lines besides. I want to tell him how happy I am: he was a friend to us in our sorrows, and he ought to know when any prosperity, or pleasure, or happiness, comes to either of us. I must tell him I can confide in you now.'

'That is a very pleasant piece of news, I am sure,' said Brandon.

'Jane will write to him from Wiriwilta, but she cannot know of our engagement till too late for the mail.'

'I think Jane formed a very shrewd guess as to my intentions, and, if she writes fully to Hogarth, will mention them. But, by-the-by, you must write a few lines to my mother. She will be delighted to hear this good news; and, as for Fanny, the idea that there will be some one at Barragong to take a motherly care of Edgar, and make him change his clothes when he gets wet, and see that he wears flannel in winter, will be very soothing to her maternal anxiety.'

XI

ELSIE MELVILLE'S LETTER

Francis Hogarth had devoted himself to public life even more assiduously after the departure of Jane than before, and had made himself more prominent in Parliament as practice strengthened his powers of debate and study increased his stock of information. He was invaluable on a committee to those who really wanted to elicit the truth; while those who had anything to conceal dreaded his searching questions and careful weighing of conflicting testimony. His own peculiar crotchet—the reconstruction of electoral districts, so as to secure the rights of minorities—to increase the purity and diminish the expense and the bitterness of elections in the meantime, and to pave the way for the elevation of the masses by the gradual extension of the suffrage, by securing that the new voters should not have all political power in their hands—was one that, of course, found little sympathy within the walls of Parliament.

'There never has yet been,' says Mr. J. S. Mill, 'among political men in England any real and serious attempt to prevent bribery, because there has been no real desire that elections should not be costly. Their costliness is an advantage to those who can afford the expense by excluding a multitude of competitors; and anything, however noxious, is cherished as having a conservative tendency if it

limits the access to Parliament to rich men. This is a rooted feeling among our legislators of both political parties, and is about the only point on which I believe them to be really ill-intentioned. They care comparatively little who votes, so long as they feel assured that none but persons of their own class can be voted for. They know that they can rely on the fellow-feeling of one of their own class with another, while the subservience of *nouveaux enrichis*, who knocking at the door of the class, is a still surer reliance, and that nothing very democratic need be apprehended under the most democratic suffrage, as long as democratic persons can be prevented from being elected to Parliament.'

But outside of the walls of the House of Commons, Francis had found many who agreed with him as to the necessity for some great change. All accounts from America, and even those from Australia, proved that the wide extension of the suffrage without some precaution to secure the minorities from extinction, tended to political degeneration, even in countries where there was great material prosperity, abundance of land, considerable advantages of education, and greater equality of condition than in Britain. The march of affairs was all steadily towards more democratic institutions, and Francis was not deceived by temporary and partial reactions. The extension of the suffrage must come, and England ought to be prepared to meet it. He was willing to take advantage of every suggestion and every discovery that might be made; and when a scheme more comprehensive than that of Sir Rowland Hill for our first Adelaide Corporation, and incomparably better than Lord John Russell's, was first launched into the world, amid many sneers that it was utopian, crotchety, and un-English, he adopted it with an enthusiasm which he knew Jane Melville would approve of. The criticism and the ridicule only strengthened his conviction of the feasibility of the scheme, and his hopes of its success. Jane was sure to be proud if he could be the means of bringing about so great a reform. They had often talked on the subject, but had never been able to devise anything comparable to this. Mr. Sinclair, with whom the matter had been gone over most carefully, was quite as

enthusiastic about it as the discoverer himself, and Francis wished more than ever that the entrance to Parliament was less expensive and less difficult, so that he might have so good a coadjutor.

Old Thomas Lowrie was dead, and Peggy and her young folks were all full of preparations for the outward voyage to Australia. Tom hoped to serve out his time to as great advantage in Melbourne as in Edinburgh; and he really was as clever and as skilful as if he had been seven instead of less than two years at the engineering. Francis had visited much at Miss Thomson's, and had seen a great deal of Mary Forrester, but not with the result that Jane had anticipated; and now, before she had made any impression on him beyond the conviction that she was an exceedingly amiable girl, the plans of the whole family were changed, and they, too, were going to Australia. As Mary had said, they had cost Aunt Margaret a great deal of money first and last. Mr. Forrester had been indolent, and perhaps unlucky; Mrs. Forrester had been occupied with the cares of a very large family, and had not the force of character of her single sister. Her eldest son had gone to Australia some time before, and though he had not made a fortune, he had done pretty well; and he was perhaps ashamed that so much had been done for his family by his aunt and so little by himself. So he wrote advising them to come out to Melbourne, at least all but John, who was now of service to Miss Thomson; and James, if he thought his business was worth staying for. If Margaret and Mary were inclined to take situations as governesses, he had no doubt they could obtain them. Robert and Henry could work for themselves, and with his help could assist their parents to better advantage than in Scotland. The family council met on this proposal, and it was ultimately acceded to, and the family were busy with their preparations to go in the same ship as Peggy and the Lowries. It seemed to Francis as if everybody was going to Australia.

He had dined out one day, and had brushed against some of the greatest men of the age, and felt himself brightened by the collision. He sat beside the most benevolent, the most enlightened, and the

most sober-minded of political economists, on the one hand; on the other by the most brilliant of French conversationalists. He—Francis Hogarth, the obscure bank clerk, who had had no name, no position, and, he used to think, no ability—was admitted on equal footing with such men as these. He had not felt so much on the occasion of his dining with the Earl, and meeting with people there of title and political influence.

After an evening passed in conversation on the subjects which especially interested him, Francis returned to his club. He sat down before going to bed with a cigar, and took up his letters. An Australian mail was in, and a letter from Jane and from Elsie. Jane's was first taken up and read. It described her life at Wiriwilta, the house, and the scenery, so far as she could do it justice; Miss Phillips's relations with Dr. Grant, and Jane's hopes that Brandon and Elsie would come to an understanding, for his manner had been very much like that of a man in love. How cautious, yet how affectionate were her expressions to himself! How she seemed to live in others, and to care for the happiness of everyone in the world, while regardless of her own and of his.

'Ah, Jane,' said he, half aloud, 'how different it would be to come home, after such an evening as this, to you; to see your dear eyes brighten at the recital of all I have seen and all I have heard; to hear your beloved voice inspiring me to more exertion and more patience. After sitting through so many party debates, so much transparent self-seeking, and so much ungenerous opposition as I cannot help seeing in Parliament, how refreshing to see, among such men as I have met to-day, the pure, genuine public spirit which Jane first showed me the example of in the midst of her hardest trials. This reform does not bring personal advantage to one of these people, and yet they are as enthusiastic about it as if their lives depended on it. It may bring fame; but, as M.—— says, 'The laurels will be late, and we will have lost the care for them by the time they fall on our heads.' The pleasure is *in* the work—the disinterested work itself—as Jane used to say. There is one half the globe between us. I cannot fancy that she is sitting over the fire

thinking of me at this moment; it is morning with her; and she is up and busy. But in my business, and in my pleasure, or my trouble, she is always in the background—if not in the foreground—of my thoughts. But then she does not love me as I love her.' And a long fit of silent musing, with the letter in his hand, followed these half-spoken regrets.

'But I must read Elsie's letter too; it appears to be long, and the first she has written to me—later in date than Jane's, which is posted in the country, and I suppose asking for congratulations—well, she shall have them.'

As he opened the envelope, and saw the curious legal-looking document enclosed, containing the certified copy of Mrs. Peck's confession, his curiosity was strongly aroused; he read it through first with surprise and agitation. Elsie's own letter was not long; it ran as follows:—

'My dear Francis,—I enclose you this, because I think you ought to know that Mrs. Peck is not your mother. I think you must have had good parents, though you may never be able to find them out. You are still as much entitled to Cross Hall, and all that my uncle left you, for you know it was given to you because you deserved it, and I am sure that he could have found no worthier heir. I had hoped very much that the evidence would have been sufficient to prove that you are not Jane's cousin, because you might then have done as you pleased without losing the property, and the position and the opportunities you make such good use of; but I fear—and Mr. Brandon fears—that it cannot be conclusively proved. We have sent you all the information we can get from Mrs. Peck. You will observe a few additional memoranda at the end of the confession. I am quite convinced that what she says is true, for I have often remarked that you were not at all like my uncle or any of his family, and you are still more unlike Mrs. Peck. Consult your own judgment about making inquiries; I know you will do rightly and well.

'You will be very glad to hear that I am engaged to Mr. Brandon, who has taken all the trouble about this affair, and I think elicited all that Mrs. Peck knows. It is most unfortunate that she is so little

to be believed, and that she wanted to get money for her information, as well as revenge on you for not answering her letter or letters. I believe I am going to be very happy, and I only wish I could make everybody as happy as myself. Give my love to Peggy when you see her, and say that I should have liked to have been married from her house rather than from any other, but I do not think Mr. Brandon will let me wait so long. Jane will be writing you all the Wiriwilta news, and about Miss Phillips and Dr. Grant. Mrs. Phillips has been very kind to me, kinder than ever she was before; and as for Mr. Phillips, you know how good he has always been to both Jane and myself. We both like Australia, even more than we expected, and I am going to try to make a good bush wife to one who loves me very much. He desires me to send his kindest regards to you; and believe me

'Always, your very affectionate friend,

'Elsie Melville.'

'Well,' said Francis, 'here is one person who cares about my happiness. If I cannot prove that Jane is not my cousin, I can at least give up the property, which never would have been left to me unless Henry Hogarth had believed me to be his son. Jane must love me—her sister must know it, or she would never have written to me thus. I will have her after a time. If I can combine the public duty and the career I have entered on with happiness, so much the better; if not, farewell ambition! She cannot blame me for such a course. Henry Hogarth wronged his nieces to enrich me, supposing me to be his son: he must have supposed it, or he would not have forbidden our marriage on account of the cousinship. If I can restore it to Jane by marriage, well and good; but otherwise I cannot keep it. To-morrow for inquiries. First a file of the *Times* for 18—; the police reports, the coroner's inquests, the passenger-list of the Sydney ship and of the American ship, inquiries at the lodging-house near the wharf—then to Edinburgh to inquire at the house in New Street, and consult with MacFarlane and Sinclair. I surely can work through it—at least I will try.'

XII

WHAT CAN BE MADE OF IT?

Early on the following morning Francis began his researches; but the *Times* and other journals of the date Mrs. Peck mentioned, which he searched through, proved quite barren of intelligence. The passenger-lists he could not find complete anywhere; the newspapers more especially devoted to these matters contained the passenger-list of the 'Lysander' bound for Sydney, for the first and second cabin, and in the latter the names of Mrs. Ormistown and Miss E. Ormistown were mentioned; but for the American ship, in which he supposed his real mother had sailed, there was no mention of any passengers except those in the first cabin; and in all probability, she being a poor woman, would sail in the steerage. There were also three vessels sailing for New York very close upon one another at the time, and he could not be sure in which the passage had been taken. Mrs. Peck said the ship was to sail the next day; but her own vessel had been rather hurried to go with the tide, and there was no saying whether that was the case with the American one. But in all the American ships there was no mention of the names of the fore-cabin passengers. Then the police reports gave no account of any complaint having been made about an exchanged child, and when he eagerly turned to the coroner's

inquests there was nothing to be seen there either. The mother had probably been too distressed with grief to observe the substitution, or too anxious not to lose her passage to stop to make inquiries if she had had any suspicion—teething convulsions are not at all uncommon among children of that age, and a stranger in London was likely to get no redress under such circumstances, even if she had the courage to attempt it. There was so little likely motive for any one to take away a living child and leave a dead one, that she was sure to have been laughed to scorn if she had suggested such a thing to the landlady of the house.

Francis, disappointed in the newspapers, next went to the lodging-house, but it had been pulled down and another substituted in its place, and of course no one could tell anything about the obscure woman who had kept it. A London Directory for 18— gave her name as Mrs. Martha Stubbs, which did not agree with the name which Mrs. Peck reported, which was Mrs. Dawson. This was a bad beginning to his search for corroborative evidence; but he put an advertisement in the *Times* and *Weekly Dispatch* for her under both names, in hopes that she might recollect something about a child dying in convulsions in her house, in the absence of its mother, just before a lodger left her house to go to Sydney with another child of the same sex and age. This, after a lapse of thirty-five years, was a desperate chance, but it was the only course open to Francis, and he took it.

Next he went to Edinburgh and inquired in New Street, in the old town, for the woman, Violet Strachan, who had let the lodgings where the real Francis Hogarth was born, and where the irregular marriage had also taken place. Thrity-five years in a city like Edinburgh, with an eminently migrating population, is a far more unmanageable period than in a country town, where people inhabit the same houses from one generation to another, and where, even if the persons whom you wish to discover are dead, there are neighbours who recollect about them. This second search was fruitless, so he could only advertise for Violet Strachan, and that he also did.

Next he went to his friend Sinclair, and opened his budget of news to him. Sinclair had been in America, and he might have chanced to have heard something of some one who had had a doubtful baby found dead on the bed just before its mother sailed. If this had been a sensation novel, Mr. Sinclair would have been sure to have known all about it, and have turned out to be the father or the uncle of his friend—he was of the age to be either; but as this is not a sensation novel, he could not throw any light on the dark subject, and could only give his sympathy, and offer to take any amount of trouble on Francis's behalf. His only advice was that he should advertise in the States' leading papers, if he really wanted to know, for some one who emigrated in May 18—, in one of the three ships which had sailed about that time, who had lost a child in convulsions that might not have been her own; requiring some particulars about the age and the house at which the death was believed to have taken place.

'It is a thousand to one against your getting an answer,' said Mr. Sinclair. 'But what makes you so anxious to prove this? It can do no good.'

'Only this, that if Jane Melville can be proved not to be my cousin, I can marry her and keep Cross Hall and my seat in Parliament. If it cannot be proved, then I must give up everything, and go to Melbourne and ask if she will have me without a penny.'

'Oh, is that it?' said Sinclair. 'I am the more bound to do all I can to help you. We cannot spare you from the House, nor from the country. But, after all, Hogarth, one woman is as good as another, and your career should not be lightly sacrificed.'

'One woman as good as another!' exclaimed Francis.

'Not exactly so; but there are many women as good as Miss Melville. I grant that she is a fine woman, and one of excellent principles and understanding; but not just the sort of person one could go into heroics about. I do not say that as a companion and friend her place could be filled up to you by such women as Miss Crichton or any of the Jardine girls, or even by Eliza Rennie. But Mary Forrester—what do you think of Mary Forrester? You should

not let such a girl leave the country. She is handsomer, younger, and every bit as good as Miss Melville.'

'She is a very fine girl, no doubt, but do not speak of her in the same breath with Jane Melville. I owe so much to Jane: if it had not been for her, I would never have been so valuable even to you.'

'Well, then, let us see what is to be done to suit your wishes. Shall I go with you to MacFarlane's?'

'I will be very glad indeed of your company,' said Francis.

Mr. MacFarlane was very much surprised at the strange business which had brought Hogarth from his parliamentary duties to consult him upon. He read carefully the document which Alice had forwarded, and listened to Francis's account of the inquiries he had made so unsuccessfully, before he ventured on giving any opinion.

'This is very possibly true, Mr. Hogarth,' said he, at last; 'indeed very probably true. I think with you that this woman, Elizabeth Ormistown, and her mother, were capable of doing anything that would bring them in money; but the secret has been kept too long—much too long. They did their work skilfully, without accomplices, and without leaving any traces of their proceedings. This confession is not worth the paper it is written on in a court of law, and you have failed in all your efforts to get corroborative evidence. There is no use in inquiring about Violet Strachan; she is dead three years ago. I paid her, on Hogarth's account, a small weekly sum, that she used to come to my office for to keep her from destitution, but that payment is at an end. The other witness could only prove the irregular marriage, which there is no doubt about, as Henry Hogarth owns to it in his will. The only evidence that would be worth anything is that of your real mother, and there is no saying if she is not dead too. I think the chances are that she is,' said Mr. MacFarlane, turning up the annuity tables for the chances of life at the supposed age of thirty-two, which Mrs. Peck had given as the probable age of her neighbour in the lodging-house, after a period of thirty-four years. 'If alive, there is no getting at her, and after all—*cui bono*?'

'I am attached—very deeply attached—to my supposed cousin,

Jane Melville. I want to be free to marry her. I am convinced that she is not my cousin, and you know the will said that it was on condition of not marrying or assisting either of my cousins that I was to hold the property. If I have convinced you of the feasibility of the case—that I am not related in the slightest degree to the Misses Melville—would not the benevolent societies to which Mr. Hogarth left his property, in case of my disobeying his injunctions, see it also?'

'One man, or one society of men, might be convinced,' said Mr. MacFarlane, 'and would make a compromise with you on very easy terms; but I doubt if five distinct corporations would do so.'

'There is no one who has any right to object, except these societies,' said Francis, 'or any object in doing so.'

'Those clauses forbidding marriage as a condition of inheriting property, or of receiving yearly incomes, are always michievious,' said Sinclair; 'they are contrary to public morals.'

'Henry Hogarth,' said Mr. MacFarlane, 'who was a clever man, and in some respects a wise man, did the foolishest things in important matters that ever I heard of. First, his marriage with that girl. I saw her once at the house he lodged in; and a glaikit lassie I thought her. Next, the education of his nieces, which was absolutely nonsensical; and then putting such a clause into his will, as if he meant that you should take a fancy to each other—for prohibitions of that kind just put mischief into young folks' heads.'

'Then do you see the absence of family likeness that Elsie relies so much upon? You knew Elizabeth Ormistown when she was young—she saw her an old woman.'

'I am no hand at likenesses,' said MacFarlane, 'and did not pay much attention to the girl; but I think both she and Henry were fair and low-featured, and you are dark and high-featured. But that is of no use either, as you know.'

'Then, by a rigid interpretation of the will, you think the societies would be able to dispossess me, if I married Jane, and could not prove this story of Mrs. Peck's to be true.'

'I think I know it pretty well by heart, but we had better turn to

it,' said Mr. MacFarlane, and he looked out the document he had himself drawn out, and read it aloud to Francis and Mr. Sinclair. 'Now you see that the great purpose and bent of Mr. Hogarth's will was to impoverish his nieces, to force them to act and work for themselves. Not merely marriage, but any other way of assisting them was forbidden. He certainly meant to enrich you, because he thought you deserved it, but in case of your not co-operating with him in his principal object, the property was to go away from you altogether. The Misses Melville have made their way in the world remarkably well—much better than I could have thought possible. I think he acted both cruelly and unjustly to them, but as they have so well conquered their difficulties, the matter had better be left as it is.'

'Then,' said Francis, 'you think that even if I had satisfactory proof from my real mother to corroborate Elizabeth Ormistown's confession, and could make it incontestably plain that I am not related to Miss Melville, so that I do not, in marrying her, marry my cousin, it would be considered in law as invalidating my right to the property—that by doing so I am assisting Jane Melville, which was forbidden as clearly as the marriage.'

'It is a very strong point. If I were the legal adviser of any one of these benevolent associations, I certainly would recommend them to contest it; at the same time, with the proof which you speak of, I would enjoy fighting it out with them. In a court of law the decision would be against you, under the most favourable circumstances; but if we took it to the Equity Courts I think your chance would be better, for there is a growing feeling there that it is not right for people to bequeath property clogged with vexatious restrictions. Yet, at the same time, all who think well of these five charitable institutions—and they are the very best-managed of the kind in Scotland—Mr. Hogarth showed judgment in his selection—will think taking the property from a man who had, according to his own showing, no right to it, for the sake of the poor and afflicted, really a good work. Public feeling will be against you where you are not personally known.'

'God knows it is not for myself that I wish to keep Cross Hall, nor yet for Jane herself,' said Francis. 'But my life lies out before me so clearly that at no period have I had more to give up than now.'

'If you had the evidence you wish for (which I see very little chance of your getting), and married Miss Melville, then, of course, the societies would come upon you. You have got possession, you might keep them at bay for years, and in the meantime you might have interest enough with your political friends to get something good in the way of a government appointment. We hear you well spoken of in the House as a man likely to distinguish himself.'

'Not in the way of getting government appointments,' said Francis—'quite in a contrary direction. But without the evidence, then, what would you advise?'

'To let the matter rest. Indeed, I think it is useless to disquiet yourself about discovering your real parents. These long-lost relations never amalgamate well. I have seen several instances of it, and they were very disappointing.'

'Then,' said Francis, 'I suppose the only thing for me to do is to make out a deed of gift to each of these societies in the order in which Mr. Hogarth left the property to them. The personal estate I have certainly trenched upon a little, but all to the benefit of the heritable estate. Cross Hall is in better condition now than when I succeeded to it. If I have given away on the very easiest terms some of the worst land on the estate, I have improved the better, and I have spent a large sum in new cottages. I have lived within my means; even my election expenses were saved out of the current income.'

'You do not mean to say,' said Mr. MacFarlane, 'that you are going to take so wild a step as this? What good end can you secure by throwing up your handsome fortune in this way?'

'Don't propose such a thing yet; think a little, Hogarth,' said Sinclair.

'I am sure the figure you are making in the House would delight my old friend Harry's heart,' said Mr. MacFarlane; 'just in the way he would have liked to do himself; getting in in such an honourable

way too. I heard Prentice say that he never saw anything so open and above board and so pure as your canvassing. If you are not Harry's son, you deserve to be, and it is no fault of yours. You are like a chip of the old block in your ways of thinking. It is quite possible you are his son after all: this woman is not to be believed one way or another. To give up all this for the sake of a pair of grey eyes, and a pair of healthy-looking cheeks that nobody ever even thought handsome, is a young man's folly.'

'Yes, and a head and a heart, and a few other things,' said Francis.

'She would never be so unreasonable as to wish or expect you to do it,' said Mr. Sinclair.

'She would not expect me to do it, I know. I cannot regret my career more than she will do; but I love her, and I believe she loves me; and, please God, we will begin the world together.'

'I was sorry for the girls,' said MacFarlane, 'very sorry. You could see that when I read the will to you; but they have really done very creditably. In spite of the most absurd education in the world, one of them got a capital situation as a governess; and the other did very well indeed, I hear, at some sort of woman's work. It's the youngest that is going to be well married in Australia, and very likely the other will do the same.'

'I think it is very likely she will,' said Francis.

'But if she is married to some one else before you go out—they do these things very quickly at the antipodes,' said Mr. MacFarlane. 'There—the first mail after their arrival, we hear of Alice Melville being engaged to be married.'

'I will trust her,' said Francis. 'She will surely wait till she hears how I receive this news. Even at the worst I can console myself with your friend, Mr. Sinclair; she will be at hand, and that is a great matter.'

'Don't give it up so rashly. I'd rather fight it out to the death than that. At any rate, you might keep possession of Cross Hall for a while till you made your way in public life,' said Mr. MacFarlane.

'The plan of action I had laid out for myself was not likely to

succeed for ten or twenty years, in all probability; and the lawsuit, if protracted to the utmost, would likely go against me at last—I see it would; and the only effect would be that the benevolent societies would come to the property when it had been reduced about one half by litigation. With all due respect for you personally, Mr. MacFarlane, I think money spent in law the very worst investment for all parties concerned, and for the world in general. No, it shall be given up at once.'

'But,' said Sinclair, 'it would be unfair to yourself to begin the world at greater disadvantage than before you were left the property.'

'Yes, I think it would,' said Francis. 'I might represent the case to them in that light. I am satisfied with your opinion, Mr. MacFarlane; but on a question of such importance, you will, of course, have no objection to my consulting another adviser—the Lord Advocate, I think.'

'Certainly, you could not have a better man,' said Mr. MacFarlane.

'Give me the will or a copy to show him,' said Francis. 'I must make a note of the names and addresses of these societies, in case his opinion coincides with yours, for I must write to each of them to send a delegate or deputation to meet me. I should see them all at once, and explain matters to them. Rather a hard matter for a shy man like myself to bring his love affairs before five charitable associations.'

'Shy!' said Sinclair. 'You are as bold and frank a politician as I ever saw.'

'Oh, politics are another matter; but until I met with Jane, I never had any one in whom I could confide—I never even knew the blessing of friendship before. She taught me to be frank, for she had confidence in me and felt for me. You see I am practising for the associations by speaking to two elderly gentlemen on the subject. Another lesson at the Lord Advocate's, and I hope to be equal to the emergency.'

The Lord Advocate agreed in all points with Mr. MacFarlane as to the legal chances of keeping the property; and although he

thought it a very quixotic thing to give it up, Francis was determined on that subject. The letters were written to the associations, and a day was appointed for his meeting a delegate from each of them, intrusted with powers to decide and act. Mr. MacFarlane wished to be present, for he had no confidence in the prudence of his client, who would be sure to show his hand to the opposing party, and let them know too soon how little there was in it, and Francis rather reluctantly consented. In the mean time he worked off some of his excitement by visiting Peggy and the Lowries to deliver Elsie's messages. She was busy, as usual, but laid aside her work at the sight of the unexpected visitor.

'Have you any news?' said she, 'for I have had no letter from Miss Jean this month, and next mail I'll no be here to get it. You look as if there was good news, Mr. Hogarth.'

'Good and bad,' said Francis; 'can you guess the good?'

'Miss Elsie and Mr. Brandon,' said Peggy. 'I see by your eyes I'm right.'

'You are a good guesser, Peggy. She is only sorry she could not be married from your house; but she did not think Mr. Brandon would wait so long.'

'Oh, I dare say no. But indeed I marvelled that he went to Australia without her, for I thought it was a thing that was to be, from the first day he spoke about her. But there's no much time lost after all. There's to be a Mrs. Brandon at Barragong at last—and what says Miss Jean about it?'

'It is Elsie herself who writes to me that it is a settled thing, and that she hopes to be very happy, and sends you this message. But what would you say if Miss Jane were to be married herself?'

'You don't say so!' said Peggy, looking surprised and puzzled. 'I never thought upon her being married. And that's the bad, is it? I wonder what man about Wiriwilta has got the presumption to even himself to her. I misdoubt she's throwing herself away, as many a sensible woman has done before her. One marriage is quite enough for me at a time.'

'Perhaps it is premature in me to speak of it,' said Francis, 'for

the Saldanha will be three months, or nearly so, on the way, and she has not been rightly asked yet.'

'The Saldanha! What in the name of wonder do you mean?'

'I mean to go with you in the Saldanha, if I finish the little matter of business I have got to do on this side of the world before she sails. But I see I must let you read my letters, so that you may judge of the news.'

'It's fine big writing,' said Peggy. 'I hope it's easier made out than what you say,' and she proceeded to read Elsie's letter and enclosure, with a running comment.

She scarcely understood the drift of the beginning of the letter, but when she came to Mr. Brandon's name she knew her ground. 'Happy! she's sure to be happy! Mr. Brandon will give her all her own way, and she does not want for sense.—That's a kind message to me; but she might have been married here if Mr. Brandon had had more gumption, and asked her before he went away.—And Mrs. Phillips is more reasonable. I'd like to see her show any airs to her now, when Mr. Brandon is by; he'll let her know her place.—And they like Australia—both of them. Who, in all the world, is it Miss Jean can have taken up with?—And so that was the way Cross Hall got his bonny bargain of a wife; he was young and simple to be entrapped with such a pair. Well, well! it was a home-coming to hear such words passing between her and an old sweetheart. I'll be bound he never wanted to see her again.—But, mercy on us! and so it was no you that was the bairn after all, Master Francis, and the old laird had really no call to care about you. But that woman should be punished. Men and women have been hanged for less guilt. I'd hurry no one into the presence of the Great Judge; but that she should be at large, boasting of her wickedness, and hoping to make siller of it, is a thing that should not be permitted.'

'Then you believe this story, Peggy?' said Francis.

'What should ail me to believe it? It's all of a piece; no woman that was not as wicked as that would make up so wicked a story.'

'Every one that I show the narrative to believes it, yet they all say that it would not hold in a court of justice; so I am going to give up

Cross Hall to the benevolent associations, as Mr. Hogarth made them his heirs, in case of my not obeying some of his directions, and I will then sail with you in the Saldanha, to begin the world afresh, and to ask Jane Melville to begin it with me.'

Peggy made no doubt that that was the only thing Francis could do under the circumstances. She did not know the value of what he lost, she only thought of what he was likely to gain.

'Well, Mr. Francis, or whatever your name may be, if that is the marriage you spoke of, I think that news is *good* too. I'm not a woman of many words, but I think you'll never repent of this, or grieve for the loss of this world's gear; and so far as my poor judgment goes, I think Miss Jean is not the woman to say you nay;' and she shook his hand warmly, and entered into his plans for beginning life in Melbourne, as neither Sinclair nor MacFarlane had done. 'There's good work to be done in Australia, Mr. Francis, and there's one there that will help you to do it. There's no doubt Providence intends to make something of you. After all this chopping and changing, it would be a queer thing if you would not rise as high at the other end of the world as you have done in this.'

XIII

NOT SO BAD, AFTER ALL

Perhaps there never was a romantic communication made to five more prosaic-looking people than the accredited agents of the societies. Middle-aged and elderly men, who, if they ever took up a novel, skipped the love passages, and in all instances preferred to read newspapers. They were very much bewildered at the purpose of their being called together. They had thought there must have been a codicil found to the very strange will of which they had had a copy sent to their societies, as being, though in a very unlikely contigency, possibly interested, and that it was possible they were to receive a small sum *in esse,* instead of the large one *in posse.* But when Mr. MacFarlane produced no codicil, but read to them gravely Mrs. Peck's confession instead, and paused at the conclusion, as if he expected them to express an opinion, they looked at each other for a few seconds, unwilling to commit themselves by initiating any remark whatever. At last the boldest of the number observed that it was a strange story, which the others agreed to unanimously.

'Do you think it is true?' said Francis.

'Perhaps it is,' said the director of the Blind Asylum; 'there is no saying.'

'Of course it does not at all invalidate Mr. Hogarth, my client's

right to the estate, moveable and heritable, of the late Hogarth, of Cross Hall,' said Mr. MacFarlane, 'for you know that was left to him by will.'

'Of course not,' said the director of the Blind Asylum; 'one can see that.'

'But what was the use of calling us all here,' said the representative of the Deaf and Dumb Asylum, 'to tell us that Cross Hall left his property perhaps by a mistake? Had he claimed as heir-of-entail or as heir-at-law the case would have been different; but it would have been our business to have found out that, or the next heir's, and certainly not the present possessor's.'

'You will observe,' said Francis, 'that I hold the property under conditions—one is, that I shall not marry either of my cousins. If Jane Melville is not my cousin, marrying her, and restoring her to the property, which she has a better right to than I have—should not invalidate my right by this will.'

'Oh, that is a very different affair,' said the Deaf and Dumb delgate. 'You want to marry Miss Melville, and to keep the estate too.'

'Yes, if I can legally. I know that if Mr. Hogarth was alive at this day, and could see this confession, he would believe it, and he would no longer see any bar to my marriage with his niece. If he could see how well and how bravely his nieces have battled with the world he would require no further trial of their fortitude or patience.'

'We would never think of disturbing you in possession of Cross Hall, so long as you fulfil the conditions of the will,' said the delegate from the Blind Asylum.

'Certainly, you need never think of it, for you cannot,' said MacFarlane.

'But such a step as you contemplate is so flagrant a violation of the spirit and purport of Mr. Hogarth's will—for, right or wrong, he never meant Jane Melville to be mistress of Cross Hall—that we must claim our just rights. This confession, given with the hope of extorting money from the supposed heirs of Mr. Hogarth, is worthless, particularly considering the character of the person who

makes it. I think you have no case whatever: do not you agree with me?' said the director of the Deaf and Dumb Asylum—one who took the greatest possible interest in the working and the prosperity of that charity, the funds of which were rather at a low ebb at this time. 'We cannot be supposed to be actuated by selfish motives; we are perfectly disinterested trustees for great public interests; but if property is left to these institutions, we would be wanting in our duty if we did not claim it.'

The other four directors took the same view of the case. None of them would agree to leave Francis unmolested, if he took the step he meditated.

'But you observe,' said Francis, 'that this will has been the cause of great injustice. In the first place, Mr. Hogarth's two nieces had been brought up as his heirs, and they were left to struggle with difficulties and hardships which were harder and more severe than any man has to go through—and for which the education their uncle had given them had not made them more fitted. In the second place, he left the property to me as supposing me to be his son. If this confession is true, I am not his son; but if I marry the woman who in that case is not my cousin, you will not allow me to keep the estate for her, so I am forced to——'

'Stop, Mr. Hogarth,' said Mr. MacFarlane, eagerly.

'I am forced to make a deed of gift to each of you, as I am really in possession of the estate. I save you all the expense and trouble of litigation, and I have to begin the world again at far greater disadvantage than when I was taken from my bank-desk and my £250 a year two years ago. I have acquired expensive habits; I am two years older, and I shall have a wife and probably a family to maintain.'

'There is a great deal of truth in what you say,' said the director of the —— Institution, for the sub-matronship of which Jane Melville had applied in vain. The other four were speechless with astonishment at the extraordinary proposition which Francis made to them. 'Litigation is long and expensive. I may say, for my body of directors, that we would be very happy to give some consideration

for the very handsome, the very generous, offer you make to us. It is not right to marry without being a little beforehand with the world; and it would be very unfair to accept of all you gained by the will without making a little compensation for what you have lost. Any personal property, books, and furniture, that you would like to keep, to the value of £200, or thereabouts, and a sum of £400 from each of us, I think would be fair, to give you a start in a new country. I believe Miss Melville is a very deserving lady. If it had not been for her youth we should have had her with us. I hope my friends here will agree with me that this is reasonable and just.'

'You get the estate too chealpy,' said Mr. MacFarlane, with warmth. 'Think that Mr. Hogarth might have kept it for ever if it had not been for this romantic crotchet; think that he might marry Miss Melville, and having possession might defy you to oust him, and drag you through court after court, and run you up £10,000 of costs, and after all the Chancery Courts would decide that he should keep it. Public feeling is against these restrictions, for they lead to people living *par amours* if they are forbidden to marry; and Mr. Hogarth's position and character would be all in his favour. You get property worth £50,000 divided amongst you, and you offer my client a paltry £2,000 out of consideration for his generosity and forbearance.'

'I am satisfied with it,' said Francis; 'and I think Jane will be the same.'

'It is too little,' said the director of the —— Infirmary, who had never spoken before. 'We must make it £500 each; and we are very much obliged to Mr. Hogarth; and we should not limit him so much with regard to the personal property. Cross Hall library was valued at more than £1,000; and as they are all such reading folk, they might take £200 of books alone. Let us be liberal, and say £700 for what he may like to take from Cross Hall.'

'If I have any voice in the administration of the property I make over to you, I should like to have it applied specially to paying your officers better—particularly in those situations which are filled by women. I know you think it right to economize your funds; and I

believe that all Scotch charities are much better managed, and much more honestly administered than those on the other side of the Tweed. But I think you pay your surgeons and your matrons very shabbily. You say you get so many applications, that it shows you do not underpay them. But it would be much better to demand better qualifications, and to pay them more highly. Out of sixty applications for a matronship worth £30 a year, there is perhaps one or two only fit for the work; and if they are fit for it, they are well worth £70,' said Francis.

'We have raised *that* salary,' said the director of the —— Institution.

'I am glad to hear it—very glad to hear it,' said Francis.

'We will take what you say into consideration,' said the director of the Deaf and Dumb Institution, who was speculating on all that could be done with a sum amounting to more than £9,000.

'I object to specify sums in making the deed of gift, or I should make some special provision on that score; but the value of money changes so much that what is a fair salary in one generation is not a fair one the next, and if salaries are fixed too high they are apt to lead to favoritism and jobbing. I dare say it would be better to trust to your own sense of honour on the matter.'

'I think you may safely do so, Mr. Hogarth. With regard to the property, I suppose we should advertise it for sale and then divide the proceeds. The payments to Mr. Hogarth must be made at once, however, as I suppose he is bound for Australia,' said the director of the Deaf and Dumb Asylum.

'Yes, in the first ship, in which some friends of mine are going,' said Francis.

'I am sure we wish you all prosperity and all happiness in the marriage you contemplate, which has been so fortunate for those in whom we are interested,' said the last speaker, and the sentiment was echoed by all the others.

'Could not you buy Cross Hall?' said Francis to Miss Thomson on the day after this matter was settled. 'I should feel half my sorrow at parting with it removed if I knew you could have it.'

'No, no; I am not going to buy a property that I cannot pay for. My father did something of the kind once, and all the time he was a laird we were poor. He sold the property at a great loss, and then things looked up again with him. I'd rather be a rich farmer than a poor proprietor.'

'If I could see you in possession of Cross Hall, and Mr. Sinclair in my seat in Parliament, I should really have very little to give up; but it appears I cannot. I have accepted the stewardship of Her Majesty's Chiltern Hundreds to-day, and the burghs will be declared vacant directly. But Mr. Sinclair cannot afford it; and he could not carry the election. His manner is not good enough; he does not conciliate people. If our scheme were carried there would be no fear of Sinclair getting in, for he is a man really wanted. He could get a sufficient number of votes here to carry him half in, and the remainder of the quota would be attracted by his original genius and upright character, which he could show by his speeches and addresses; and we hope to make a seat in Parliament a much less costly affair—£50 or £100 should cover it all. But I fear the burghs must fall back on either the Duke's nominee or the Earl's.'

'Then are you more sorry to leave your people at Cross Hall, or your parliamentary duties?' said Miss Thomson.

'The people at Cross Hall I think are really in a much better position than when I came; and, perhaps, it is as well for them to be left to work out things for themselves. I have become much attached to them, but perhaps if I stayed there, they would depend too much upon me. But in Parliament, I have not yet broken ground in the work I had set myself to do: and I confess that I do regret it, both for my own sake, for the sake of my friends who depended on me, and for the sake of the dear old country itself. There may be more able men and more energetic men in Parliament; but I am sure there are none whose heart was more in the work than mine. But that was Jane's doing. I know if she had not urged these matters on me, I would very likely have spent my life in indolent enjoyment. Without the one drop of bitter in my cup, in the sufferings of Jane and Elsie, I never could have felt the

responsibilities of wealth. I should have made a fine picture-gallery at Cross Hall, and probably acquired a name as a man of good taste, but the higher objects of life would have been lost sight of.'

The farewell address to his constituents was next written and read, with genuine sorrow on both sides. The farewells at Cross Hall were taken, and the establishment broke up; but Susan (the housemaid), when she heard that the master was going to Australia, with the purpose of marrying Miss Jane, begged to go with Peggy Walker's family, in hopes of being engaged in the service of the best master and the best mistress she ever saw. And her request was acceded to.

Next came the journey to London, and the preparations for the voyage, and the hardest task of all—the parting from the friends and the objects he had so much at heart there.

He had written a full explanation of his conduct to his coadjutors in London on his resigning his seat; and, though there was no reproach, there was a great deal of regret, for there was not another man either able or willing to take the part which Francis had purposed to hold for any number of years in which he might be in Parliament.

XIV

MEETING

Jane Melville was very much surprised at the extraordinary news that Elsie wrote to her with regard to Mrs. Peck's revelations to herself and Mr. Brandon. Though she was quite prepared for a very interesting letter on their own private affairs, she felt this touch her still more nearly. She was sorry that Elsie had written to Francis on the subject without consulting her, and that she had to wait a whole month before she could assure him that this confession made no difference in her feeling of regard and affection towards him, or in her pride in his career, saying that she hoped he was now satisfied that he was the son of honest and loving parents, though unknown ones; rejoicing that he had got quit of such a mother as Mrs. Peck; and expressing the pleasure with which she read his speeches, and her interest in the objects with which he had in a measure identified himself. She tried to think that all was with them as before, and that, though no longer his cousin, she might continue to be his affectionate and sympathizing friend.

Elsie's marriage gave to her sister great and unmixed pleasure. It took place very shortly after Brandon had obtained her consent, and Emily and Jane went to Melbourne to act as bridesmaids; and Edgar, too, was needed on such an occasion as this. Although there

were twenty miles between Wiriwilta and Barragong, the sisters contrived to see a good deal of each other. Mrs. Phillips was kinder and more cordial to the Melvilles than before; and now that Elsie had an ascertained position as Brandon's wife, even Miss Phillips could not condescend quite so much to her.

During Brandon's honeymoon, Dr. Grant had got matters in such excellent train that he made his proposal in due form, and was accepted; but there could not be such promptitude in carrying it out as in Brandon's case, for he could never think of taking a lady of Miss Phillips's pretensions to Ben More without making considerable additions and improvements on it, and the masons and carpenters were very slow about their work. The pangs occasioned by delay were sweetened by frequent and long visits; and the plan of his house, and of the garden which he was laying out and planting, was constantly in the hands of the betrothed lovers for mutual suggestions and admiration. At last the day was fixed, and it was to be a very grand affair. There was to be a special licence, and she was to be married from her brother's house, as there was no English church within reasonable distance. The Lord Bishop of Melbourne was to come out to perform the ceremony, and all the neighbours from far and near were invited;—the Ballantynes and some of their town acquaintance besides. There were to be thirty-five at breakfast; and little or nothing could be had from town, so there was an extraordinary amount of cooking going on at Wiriwilta. Mrs. Bennett, who was worth any two of the women servants in the house, was going hither and thither, and surpassing herself in her culinary successes. Emily was instructing Harriett how she was to behave on the following day as bridesmaid, for the two little girls were to support their aunt on the trying occasion; and after officiating in that capacity at the marriage of her favourites, Brandon and Alice, Emily felt quite experienced on the subject. Their dresses were very pretty; and as for Miss Phillips's, it was magnificent, for she thought, if there ever was an occasion on which one should be richly dressed, it was on an occasion like this. Mrs. Phillips had been persuaded for once to allow her sister-in-law

to oushine her, at least so far as she could do so.

Jane was as busy in the kitchen as any one; when she was called away by Miss Phillips, to be consulted as to how her veil should be disposed of, for Mrs. Phillips had declined to give an opinion—and there were two modes of arranging it that she was doubtful about. Could not Miss Melville settle that knotty point?

'I really cannot say; one seems to me to look as well as the other,' said Jane.

'That is very unsatisfactory,' said Harriett. 'I know they are not equally becoming.'

'Elsie will be here this evening,' said Jane, 'or early to-morrow morning; and I am sure she will be most happy to give the last touches to your dress. Her taste is good, and you know how wretched mine is.'

'Well, I suppose I must trust to that; but I should prefer to have everything settled to-day, so that my mind might be quite easy. I should not like to look flurried to-morrow. I must ask Dr. Grant when he comes in. Perhaps he will give me an idea. Your sister's dress was very simple, she told me; but then the affair was so hurried—there was no time to make preparations. We have not that excuse, thanks to those tiresome tradespeople. But Alice and Brandon seem to get on pretty comfortably.'

'Very happily, I think,' said Jane.

'Oh, yes, he is good-natured enough, and I dare say, very kind to her, and she seems quite satisfied. But I have been just thinking how difficult it would have been for me to have been suited in such a colony as this if I had not been so fortunate as to meet with Dr. Grant. Being a professional man, he is necessarily an educated man, and you know how much that weighs with me; and he has the manners of a gentleman, which are also indispensable to my happiness in marriage. None of your rough, boorish bushmen, who can only talk of sheep and cattle, could possibly have done for me. Then, his family connections are most unexceptionable; my own relations cannot feel in any way compromised by such an alliance. The near neighbourhood (as I suppose it must be called) to

Wiriwilta, and even to Barragong, makes it very pleasant. I should not have at all liked marrying to be at distance from my brother and his family. Coming out, as I did, on their account principally, it would be dreadful for all of us if we were separated. I am sure I am quite pleased, too, to have your sister and Brandon as neighbours. Alice looks quite a different person now she has a house of her own. I don't call her pretty—I never did; but she looks very well indeed at Barragong, and seems to get on wonderful well, considering.'

'Considering what?' was about to come from Jane's lips, for she had never liked Miss Phillips's condescending way of talking about her sister; but she checked herself, for it was no use to argue with the bride on the eve of her wedding-day, and gave an indifferent and conciliatory reply; but the conversation was here interrupted by the entrance of two old friends, not any of the party invited for the morrow, but two large beautiful dogs, who ran up to Jane with the wildest expressions of canine delight.

'Oh, Nep! oh Flora!' said Jane, 'where have you come from? Who can have brought you here? Poor old fellows! dear old fellows!' And the favourites from Cross Hall laid their happy heads in her lap, and rejoiced in their old mistress's caresses.

'What beauties!' said Miss Phillips; 'but I do not like dogs in the drawing-room.'

'I will take them out,' said Jane, trembling with wonder and agitation. She went out of the room, and at the hall door, which stood (bush fashion) hospitably open, she saw Francis standing, allowing Nep and Flora, who seemed to know there was a friend in the house, to make an entrance and introduce themselves. She extended her hand, but he clasped her in his arms.

'Not farewell this time, dearest Jane. I have come for you, and I will not be refused. When we parted I said you knew I loved you, and now I believe you love me. I have given up everything—the property, the seat in Parliament; and now that I have no career to relinquish, perhaps you will acknowledge that you love me?'

'Oh, Francis, I have always loved you! but I could have lived

without you all my life if I had thought it for your good and your happiness. I could not bear to be your stumbling-block. But is it really the case? did you believe that strange story? have you given up what you made such good use of?'

'Come out into the garden with me, and I will tell you all about it;' and Francis led Jane where they were more secure from interruption. Flora and Nep followed them in the greatest exuberance of spirits.

'I had to stay one day in Melbourne, and found that I could get a situation there as accountant in a merchant's office, at £300 to begin with. I had Mr. Rennie's testimonial to speak for me. It is not so much as my £250 in Edinburgh; but will you marry me on that?' said Francis.

'I would marry you on less,' said Jane, 'for my own part of it; but you care more for comfort and luxury than I do. If you will consent to be cheerfully without what we cannot afford, I will do my best.'

'I have been roughing it a little on board ship; you may ask Peggy and Mary Forrester if I have not. But I hope to get on, for your sake, if not for my own. I feel just like a boy again beginning the world, and feeling it is all his for the winning.'

'But your plans—your ambitions—are they all given up? You know the property was really yours—as much yours without a name as with my uncle's. I am sorry you were so rash.'

'No, Jane, don't be sorry; don't be anything but very glad. I never was so happy in my life. I left all my regrets on the other side of the world. Now, when I have your hand in mine, your heart in my keeping, when you have promised to give yourself to me, I will not feel that I have cause for anything but devout gratitude to our Heavenly Father, and humble but confident hope that He will bless our union. My dearest love, do look in my face and say you are happy.'

'Yes, I am happy,' said Jane, 'very happy. Thank God for all his goodness.'

'But what are we to do for a name? I ought not to be Hogarth, or Ormistown, or Francis either. Can you give me a new name to

begin our new life with?'

'I think we will still call you Francis Hogarth; it is the name I learned to love you by, and I think if my poor dear uncle saw us now, and saw how we love each other, he would be pleased that my husband should have his name. Then you have really given up everything?' said Jane, who could not at once believe in the fact.

'To the benevolent societies. But they behaved very handsomely, and gave to me—or rather, to you—a sum of money sufficient to better our position. I have not only the £300 a-year—I have £2,500 besides, and a lot of things from Cross Hall to furnish a cottage with. I had to leave the horses, but I thought you and Elsie would like the dogs. Susan helped to pack the furniture; and I have brought her out to go into your service in any capacity. I suppose we can afford to keep one domestic on our small means, even in Melbourne.'

'I suppose the rest of the establishment were sorry to lose a good master,' said Jane; 'and the labourers, too—what about your arrangments there?'

'The cottages were built and the allotments made over securely, and I think they are the better, and not the worse, for my two years' tenure of Cross Hall. As for the political and social reforms, I have no doubt that there are five hundred men in England as good as me. Sinclair is as good an apostle of my crotchets as I could be, only he is not in the House. I will not be so insincere as to say that I did not give up my parliamentary life with the greatest regret. That really was *the* sacrifice. You must be very, very kind to me on that account; but you know that I could not, as an honest man, keep property which had been bequeathed to me under such a mistake. You would not have done it under the circumstances. I tried to save it for you, to whom it ought to have been left; but after consulting the best authorities I found I could not do so, for your uncle's will was so distinct in excluding you from any benefit from his estate. So, Jane, you must say that you are glad. Don't look as if you were anything but my guiding-star—the life of my life—all the world to me. A hindrance, a stumbling-block! Without you I should have had

no high aims, no noble ambition. If I had done little or nothing, I have learned a great deal; so

'"Love me for the sake of what I am,
And not of what I do."'

'You know that I will be only too happy to be your wife, Francis,' said Jane.

'And perhaps if I get on well here I may go into political life in the colony and do the work I was sent into the world for at the other end of it. Then when are you going to give yourself to me?'

'As soon as I can possibly leave this family. We must let Mr. Phillips know immediately. How surprised Elsie will be!'

'Not so much as you are, I fancy. Bless her for writing me that letter; there is not one of yours that I prize more. But with regard to the Phillipses, Miss Marry Forrester, I think, would be very happy to take your place; and, from all I can see of her, she will do admirably. Did you really want me to fall in love with her?'

'I wanted you to be happy, and I thought she could make you so. You do not understand how unselfish a woman's love can be. Then, if Miss Forrester can take my place here, there need be no delay.'

'You make none on your part, like a good, honest girl, as you are.'

'Why should I? We have loved each other for two years. Our wedding will be the simplest affair possible. Why should I pretend to wish to delay what will be my happiness as well as yours? Oh, Francis! though I could not have wished you to make the sacrifices you have made for my poor sake, yet, now that it is done, it is not a half-heart I give you. I will try to give you no cause to regret what I have cost you. Oh, how glad I am to be able to tell you frankly how dear you are to me!'

EPILOGUE

It is Christmas-day, 186—. Jane Hogarth is busy making arrangements for a quiet family dinner party, in her pretty house, not far from Melbourne, a little annoyed because the season is so backward that no fruit is to be had for love or money; but, on the whole, certain that things will go off very well without it. Francis has succeeded very well in Victoria. His talents and industry made him very valuable to the mercantile house he went into. In the course of a few years he put his capital into it, and got a partnership, which, now that the principal was absent on a visit to England, was on equal terms. The Brandons and Hogarths exchange Christmas visits with each other, and this year it is Jane's turn to be the entertainer, and Elsie with her husband and children have come down from the bush to have a little gaiety in Melbourne.

This occasion was one to be especially remarked on, for there was a bride to be honoured in the person of pretty Grace Forrester, whom Tom Lowrie, now a rising engineer, had succeeded in winning as his wife. All the Lowries had made good colonists; the eldest girl had married respectably; the second assisted her aunt in the shop, which she had recently enlarged and improved; but Tom's prospects were better than those of any other of the family, and fully justified Jane's hopes and expectations. There is no saying

where he may stop in his colonial career. Peggy, now called Miss Walker universally, except by one or two old friends, was to accompany her nephew and his wife. Is it really Peggy whom we see at Mrs. Hogarth's door with the dress of rich black silk, destitute of crinoline, and the bonnet, in these days of tall bonnets, flattened down in contempt of fashion, but still of excellent materials?

She is a better-looking woman in her older days than when she was younger. Brandon declares that in time she will turn out quite a beauty, and takes more interest in the caps that his wife makes as a regular thing for Peggy—four every year (nobody can make them to please her as Mrs. Brandon can do)—than in any other of her attempts at millinery.

Another member of the party was Mr. Dempster, who had just come over from Adelaide. He had been seized on by Francis, and begged to accept of a little corner of their somewhat crowded house.

There are a number of very bright faces collected round the table. How many recollections of early difficulties faithfully wrestled with and overcome, throng upon our friends at such an hour of meeting!

Peggy was disposed to improve the occasion. 'Well,' said she, 'to think of us all being together in this way after all we've come through! I'm not speaking of you, Mr. Dempster, for I know none of your harassments—but when I mind of the night when Miss Jean and Miss Elsie sat in my little room, so downcast, and so despairing, and I told them about all my troubles just to hearten them up a bit, and to show what God had enabled me to win through, little did I think of how the Almighty was leading us all! You mind well of how I spoke of Miss Thomson that night, and of the money she gave for my help when I was in sore straits how to provide for my bairns. And to think of my Tam being married on her niece! It's no for worms like us to be proud, but to be connected with such as Miss Thomson is a cause of thanksgiving.'

'And I have had a letter from Aunt Margaret, and so has Tom,' said Grace, 'and she is quite pleased with our engagement. She says she knows that as Tom has raised himself so far by his own

industry and abilities, helped by the education his good aunt gave to him, that there is no fear of his ever falling; and she said Tom's letter to her is the best thing of the kind she ever read.'

'Mrs. Hogarth taught him to write letters,' said Peggy; 'and really when he reads out anything to me that he has written, it reads like a printed book. As for Miss Thomson's own letter, it deserves to be printed in letters of gold; but mind, you young folk, not to be overmuch set up about being married, and all your friends being so satisfied. It is a great good Providence that you have happened so well; but all folk have not your good luck. You must not look down on your sister Mary—who is the best of the whole bunch of you, I reckon—because she is six years older than you and not married yet.'

'Oh, auntie!' said Grace,—'with such a maiden aunt as I have, and such a maiden aunt as Tom has, you never could dream of my looking down on old maids, or fancying I can be compared to Mary.'

'Bravo! Mrs. Lowrie,' said Brandon; 'I wish I could find any one good enough for Miss Forrester, but I cannot.'

'Mr. Sinclair cannot comprehend my going off before Mary. He says, if he does not hear news of her in two years' time, he must come to Australia for her himself,' said Grace.

'There is likely to be another wedding ere long, at Wiriwilta, however,' said Brandon.

'Emily,' said Peggy, 'Grace was getting word of it from her sister. She's young yet.'

'So she is, and so is Edgar; but it is a settled thing. A year's engagement—or something of that sort. Mr. and Mrs. Phillips have consented very handsomely, but Mrs. Grant thinks that, with Emily's beauty and education (for Miss Forrester has certainly brought her on wonderfully), she should make a better marriage.'

'But, for my part, Frank,' said Brandon, addressing his brother-in-law. 'I do like to see young people falling in love in this natural way, and willing to begin life not just as their fathers leave off. I talked to Emily like a father, and told her what she could expect until they worked for it; and she gave me a kiss, and said that she knew quite

well that she could not have everything just as it was at Wiriwilta, but if there was twice as much to give up she would do it; for, as she said very charmingly, "I am very fond of Edgar, and Edgar is very fond of me." To see people beginning life in a love-marriage so young as the happy pair in company, or even younger, as in the case of Edgar and Emily, is very refreshing to old fogies like you and me, Frank, who began our married life a good deal on the wrong side of thirty, and whose eldest children look out for white hairs in our heads. The only consolation I have for not being happy younger is, that if I had married before I should have married some one else, and that would never have done. Elsie might have taken me a year before she did, however. I have never quite forgiven her.'

'And the young people are very fond of each other,' said Peggy. 'All very right, but I don't like to see them make too much fuss. Tom and Grace are very ridiculous whiles.'

'Well, I must say I like to see it,' said Brandon. 'I quite enjoy seeing Emily stealing out with Edgar in the gloaming, and meeting him in the hall when she hears his knock, and getting into corners with him. Harriett, who has some notion what the thing means, has patience with it, but Constance, who is younger, despises all this philandering. I said to her the other day, when she was expressing her disgust at these proceedings, "Ah, Constance! three years or so, and you will be doing just the same. I have another nephew coming out next month, and a fine fellow he is said to be. You'll be just as foolish." "You'll see me boiled first!" said Constance, with a vehemence which startled her aunt Harriett, and brought down a serious rebuke, though she herself thought the young people rather ridiculous, to use Peggy's phrase. But I know very well that one great reason for Emily's fancy for Edgar is her wish to call Elsie and myself aunt and uncle. I think it likely that that weighed with you, Mrs. Lowrie.'

'None of your nonsense, Mr. Brandon,' said Peggy. 'Who would care to be connected with an old woman like me?' and yet she was pleased with Brandon's remark, notwithstanding.

'Well, joking apart, I think it is really a great thing for a girl to

marry into a family where they are prepared to love her, and to put the most charitable construction on all she does and all she does not do,' said Brandon.

'But, Mr. Hogarth,' said Mr. Dempster, 'you promised at this family party to tell me the whole story of which I have got some separate threads. You recollect that we had some curious revelations one evening at a *séance* at my house in London. Shortly after I returned to Adelaide, I met in a wayside inn an old woman whom I took to be your mother, who entered into conversation with me; but as the spiritual directions had been to have nothing to do with her, I did not inquire sufficiently to get much information from her. Some time after that, I heard of your giving up your property in Scotland, sailing for Australia, marrying your cousin, and settling here; but what connection these three things have with each other, I never knew. Will you be good enough to explain?'

'The spirit was in the wrong on that occasion in two important particulars. The letter I had in my pocket was from Mrs. Peck, but she was not my mother; Mr. Hogarth was not my father,' said Francis.

'Not your mother! not your father!' said Mr. Dempster; 'can you prove that?'

'No; but I am quite convinced of it,' said Francis.

'I would believe the spirits always, if I had no positive proof to the contrary,' said Mr. Dempster.

'Mrs. Peck confessed to Brandon that as her own child died suddenly she had picked up another, with the view of imposing on Mr. Hogarth and getting a handsome allowance from him; but when he saw me he preferred keeping me out of her hands, and educated me, but never loved me,' said Francis.

'I would not believe that woman on her oath,' said Mr. Dempster; 'and I know her motive. She wanted to get something out of your cousins, and for that purpose invented this confession. That would never shake my belief in the spirits. Look at the way in which those names were spelled out—you were convinced of the truth of it at the time.'

'My dear sir,' said Francis, 'I certainly heard and saw a great many things which I could not explain. They seemed to echo my own thoughts marvellously correctly, but whenever I was at fault, they, too, were misinformed. Elsie had been suspicious beforehand that I was not Henry Hogarth's son. Mrs. Peck's confession was consistent and probable; she stuck to it as being true, to her dying day. I went to see her on her death-bed, and she declared that, as she hoped for forgiveness, I was not her child or Mr. Hogarth's; so that, though I never got any clue to my real parents—for she did not know my name, and the advertisments which I put into American papers were never answered—thirty-five years being a lapse of time in which such matters cannot be traced—I am morally certain that I am not Jane's cousin, and consequently that the spirit was wrong. It might be mesmerism, or extra-ordinary quickness of sight; for though I tried to pass over the letters which spelled out the names, a very practised eye might observe an infinitesimal hesitation over the particular letter;—but of one thing I am certain, that if Henry Hogarth had been there in the spirit, he would have been able to tell me both that he was not my father, and also whose son I really was, which information I wished to obtain.'

'But did not the spirit say you were to have happiness after a time,' said Mr. Dempster, triumphantly, 'and have you not got it?'

'Certainly I have; and if it had any hand in bringing it about I am very grateful to it,' said Francis, looking at his wife with pride and pleasure; 'but I think we owe our happiness very much to each other. The will, which was as unjust and absurd a one as could have been made, indirectly did us service. I am quite sure that but for the singular relations in which I was placed I never could have known Jane, and could not have loved her.'

'If Elsie had been left £20,000 I never should have dared to have looked up to her,' said Brandon; 'and what a loss that would have been to her, not speak of myself! It is a hundred chances to one against two heiresses getting two such good husbands, and keeping all such capital friends as we do.'

'It is quite true,' said Jane; 'my uncle's will has resulted in more happiness than even he could have hoped for.'

'Though he certainly would not have contemplated with equanimity the passing of Cross Hall into the hands of Mrs. William Dalzell, whose trustees invested her fortune in it when it was sold by the benevolent societies to whom I relinquished the inheritance,' said Francis. 'Dalzell does not make so bad a landlord as we expected, particularly as he has not much in his power. The proceeds of the sale are doing good to the sick and afflicted, while we are quite as comfortable without it.'

'I cannot think enough of the Providence that has made good come out of evil,' said Jane. 'But with regard to the rappings, Mr. Dempster, the oracular sentences that all would be well in the end, and that Francis should be happy after a time, were of the vaguest description, while on positive matters they were decidedly misinformed.'

'It might have been a lying or mocking spirit,' said Mr. Dempster; 'my faith in the truth of these manifestations is not to be shaken by what you say.'

'I wonder if your spirits could tell us if Grant is in for ——, and his majority? The election must have taken place, but no one in the room knows of it; that would be a crucial test, as Jane calls it,' said Brandon.

'In such a company of unbelievers,' said Mr. Dempster, ' we could not get up a *séance*, and what is more, we have no medium.'

'It is well that Grant goes out of his own district,' said Brandon, 'for he would not stand a chance there; and now he is promising to those strangers anything and everything. With all Grant's aristocratic feelings, and his wife's too, which are still stronger, their desire that he should have a seat in the Assembly, now that McIntyre is in, seems to drag him into as low depths as any one. I cannot see why they should be so anxious about it, unless it is that, since they cannot afford to go home, they want to take as good a position here as any of their neighbours. Grant's affairs will suffer if he has to be so much in Melbourne, and at best he will make a

very fourth-rate legislator.'

'I think he is naturally "indifferent honest,"' said Francis. 'At least, he is disposed to be honest, but canvassing is very different work here as well as in Britain.'

'You should really get into our Assembly, Frank,' said Brandon, 'to give the natives here the benefit of your experience. How great you would be on a point of order or a question of privilege!'

'I wish Francis had time to give to parliamentary duties,' said Jane. 'I live in hopes that when Mr. —— returns, he may try his fortune in the political world here. If representative assemblies would limit themselves to what really concerns such bodies, it would not be so heavy a tax upon people in business to give their time to the public; but they will meddle with things that ought to be let alone, and endless floods of talk on such matters take up much valuable time.'

'Then Mr. Hogarth's public spirit has not been gently smothered by a happy marriage and a fine family of children? That is the modern view of the case,' said Mr. Dempster. 'Nothing great is done by married men, unless they are unhappily mated.'

'A most ignoble view of a wife's duties,' said Jane.

'My wife would never smother any public spirit I may have,' said Francis. 'She had too much to do with the birth of it, not to cherish it as fondly as any of her other babies; but I fear that, till my friend Mr. Hare's scheme is carried, I could not get a majority in Victoria. We want the reform very much here, and in all the colonies; and as yet, it has been failure, failure, failure.'

'And if such men as you do not get in, Frank, it will never be carried. Grant is stupid—thoroughly stupid. I talked to him for four mortal hours on the subject, and made it plain to the meanest capacity, that though we wanted a representation of minorities, the minority in the House would faithfully represent the minority out of doors, and not be able to defeat the majorities, as he was convinced it would do. I put it down in black and white—proved it with figures. Elsie and I made fancy voting-papers, and I acted as returning officer, and showed the thing as clear as day; but though

he drank a bottle and a half of sherry during the process, he was just as wise at the end as at the beginning. Now I don't call myself at all clever, but when Frank explained the method of voting to me, I saw it all in a minute—and you, Tom—did not you, too? but then you are rather a genius.'

'It is as plain as a pikestaff,' said Tom Lowrie.

'Walter thinks, because he has not read very much, that we must think him stupid,' said Elsie, 'when he really has the quickest apprehension of all sorts of things.'

'Dr. Grant will, perhaps, take up the meaning of Hare's scheme when the newspapers have advocated it for years, and it has been familiar to all the people around him,' said Francis, 'or he may vote for it without understanding it, when it becomes a popular cry.'

'But to have to stir such a dish of skimmed milk to honourable action!' said Brandon. 'Frank, you really must stand for our district. I fancy McIntyre will go home by the time your partner comes back, so we will have a vacancy. I will canvass for you, and so will Edgar. It would be a credit to us to have a real British M.P. as our representative, and then you could push your grand idea, as you intended to have done in England, before love routed ambition. As you say, the result has hitherto been a failure in the colonies, but the contest should not be abandoned.'

'I hear that the movement makes slow progress in Britain,' said Francis, 'but still it makes progress. It is too great a change there, and there are so many vested interests which consider such a reform would interfere with their prescriptive rights. On the Continent it makes more way; and, perhaps, as my French friends say, the discovery may be first carried into practice there; but I had hopes of its success in the colonies. There is so much less to disturb here that a change from exclusively local to general elections would not be difficult, if we could only make the idea familiar. All we see in America, all we see in political matters here, only show how much easier it is to reform before abuses go too far. I should very much like to try your district, Brandon, and will be very glad of your services when the time comes; and so I should feel that my work

had been postponed, but not altogether given up.'

'If we could carry the measure by a *coup de main* in any one of the colonies, and bring it into working, the whole world would be the better for it,' said Brandon.

'There can be no carrying it by a *coup de main*,' said Francis. 'Every inch of the ground must be fought here, as in Britain, but the extent of ground is shorter.'

'I have grown much more patriotic since I was married,' said Brandon. 'The place where you have a real home—the birthplace of your children—and where you hope to see them grow up—becomes very dear to you. And here are the youngsters!'

Little Maggie Brandon (so called in compliment to Peggy) seemed to know by intuition that there was something for her in the pocket of the worthy woman, and went to her at once; and the others distributed themselves according to their several likings.

'Well,' said Peggy, 'I've often thought to ask you before, Mrs. Hogarth, but how are you going to educate your lassies? What are you going to do with them? and you favour lassies in both families—two to one in each of them.'

'Very much as we were educated ourselves,' said Jane; 'with more care taken for the cultivation of their natural tastes, but the ground-work will be the same.'

'That education has certainly turned out admirable wives,' said Francis.

'Speak for yourself, Frank,' said Brandon; 'but my wife spoils me, and everybody in the house. There is a sad want of vinegar in her composition. She cannot scold her servants—the mildest approach to it that she ever makes is by saying, "Mr. Brandon does not like such a thing," or that "Mr. Brandon would be displeased if they do not attend to such another." The idea of making a bugbear of me is very ingenious, but I fear not very efficacious, for I know they see through it. As for me, a penitent recollection of a conversation in an English railway carriage has stopped her mouth for ever, and she never gives me a hard word, however I may deserve it; and for the children, the less we say of them the better.'

'But, Walter, I can keep my servants, and they really do very well; and the children are good enough, and so are you; so there is no need to scold.'

'That is where the dangerous part of this subtle flattery lies; it is so perfectly sincere. But I suppose we get along pretty well, considering, as Mrs. Grant would say; and I really think her household would be more comfortable if she took a leaf out of my wife's book. Her servants will not stay three months with her, and she has three of the most spoiled, exacting children I ever saw—far worse than their cousins at Wiriwilta were in their worst days. The Phillipses had spirit, but the Grants have none, except perhaps the spirit of discontent. I think we might do worse, Peggy, than educate our girls to resemble their mothers.'

'But,' said Jane, 'we must make some provision for them also, if we can. I suppose that I could have got on as well as you, Francis, if I had been a man.'

'Yes, there is nothing I have done that you could not have done as well. I have as much perseverance as you, but not so much energy. It is likely you would have made a better figure in the world than I have done.'

'But I could get nothing to do but to take a governess's situation; and wonderfully lucky I was to get it. Mary Forrester is a much better governess for Mr. Phillips's family than I was. Elsie could only maintain herself as a milliner or as a lady's maid; and yet Elsie, placed as a clerk or bookkeeper in a bank or merchant's office, would have filled the situation as satisfactorily as half the young men I know.'

'Then you have not quite given up your notions of woman's rights?' said Mr. Dempster. 'For my part, I think the best right a woman has is the right to a husband.'

'That is a right she cannot assert for herself,' said Jane, smiling. 'One would think, to hear people talk on this subject, that the entreaties for work and independence come from those who in their youth disdained faithful lovers, and perversely and unnaturally refused to love, honour, and obey. I think, on the contrary, that the

women of our century are only too easily won, and cannot be charged with any unnecessary cruelty to lovers. I do not think that you increase the number of happy marriages or lessen the number of mercenary unions by making the task for a single woman to maintain herself honestly and usefully such very uphill work.

FOR THE BEST PAPERBACKS, LOOK FOR THE

PENGUIN

Her Selection:
Writings by Nineteenth Century Australian Women edited by Lynne Spender

Nineteenth-century Australian women writers were published widely in magazines, newspapers and books in Australia and abroad. Their writings provide an insight into the lives of women, the opportunities and obstacles, the hardships and the successes. This lively collection brings together works that have been unavailable for many years.

Included are works by: Georgiana Molloy, Louisa Lawson, Annabella Boswell, Mary Fortune and 'Tasma'.

A Bright and Fiery Troop:
Australian Women Writers of the Nineteenth Century edited by Debra Adelaide

Who was the most popular detective story writer of the nineteenth century? A woman, Mary Fortune.
Who was the internationally famous botanist and artist who also wrote novels? A woman, Louisa Atkinson.
Who wrote the first convict novel? A woman, Caroline Leakey.
Who wrote the first novel with an Aboriginal protagonist? A woman, Catherine Martin.

This book opens up the hidden history of Australian literature and is the first critical appraisal of the major Australian women writers of the nineteenth century.

The book includes photographs.

BOOKS BY JESSICA ANDERSON IN PENGUIN

Tirra Lirra by the River

A beautifully written novel of a woman's seventy-year search to find a place where she truly belongs.
For Nora Porteous, life is a series of escapes. To escape her tightly knit small-town family, she marries, only to find herself confined again, this time in a stifling Sydney suburb with a selfish, sanctimonious husband. With a courage born of desperation and sustained by a spirited sense of humor, Nora travels to London, and it is there that she becomes the woman she wants to be. Or does she?
Winner of the Miles Franklin Award.

Stories From the Warm Zone and Sydney Stories

Jessica Anderson's evocative stories recreate, through the eyes of a child, the atmosphere of Australia between the wars. A stammer becomes a blessing in disguise; the prospect of a middle name converts a reluctant child to baptism. These autobiographical stories of a Brisbane childhood glow with the warmth of memory.
The formless sprawl of Sydney in the 1980s is a very different world. Here the lives of other characters are changed by the uncertainties of divorce, chance meetings and the disintegration and generation of relationships.
Winner of The Age Book of the Year Award

Last Man's Head

Detective Alec Probyn has his enemies too. His recent stand on police violence has led to his being suspended from duty. He has a growing suspicion that a vicious crime is about to be committed. All the more disturbing as the suspect and the victim are both members of his own family.
How can Probyn prevent this crime and its shattering consequences? In the savage resolution he discovers that his anti-violent stand has not magically cancelled out the violence in himself.

FOR THE BEST PAPERBACKS, LOOK FOR THE

PENGUIN

An Ordinary Lunacy

When David Byfield sees Isobel for the first time at a party, he decides that he has fallen in love with her. An attractive and successful lawyer, David is being groomed for a political career; his experience with love and intimacy, however, is limited.

Months after the party, Isobel's alcoholic husband is found dead in their shabby apartment, an apparent suicide. Then Isobel is accused of his murder and David steps up to defend her both as lawyer and friend. But Isobel's case is more than he bargained for . . .

Set in contemporary Sydney, Jessica Anderson's first novel is a perceptive and witty portrait of men and women caught between their desires and their obligations, and the choices we all make for – or in spite of – love.

The Commandant

In the 1830s the penal settlement of Moreton Bay on the Brisbane River is under the command of Patrick Logan, a fanatical disciplinarian. In his charge are convicts whom no flogging can break. But in spite of his precautions some still escape to the bush and take refuge with the Aborigines. Logan's administration has been denounced by the liberal press in Sydney, but he scorns such criticism. How can it harm him when he has governed according to the rules?

He cannot continue to ignore the growing opposition to his harsh discipline after the arrival of his wife's younger sister, Frances O'Beirne, a girl imbued with radical ideals. She cannot accept the brutality of chained and toiling men, punishment parades and the lash, and it is she who precipitates the crisis from which the final drama springs.

BOOKS BY THEA ASTLEY IN PENGUIN

Hunting the Wild Pineapple

Leverson the narrator, at the centre of these stories, calls himself a 'people freak'. Seduced by north Queensland's sultry beauty and unique strangeness, he is as fascinated by the invading hordes of misfits from the south as by the old-established Queenslanders.
Leverson's ironical yet compassionate view makes every story, every incident, a pointed example of human weakness – or strength.

Beachmasters

The central government in Trinitas can't control the outer island. But then neither can the British and French masters.
The natives of Kristi, supported and abetted by some of the *hapkas* and *colons* of two nationalities, make a grab for independence from the rest of their Pacific island group. On their tiny island, where blood and tradition are as mixed as loyalties and interests, their revolution is short-lived. Yet it swallows the lives of a number of inhabitants – from the old-time planters Salway and Duchard, to the opportunist Bonser, and the once mighty *yeremanu*, Tommy Narota himself.
Salway's grandson Gavi unwittingly gets caught up in Bonser's plans and, in a test of identity too risky for one so young, forfeits his own peace.

An Item From the Late News

Wafer, who saw his father blown apart by a bomb in the second world war, and who grew up under the shadow of the nuclear bomb, seeks to spend his middle years in a place of solitude where he can prepare for the inevitable . . .
Allbut, scarcely a dot on the map in the vast Queensland outback, seems to be the perfect place.
But Wafer's peace-loving ways are not understood by the clean and decent locals and when it comes, the final blast is not the one he expected.

Asper Nation

OTHER BOOKS BY MARC EDGE

Pacific Press: The Unauthorized Story of Vancouver's Newspaper Monopoly

Red Line, Blue Line, Bottom Line: How Push Came to Shove Between the National Hockey League and Its Players